STAR TREK READER'S
REFERENCE TO
THE NOVELS: 1992-1993

ALVA UNDERWOOD

VOLUME 7

authorHOUSE®

AuthorHouse™
1663 Liberty Drive
Bloomington, IN 47403
www.authorhouse.com
Phone: 1-800-839-8640

First published by AuthorHouse 12/15/2011

ISBN: 978-1-4634-4781-6 (sc)
ISBN: 978-1-4634-4782-3 (ebk)

Library of Congress Control Number: 2011914801

Printed in the United States of America

Preface:

What began as a source of information for myself has grown to seven volumes. This volume continues the research into the novels of the original series. Though no Star Trek weekly tv show runs today, the world of Gene Roddenberry is kept alive through reruns and novels. This volume is my contribution to keeping that world alive, just one of many. *Star Trek Reader's Reference to the Novels* is available in six volumes. Volume one covers 1970-1979; volume two covers 1980-1983; volume three covers 1984-1985; volume four covers 1986-1987; volume five covers 1988-1989; volume six covers 1990-1991. This continued effort provides helpful information for the professional and amateur writer who want facts handily available when writing a novel and need to document a mission according to dates and events of other missions or simply wish to refresh a memory. Readers who enjoy the novels will find these volumes of interest. This seventh *Reference* offers brief information about a variety of items ranging from characters to missions to quotes to stardates of the missions. With careful attention to accuracy, I provide a storehouse of information and a fascinating look into the Federation and StarFleet world.

Format:

Each character, place, event, reference, allusion, quote, and stardate found in each novel of this group is documented beginning with the identification of the novel in which the entry appeared and followed by general information about the entry. If an original TV episode is connected to the information, that episode is identified. Movies are identified only if the novel mentions information also found in the movie and the movie novelization is in the group being referenced. Only those movies made before the date of the information in the novel and the novel's publication date are considered. Included are entries with which any reader is familiar and many with which he is not. Biographies of all seven major characters are included and a plot summary for each novel referenced.

Each piece of equipment of *Enterprise* has not been indexed since I assume the reader of this *Reference* will be a STAR TREK fan and thus familiar with the item. However, when a piece of equipment is entered, it has a novel identification accompanied with a description and should be assumed part of the ship. The information included will illustrate why it was referenced. In some cases an item of equipment is included when extensive information has been found to provide a broad entry. When this occurs, the item generally is related to a mission and therefore the novel is identified. Chronological order of missions has not been followed for any of the *References*, for to do so would be difficult. Many of the novels do not have references to TV episodes or other missions already novelized that would help determine its place in the chronology. I have ordered the *References* according to novel publication, grouping them generally to their publication date. Also, I have kept the information confined to what is offered in the group of novels. For example, although the cloaking device will be used for Captain Siko's ship, the *Defiant*, I have not noted that in the entry. First, because I have not referenced any of the DS-9 novels and second, because that development will come many years after Kirk's missions. Other helpful sections are included in this *Reference*. A list of the novels referenced is included and identifies novels, the authors, and the novels' publication dates. An abbreviation page is included for easy use and identifies those abbreviations used in the *Reference*. Each entry consists of information in an established order. First is the entry followed by the abbreviation of the novel it appears in, then a full explanation with additional information if identified. Generally all entries are credited to a novel source. Sometimes information within the entry will have a source listed that has expanded or explained the entry. Appendices supplement information in the body of the *Reference*. An appendix for stardates identifies each novel alphabetically and then lists the stardates in the order they appear in the novels. An appendix for quotations is provided. Novels are in alphabetical order with the quotes from each novel given in the order they appear in the novel. Identification of the speaker and purpose of the quote is given when known. When an original source of the quote is known that too is included. Other appendices are included as warranted by the content of the entry section. For this seventh *Reference* the manifest for the Great Starship Race is included and a list of the names and information about the group of Klingons who appear in *Faces of Fire*, the novel by Michael J. Friedman. Klingon words from Victor Milan's *From the Depths* is included. Two sections of the Appendices that remain the same from *Reference* to *Reference* are "Crew Compliment" and "Diversity of Stars." Documentation is provided where needed. If the source is another novel then the author's name and a word from the title is provided. If the source is another reference then the author's name, a word from the title, and a page number is given. For example: Trimble 242 refers to Bjo Trimble's *Concordance* page 242. When an asterisk with an abbreviation appears it refers to a TV episode, animated episode, or movie and can be identified in the Abbreviation listing. In keeping with STAR TREK's concept of a united earth, I have employed the term "Terra" to designate the third planet of the Sol system. This avoids the misunderstanding that could occur with the term "earth" that some authors use for the planet and for the soil of a planet. Frequently a SEE appears and refers the reader of another entry in the *Reference*. CONSULTs are provided when a previous novel or TV episode has mentioned the entry or has information that expands the entry. A full bibliography identifies all sources referred to, extracted information from, and used to supplement information referenced. Any errors pertaining to information, documentation, and credit are solely the author's, who accepts full responsibility.

Acknowledgments:

To continue this series of *Star Trek Reader's References* requires a lot of time and energy. To those who have wondered why I spend my time with a fictional world, I say that it gives a positive view of a chaotic world and I like the "good guys to win, always!" To say that I did it all on my own is not true. I've received support from my sweetheart Bill, and though he laughs at my concentration on a fictional world has encouraged me on my every step. Thanks go also to two wonderful and capable women: Shelly Wentzell for research help and Mary Enslen, a friend who has a good eye for grammatical errors.

Novels:1992-1993

Abbreviations

*AF	"The Alternative Factor"
*Ap	"The Apple"
*AT	"Amok Time"
B	*Enterprise Blueprints*
BD	*Best Destiny*
*BFS/a	"Beyond the Farthest Star"
*BT	"Balance of Terror"
*CC/a	"The Counter-Clock Incident"
*CK	"Conscience of the King"
*CL	"And the Children Shall Lead Them"
*CMn	"The Corbomite Maneuver"
*CX	"Charlie X"
DC	*Death Count*
*DD	"Devil in the Dark"
Di	*Disinherited*
*DMa	"The Doomsday Machine"
*Dv	"Day of the Dove"
*DY	"The Deadly Years"
*EI	"Enterprise Incident"
*EM	"Errand of Mercy"
*FC	"Friday's Child"
FD	*From the Depths*
FF	*Faces of Fire*
*FW	"For the World is Hollow and I Have Touched the Sky"
GSR	*The Great Starship Race*
*GT	"The Gamesters of Triskelion"
IE	*"The IDIC Epidemic"*
*IS	"Immunity Syndrome"
IT	*Ice Trap*
*JB	"Journey to Babel"
*LG	"What Are Little Girls Made Of?"

ly	light years
*Mi	"Miri"
*MT	"The Man Trap"
*MTT/a	"More Tribbles, More Troubles"
*MW	"Mudd's Women"
*NT	"Naked Time"
*OA	"Operation Annihilate!"
*OUP/a	"Once upon a Planet"
P	*Probe*
*PLW	"Private Little War"
S	*Sanctuary*
SG	*Shell Game*
*SL	"Shore Leave"
SS	*Shadows on the Sun*
ST	*Starship Trap*
*TT	"Trouble with Tribbles"
*TW	"The Tholian Web"
UC	*The Undiscovered Country*
*UC	"The Ultimate Computer"
UFP	United Federation of Planets
*WGD	"Whom the Gods Would Destroy"
*WEd	"The Way to Eden"
*WF	"Wolf in the Fold"
WLW	*Windows on a Lost World*
*WNM	"Where No Man Has Gone Before"
*Yy/a	"Yesteryear"

Abaco Islands (GSR)–Located northeast of Bahamas; one of a group of islands. SEE *El Sol*.

ABC murders (Di)–A method of killing someone and disguising it by murdering several unrelated victims. Kirk accused the Parath'aa of doing this by striking colonies in the Alpha Xaridian system, including the intended colony.

acetylcholine test (ST)–Test used for patients believed to have angina pectoris; also used for normal coronary angiography.

Adirondack Mts. (SG)–Located in northeastern New York state, Terra, these mountains extend southward from the St. Lawrence River Valley and Lake Champlain to the Mohawk River Valley. Sparsely settled even now, the area exists in a near primitive state conserved by law. McCoy's childhood memory, recalled by Scotty's telling of ghost stories, involved his spending a camping trip with a flashlight as comfort against frightening things of the night.

"Ah ii ya" (WLW)–Exclamatory term Talkia Nyar uttered on first spotting the anomalous tricorder readings which led to the discovery of the first of many transit-frames on Careta IV. The phrase may be compared to "eureka!"

Aifor (SG)–A young Romulan Dr. Rinagh treated for knifeweed wounds.

Aileea (FD)– See dinAthos, Aileea.

Akaar, Teer Leonard James (FD)–The son of Eleen and Teer Akaar and future leader of the Ten Tribes of Capella V was born in 2267. Dr. McCoy aided Eleen in delivering her son whom she named Leonard James Akaar to honor Dr. McCoy and Captain Kirk. She ruled as regent until his coronation (*FC; Okuda and Okuda *Encyclopedia* 4). McCoy's memory of this event was triggered by Kain who was carrying a *kligat*. SEE Kain; *kligat*.

Akbar, Ravi (Di)–StarFleet Academy cadet who served as Chekov's First Officer during Chekov's *Maru* test.

Alalpech'ch (FF)–A vassal world of the Klingon Empire which supplied the *Kadn'ra* and crew with updated photon torpedo launchers.

Aldebaran *kigris* (FF)–A beast native to an Aldebaran world. McCoy worried that the smell needed to keep the cubaya from sacred places might not work although he suggested the *kirgis*. SEE cubaya.

Aleph (ST)–Dr. Omen believed he had built a "better mousetrap" and declared his device was a weapon to rid the galaxy of war. Taken from the first letter of the Hebrew Alphabet, the term, Spock explained to Kirk , "noted the transfinite number, any part of which is as large as the whole." Dr. Omen identified the Aleph as "an ancient cabalistic symbol pointing to both Heaven and Earth, showing that the lower world reflects the higher." On further questioning by Kirk, Dr. Omen declared that his Aleph was "named after a literary construct in a story by a twentieth-century writer named Borges [who] described his Aleph as a single mathematical point, a nexus where all parts of the universe touch." Once Omen's machinery was working, he pursued starships regardless of what group they belonged to, admitting to Kirk that he had sent Romulan, Klingon, and Federation ships through an Aleph, declaring with complete indifference that he was "not certain where they go... [and that he had] killed no one. The ships just go where they will no longer bother anyone." When asked about the lives of the crew, he answered: "They are not my concern. In sacrificing their hundreds of lives, I am saving thousands, millions." Dr. Omen believed the Federation and its military-prepared ships were the main culprits in the continuing battle among governing entities. Dr. Omen worked for the Federation for many years, helping to develop new weapons and improving old ones, but with the death of his daughter on a Federation ship, he turned his genius to developing a superior weapon to rid the galaxy of starships, particularly those carrying and using weapons. Once he confirmed his calculations, he purchased an asteroid, had it hollowed out, built to his specifications, and named it *Erehwon*. SEE *Erehwon*. *Enterprise* crew logs revealed startling information about the Aleph. Kirk and Spock both recorded thatOmen's machinery created extremely small dimensions on demand. An Aleph began as "a tiny spot of light, like a spinning diamond" and as it grew, "across its surface could be seen uncountable objects, scenes, people," Kirk wrote in his report, adding "I had no time to study it, but in the few seconds [I had] I saw Lt. Foss down in his cabin, a green hill on some planet-like earth, the glare of a star's interior, colorful spider creatures crawling across bare rock in a single line that extended to the red horizon, a child with an ice cream cone – all this and more – all at a single point." Kirk's memories of his exposure to the Aleph had let him see "the face of every crew member on the *Enterprise*, the contents of their closets...the harsh and nervous dazzle inside the warp engines, the lattice structure of dilithium crystals, and individual dilithium molecules." Spock's report noted that a ship struck by an Aleph felt no impact, and once an Aleph locked onto a targeted ship it would pursue it anywhere at any speed, even into warp. *Enterprise* logs also revealed that when struck by an Aleph, the ship and the Aleph entered a space occupied only by these two entities. Mathematics of the Aleph suggested that the other side of an Aleph was a random point inside the universe of universes, at least according to Spock, who added "the destination is random." What every crew member's log revealed was extreme fatigue and hallucinations ranging from pleasant to horrifying.

By the end of the first day's watch, the engineering report indicated ship energy was down by 15% and that everyone aboard suffered from continued energy drain. In seeking a way out of their situation, Kirk accepted all theories. Spock's proved to be the best for he theorized the possibility of employing Payton's implant (the only sensor still working) which, once modified, could record images from the Aleph though those images would be hints of gross structures and details would be lost. With Kirk's permission and Payton's compliance, Spock and Engineer Scott modified Payton's recording equipment. SEE Hazel Payton. Their report included their statements that they knew Payton's equipment (memory argumentation/cranial interface) was "not sophisticated enough to pick up the Aleph's infinite subtleties," yet it was all that was available. With Payton staring into the Aleph and Spock recording the view, he and Scott gained additional understanding of how the Aleph worked, enough to formulate a theory about getting out of it. Although changing focus of attention allowed for seeing items, their joint reported indicated "the viewer [still] would see everything at a single point with no confusion, with no overlapping with no crowding. Each thing, each action was discrete, alone, a universe among universes, an inspiration for new philosophies." One portion of Spock's report reads: "I saw Captain Kirk pacing on the Bridge, crew members drinking coffee, [my] father pondering the words of an ancient Vulcan scribe..."and noted " I could look over my own shoulder." With the data gathered, Spock began to hypothesize how the Aleph worked. As he explained to Kirk and McCoy, the data had to be selective and input manually into the ship's computers, adding "We have no way to know what is on the other side. The destination may be changing from instant to instant," and the universe on the other side may also be incompatible to "the one in which we find ourselves." Kirk's decision to deliberately enter the Aleph, rested on the certainty of death to everyone aboard, including the ship. "Given the alternative," he wrote in his report, " I preferred to take a chance." The second trip through the Aleph landed the *Enterprise* in an universe occupied by Klingees who did not welcome them. SEE Klingee. Kirk used the Aleph to discover a way past the Klingee Fleet and enter the Aleph a third time. Spock's continued study of recorded Aleph images gained him knowledge that led to calibrating "a proper formula for re-tuning the warp engines...[which] by normal engineering standards the specifications are rather bizarre." Spock's calculation that the Aleph would soon lose its stability also revealed that any ship entering the Aleph pulled it and the Aleph into the universe created, both arriving together. This happened to the *Enterprise* on its return to its proper universe and time following Kirk's confrontation with, and the gaining of entrance to the Aleph from, the Klingee captain. Confronted with the return of Kirk and the *Enterprise*, Dr. Omen created an Aleph into which he entered. His parting words indicated his resignation to the inevitable: "The galaxy is full of weapons experts and sooner or later, you will study [it]...[and] if you take me alive, you will force me to make weapons of war again. I cannot allow either to happen [so] for the sake of all the children....Perhaps we will meet again in a better universe." Since *Enterprise's* sensors didn't work properly inside the Aleph-constructed space, Kirk had no way of determining exactly how long the ship had stayed in the initial Aleph, but he estimated it was two or three days, given the time necessary to devise a possible solution. This is what he entered in his report. He also recorded, after recovering from his exposure to the bizarre effects of the Aleph, that he retained the memory of the experience and the scenes he'd viewed, the electronics buried in the corridors, "the nearly invisible nick in the intercom button at one corridor intersection...I even knew what crew members kept in their closets...picked at their fingers...pulled their ears or rubbed their chins...." Kirk's report ended with his statement that the Aleph "is a weapon [and] the ultimate spy apparatus. Whoever has one can, with the proper equipment and training, see anything." Spock's conclusion, one he stated to Kirk and Kirk incorporated into his report, declared the "Aleph...an extraordinary topological construction representing a unique scientific achievement [that] deserves to be studied... by a team of scientists and mathematicians." Concerned about the probability that the Aleph could lead to the complete loss of privacy, Kirk ordered the destruction of the only remaining Aleph and concluded his report with the statement that his action had been made with the full cooperation of all the crew. An addendum included praise for Spock, Scotty, McCoy, and passenger Hazel Payton with a notation that said remarks had been added to their files.

Alexandria (GSR)–This entrant in the Great Starship Race named in honor of the original schooner and captained by Pete Hall had interior parts made of wood from the original *Alexandria*, a Baltic trader schooner built in Sweden in 1919 and sold in 1939 and renamed the *Linda*. The *Linda* came to America in 1975 and took part in Operation sail in 1975. Acquired by the Alexandria Seaport Foundation, the ship participated in several races and tall ship reunions before being sold in 1996. Though unseaworthy, the new owner took the *Linda* to sea, and she sank off Cape Hatteras, North Carolina. Captain Kirk, fearing *Alexandria* had been taken captive, transported an armed boarding party with orders to take control of the ship, assume command under StarFleet authority, and use the ship to erect a Section Three security blockade from which to search every passing ship.

alien (UC)–A prisoner at Rura Penthe appeared to Kirk as a brightly painted horned toad with scaly hands, horrible growths on his chin, and sex organs in his knees. He and Kirk fought, with him winning until Kirk kicked him in the knees.

Alion (IT)–Taller than the average native Kitha of the planet Nordstral and born at the equator, he went north to create a power base from which to force off-worlders to leave the planet. He spoke excellent Standard and called himself Speaker of Fishes. Motivated by religious reasons, but mostly through greed, he killed several crews of landing vessels, blaming their deaths on the fluctuating magnetic fields. He was killed by a kraken. SEE Nordstral; kraken.

Alloseng (S)–Home planet for Renna. SEE Renna.

Alpha-329-ch-omega (WLW)–Master file in *Enterprise's* computer containing data on the events at Careta IV. Dara Niles monitored this file, constantly updating and adding data as it became available. SEE Dara Niles.

Alpha and Beta Xaridian Systems (Di)–These neighboring systems suffered additional attacks four months after the initial attack.

Alpha Centauri (GSR)–One of the nearest stars to Terra's solar system, some 4.3ly from Sol. SEE Port Apt.

Alpha Gederic Four (SS)–Designation for the Ssan planet, a cloud-covered world.

Alpha Maluria Six (FF)–This class-M planet with a single moon is located in the Alpha Maluria system to which Ambassador Farquhar was to be delivered by the *Enterprise* in order to mediate a civil conflict. Although a Federation planet, numerous occasions of social unrest between two main religious groups appeared to be escalating into a civil war.

Alpha Xaridian system (Di)–Five planets orbit the star Alpha Xaridian. Alpha One was devoid of life; Alpha Two was the site of a colony attacked by unknowns; Alpha Three was also devoid of life; Alpha Four was the site of an atomic war that extinguished all planet life; Alpha Five is populated by people calling their world Parathu'ul, meaning "Our World."

Alpha Xaridian Two (Di)–Second of five planets. The colony here was attacked by unknowns and equipment items taken. *Enterprise's* investigation of one mystery revealed another. Both eventually led to the solving of both. Administrator Jeff Gelb expected, as did the survivors, that the Federation would apprehend the attackers.

Alphonse and Gaston (P)–Bumbling pair of Frenchmen characters from a Terran comic strip created by Frederick Opper in 1901. Alphonse was short while Gaston was tall. From the strip came the saying "After you Alphonse. No, after you Gaston." The pair had difficulty determining who would go first. Their routine consisted of a situation in which one refused to act until the other did. Kirk was reminded of these characters by the actions of the Probe which shifted direction when *Enterprise* did. Kirk told Sulu the Probe was playing an interstellar version of Alphonse and Gaston.

Altairian devil (ST)–Possibly eatable. A glowing, tentacled life-form encased alive in a twisted green bottle. The liquid is drunk. Kirk admitted he tried it once and had to endure, for a day and a half, screams only he could hear.

Amagh (FF)–Klingon captain of the *Ul'lud*. SEE fireblossoms.

America's Cup (GSR)–A sailing regatta that claims to be the oldest active sailing sport which predates the modern Olympics by forty-five years. The first race was won by *America* in 1851, competing against fifteen others in a fifty-three mile regatta around the Isle of Wright (Terra). *America* won eight minutes ahead of the second contestant. The trophy presented to the winner was described as an ornate sterling silver bottomless ewer. A similar trophy has continued to the awarded. In his opening remarks, John Orland summarized the history of such contests by including mention of the America's Cup, emphasizing the Great Starship Race was in the same category. SEE John Orland.

Ames (GSR)–Bulky framed and heavy-set captain of *Haunted House*, a private vessel and an entrant in the Great Starship Race.

Amnita system (UC)–Praxis is a moon of this system located in Klingon territory. SEE Praxis.

"amumtu" (Di)–Possibly Swahili for friend.

Andorian (DC; GSR)–Identified as a humanoid race and member of UFP. Johnson (*Worlds* 22) declares Andorians were the third intelligent race to be contacted by the Federation.

However, other historians disagree. CONSULT Goldstein and Goldstein. Native to the planet Andor, Andorians have an internal skeleton and a limited exoskeleton which adds strength and protection to the limbs and torso (Johnson *Worlds* 22). Adults are generally white-haired with pastel eye coloring. An Andorian blush leaves the skin a light lavender (Graf *Death*). Other interesting features include intensity-sensitive rods in the retina, fully functional dual antennae (Trimble 126), and a well developed auditory ability. Johnson writes that the race is incapable of discerning color through their eyes but that the "dual antennae house auditor receptors and a complex matrix of light-sensitive cones." Furthermore he describes their vision as quadriscopic resulting in superior depth perception. They can also hear on a wide range of frequencies with their nondirectional antennae. A notable characteristic is the position of the head. When bowed and slightly titled, the Andorian is "listening" intently. Quite possibly the antennae extended toward the speaker provides a better viewing of the infrared wavelengths coming from the speaker. Thus it allows for additional "reading" of the speaker beyond the vocalization. In addition to this note, Johnson (*Worlds* 22) also writes that the antennae tilted toward someone is a gesture of respect while a chin titled upwards signals disrespect. The gesture of both thumbs, together, pointed and focused at another is a gesture of contempt (Graf *Death*). To the surprise of the xeno-anthropologists who read the initial reports, Andorians "do not have veins in their circulatory systems, relying when necessary on intramuscular injection" (*WDG; Trimble 126). Johnson (*Worlds* 22) includes the notation that all Andorians are ambidextrous. Several sources indicate that "an Andorian accent sounds like a soft lisp" (*GT; *JB; Trimble 126). An interesting item of information resulting from a Vulcan mission reveals an Andorian cannot be resuscitated but it is not known whether this is due to physiology or religion (Lorrah *Epidemic*). The leading Federation historian declares Andor's history of savage warriors and repeated conquests indicates they are "a violent race though ruled by reason." She adds that their "strength and fighting ability [are] masked by soft voices and slender builds" (Trimble 126). Johnson includes the note that "once [these emotions are] released Andorian savagery and fighting ability is almost unequaled." Furthermore, he states that Andorians are known to have few sympathies, though they do admit to being a violent race who "place high value on family relationships and obligations, [and] often [place] them above public duty. This strong sense of family duty accords family and family obligations and relationships the highest attention, even to the exclusion of public duty" (*Worlds* 22, 23). They also have an obsessive habit of paying debts. Andorians are members of the Federation and in 2267 as UFP members, they sent a diplomatic delegation to the Babel Conference (Okuda and Okuda *Encyclopedia* 12; *JB). Several Andorians presently serve on StarFleet ships and in administrative offices of StarFleet command. Discovered after many years of contact is the fact that Andorians have had no lawyers for a thousand years, seeing no real need for them until Andor became a UFP member (Reeves-Stevens *Memory*). The supreme deity of Andor is known as "Great Mother Andor." An interesting footnote about this race is that its population is falling and fear is building that they will become extinct (Lorrah *Epidemic*).

Andorian (S; FD)–Native people of Andor. SEE Errico.

Andorian Reserve Fleet (DC)–Andorian space military has two divisions. The chief division is composed of military ships with other Andorian ships held in reserve in case of an emergency should the military group require support.

Andorian *tagg* (FD)–A food item possibly vegetable. Kirk enjoyed a meal of tournedos of beef with asparagus tips and steamed tagg shared with Moriah Wayne.

Andrachis, Shil (SS)–This native born Ssan could boast of having a grandfather who was a policeman and a father who was an assassin. As a protege to High Assassin Moboron, Shil was injured during an attack on a civilian location. McCoy, sent to help the injured, saved Shil's life though in doing so he violated the assassin code. When Moboron was killed, Shil became High Assassin and sought to reinstate the assassin tradition on Ssan with unprovoked killings. The Federation sent *Enterprise* to seek a peaceful settlement. During an attempt to rescue Kirk and diplomat Jocelyn Treadway, her husband Clay wounded Shil. To uphold their traditions, another assassin killed him.

Anneke (P)–This female, protege to Andrew Penalt, was dark skinned and reed-slender.

antidissolution shielding (GSR)–This type of shielding employed on *Ransom Castle's* aft 1/3 of the ship prevented beaming into or out of the shielded area.

antimatter powerplants (BD)–Starship power plants orbit thousands of miles out from Terra because of their size, appearance, and danger which prohibit placing them on Terra. Power generated by these plants is tight-beamed to Terra's surface for use.

anti-proton flushback (BD)–This unnatural occurrence is known to occur only in the explosion of warp engines.

Antonoff (GSR)–*Enterprise* ensign at Navigation when *Enterprise* "rose" above the cloud formed from a million-year-old explosion.

Antronic, Nem (SS)–Had become master governor of the province of Tanul seven days before *Enterprise* arrived.

Aora (FF)–Klingon sent to search for the missing colony children on Beta Canzandia Three. He and Gidris fell into a deep pit-trap set by Spock and the children. Both men were killed by Vheled. SEE Vheled.

Appenfellen, Helmut (GSR)–Captain of the ship *Drachenfels*, an entrant in the Great Race.

April, Robert (BD)–April was the captain of the initial shakedown cruise of the soon-to-be named *Enterprise*, launched, according to historians Okuda and Okuda in 2245 (*Chronology* 31). His blue eyes belied his forty years. Although suffering from a rare blood deficiency that left him always feeling chilly (he wore a heavy cardigan when on the Bridge), he was still quite capable of commanding missions. StarFleet gave him an untested ship and the unusual mission of rescuing the stranded colonists on the *Rosenberg*. CONSULT *The Final Frontier* by Diane Carey. To do this, April assembled his own top-notch crew: Dr. Sarah Poole (whom he later married); Leo Brownell, Chief Engineer (age 70); Graff and Saffire (wunderkid engineers who turned out to be spies); Drake Reed, Chief of Security; Antony Wood (21-year-old engineer), second in command to Brownell; and George Kirk (First Officer and father of James T. Kirk). Poole was sweet-talked into being the ship's doctor, but Kirk and Reed were kidnapped on April's orders. April needed Kirk to help curb his idealism, especially when the ship warped, unexpectedly into Romulan space. When the rescue mission ended, April married Poole and helmed the ship for a five-year mission of deep-space exploration before passing a finely-tuned starship, now christened the *Enterprise*, into the capable hands of Captain Pike. April retired shortly after his final assignment. Historian Bjo Trimble (127) writes that April served twenty years as a Federation ambassador, fully retiring at age 75 after saving the *Enterprise* from a negative universe (*CC/a). In BD, April is about forty and described as lean and casual, a "happy, broad gauged English string-puller" whom some of the crew called Uncle Robert, as he was very good at handling young StarFleet inductees. His resume indicates he had been part of a group study to implement starship designs and includes a notation to the effect that Captain April believed in and supported the Prime Directive. In a mission detailed in *Flag Full of Stars*, Nan Davis of World News conducted an interview with retired Captain April, age 80. In commemorating Apollo Day, he spoke of StarFleet Command's decision to renovate the *Enterprise* rather than build a new cruiser. In the mission about Faramond, (*Best Destiny*), he was asked to initiate digging at Faramond and guided *Enterprise* during the Faramond expedition. By allowing George Kirk to bring his son Jimmy on to the ship, April showed his understanding towards a misguided youth. In speaking to young Jimmy Kirk about the *Enterprise* he declared: "she's a testimony to how much good mankind can do...we're going to climb aboard...to head out...like pioneers who went out...." April attempted to reach the angry Jimmy Kirk by offering his philosophy about humanity. "Humanity," he said, "is all right. Mankind is cunning and artful, enthusiastic, and ultimately smart. [They] blunder from time to time, sometimes a little butterfingered while we build on some unclear vision, but we always learn from our blunders and we rarely forget. And we never <u>ever</u>...stop trying." When Jimmy wondered what value humans had, April had this to say: "What good are humans? Humans have been the only ones to reach out and ask others to join us in our common future. We're the only ones to initiate a galactic unity." When Jimmy sarcastically accused his father of always choosing space over family, April suggested he think about the fact that "space is a jealous concubine. It demands a whole heart from those of us who tend it. The Federation doesn't have an iron-bound coast. It's incumbent upon StarFleet to constable the settled galaxy wherever we're called upon. Our colonists depend on us, as do our allies, and anyone else who needs help, friend or foe...so many fragile details to tend...." Kirk remembered April's words.

April's group (BD)–Members of the Liaison Cutter #4 were April, George Kirk, Ensign Veronica Hall, Jimmy Kirk, and two engineers Thorvaldsen and Bennings.

Arc (UC)–Home planet for Martia. SEE Martia.

archeology teams (P)–In an agreement between Romulans and Federation envoys, groups paired off and employed the Federation tricorder to conduct an initial survey of the site on Temaris Four. All recordings were transferred to the *Enterprise* and the *Galtizh* computers each day. SEE Temaris Four.

Arcturian yoga (DC)–Yoga is a system of exercises and a discipline for attaining bodily/ mental control. To do this form of exercise requires two sets of arms.

Arkazha, Mona (FD)–A native Variant of the planet Discord. She was the representative for the Deep-Ranger Syndicate and a member of the Freefolk trio who initially met with Kirk and Commissioner Wayne. Her accent indicated Russian ancestry. Kirk described her as a "squat being, hairless with rubbery-looking black skin" a broad face and no external ears just holes on the side of her head. SEE Variants; Discord.

Arn dreamtalker (SG)–Native of Arnheim Land of northern Australia, Terra. A powerful shaman figure capable of divining the future through the use of divining bones.

Artful Dodger (BD)–Character from Charles Dicken's novel *Oliver Twist*. Nickname Captain April applied to Jimmy Kirk.

Arthur's Grail (SG)–Various Terran writers have reworked tales about this object of legendary quest by the Knights of Arthurian romances. The best known is by Thomas Malory in the 15th century, *LeMorte d'Arthur* (1485). The grail, an object of great value, is often described as a wide-mouthed or shallow vessel used by Jesus at the last supper. The illusion crossed McCoy's mind as he looked out the window of the space station and saw the *Enterprise* drifting in space, a thing of great beauty.

Article 184 (UC)–Section of Interstellar Law under which Chang arrested Kirk and McCoy, charging them of assassinating Chancellor Gorkon.

Ascendancy (P)–Term meaning "dominant influence" was given to those civilizations that rose to control large expanses of areas and which influenced the areas they had already declared theirs. On this particular mission it is the Erisian Ascendancy to be studied. SEE Audrea Benar.

assassin blood (SS)–A virus that infects those who choose to be infected and in, times of stress to its host, stimulates "the adrenal medulla" resulting in "supernormal increases in the speed and force of the heartbeat, dilation of the airways to facilitate an incredible rate of breathing and oxygenation, widening of the vessels supplying blood to the skeletal muscles...in short, the individual becomes a superman," according to Vincent Bando's medical reports. The natives call it bloodfire for the way one reacts under its influence. Assassins accept injection of the virus to enhance their physical powers. A variant strain is a biological time bomb that may at any time cause instantaneous and irreversible cardiac arrest. However, if the anti-viral medicine is injected within a few minutes of the onset of symptoms, the victim will recover. Dr. Bando injected the young assassin Andrachis with the viral strain, but McCoy countered its effects and saved Andrachis' life. SEE Shil Andrachis.

Assassin Wars (SS)–Daily battles conducted between the assassins led by Li Moboron and those hired by the Ssan government raged until Moboron was killed.

Atanakian (FD)–A sentient race living within Federation territory. Generally adults reach two meters in height, have long jointed antenna, and huge yellow self-luminous eyes which are used in communicating. Color varies among the race but a green chitinous colored head denotes a male. SEE Bill.

Atlantis (S)–Mythological place located on Terra. McCoy linked it to Sanctuary believed to also be a mythological place until Kirk, Spock, and McCoy spent time there.

ATS *Shras* (DC)–Docked at space station Sigma One, this Andorian ship captained by Pov Kanin was a passenger transport ship with orders to run as a sensor ghost. Its five decks each had a narrow corridor that ran the length of each level and accessed multiple rooms. A manual access shaft at either end of each corridor connected the levels. A tear-shaped bridge had a forward viewscreen. Sulu took command per StarFleet regulation and piloted the craft to save the *Enterprise*.

Atzebur (UC)–This slender Klingon female, and daughter of Chancellor Gorkon, became Chancellor at his death and continued his policy of pursuing peace with the Federation. She had waist-length black hair held back by a silver skull ornament. Though she loved Kesla, she didn't trust him. SEE Kesla.

Auditor General (DC)–Subdivision personnel from this office was assigned to audit the *Enterprise* and were aboard during the incident of *Death Count*. During their stay on board, McCoy declared to Kirk that "their (auditors) idea of improving efficiency means enforcing every regulation some bureaucrat ever dreamed up."

Auk-rex (S)–A space pirate who attacked a variety of vessels but took only cargo. To cripple a vessel, the attacking ship always hailed the vessel by code but never with visual. This hailing allowed the ship's computer to be compromised and the pirate took all relevant data from it as well as any cargo. Ordered to stop the pirating, *Enterprise* trailed the ship to Sanctuary intending to capture it and its crew. After the vessel crashed on Sanctuary, Kirk learned Auk-rex was a female named Renna whose home planet was Alloseng. Kirk and group were able to devise a way to leave Sanctuary, and Kirk offered her the chance to leave, but she chose to stay on Sanctuary. SEE Sanctuary.

Australia (P)–Terra's southern continent and location of the New Cetacean Institute at the Great Barrier Reef. CONSULT *The Voyage Home* by Vonda McIntyre.

Australia aborigine (P)–These native Australians believe their totemic ancestors walked the land mapping it geographically and musically, "laying down trails of song with their footprints, so that if a thousand years later someone learned the songs, he could find his way unerringly across a land he'd never seen," Dr. Benar explained to the *Enterprise* briefing group.

autopsy procedures (WLW)–Standard Federation policy dictates that a corpse be placed in a crynoic-stasis field to preserve it. Dr. McCoy, knowing StarFleet would find the two specimen of Kh!lict of great interest, did everything necessary to preserve the corpses. SEE Kh!lict.

Axanar (FD)–On this planet StarFleet Captain Garth won a major battle in 2250. James T. Kirk was an ensign when he first visited the planet as a member of the peace mission. Kirk warned the authorities that the young Klingon Kain intended to steal an Axanar holy relic. They apprehended Kain who suffered great humiliation and never forgot what Kirk had done to him. For Kirk's actions during that time, the government awarded Kirk the Palm Leaf of Axanar Peace Mission (Okuda and Okuda *Encyclopedia* 26). SEE Kain.

Axanar Peace Conference (FD)–Held on Axanar following the decisive battle won by Captain Garth which led to peaceful negotiations. Ensign James T. Kirk was a member of the negotiating team.

axial shield generator (WLW)–A shielding device believed, as suggested by Chekov, to shield the first anomaly discovered on Careta IV. Spock declared it to be "a device of completely alien manufacture," a supposition, he added, "supported by the rest of our findings on this planet."

Azmuth (P)–Romulan vessel that followed the Probe once it crossed into Romulan space. The ship sent information of contact to Romulus.

Baker (IT)–Female member on the Nordstral orbiting station *Curie* whose sufferings from the effects of the strong magnetic fields led her to commit suicide.

Bahtain (P)–A three-stringed Romulan musical instrument Jandra was required to play at the Praetor's funeral.

Baila, Jerome (Di)–A tall slender man with chocolate complexion born in Africa at Potaya near Lake Nyasa. His parents and other villagers followed the teaching of Beccah Talulu. Though allowed a basic education, he was denied further schooling. To learn, he stole books from booksellers' wares whenever he and his parents went to the neighboring town. At age eleven he ran away from home, going to an aunt's home in Quelemaine. When his parents were notified of his whereabouts, they refused to allow him to come home and considered him dead. His aunt provided him schooling. Though he had to take the Academy exams twice, he entered the Academy and distinguished himself. He served under Commodore Wesley and aided Lt. Cmd. Uhura in the dealings with Rithrim. When the issue of marauders attacking colonies was resolved, Baila requested permission from Wesley to remain on Rithra and help them solve their issue with the fifth caste. SEE Rithra.

Bailey (Di)–An *Enterprise* navigator who had once gotten into trouble.

Bainin cardigan (BD)–Heavy wool sweater Captain Robert April wore when on the Bridge. Made of 100% merino wool, the best cardigans, sometimes called fishermen sweaters, are made in Ireland, Terra. The bulky garment with prominent cable patterns is generally cream-colored with two roomy packets

balloon (S)–Spock theorized the only way to escape Sanctuary's shields was to employ a balloon. McCoy became enthusiastic and helped develop the form and the "basket" to ride in. Spock calculated the planet's shield existed to the altitude of 30 kilometers and tested his theory that the shields were programmed to repel driven flight by using a small weather balloon. Once this balloon rose beyond the 30 kilometers, Kirk decided a balloon, powered by hydrogen, would get him and his people above the limit. Passengers would need pressure suits. Belket drew up the blueprints and used tri-polymer sheeting for the balloon panels to be zero pressurized to allow for gas expansion as the balloon rose. Errico produced three pressure suits. McCoy devised a nylon hammock to create the "basket" attached to the balloon and to serve as the passenger container. He also provided ballast by loading food and water supplies, explaining "If...we come down on land we might need food and water...." Balloon and passengers got high enough to call the *Enterprise* and be rescued by Scotty. SEE Belket; Errico.

Bando, Vincent (SS)–Chief Medical Officer during the mission to Ssan. According to Janice Taylor, one of the five trainee doctors, he was "the toughest chief medical officer this side of Alpha Centauri." Described as a blunt man with squared-off features, close-cropped iron grey hair, and a thin-lipped mouth, Bando instilled fear in new medical personnel. McCoy, who served under him during the Ssan crisis, always remembered Bando's words: "It takes more than compassion to make a good doctor. It takes anger too, and plenty of it. Anger at the circumstances that create the misery you've got to deal with. Anger at the people who create these circumstances. Anger at the whole damn cosmos for giving birth to the kind of beings who could be so miserable in the first place." When nervous Bando cracked his knuckles or when he was anxious to get to a more pressing need. He hated Ssan assassins and attempted to attack Moboron, High Assassin, during a killing spree in a children's hospital. He also attempted to kill the young assassin Shil Andrachis while he was in the medical ward recovering from wounds. McCoy and the other trainees stopped Bando and spared Andrachis' life. Bando was put under house arrest and turned over to Captain Pike for transport to StarFleet Headquarters for trial.

banned list (P)–Sometime during a civilization's life, its governing force creates a list of books, musicians, music, etc. considered discomforting to the status quo. These are placed on a banned list. The Romulan Empire has several lists of banned items pertaining to several categories.

Baraffin, Harn (SS)–Native Ssan assassin who killed Master Governor Dathrabin per orders from Andrachis.

Barrasso (DC)–*Enterprise* crewman; member of Chekov's Security force.

Barrier Reef (P)–Also known as the Great Barrier Reef. It extends for 1,250 miles along the northeastern coast of Australia some 10 to 100 miles off the coast. Consisting of thousands of individual reefs, shoals, islets, it was created by living creatures whose skeletons slowly built up the reefs. In the early 20th century it became a tourist attraction and so many visitors came that eventually the Australian government designated the entire reef environment protected by law. It remains so today.

Barrows, Tonia (FF)–She and McCoy experienced an incident on an amusement planet in which McCoy had attempted to save her from being abducted (*SL). She sculpted a knight on a rearing charger and gave it to him shortly before her transfer to the *Potemkin*.

Basco, John (IT)–A saint with whom Risa, an employee on a harvester, carried on conversations. SEE Risa.

Bass (ST)–Broad name for several Terran English beers originally brewed in Burton Upon Trent. Associated with pale ale.

Beauregard (Di)–A temperamental plant Sulu once tried to raise.

Beauvois, Tom (BD)–This member of Jimmy Kirk's gang of juveniles had no goal in life and was considered to be a punk. SEE Jimmy's group.

Beethoven Festival (P)–The works of Ludwig Van Beethoven, a Terran, have never gone out of style. Music festivals still offer live performances of many of his works. Hardly a year passes that someone somewhere isn't presenting such a festival, even off-world.

Beethoven's *Seventh* (P)–Reference is to Ludwig van Beethoven's *Symphony No. 7 in A Major* (1812). One critic denounced it as "demoniac...with...expanded scherzo and trio, blazing finale, and spirited first movement preceded by a long modulatory introduction" ("Beethoven" *Britannica*). When Uhura went to inform Dr. Audrea Benar that she had been requested by the Romulans to be part of the archeological dig on Termais Four, the orchestra was in rehearsal for the presentation of this symphony. SEE Audrea Benar.

Belesov V (WLW)–A planet visited by archeologists who studied remains of a civilization. The *Enterprise* assistant historian who examined wall decorations and reported his findings to Spock admitted to touching a center medallion on the wall, explaining that the carvings on Careta IV reminded him of those on Belesov V which were designed to hide passageways in the royal audience chamber.

Belket (S)–Humanoid albino who helped develop blueprints for the balloon. SEE balloon.

Bell Book (BD)–In the early sailing days, and up to the time Terra began moving into space, each ship kept a complete log book that recorded all the ship's activities, especially those activities associated with ship propulsion. As Terrans moved into space, they continued the tradition. All StarFleet Command ships continue to daily record ship activities pertaining to the engines. The Chief Engineer keeps a separate Bell sheet for each day's shift with dates, names, times, and activities recorded, and though Engineering has general control of its own Bell Book contents, its activities are included in the Bell Book report presented daily to the captain. When Watch shifts change, the captain's yeoman presents the report to the captain, or ranking Bridge personnel. The report is looked over and signed off. The official Bell Book contains a complete log identifying the entire history of the starship for the life of the ship. The Bell Book is presented by the out-going captain to the in-coming captain. In BD, the President of UFP, in one of his last conversations with Captain Kirk, told Kirk that he would be glad to sign the Bell Book for *Enterprise* 1701-A in appreciation for all that Kirk and his crew had done for the Federation.

Benar, Dr. Audrea (P)–As an archeologist she was drawn to the mystery of Ascendancy and worked on two different Ascendancy worlds, including recordings from Temaris Four. She and her teams wrote numerous papers about the Ascendancy. Her study of the Ascendancy led to the development of formulas relating to it, particularly to the Erisians. Dr. Benar was working at Kalis Three where she and her team were captured by Romulans who "experimented" on them. Dr. Benar lost her brother to the Romulans, but she managed to escape and eventually went to Vulcan where she learned to deal with her rage and hatred. Her studies of Vulcan logic helped rebuild her mind, and she began wearing the typical Vulcan dress which accented her dark hair and slender build. She came to the Lincoln Center Philharmonic two years before the mission detailed in this novel as an expert on the *tlakyrr* and was considered an excellent conductor, concentrating on Beethoven. The Lincoln Center Philharmonic Hall where she worked for many years considered her a "treasure," according to Maestro Carmen Espinoza. When another Ascendancy world was discovered and surveyed by a team of Romulans and Federation representatives, the Romulans requested a Federation archaeologist, namely Dr. Benar, to be on hand as one of the leaders. She was able to apply her formulas to discover the Exodus Hall on Temaris Four. After the conclusion of the mission, Dr. Benar returned to conduct the Lincoln Center Philharmonic Orchestra's first performance of two aspects of the Probe's language. SEE Probe.

Benar's tool (P)–Used to excavate buried artifacts, this small short-range, phaser-like devise was programmed to distinguish between organic and inorganic materials, even if fossilized. SEE Dr. Audrea Benar.

Bendilon (WLW)–Home world of Dr. Meredith Lassiter. This colony, designed by humans who settled it in the early days of spaceflight, was modeled on the Australian aborigines and the Amerind peyote cults. Extremely difficult to study for the researcher either "vanished" into the culture or was never given information on the culture. Outsiders often referred to the colony as Space Haven or Dreamtime.

Beneon (GSR)–This native of Gullrey and one of two Whistlers at the last Whistling Outpost was the first to identify a signal believed to be coming from a supposed asteroid . In reality, the signal was from intelligent life. She discovered it was coming from the USS *Hood*. For her discovery, her government insisted she participate in the ceremony marking Gullrey's entry into the UFP. SEE Whistlers; Vorry.

Benning (BD)–SEE Dennings.

Beppe, Captain Marco (SG)–The fiercest pirate ever to plunder Italy's coastline and rumored to have scuttled his last ship causing the deaths of half his crew rather than give up his spoils. His ship the *Stephanie Emilia* was found abandoned off the coast of Scotland. He was found dead and given a burial at sea. Scotty once mentioned he had seen an oil portrait of Captain Beppe in an Edinburgh museum, saying "He was the very picture of a storybook brigand, with his size and curly dark hair and beard, but there was no touch of romance in the reality of him."

Berganza (Di)–This *Enterprise* ensign was a biophysicist who dated Pitharese, also a crew member of the *Enterprise*.

Beria (UC)–Klingon Kesla had been aboard this ship when it was attacked by Romulans who killed the captain and most of the crew. SEE Kesla.

Bernhard, Judge (SS)–Native of Georgia, Terra, whom McCoy knew as a fair but hard judge.

Berriman (Di)–A pretty redhead helmsman on the *Lexington* under Commander Robert Wesley.

Berth 416C (DC)–Docking berth at Space Station Sigma One assigned to the *Shras*. SEE ATS *Shras*.

Best Destiny–Novel by Diane Carey. Two plot lines interwoven by a common thread. An SOS message from the *Bill of Rights* and an interception of a flushback alerted Captain

Kirk to impending trouble. This and the mention of Faramond caused Kirk to recall his experience aboard the Liaison Cutter 4, his efforts to help his father and Captain April survive a run-in with pirates, and the events that led to his decision to enter StarFleet. Forty years later he met Roy Moss whom he, at age sixteen, had bested on the pirate ship. Again Kirk stopped Moss and his plans to employ ancient Faramond machinery about which he knew little.

Beta Aurelon Three (SS)–McCoy along with other neophyte trainees were sent to this planet suffering from a mysterious plague that threatened to decimate the population. SEE five doctors.

Beta Aurelonites (SS)–Natives of the planet Beta Aurelon Three.

Beta Canzandia Three (FF)–One of several planets in a system sitting on the edge of Federation space. The climate is on the cool side with a surface scarred by fissures of all depths. Klingons named it Pheranna. Chosen by the Federation as the site to employ new terraforming technology, the planet became home to a small research colony. SEE Yves Boudreau.

Beta Damovon V (Di)–Chekov was a member of a landing party to this planet.

Beta Ganymede (Di)–A series of asteroids in this area affected the arrival time of Wynn Samuels to greet Captain Wesley and Lt. Uhura as they came aboard the *Lexington*. SEE Wynn Samuels.

Beta Herculian (DC)–Binary star system; part of Chekov and Sulu's space simulation program they played on Sigma One Station.

Beta Quadrant (UC)–One quarter of the Milky Way Galaxy. Most of the Klingon and Romulan Empires occupy this region though parts of the UFP spill into it. *Excelsior* was on a scientific mission in Beta when it detected the explosion of Praxis in 2293 (Okuda and Okuda *Encyclopedia* 43).

Beta Xaridian Four (Di)–Fourth planet of this system. The Federation colony chief administrator was Sharon Jarvis at the time of this mission. Most of the population of the colony were women. This colony suffered an attack from an unknown assailant who was driven off.

Beta Xaridian Six (Di)–A colony on this planet in the Beta Xaridian system was hit by attacks from unknowns. The third colony to be hit in the system.

Betts, Marilyn (ST)–Second mate on *Ransom Castle* captained by Nancy Ransom.

Bhutto (DC)–*Enterprise* lieutenant who worked flight control navigation and also served on the Bridge in a shift with Sulu and Uhura.

Big Rex (BD)–SEE Rex Moss.

Bilindian flu (WLW)–A very uncomfortable illness. Kirk compared its symptoms to how he felt after recovering from exposure to suldanic gas.

Bill (FD)–An Atarakian who stood 2 meters tall, had huge yellow eyes, and a large green chitinous head. He owned and ran Min and Bill's Pub on Starbase 23. SEE Atarakian.

Billiwog (S)–One of many who came to Sanctuary to escape being imprisoned and learned Sanctuary wasn't quite the Eden reported. This humanoid with facial hair built boats to occupy his time. He helped Kirk, Spock, and McCoy escape from the Reborning ritual and became part of the community at the Graveyard of Lost Ships.

Bill of Rights (BD)–SEE *USS Bill of Rights*.

Biminath, Dal (SS)–A legendary Ssan High Assassin; predecessor to Li Moboron.

Bird-of-Prey (UC)–Klingon ship deployed by the Klingon Defense Force. A prototype of a Bird capable of both atmosphere entry and landing had been built with several types of new systems and equipped with an improved cloaking device. This experimental ship, developed prior to 2293, was designed to fire its weapons while cloaked. General Chang commanded such a vessel and used it to obstruct the Khitomer peace conference. SEE Chang.

Blackjackel (GSR)–One of the entrants in the Great Starship Race.

Blackington, Ian (GSR)–Captain of a merchantman and an entrant in the Great Starship Race.

Blaine, Leo (GSR)–StarFleet retired and now captain of the *Cynthia Blaine*, an entrant in the Great Starship Race. He ran the ship under the flag of the company his mother founded.

bloodfire (SS)–SEE assassin blood.

Blue Hell (SG)–Translated Romulan phrase.

Bluenose W (GSR)–Canadian ship entrant in the Great Starship Race; captained by Sinclair Rowan for Canada and Great Britain of Terra.

Blue Zone (BD)–Designated area around a neutron star that a computer-enhanced image showed as Blue. No ship was able to enter the Zone and survive its gravity, radiation, temperature, and solar wind which could rip through a starship's shielding. SEE *Shark*.

Bois de Boulogne (FF)–A park in the outskirts of Paris, France on Terra. On Beta Canzandia, this "... the grandest forest" on the world, according to Yves Boudreau, was a cluster of fifty golden-needled conifers, none more than twelve feet tall. All were hybrids – half Aldebaran *eristor*, half Marraquite *casslana*. The plants had responded quite well to the G-Seven unit, but at the time of Kirk's visit the trees had not begun producing oxygen at the rate expected. SEE G-Seven unit.

Boles (GSR)–*Enterprise* lieutenant on the Bridge at the Engineering Station; Kirk relieved him for his hesitancy in reporting on the Romulan ship.

Bonanno, Margaret–Author of *Probe*.

Book of Death (P)–On the death of the Romulan Praetor, thousands came to see him in his sarcophagus and to sign the book indicating their loyalty.

boreal winds (IT)–Extreme north winds. Nordstral natives, subjected to these, often suffered death and destruction to their settlements.

Borges (ST)–A 20th century writer from Argentina described as involving "the reader in dazzling displays of erudition and imagination, unlike anything previously encountered in the short story genre" ("Borges" *Britannica* 2000). In a collection of short stories entitled "The Aleph and Other Stories" (1933-1969), he introduced the concept of an Aleph as a single mathematical point. SEE Professor Omen.

Bosco, John (IT)–Born on August 16, 1815, in Sardina, Terra, he was canonized as a Catholic saint for his pioneering work in educating the poor and as the founder of the Salesian Order on April 1, 1934. One of the Nordstral Pharmaceutical's employees who had been exposed to heavy magnetic fluctuations believed she was talking with this saint.

Boswellia (UC)–A sector bordering Klingon space. SEE Valeris.

Botanical Gardens (P)–Identified on the Blueprints for *Enterprise* 1701 were several areas for studying, growing, and enjoying a variety of plant life. A fully equipped research lab was located on Deck 2 with a second area on Deck 7, forward, dedicated to the growth and study of many plants. On Deck 8, identified as entertainment/recreation, was a large area, nearly 1/3 of the deck, dedicated to a park-like area. Paths weaved through a great variety of plants. Scattered throughout were benches discreetly placed for privacy. This area was open to all crew most anytime of the day. Crew assigned to the botany sections had duties that entailed maintaining the plants and policing the areas, including removing and replacing plants as required. Deck 18 forward had two areas strictly devoted to the botany section and the hydroponics lab. Both were dedicated to research. A small area on Deck 17 forward labeled Botany hi-bay also was for research. CONSULT *Enterprise* Blueprints.

Boudreau, Yves (FF)–A tall, distinguished-looking gentleman with deep-set eyes noted for speaking his mind. His many publications and persistent lobbying led to the establishment of a colony on Beta Canzandia. As head of the research colony on Beta Canzandia and the leading terraformer, he employed his latest devise, a G-Seven unit, to increase planet growth and increase oxygen output. His lab in the largest central dome had 32 workstations for staff members.

Bovary (WLW)–*Enterprise* ensign who volunteered to accompany Kirk through the transit-frame. Placed in the body of a Kh!lict, he was killed in a duel with another Kh!lict. McCoy autopsied the alien body and determined which human occupied it.

bowling alleys (P)–On *Enterprise* 1701 this area was located on Deck 21 aft of the food preparation facility. Six regulation lanes with two recreational seating areas nearby provided opportunity for those who enjoyed the sport. When Kirk escorted Romulan Captain Hiran on a tour of *Enterprise*, he showed him this area and other recreation areas on Deck 8. CONSULT Blueprints.

bowling lanes (P)–Recreation facilities available on the *Enterprise* located on Deck 21 (B).

Boy Scouts (BD)–A boy's organization founded in 1908 in Britain, Terra, was devoted to good citizenship, chivalrous behavior, and skill in outdoor activities. Boy Scouts often used the rope bridge across the Skunk River, Iowa. SEE Jimmy's group.

Brache (DC)–*Enterprise* shuttlecraft Chekov used to nudge the *Clarke*, another shuttlecraft, out the hangar bay before the bomb on the *Clarke* exploded. *Brache* was wrecked when Chekvo attempted a hurried return landing.

Bracken (IT)–A stocky dark-haired man stationed on Nordstral station *Curie* who, suffering effects of Nordstral's magnetic fields, played an imaginary harp and believed he was a famous Scottish Highlander. He had worked on the *Soroya*, a plankton harvester in the icy Nordstral oceans. SEE Rory Dall Morison.

Brahmson (DC)–Chief of Security on Space Station Sigma One.

Bravo Station (Di)–One of several planetary defense installations located on Gamma Xaridian colony; destroyed by attacking Rithrim. SEE Rithra.

Bremerton, Oregon (BD)–Destination of Jimmy Kirk and his gang. Also location of a port dock for the dynacarrier *Sir Christopher Cockerell.*

Brennan (GSR)–*Enterprise* security officer and member of Kirk's boarding team to the *Ransom Castle.*

Brewster, Dr. (ST)–This adult Horta male was the supervisor of a team on Pegasus IV who studied pools of intelligent mud. SEE G'lops; Pegasus IV.

Briggs, Benjamin Spooner (SG)–Captain of the *Mary Celeste* in the 1870s. He, his wife, and baby daughter sailed on the *Celeste* and were lost. Only a drifting, empty ship was found.

Brotherhood of Aliens (UC)–Prisoners held at Rura Penthe who are non-Klingon band together to survive. Kirk was accepted as a member.

Brother's Keeper (GSR)–This hospital ship under the control of its flight master who issued the orders was an entrant in the Great Starship Race under the command of General Christoff Gogine.

bubble and squeak (DC)–Refers to the sounds made when frying a dish of potatoes, cabbage, and meat. Scotty once told McCoy that his father used this to threaten the children so it must have held a negative impression.

buffalo (ST)–Term is accurately applied to the cud-chewing mammal native to Terra's Indian continent but mistakenly applied to the same-sized mammal of the North American continent. As an authority on all things American western, Commodore Favere of Starbase 12 should have told his guests they were eating replicated bison meat. However, he used the term buffalo.

Burgoyne, Angus (BD)–This native Australian was captain of the pirate vessel *Shark*. Roy Moss killed him because he thought Burgoyne had attacked him. SEE Roy Moss.

Burke (UC)–An *Enterprise* ensign with an undistinguished record was pals with Samno. Both had a hatred toward Klingons, and both were killed by Valeris to prevent anyone learning they had killed Chancellor Gorkon. SEE Valeris.

Burns, Robert (P)–National poet of Scotland, a Terran nation associated with Great Britain. Being Scottish, Chief Engineer Scott always remembered Scotland's greatest poet with a birthday party at which he insisted on serving haggis.

Butler, Samuel (ST)–Terran author of the book titled *Erehwon*.

Byrd Station (IT)–Harvester stop located on Nordstral. Kirk and a group meet Captain Manderville here.

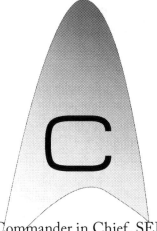

C-in-C (UC)–Abbreviation for Commander in Chief. SEE Smillie.

Callas (Di)–Captain of the *Potemkin* during this mission.

Camp Khitomer (UC)–SEE Khitomer Accord.

Canopia sector (DC)–*Enterprise* was scheduled to conduct three separate planetary explorations in this section before the events of this mission.

Capella IV (FD)–Trimble (137), who describes this planet as small, "predominantly greenish blue with red seas...rich in topaline" that has caused both the Federation and the Klingon Empire to mine the planet, also mentions that "one of the most beautiful flowers in the galaxy grows here" though "it has a life span of a few hours." This planet was also the sight of a Klingon attempt to incite the natives to war against Kirk's forces (*FC).

Cape Sorrow (FD)–Mountain located on Discord named by the Klingons. SEE Discord.

Capoeira (FD)–Afro-Brazilian art form combining elements of martial arts, music, and dance believed to have been created by African slaves brought to Brazil after the 16th century. Originally the participants formed a circle, playing instruments, singing, dancing, and taking turns sparring in pairs in the center of the circle. Action was marked by acrobatic play, feints, takedowns, leg sweeps, kicks, and head butting. Some historians insist the purpose of the dance was to improve fighting abilities in preparing participants for war readiness. In time the dance developed into a more rigid form of martial art, but with a less deadly aspect. By the time Sulu began practicing *capoeira*, opponents with blades strapped to their ankles faced each other and delivered non-lethal blows and parries in time to music by swinging their legs high in attack to see how close one could get to the other without inflicting damage. Flexibility and rapidity of movement is most important ("*Capoeira*"). Sulu compared *capoeira* to Orion dance-fighting, telling Kirk he was working his way through the variety of martial arts.

Captain Hogwild (GSR)–Derogatory term Nancy Ransom called Kirk.

Careta IV (WLW)–StarFleet's initial charter called for exploration of space, mapping and exploring as its ships ventured outward from Headquarters. As part of this plan, Kirk and the *Enterprise* had been assigned to escort a group of twenty researchers to the

Dulciphar star cluster to investigate a report of possible Meztorien culture ruins. Other records confirmed the area around Careta IV to have once harbored densely populated civilizations, and Kirk's survey team identified the Careta system as a promising area of study. Spock's summary of the survey data, delivered at the first briefing with Kirk, declared the system's star was "classified as F 9...gradually fading for the last 500,000 years...orbited by 10 planets, most of them small...a broad zone of widely scattered asteroids between the fifth and sixth planets. The third and fourth planets [are found to be] in the habitable zone...[with] climates [that] are marginal...[none of the surveys indicated] the presence of intelligent life." When questioned by Kirk about the asteroid belt, Spock reported the "possibility exists that artifacts remain. The Meztoriens often established orbiting habitats...that they otherwise did not occupy." He estimated "7.25 days to scan the belt" to ensure nothing had been missed. Spock also reminded Kirk that their orders were to look for Meztorien ruins and that the numbers of "orphan archaeological sites" reported in the quadrant may have no context. However, Spock declared the fourth planet was viable for ruins. It became the target of study after a brief survey revealed ruins. The briefing of ship's officers, those who were to lead teams to the surface, concurred that Careta IV was a planet worth investigating. Spock's science reports included data that the planet was "a class-M with a gravity of 0.85 of Terra [with an] oxygen content...below optimum for humans [but] well within range tolerated by Vulcans." Other information revealed the planet had a cool climate with sparse vegetation and low rainfall suggesting arid conditions. Additional scans revealed Meztorien ruins and several anomalies scattered around the planet. Five of the largest sites identified as Sites 1-5 were scanned for more detail. Following the conclusion of the initial mission to Careta IV, Kirk, with consensus of all involved except Dr. Kaul, made the recommendation to the Federation Council that the Careta system, especially Careta IV be quarantined. SEE Careta IV ruins; Kh!lict.

Careta IV landing team (WLW)–Twenty-three personnel from the *Enterprise* composed the landing team. They surveyed areas, made scans, and generally determined the ground situation. The group consisted of Kirk, Spock, McCoy, Chekov, Uhura, Scotty, Sulu, and McBenga, as well as ship's linguist Nadia Hernandez, ship's historian Tallieu, biologists Lt. Jylor, Dara Niles, and Ensign Bovray. Engineer Terrenson and alien technology expert Temren Knealayz were included along with security members Bradford Nairobi, McGaven, Timmons, and Lt. Jacobs. Archeologists Dr. Abdul Ramesh Kaul and his assistants Talika Nyar, Meredith Lassiter, and Anton Kordes accompanied them. Of this group, Bovray and Nairobi lost their lives on this mission. SEE transit-frame.

Careta IV ruins (WLW)–Two areas, Site J3 and Site N4, were determined to be the best choice to investigate first. Initial orbital scans showed Site J3 to have less weathering and more shelter as well as better preserved artifacts. The scan also revealed buried structures whose age was estimated in excess of 100,000 years. Once teams were on the surface, their scanners revealed the ruins were twice as old. A transit-frame at this site caused Kirk's people a lot of trouble. Consensus was the Meztoriens had explored this system, discovered the Kh!lict ruins and then elaborately concealed them with massive rubble piles and jamming fields. Both had remained in place for thousands of years. When the *Enterprise's* crew excavated the site of the anomalous sensor readings, they discovered "four huge basalt slabs standing on their edges, capped by a fifth" twice as tall as Captain Kirk, and forming a cube with a near impossible hint at how it had been constructed. The exposed cube did not register on scanners. Scotty's group of engineers rigged up a winch and pulley system to pull the blocks apart. Their efforts resulted in the release of suldanic gas that nearly killed them all. The object within the shielded block was described by Dr. Lassiter as "about two meters high and four meters long, but only ten centimeters thick." Kirk detailed in his report that one side was a metallic blue-grey unmarred surface while the other resembled "a pair of plate-glass windows enclosed in a flat black frame" and added that "the glass window side seemed to reveal a lifelike landscape with knee-deep grass. The glassy sheen of the window-like surface was the only thing that differentiated it from its background." The other side remained blank, suggesting a one-way viewing. Once uncovered the power levels steadied after 7.3 hours. Temperature changes were noted whenever anyone came close. Touching the dark side produced a tingling that repelled the touch by its force field. According to Chekov's report, the glass-like surface produced a soothing warmth and engulfed his arm, making it difficult to pull away. Chekov and Taika Nyar experimented with throwing non-organic objects at it, but none penetrated. Inadvertently they fell "through" the transit-frame, emerging re-constructed as crablike beings. Uncertain how to rescue Chekov and Nyar, Kirk took three security guards and entered the same transit-frame while Spock and his team began identifying other transit-frames. Another area on the planet revealed a hidden complex, its entrance partially destroyed. Spock and his seven team members concentrated on it after discovering decorative carvings that had once surrounded an entryway. A large cavern, once hidden, lay exposed by rock slides. Their scans "showed alien prisoners being slaughtered on low blocky alters" as one report stated. Spock reported that some of the scenes revealed "ritual sacrifices" of "eviscerated, flayed, and dismembered bodies of half a dozen non-Kh!lict races, including two known only from single, isolated occurrences." Inspection of this cavern revealed bits of metal and pink damaged columns. Here partially destroyed carvings showed "scenes of mass sacrifices and ritual murders" and were estimated to be 300,000 years old. Spock estimated the cavern was as large as the *Enterprise* hangar deck. The blast that destroyed the entrance also destroyed much of the cavern. Pushing a central medallion opened a door, protected by a force field, into a corridor whose walls were a "mottled rusty beige" with a low ceiling. Doors that led to various rooms bore "deeply carved pictures of violent and brutal scenes." Some depicted "mass sacrifices." Some of the victims were known races. This corridor was labeled to be in "pristine condition" and was considered a "still-functioning library." The rooms, most of them, were empty or had piles of fibrous debris or "sandstone slabs which resembled narrow waist-high, backless benches." Some objects resembled "desks or tables made of blocks of limestone." None of the rooms seemed to have a light source though they were lighted. One of the landing team noted that "150 meters from the entrance first cross-corridor" were a number of cross-corridors, that indicated this cavern was a master complex. The conclusion was that this structure was the "ceremonial entrance... designed to awe and intimidate" visitors. Rooms nearer the entrance probably were meeting rooms. Spock's conclusion to his report stated that the Kh!lict were a highly repressive society with an extreme degree of paranoia. All those involved in studying this cavern noted the difficulty they had with their scanners due to the shielded walls. *Enterprise's* sensors also had difficulty keeping a fixed position on the "complex cut from solid rock." Dr. Lassiter wrote in her notes that the there had been no attempt to alter colors or textures, that function of an area or room appeared to correlate to color and rock type, that some corridor rooms connected to other similar rooms, that two rooms straddled the fault line, the door of one such room "depicted scenes of tortures, sacrificial slaughter, ritual brutality with such precise and graphic detail" that the interpretation was correct. Spock's report revealed an entrance door that swung open onto "a long and narrow room with a fault line bisecting its entire length." In the center was "a block of grey limestone spotted with purplish stains on its top, sides, and floor." Beyond the limestone block, sensors became affective and Spock was able to reveal the controls of a transport system that sent the group to another area. They arrived in "a huge amphitheater-like room lit...by small diffuse lights...in the rafters of the high, vaulted ceiling...at one end of the arena floor was a broad ramp leading to an enclosed area whose doors were plain and unadorned." Spock concluded that within a few minutes of their discovery of an intra-building transport system, the system transported them to the control center, "an arena encircled by wide tiers that stepped upward, with squares, rectangles, and strangely shaped boxes [that] filled the space on each level." The arena appeared to be a Holy of Holies. Equipment here contained "information that programmed, directed, and controlled the Kh!lict people with a completeness made possible only by the unique construction of the Kh!lict brain," Dr. Lassiter wrote in her report, adding that banks of machinery whose "controls were laid out on the sloping surfaces were designed to be manipulated by Kh!lict claws, [and] several limbs were needed to activate the machinery." Nothing was identified by a written language. "Consoles were color-coded" with small readout devices "that displayed the colors of the spectrum on a two-minute cycle." A door opening out from the arena had to be activated by a Kh!lict's pincers on the precise spots and once done the walls went transparent. Kirk wrote in his report that the revealed room featured "two tiled misshaped consoles that were the master units that directed everything in the complex. The floor plan was a snarled maze through pillars of consoles guarded by a distortion field. The main control console for the transit-frames was on the wall. Only one console remained active in the room. Control room machinery could only be operated by a female Kh!lict." Kirk and Spock considered destroying the unit. However, Spock, after much study, concluded the *Enterprise* had no way "to sever the links between the Kh!lict devices and their power sources." He also was uncertain if a photon torpedo would be able to do so and concluded the devices were protected because only a Kh!lict female could activate them.

Carey, Diane–Author of *Best Destiny*.
Carlos (BD–SEE Carlos Florida.

Carter, Councilor (ST)–Female counselor and chairperson of the committee on StarFleet Operations. She requested that Hazel Payton be taken on the *Enterprise* during its search for the secret weapon. SEE Hazel Payton.

Carter, Nancy (SS)–Wife of archeologist Robert Carter. She was killed prior to 2266 by the last surviving member of a race on planet M113 who assumed her image. Kirk was forced to kill it to save his crew. Nancy and McCoy had once been very close (*MT). In SS, Jocelyn, McCoy's former wife, told Kirk she had known about Nancy Carter.

Cartwright, Admiral (P; SG; UC)–A dark complexioned man. For a short while he commanded a starship on patrol along the Romulan/Federation Neutral Zone. His opinion of Romulans was as low as his opinion of Klingons. Certain dealings with Klingons during his captaincy led to his hatred of and fear of all Klingons. He rose to become an admiral and then director of StarFleet Headquarters. When the Probe attacked Terra in 2286, he attempted to direct emergency actions. A few months after this incident, he called Kirk to his office and played a message from a friendly Romulan detailing chaos in the Empire and ordered Kirk to conduct personnel to Termais Four. Both incidents involved the Probe. In SG, Cartwright was kept informed by Kirk concerning the discovery of the derelict Romulan space station *Reltah*. In UC, he opposed any negotiations with the Klingons and called Kirk to Headquarters to meet with Rear Admiral Smillie and receive orders. When Kirk and McCoy were extradited to Qo'noS, he counseled retrieving them even if it meant going to war. Cartwright conspired with the Klingon General Chang and with Romulan Ambassador Nanclus to assassinate Chancellor Gorkon during peace talks in 2293. He also knew about the planned assassination of Atzebur and President Ra-ghoratrei. Kirk and team foiled the plot, and Cartwright was arrested along with the others.

Carver (P)–One of two ensigns Kirk requested to be with him when he met Penalt and his staff. Kirk sent Carver to help Scotty board the archaeology shuttle. SEE Smith; Penalt.

Carey, Diane – Author of *The Great Starship Race*.

Casanova (BD)–Term often applied to James T. Kirk. Both men were known for seducing women.

Caskie, Lou (BD)–Navigator on the pirate vessel the *Shark*. He had arthritic legs and was nearly toothless. One of possibly three crewmen taken from the *Shark* by StarFleet.

Catulla (P)–Theta Pictoria orbits a medium-sized red-orange star with nine planets of which Cendo-Prae or Catulla is the sixth. Its mass is comparable to Terra's though it has two moons, Millar and Milar. A thriving humanoid population of nearly 9.5 million enjoy a high-level of technological development. In the dim past a nuclear war nearly wiped out the entire Catullan world, leaving much of the land sterile, food supplies almost non-existence, and the people in danger of losing their culture. Since that time Catulla has focused much of its energy toward regaining what had been lost. The recent leap in recovery is credited to Ambassador Tongo Sil of Catulla. His devotion to the study and implementation of space science and interplanetary relations, especially with Federation help, has led to several decades of social rest. The planet's main industry, the building of warp spacecraft bodies, is located on the northern edge of the continent of Tesaker with other facilities in orbit (Johnson *Worlds* 42).

Catullan (P)–The home world of this species has been a member of UFP since 2269 (Okuda and Okuda *Encyclopedia* 68). A Catullan silver-haired female was a member of the Federation archaeology delegation to Temaris Four.

Catullan liquor (UC)–An extremely fiery liquor that Klingon Kesla preferred when he attempted to relieve his boredom. SEE Kesla; *qrokhang.*

CBB (Di)–An intra-ship Computer bulletin board for posting messages for the crew. The board was open and available to all ship members.

Cecil, Robert (DC)–He and Chekov were at the Academy at the same time and became good friends. Chekov remembered him as a brilliant person whose blond hair and pale eyes made him easily spotted in a crowded room. He served as science officer on the *USS Kongo* and died attempting to seal a containment field breach.

Central Septum (P)–The Romulan Praetor's body lay in state in the Hall of Columns in the capital city of Romulus.

Chablis (ST)–Wine served at Kent's dinner held aboard the *Enterprise*. SEE Kent.

Chagall, Marc (UC)–This Russian-born painter, print maker, and designer was born on July 7, 1887 and died on March 28, 1985. His work, especially "I and the Village," changed the image of psychic reality in modern art. One critic wrote that his colors were thin with whimsical elements that frequently portrayed images upside down and sideways (*Britannica*, 2000). Spock had an original Chagall, (10 by 13 inches) *Adam and Eve Banished from Paradise*, in his *Enterprise* quarters. When Valeris asked him what was being portrayed, he told her it illustrated Terra's mythological story of Adam and Eve's expulsion from Paradise.

Chaiken (DC)–This female auditor, one of several sent to access *Enterprise*, shared quarters with Gendron. Sulu found her and Taylor, another auditor, murdered. SEE Gendron.

Chak (Di)–Parath'aa commander of the five ships carrying the plasma cannon for an attack on Cygni Maxima.

chameloid (UC)–Shape-shifting life-form. SEE Martia.

Chang (UC)–Chief of Staff to Klingon Chancellor Gorkon. Though short in stature for a Klingon, he made up the height in a forceful personality. His bald head displayed the bony ridges, and a small wisp of grey hair at the base of his head gave him distinction. His left eye, lost in a battle, was covered with a dark patch. He earned the nickname "Chang the Merciless." This proud warrior feared the end of military strikes and disapproved of any attempt at peace between the Empire and the Federation. He greatly admired the Klingon version of *Hamlet* and quoted from it. Conspiring with Admiral Cartwright of the Federation and Romulan Ambassador Nanclus, he disrupted the initial peace talks by firing on Gorkon's ship from a cloaked ship hidden beneath the *Enterprise* thus making everyone believe the *Enterprise* had fired. Then he lied to Atzebur about Kirk's part in the murder of Gorkon. He died aboard his ship *Dakronh*, when Kirk destroyed it.

Chapel, Christine (P)–This beautiful blond Terran female was a research biologist who held several degrees, one of which was in bio-research. She had already completed several years of StarFleet service before signing aboard the *Enterprise*. After her finance Roger Korby had been reported lost on an expedition, Chapel entered the Service as a means of searching for some indication that he was still alive. Eventually she located him and learned he had deposited his mind into an android body. A confrontation with Kirk led to Korby's death (*LG) and the severing of all of Chapel's emotional bonds with Terra. She chose to remain on the *Enterprise*, settling into the role of nurse to Dr. McCoy. In later years she again experienced the androids that Korby had found when she, along with other *Enterprise* crew were captured and duplicated (Friedman *Double)*. Her rank when she came to the *Enterprise* was as a lieutenant. Over the years she earned several promotions. Her quiet dependable character, the depths of her training, and the steadiness she showed in emergencies, made her invaluable to Sick Bay. She continued to be a positive force on the ship and in the medical area. Dedicated to being the best medical person she could be, Christine continued her medical studies. During the mission involving Dr. Omen, she monitored Kirk's physical condition while he stared into the Aleph. When he broke off contact, she helped him to Sick Bay and couldn't understand why he kept thanking her (Gilden *Trap)*. Dr. McCoy sometimes left her in charge of Sick Bay. She was in charge one time while he was on the Romulan space station. Another time she healed Kirk's broken ribs received during a Romulan attack (Crandall *Shell)*.

Charlie X (P)–Kirk was reminded of his encounter with Charlie (*CX). Thasians rescued a three-year-old child, the only one to survive a transport crash on Thasus in 2249 and gave him extraordinary powers to help him survive. When he came aboard *Enterprise*, his inexperience with humans and his powers made it undesirable to keep him aboard. The Thasians returned him to the planet where *Enterprise* had found him (Okuda and Okuda *Chronology* 32).

Checkers, Lt. (IT)–Name Nordstral station manager Nicholai Steno deridingly called Chekov.

Chekov, Pavel Andreievick–StarFleet Serial Number: SE 658-749. Chekov, an only child (*WM), was born in Puskino, Russia, a Terran town near Moscow, to Aleksei Mikhailovich Chekov and Catherine Rykova (Rostler "Chekov" 6). One historian establishes his birth date as September 19, 2242 or sd1290.7 (Mandel *Manual* 29) while another gives the year as 2345 (Okuda and Okuda *Chronology* 31). According to information obtained from one *Enterprise's* mission, Chekov was raised on the planet Novy Riga (Larson *Pawns)* and moved back to Terra. His record states he graduated from high school in Volgograd, Russia (Kagan *Song)*. Mandel, an early biographer, writes that he entered StarFleet Academy at age eighteen as part of an exchange program by Moskva University and transferred to Command Training School where his navigation instructor Lt. Arex awarded him special honors. Within three years, he graduated *cum laude* with a grade average of 3.6 (Rostler "Chekov" 6). His *Kobayashi Maru* test captaining the *Yorktown* sent to rescue a stranded ship resulted in his choosing to blow up his ship rather than surrender to the attacking Klingons. A biographer who researched his love life during his Academy years discovered Chekov became involved with Irina Galliulin, but they both considered themselves too young to make a commitment. Chekov wanted to pursue service in the Fleet, while Irina, who had frequently told him she was uncomfortable with the regimented life StarFleet required, wanted a more self-centered life. They met later when Dr. Servin and his group who were searching for a mythical planet called Eden came on board *Enterprise*. Again neither could quite commit to the other's dreams (*WEd). When Chekov finally decided to seek a commitment, he contacted Irina only to learn she was already involved and didn't wish to pursue a relationship (Dillard *Country*). At age twenty-two, Chekov arrived on the *Enterprise* as assistant to Mr. Spock, commander of the Science Department (Mandel *Manual* 29). For a brief time he served on the USS *Lermontov*, a galactic cruiser, sd6019, but returned to the *Enterprise* on sd7808 (Mandel *Manual* 29). Within the year, sd3478, following the death of Lt. Cmdr. Gary Mitchell (*WNM), Kirk, who had already had several navigators, believed Chekov ready for the position of Chief Navigator. Since the *Enterprise* was his first Fleet assignment, he set himself the task of learning the ship aft to stern, port to starboard. He found the best way to do this was to serve duty time at various stations. An *Enterprise* duty he found enjoyable was working with Dr. McCoy to update the ship's musical library. Although he recommended only Russian composers, he did understand why McCoy wanted a variety (Bonanno *Probe*). To further broaden his experiences, he requested additional responsibility and was appointed Second Ordnance Officer under Spock's supervision. He served at various Bridge stations, and frequently took over Spock's Library-Computer Station when Spock was off the Bridge or in Bridge command. Since Chekov showed a logical mind, Spock often gave him special projects. His on-the-job training paid off. Kirk frequently took him on landing parties and believed he had starship command potential. At one time while Kirk and Scotty were enjoying the pubs on Starbase 32, the ship had been left in the hands of Commodore Snodgrass while her crew was busy updating key elements of *Enterprise's* weapon. She left Chekov in Bridge control. He delivered a priority message from Admiral Satanta to Kirk who signed off with "Carry on, Captain" (Milan *Depths*). As one of the youngest crew members, Chekov frequently was "dragooned" into service at social functions as an extra male (Gilden *Trap*). His personal, medical, and military records contain interesting material. The file included several reprimands for fighting. He was involved in a brawl on Space Station K-7 which Kirk noted. It also included a reprimand from Kirk related to his actions during a battle with Rithra raiders. When Kirk ordered a maneuver, Chekov questioned it. Kirk relieved him from the Bridge and confined him to quarters. Searching for redemption for his Bridge action, Chekov created a graphics program composed of all the sensor scans taken during the Rithra raid on *Enterprise*. It proved valuable in determining how to combat the raiders (David *Disinherited*). His psychological profile, while noting that he was intelligent, witty, and excitable, also stated he exhibited a basic insecurity hidden under "flagrant nationalism and...pride in his Soviet heritage" (Mandel *Manual* 30). It also included the note that his admiration of Captain Kirk bordered on idolatry, and he often effected Kirk's mannerisms (Roddenberrry, 250-251). The medical file references a list of medical treatments. During his first months on *Enterprise* (the year is recorded as 2267), Kirk included

Chekov on a landing party to Gamma Hydra IV. All were exposed to an aging disease. Only Chekov did not become infected because a sudden surge of adrenaline caused by the sight of a dead colonist protected him (*DY; Okuda and Okuda *Encyclopedia* 73). He faced near death on Nordstral when Kirk sent him, Uhura, and three Security men to search for missing personnel of Nordstral Pharmaceuticals. They faced deadly cold and bitter winds to discover Nordstral's secret, and during that period, he was bitten by a kraken and came close to dying (Graf *Ice*). During another mission, Chekov suffered from ADF syndrome (Kagan *Song*). A fractured shoulder and several puncture wounds, one that damaged a lung, required he spend several weeks in regeneration therapy (*GT). Minor cuts and bruises received during a brawl on Space Station K-7 were treated by Dr. McCoy (*TT). The experience of having a Ceti eel thread itself via his ear canal to a position near the brain stem affected him for several months afterwards although McCoy treated him immediately the eel left the ear, and Kirk destroyed it (McIntrye *Khan*). Unusual things have happened to Chekov. Sent back in time to Terra during its World War II, he experienced several battles and was awarded a third-class medal as Hero to the Soviet Union. A second medal was awarded posthumously by Stalin in a Kremlin ceremony (Kramer-Rolls *Home*). He and several other crew members were duplicated as androids and came close to death (Friedman *Double*). The most harrowing, according to Chekov, had to be on Careta IV when he spent two days in a Kh!lict body (Mitchell *Windows*). Exposure to an entity from Beta XII-A had him imagining he had a brother named Piotr (*Dv). Chekov's biographers are quick to note some of his more unusual missions which they discover in his records. At the time of the encounter with Khan, Chekov was serving on the *Reliant* (McIntyre *Khan*). He was the navigator for the Bridge group that followed Kirk back to Genesis to rescue and return Spock's body to Vulcan to be reunited with his *katra*. He again served as navigator when Kirk and company went back in time to Terra's 1980s to collect two humpback whales and return with them to the future. Chekov was a novice in the crew when Kirk and ship went to Rithra (David *Disinherited*). At the conclusion of Kirk's five-year missions, Lieutenant Chekov was left wondering what direction he should take. He knew most of the Bridge crew would be retiring soon and he had no desire to serve aboard *Enterprise* without his friends. His attempt to re-establish a relationship with Irina Galliulin had been rebuffed when she informed him she was in a relationship with another (Dillard *Country*). The choice was delayed when he stayed on board after Kirk learned StarFleet Command intended him to escort Chancellor Gorkon's flag ship to the peace talks. As part of Security, Chekov helped search for the ones who had killed Gorkon (Dillard *Country*). After this incident, Kirk moved to the Admiralty, and Chekov applied to the Academy for Command classes. A later historian discovered he was considered too young, but was accepted to Security Training as an ensign (Graf *Traitor*). His Security training was grueling but he succeeded and in the mission identified as *Shell Game* by its writer, Chekov was head of Security on *Enterprise*. Between the time Kirk "retired" into the Admiralty and emerged to once again captain a ship, Chekov completed his Security training and Command Training and was assigned to Captain Terrell's *Reliant* as its First Officer.

Quite possibly his first assignment as Chief of Security occurred during the mission to Careta IV (Mitchell *Windows*). Opportunity to again serve with Kirk came when Kirk regained a ship captaincy and began running missions. Chekov requested duty with him and became *Enterprise's* Chief of Security (Mitchell *Windows*; Crandall *Shell*). The mission to Careta IV was one of the first he participated in after arriving as Chief of Security (Mitchell *Windows*). He displayed nerve and quick thinking during the events recorded in *Death Count*. Chekov, as head of Security, was alerted to a bomb's location on the ship and was able to encase it to lessen its destructive force before taking actions to solve the mystery of both the bomb and several deaths on board (Graf *Death*). Chekov would be the first to admit that his life among the stars was never dull for very long. He and Sulu formed a bond of friendship that extended throughout their lives. In the years following Kirk's death, the two kept in close touch with the other Bridge officers and frequently had time to visit. An early biographer noted that Chekov earned four commendations, including the StarFleet Unit Citation, with Cluster. That historian also mentions six awards of valor and three Academy demerits. The same writer indicates Chekov served on two other StarFleet ships prior to moving to *Enterprise* (Rostler "Chekov" 6-7). These two can be considered to have been training ships. Arriving as a dewy-eyed lad barely out of his teens, Chekov grew into a man that Kirk was proud of, Sulu admired for his youth and bravery, Uhura loved for his joy of life, and McCoy found always ready to give credit to his mother country for any and every thing.

Chekov's office (DC)–Now Chief of Security, Chekov's office was on Deck 5 which contained an equipment cabinet, a work terminal, a small desk and two chairs.

Chekov's task (Di)–Kirk assigned Chekov to initiate a search, starting in the Xaridian system, to determine who in the area could supply small ships for attacking Federation colonies. Chekov began by running astrogation maps of the systems, including all the colonies and marking those that had been attacked. Then he added theoretical limits to the raiding ships. By doing this, he was able to narrow the search to five or six populated solar systems, including Parathu'ul. His project alerted Spock and Kirk to the fact the Parath'aa had requested admission to the Federation and had been denied.

Chekov, Vanya (SG)–Uncle to Chekov.

Cheshire Cat (SG)–Allusion to the disappearing cat of the children's novel *Alice in Wonderland*. McCoy, having won a verbal battle with Spock about Spock's curiosity concerning the Romulan space station just discovered, awarded Spock with a smug look and a grin similar to the Cheshire Cat's.

Chiltons (FF)–Family members of the terraforming team on Beta Canzandia.

Chin Gatling (FD)–Type of weapon Aileea dinAthos recognized as a heavy pair of machine guns employed by the Stilters. A very early version, 12.7 by 108 mm caliber four-barrel Gatling gun (a repeating shooter), was developed the Terran Soviets.

Chinit Clan (IT)–One of several Nordstral Kitka groups. They believed their god did not care for humans, only for them. SEE Nordstral; Ghyl.

Chinatown (P)–Area located in San Francisco, Terra , began to attract Chinese immigrants following the establishment of a business by two immigrants in 1948. Sulu and Kirk had set a time for a tour, but Kirk was called to Admiral Cartwright's office.

Chorrl (FF)–Klingon crew member of the *Kadn'ra* and member of Captain Vheled's team searching for the five children hiding in the hills of Beta Canzandai. Chorrl was killed by his shipmate Grael. SEE Grael.

chrondnikos (FF)–Harvested from the alien fir trees and made into a casserole of oily yellowish fibers.

C-Lift (UC)–One of several elevators used to deploy the prisoner/miners on Rura Penthe. Martia directed Kirk and McCoy to this one for their escape.

Citadel (P)–Building in Romulus capital. The translated term is considered to identify a near impregnable fortress attached to the seat of government. SEE Jandra.

Clancy (GSR)–Crew member of the *Ransom Castle*, probably killed by boarding Romulans.

Clark (ST)–Female lieutenant and one of two women seated next to Spock during Commodore Favere's dinner. After the evening entertainment she insisted Spock escort her home.

Clark, Louise (GSR)–Cook on the *Ransom Castle*; killed by boarding Romulans.

Clarke (DC)–One of *Enterprise*'s shuttles. Destroyed when its engine core was damaged by an overloaded phaser. To save the ship from an explosion, Chekov employed the *Brache* to maneuver the *Clarke* from the hangar into open space where it exploded.

class B jamming field (WLW)–Designation of a powerful shield able to withstand extensive bombardment.

Class-J freighter (ST)–A gutted freighter of this type was used in Dr. Omen's experiment with deflectors. He tested his latest development of phased field generators. *Enterprise* fired a torpedo spread onto the freighter but its shield strength dropped by only 2% with no perceptible damage noted. Later the freighter was discovered to have large jagged holes throughout the hull which had an appearance of an empty basket. Its condition was later learned to have been created by Omen's phased deflectors that caused changes in the crystalline structure of metal, causing the hull to disintegrate over time.

Cochrane, Zephram----History records Zephram Cochrane was born in 2030 (Okuda and Okuda *Chronology* 19) and is credited with the design and completion of specs for space warp drive, completing a prototype ship that demonstrated its ability to fly at warp speed. The first test was conducted on April 4, 2063 (Okuda and Okuda *Encyclopedia* 81). In another source by the same historian the test date is identified as the year 2061 (*Chronology* 20). The first date could be that of the development while the second refers to the initial trial run. Biographies and histories of this period confuse events in Cochrane's life. The Goldsteins (*Chronology* 52-53) indicate the discovery of intelligent life in the Alpha Centauri System occurred in 2048 and imply that Cochrane may have been a member of the discovery crew. Reading between the lines of the Goldsteins' history, the idea is suggested that Cochrane may have developed his warp drive specs during the six-year period of travel. They record that by 2055 the first test was run and proved successful with blueprints for future ships appearing on the drawing boards. The first interstellar application is believed to have occurred on the UNSS *Powell* which returned Cochrane to Terra (Goldsteins *Chronology* 69). Okuda and Okuda (*Encyclopedia* 80) differ with the Goldsteins and believe the invention occurred in 2063 when Cochrane, working with an engineer named Lily Slone, constructed his own ship in an abandoned missile complex in North American and conducted his first flight with her help. Speculation is that between the time Terra began applying Cochrane's theories and the first warp drive ship emerged from drydock, Cochrane had already moved permanently to Alpha Centauri. One historian called him Zephram Cochrane of Alpha Centauri (*Mt), and another historian indicated that Cochrane was born on Terra and emigrated to Alpha after the invention of the warp drive, possibly employing it to propel his ship (Okuda and Okuda *Chronology* 20). Regardless of the facts, his test flight attracted the attention of a Vulcan ship whose crew reported Terra's technological level had reached interstellar flight and should be investigated. Vulcan made official contact a few weeks later and Terra was considered a space-faring world. Soon Cochrane discovered his work being interrupted by too many adoring visitors wanting to meet and shake hands with him. When the public proved to be absorbing too much of his time, he determined to find another place, less accessible, and thus took himself to Alpha Centauri and established a laboratory where he continued work on the warp drive. Even here, he was bothered by well-wishers, and at age 87 determined to get away from all the adulation. Telling no one his destination, he set out alone in a shuttle craft. Within days the ship's signal was lost. After exhaustive searches by authorities, Cochrane was pronounced dead in 2117. In a few years numerous plaques commemorated his contributions. Okuda and Okuda (*Encyclopedia* 80-81) state Cochrane "revolutionized space travel" and his name became "revered throughout the known galaxy" with planets, universities, and children named after him. The area of Montana, Terra, from where he flew the first warp-powered flight, is now a planet shrine to both Cochrane and Slone. A statue was erected in his honor and he became one of few people to be awarded the Dynastic Liberation Prize (Marshak and Culbreath *Fate*). However, Cochrane did not die in space 150 years before Kirk's mission (Trimble 142). In 2267, Kirk found him alive but could hardly believe the man he met was 237 years old (*Mt). Kirk described him as dark-haired, handsome, and healthy. Kirk's log does not remark about his appearance other than what he included in his report. Cochrane told Kirk that he had suffered radiation poisoning in a space accident and regained his senses on the planet where Kirk found him. An entity Cochrane called Companion rescued him and restored him to his early mature years. In his log, Kirk theorized that Cochrane's altered appearance may have been the Companion's attempt at an idealized self-image it had "read" from Cochrane's mind (Okuda and Okuda (*Encyclopedia* 80-81). Though Cochrane, at first, determined to leave the planet, he changed his mind when he learned the Companion, in order to be more acceptable to him, had assumed the body of the dead Commissioner Nancy Hedford. The transformation restricted her to living a normal life on the planet. Cochrane, learning that the Companion had chosen her action out of love for him, chose to stay with her. Before Kirk left, Cochrane did speak with him about his remarkable discovery. To a question Kirk posed, Cochrane merely replied: "Don't try to be a great man, just be a man, and let history make its own judgment" (Okuda and Okuda *Encyclopedia* 81). Kirk probably informed him that a monument to him and his invention had been erected in Montana, Terra, to commemorate that first flight. Before Kirk, Spock, and McCoy left Gamma Canaris N, they agreed to keep the truth about Cochrane secret. Although Kirk had to leave a log of events, he shielded it. Only after Kirk's missions formally ended did a full entry become part of Federation's data base for the *Enterprise* missions. Years later the record was opened and made available to historians.

Code Blue (UC)–Medical term for an emergency. Sickbay called a Code Blue for crewmen Burke and Samno to lure their killer out of hiding. SEE Valeris.

Code One Emergency (BD)–StarFleet order that alerts the entire crew to report to their respective areas and station assigned duties.

Code Three (IT)–StarFleet code refers to a potentially dangerous ground situation. Chekov invoked this rule before the initial meeting with Alion. SEE Alion.

Coffey (DC)–*Enterprise* crewman and Sweeney's bunkmate who packed Sweeney's personal belongs for shipment home. SEE Sweeney.

colony forms (FD)–Discord's "true natives inhabit Venus-like micro-environments of volcanic vents" at the bottom of Hellsgate. As a colony of microscopic forms they are telepathic. Subjected to their probing, Spock effected communication and learned of the Klingon warship hiding in the depths of the sea. SEE Discord.

Columbia (WLW)–One of *Enterprise's* shuttlecraft.

Committee-to-get-things-done (Di)–Humorous remark by Delacort about the original committee established by the colony on Gamma Xaridian. SEE Delacourt.

Communicator (P)–One of many names given to the Probe. This one suggests a knowledge-seeking dialogue. SEE Probe.

Concert (P)–Jandra and Dr. Benar collaborated on a concert based on the two clear messages, "there is no danger" and "we will talk," sent from the *Enterprise* to the Probe. The music was played by a single augmented keyboard that allowed Jandra to play both messages/music while other messages/songs were played by the orchestra conducted by Dr. Benar. The music score is difficult but quite beautiful. Kirk realized when he heard the concert that the two messages had been reversed: "we will talk...there is no danger." He hoped this message conveyed to both the Federation and the Romulan Empire.

Coney Island (SG)–An amusement area in the southern part of Brooklyn, N. Y. , Terra. It opened in 1920 and soon became the best known amusement area in the United States, offering a large Boardwalk fronted by a sand beach on one side and rides, exhibitions, restaurants, and souvenirs on the other. In time the entire area was destroyed by weakened foundations and encroaching seas. Ensign Hallie had remarked that the darkened Romulan space station reminded her of an amusement park at night. Her remark made McCoy recall seeing tapes of Coney Island before its destruction.

Constellation (Di)–Commodore Decker captained this ship (*DMa).

Consul of Foreign Ports (GSR)–Representative on Starbase 10 who took control and responsibility for cargo any of the race entrants were carrying and stored them in a bonded warehouse on Starbase 10.

Coral Sea (P)–A group of islands east of Queensland in the great Pacific Ocean on Terra is bounded on the north by an area known as the Solomon Sea and south by the Tasmen Sea. Discovered by James Cook, the area acquired its name based on the numerous coral formation highlighted on its western side by the Australian Great Barrier Reef. George and Gracie, two humpback whales, lived here in their new Cetacean Institute.

Corey (SG)–One of two Security guards sent by shuttle to rescue the landing party from the Romulan space station *Reltah*. SEE Jaffe.

Cortez (Di)–*Enterprise* ensign at the Bridge Engineering station when the ship made initial contact with the raiders in the meteor swarm in the Gamma Xaridian system. He was injured during the battle.

cortico-snyaptic modulator (WLW)–Medical device designed to stimulate, excite, and modulate electrical impulses in the brain. It can be calibrated for several alien brain patterns as well as for human.

Corus (GSR)–Romulan navigator on the *Scorah*; killed in fire between *Scorah* and *Enterprise*.

Cossacks (FD)–These atmospheric vehicles with chubby wedge-shaped hulls full of weaponry clumped together are identified as Stilters' ship. Four of them are carried and deployed from Goebbels, a "mother" ship. SEE Stilters.

Coss, Peter (Di)–This tall, boney man with pale skin and straw-colored hair was the *Lexington's* chief surgeon on this mission. When notified of the medical problem the Rithrim were having, he extended the facilities of the ship's Sick Bay. SEE Rithrim.

Cotswolds (BD)–A stretch of hill country known for its stone walls, cottages, and mansions accenting the wooded area located in the middle of England, Terra. Captain Robert April was familiar with this area.

Court Recorder (UC)–All StarFleet vessels, particular cruisers have a crewman who records vital information given by witnesses. A court recorder was called to Sickbay as a trick to lure the murderer of Burke and Samno out of hiding. SEE Burke; Samno.

Cousteau (IT)–One of three submarine plankton harvesters employed in the icy Nordstral seas.

Coventry (BD)–City in central England, Terra. Captain Robert April had fond memories of this place.

Creation Play (WLW)–A notable stage presentation presented by Deveron 5 depicting their beliefs surrounding the creation of their world.

Crockett (ST)–Federation scout ship destroyed during a battle with Klingons. SEE Barbara Omen.

cubaya (FF)–Migratory beasts native to Alpha Maluria Six described by Kirk as fat and clumsy "like small walruses with short muscular legs instead of flippers" and "coats ranging from russet to very dark brown. They look ugly and smell ugly." Their main enemy is the gettrex. SEE Manteil/Obirrhat quarrel.

Cygnus Eridani (DC)–*Enterprise* intercepted a distress call from this star system and discovered the *Umyfymu*, an Orion freighter posing as unarmed and in need of help. Ship's sensor revealed it to be a T-class Orion destroyer disguised as a freighter.

Cynthia Blaine (GSR)–Entrant ship in the Great Starship Race commanded by Leo Blaine who had named it for his mother. It flew the flag of the Blaine Aerospace Company.

crystals (P)–The Exodus Hall discovered intact on Temaris Four held a crystal seated on a high pedestal with its lattice structure intact. Its internal structure, Spock wrote in his report, revealed a set of mathematics "with a progressive series of examples to contextually define the symbols, starting with simple addition and subtraction and ending with a form of vector analogies." He theorized this was a tutorial that ended in "a series of coordinates...using Temaris...and the galactic center as reference points...." In the center of the Probe a similar globular crystal was found, buried in ice. Each of its facets was "divided into a series of irregular polygons [and] housed in a room nearly a kilometer tall and three to six kilometers wide with a circular tunnel leading off that served as an entrance." Sonic holograms portrayed on the ceiling revealed immense leviathans. SEE Crystal Wisdom.

Crystal Wisdom (P)–Information held within the Probe's crystal. The crystal contained the history and wisdom of the Probe's creators and produced the sonic holograms of hundreds of leviathans and the sounds that were their language. This information also contained references to the first and second Winnowing. SEE Winnowing. Though the Probe could find no living creator, it revealed the story of its sun and planet's destruction from an asteroid.

Curie (IT)–Orbital station located at Nordstral. Nordstral Pharmaceuticals built and serviced this station commanded by Nicholai Steno. Interior was painted an "institutional pond-skum grey" (McCoy's words) with no wall decorations. Transporter station room was small and staffed by one person. During Kirk's mission to Nordstral, the station's community recreation room housed those employees considered "insane."

customary dispatch (BD)–The quick, lawful, diligent loading and unloading and discharging of vessels from docking stations is a formal order covering all actions and details of such work.

cyclor (ST)–A weapon that propels whatever it hits in the opposite direction. Klingees that Kirk met in the second Aleph used one to repel the *Enterprise*, throwing it about 500,000 kilometers from its original spot. After Kirk mentioned to the Klingee Captain Iola that his cyclor had a microscopic crack, Kirk was granted permission to approach the Aleph. Back in his own time, Kirk informed Klingon Captain Torm that StarFleet knew about their cyclor. Torm immediately contacted Qo'noS.

Cygni Maxima (Di)–A yellow star with seven planets and two asteroid belts. Originally charted by the *Hood* seventeen years before this mission. StarFleet declared it off limits because its culture was below any in the Federation. The Parath'aa intended to subjugate the system.

Dab (Di)–A small, short squat female with exaggerated musculature in the hip area was a native of Rithra. She featured a short stiff-looking almost spiny crest. As head of the procreation center threatened by flowing volcanic lava, she appealed to Commodore Wesley for help though at first she looked to her governing council for leadership.

Dagger (FD)–Klingon battle cruiser captained by Kain, commanding officer of the Klingon Imperial advisory detachment to Discord. Hoping to stop the assault on his ship, Kirk beamed himself and six men on board. They soon learned the ship had twelve crew on board: two on the Bridge, four in Engineering, and six at phaser and disruptor batteries. Kirk had to destroy the ship to save his crew and ship.

dag-jumag (FD)–Tellarite form of martial arts. Sulu told Kirk that to get *dag-jumag* right, "a human-sized person has to practice it on his knees, which gets wearing."

Dahl, Jackson (UC)–Biologist member of the Themis project who suffered a broken spine in a Klingon raid. He and Kawam-mai Suarez were lovers.

Dailey, Christopher (DC)–Assistant engineer on the *USS Kongo*; killed in a containment field breach.

Dajan (P)–Romulan male; twin to Jandra and younger brother to Keelan. Their parents were forced to commit suicide after Keelan's failure on Kalis Three. Dajan was considered handsome because of his dark curling hair and dark green eyes. As a young enthusiastic archeologist, he embraced much of the leading thought generated by the Federation concerning new evidence about ancient civilizations. Because he supported this, he was required to undergo a lengthy time in a rehabilitation center but after a few years was declared rehabilitated and labeled Orthodox. "You are under consideration for a project worthy of your August talents," so read the papers taken from T'lekan where he had been working. Sent to Termais Four, he worked with Dr. Benar, telling her that he managed to study the few archeology papers that filtered through censorship and thus knew of her thesis about Exodus Hall. He defected from Romulus along with his sister.

Dakronh (UC)–Klingon military vessel that took five years to build. It was equipped with the latest innovative cloaking device and commanded by General Chang who kept it cloaked and hidden beneath *Enterprise* from which it fired on *Kronos One*. In a final confrontation with *Enterprise*, Chang's extreme confidence that *Enterprise* could not harm it, and being unable to see the possibility, he ignored raising shields even when he saw the launch of an *Enterprise's* torpedo especially tailored for *Dakronh's* warp signature. The ship was damaged so badly that its warp core exploded, killing everyone aboard.

Daran V (GSR)–Valdus, a Federation agricultural intermediary from this planet, had died six years before the Great Race. Not the same Valdus Kirk encountered. SEE Valdus.

Darcy (P)–Young oriental lieutenant on *Enterprise* whose Bridge duty position was the Science Station.

Darnel invasion (WLW)–Alien race believed to have invaded the Meztorien sphere of influence and brought about the collapse of the Meztorien civilization. Events occurred more than 100,000 years before *Enterprise's* Careta IV mission.

Darnell, Jocelyn (SS)–Leonard McCoy's first wife and mother of Joanna. Following their divorce, she married Clay Treadway, her high school sweetheart. She and McCoy attended high school together but didn't really meet until the prom. Both were seventeen. Asking her for a dance led to McCoy's escorting her home. They began dating, and though her family and Clay's expected her to marry Clay, she preferred McCoy. Following graduation, they married and had a good marriage for nearly three years. McCoy's medical studies began interfering with their social life and led to her having an affair with Clay and then divorce which McCoy did not contest though it meant not seeing his daughter very much. Her parents had the marriage annulled. Jocelyn attended college, earning her own way. Twelve years prior to the Ssan mission, she and Clay joined the Diplomat Corps and then married. While on the way to Ssan, she admitted to Kirk that she had always loved McCoy and didn't know how to restart their association. When Clay insisted that he and Jocelyn be beamed to a meeting with the assassins, Kirk insisted on going along with two Security officers. Shortly after beam in, the assassins killed a Security officer. Kirk called for a beam out and Scotty took Spock and Clay Treadway. Kirk and Jocelyn were captured. In an effort to save them, a rescue team from *Enterprise* was the trigger that led to her death.

Dasur (FF)–One of four Manteil governing ministers of Alpha Maluria Six during the quarrel between the Manteil and the Obirrhat.

David, Peter –Author of *The Disinherited* in conjunction with Michael J. Friedman and Robert Greenberger.

Davidson (DC)–Female member of *Enterprise's* Security. Chekov ordered her to put Security on alert after finding the bomb. Purviance killed her. SEE Purviance.

Davis (IT)–Captain of the *John Lilly*. He was effected by Nordstral's magnetic fields.

Dax (UC)–A Zeosian ensign on *Enterprise* nearly accused of being one of Gorkon's assassins until it was discovered that he had large webbed feet that would not fit the incriminating boots found in his locker.

daystromite (ST)–A mineral whose identification was made by Richard Daystrom. A Federation survey reported Pegasus IV was composed of over 10% daystromite.

Dazzo (BD)–Klingon crew member of the pirate vessel *Shark*. Jimmy Kirk, who described him as being "built like a New York City antique fire hydrant," was able to kill him by fixing Hall's artificial hand to his throat. SEE Veronica Hall.

Dead Head (Di)–Nickname given to the Parath'aa. SEE Parath'aa.

Death Count– Novel by L. A. Graf. The disappearance of an Andorian physicist fueled tension between the Orions and Andorians and nearly caused a stellar war. Sent to Starbase Sigma 1, located on the edge of Orion/Andorian space, Kirk, ordered to patrol the border, was challenged to do his duty while submitting to the idiocy of efficiency tests. Kirk faced the near destruction of the *Enterprise* by a bomb, a shipboard saboteur, the near loss of Chekov, and the murder of three efficiency experts. Working with his crew, he put all the data together, averted a war, caught the saboteur, discovered Chekov was still alive, brought the quarrel between the Orions and the Andorians to a safe conclusion, and saved the *Enterprise* for another mission.

Deck 2 (ST)–Location of the Physics Lab on the *Enterprise* 1701.

Deck 3, Cabinet 27 (ST)–Location on Starbase 12 of Hazel Payton's quarters.

Deck 6 (ST)–Location of a rec room on the *Enterprise* 1701 designated as officer's country.

Deck 6, Sector 3 (DC)–Ship's intruder alert reported someone at the auditors' quarters. Sulu, Uhura, and 50 other crew had quarters near this location. Three crew quarters were lost to space when the bomb exploded.

Deck 17 (ST)–Location on the *Enterprise* for the crew's messroom with observation galley.

Decker (Di)–Captain of the *Constellation* (*DMa). He had one child: Will Decker.

Deep-Sea Research Station Five (FD)–Research facility established on Discord and anchored beneath the Southern Ocean not far from Hellsgate Rift. SEE Hellsgate Rift.

defection protocol (P)–Anyone seeking asylum with the Federation is required to formerly request it, with the request being handled by the most senior officer available. In this mission Ryan Handler, Ambassador Riley's assistant, accepted Dajan and Jandra's request and initiated the logistics required to begin the procedure. SEE Dajan; Jandra.

deflector shield (BD)–Roy Moss claimed to have invented the shields employed on the early StarFleet starships but the technology came from Faramond and its deserted cities. *Enterprise's* shields were "made for a savage unsettled galaxy" and were meant to guard against the unknown. The old shields were able to be tuned specifically for the need. On his recommendation, after Kirk became an admiral, as a compliment to the new shields, these old shields were kept and implemented on all ships coming out of StarFleet drydocks.

Delacourt (Di)–This white-haired, elderly administrator of the Gamma Xaridian colony was killed when raiders destroyed the colony.

Delanath Four (SS)–Planet known for its unusual invertebrate with a virus symbiot.

Del Gratia (SG)–Ship whose captain, David Reed Morehouse, found the abandoned *Mary Celeste*.

Delta Vegans (BD)–Diplomats on board April's *Enterprise*. Acting captain Lorna Simon ordered Lt. Reed to have them off ship immediately as the ship was leaving to search for Captain April. SEE Lorna Simon.

DeLeon (SS)–This young, slender, fine-boned man with jet-black hair and a thick mustache was an *Enterprise* doctor in McCoy's Sick Bay. He endured McCoy's medical stories.

Demarris (BD)–McCoy mistook this name for Lt. Devereaux.

Denaya 4 (WLW)–Planet noted for its abstract art.

Deneb II (WLW)–Planet colonized by humans. An unknown entity murdered several women before going on to Argelius II in 2267 (Okuda and Okuda *Encyclopedia* 112).

Denebian lemon catus (DC)–Native flora of Deneb. Sulu kept a couple in his quarters but they were destroyed by the hull breach on Deck 6.

Denebian slimedevil (FD)–Deneb A is home to a host of unusual life forms, given its vast oceans and swampy seas. The slimedevil, a carnivorous animal, is the most well known. This amphibious, fast moving predator feeds on sea life, locating it with a form of natural radar and spearing its prey with large, forklike foreclaws. The devil has two main parts, a head and a torso. The triangular-shaped head has a "radar" central organ in the forehead between very small eyes. A large slit mouth has rows of needle-sharp teeth, and a long snorkel-like extension on its head is used for breathing while partially submerged (Palestine 98). The torso has a forward hump and tapers to the rear. Two long articulated rear legs provide leverage and speed while the two forward legs have foreclaws for grasping and spearing. Protruding spines, numbering usually eight, rise from the top of the forehead and may provide a means of moving through debris-laden swamp waters. Generally the large devils range in length from a few centimeters to one to two meters in length, weigh from seven to twenty-six kilos and live, on the average, seventeen years (Johnson *Worlds* 30-31). Extremely large devils do not exist in large numbers, and attacks on humanoid natives are rare. In FD, when Kirk was confronted with Moriah Wayne's accusation that Sulu had a "possibly dangerous life-form in his quarters," Kirk humorously questioned if it was a slimedevil.

Dennehy (SS)–One of Scotty's fledgling engineers on this mission. He and Joe Christian talked about Jocelyn (McCoy) Treadway.

Dennis (WLW)–Medical technician on this *Enterprise* mission who helped McCoy and Chapel dissect a Kh!lict.

Dennings (BD)–Male engineering technician on April's *Enterprise*. Name could have been Jennings or Bennings.

DesRosiers (BD)–This lieutenant was the Navigator on *The Bill of Rights*

Destruct sequence (SG)–The code employed on several occasions by Kirk is as follows. Captain's code: "Destruct sequence: one, code one-one-A." First Officer's code: "Destruct sequence: two, code one-A-two-B." Third officer: "Destruct sequence: three, code one-B-two-B, three." This voice activated sequence differs slightly from the code employed in *The Search for Spock* by Vonda McIntyre. The code may be occasionally changed on StarFleet order to keep it secure.

Devereaux (BD)–Female ensign working at the Bridge Science Station noted the incoming anti-proton flushback and alerted Kirk. SEE flushback.

Deveron 5 (WLW)–Planet noted for its Creation Play.

Devil in the Sea (FD)–Reference is to a giant marine animal considered a mythological creature on Discord. Aileea, a Swimmer quite interested in ocean depths, became aware of something unknown in the deepest ocean area that, when finally discovered, proved to be a huge Klingon battlecruiser. SEE Aileea dinAthos.

Devin (SG)–*Enterprise* ensign on helm duty when *Enterprise* intercepted the drone sent out in the late Terran 20th century.

Diaz (SS)–A stocky dark complexioned *Enterprise* Security officer. He and Security officer Peterson were members of the initial landing party to Ssan composed of Kirk, Spock, Alan and Jocelyn Treadway. Diaz was killed by Ssan assassins.

diazilyrion (WLW)–A euphoric drug that eases inhibitions and induces a sense of serenity similar to the early stages of inebriation. McCoy included this in the nutritional supplement he provided the Kh!lict, especially the one Kirk inhabited. SEE Kh!lict changelings.

dilithium (UC)–The hardest and most rigid mineral known to the Federation. Atomic weight is 315; atomic number is 119; atomic symbol is Di. CONSULT *Star Trek Reader's Reference to the Novels: 1980-1983*.

Dimitrios (BD)–SEE Demarris.

dinAthos, Aagard (FD)– Native of Discord married to Sanabar and father to Aileea. He died in a Stitler raid on his ranch. SEE Sanabar.

dinAthos, Aileea (FD)–This native of Discord in her early thirties had green hair and gill slits on both sides of her neck. She was a Variant. She, Jason Strick, and Mona Arkazhe were the first three to accept contact with Kirk because Discord had no planetary government. She ran Secruiteck, a quasi organization that attempted to handle crimes on Discord. She and her organization were born out of the situation with the Susuru. She escorted Kirk and Dr. McCoy around the Variants' cities, helping them understand the situation.

Dini (Di)–One of several working at Bravo Station defense system on Gamma Xaridian. Killed when raiders destroyed the settlement.

Diplomatic Corp's Security Division (BD)–George Kirk was a commander in this division. According to him, his division often was "called to deal with unstable cultures, unknown sectors, border disputes, angry representatives, and assassination attempts."

Discordians (FD)–Humanoid natives of Discord. SEE Variants.

divining bones (SG)–Bones of a person or an animal believed to hold magical powers to foretell an event. SEE Arn dreamtalker.

Diplocorps (P)–Shortened form of Diplomatic Corps, a branch of the Federation.

Dirat (FF)–Klingon crew member of the *Kadn'ra*.

Disinherited, The–Novel by Peter David, Michael J. Friedman, and Robert Greenberger. A series of attacks on peaceful Federation research colonies required the attention of *Enterprise* and *Lexington*. Kirk investigated the attacks while Uhura worked under Commodore Wesley's command to help with diplomatic translations of the Rithrim language, a mixture of verbal and sign. She helped discover the problems were created when Rithra requested Federation membership. Rithra had five castes and had over the years attempted to eliminate the warrior caste. Without need for their expertise, the warriors went off planet and soon found their services were required by Parath'aa who had been denied Federation membership. Kirk learned that the Parath'aa had hired Rithra warriors to raid Federation colonies and steal technology. Together Kirk and Wesley resolved the problems.

Discord (FD)–Native name given to the 5th planet orbiting a star the Variants call Eris in the system officially called Joan-Marie. The planet is a water world with less than 3% land mass. The first Federation survey reported by the UES *Hernan de Soto* recorded the following information about the class M planet. It orbits its star at 3.13 AUs with a 3.996 standard revolution. A diameter of 12,775 kilometers produces a 1.2 Sol gravity. The rotational period is 55.905 seconds (15 ½ hours) or as Spock later verified "15 hours, 31 minutes, and 45 seconds" Terran measurements. Although the atmosphere is 78% nitrogen, 20% oxygen, 2% argon and traces of CO_2 and H_2O, it also contains high concentrations of sulfur compounds depending on proximity to volcanic areas. Average daytime temperatures hover at 311F or 38C at latitude 30. High radiation combined with a powerful magnetic field makes an inhospitable planet. A major redeeming feature is the heavy concentration of various metals in the crust. Chains of islands, none continent size, offer limited land mass. The *De Soto* also recorded "colossal electrical storms, huge lightning discharges, heavy heat, humidity, gravity" and a "high UV output from the sun." In Spock's report filed much later, he included his observation about the variety of marine life found on this planet, though some had been identified by the initial survey. Hinds, three-meter aerial life forms having six red wings, were called dragonflies. They have a high-energy, high metabolic rate, and pump air through exhaust spiracles which emerges slightly cooler than steam. Hunting in pairs, they seek marine life. Another marine type, herded and guarded by robot "wranglers" owned by Variants, is called a prawn though its resemblance to a Terran animal by the same name is misleading. An individual adult prawn can reach two hundred tons or more with a length of 50 meters and employ propulsion membranes that run like ribbons along either side of its ventral carapace. Its shell is cool and hard to the touch. These prawns cluster in pods and eat microscopic sea life as well metabolizing metals from the crust. A variety of life forms range from steel-spined worms that look like demon caterpillars to brightly colored blobs that resemble jelly to tangles of knotted grey string to fat plum yellow nodules and three-eyed raft-dodger fish. Giant swimming insects and swimming eel-like ribbons populate Discord's oceans along with other marine life similar to plesiosaurs, sharks, reptilian orcas, and giant squid. Colonies of microorganisms clustering around volcanic vents were discovered by *Enterprise* to be intelligent and indigenous to the planet. Relatively little attention was given to any additional natural life forms until after planetfall was made by a group of humans. SEE Variants. Two different sentient beings came to the planet: Variants and Susuru. Variants, who chose this name for themselves, are of human stock. They left Terran in 2072 at the height of Terra's Third World War to escape extermination for they were genetically mutated humans, results of genetic experiments conduced by laboratories under the rule of Khan Noonien Singh. In order to choose, or retain, their physical forms, they left Terra following UN Resolution 51 of the year 2038. Part of this Resolution declared "that no one could be held liable for the acts of their ancestors." A rider to the Resolution confirmed human status on those "human-variant strains who had been created in the gene research laboratories...." However, few of the variants were accepted into society. When suggestions of placing them in "protective custody" became vocal in most nations, the variants decided their freedom lay in leaving Terra and seeking their own planet. Details are sketchy about the means of leaving Terra, but in the aftermath of the Khan disaster, few people were interested in what happened to his "research" subjects. The group spent several years in space before arriving at the system whose star they named Eris and the planet Discord. Once the decision was made to settle here, those early settlers accepted the necessity of adapting to the environment rather than attempting to change it. By applying genetic manipulation, their descendants developed into a great variety with each group being adapted for specific tasks in specific environments. The range of Variants extend from "hulking humanoids covered in pliable grey armor plates" to men and women the size of Terran children ages 10 to 12 to "normal" looking humans. Varieties include human appearance with green hair and gill slits on each side of the head and a fringe of fur running down each arm from wrist to short ribs. Some are squat and hairless with rubbery-looking black skin and webbed feet and hands, with slits for a nose and no external ears. They appear quite like an amphibian. One group resembled half human, half feline. Distinct groups of Variants are known by their chosen designations. Grunts, once bred for heavy labor, were given great strength, endurance, low volition and low intelligence. On Discord, once freed to reclaim their wills and intellects, Grunts chose to retain their body styles but enhance their intelligence. Grunts now perform physical tasks, often performing on "autopilot," leaving their minds free. They are considered the planet's greatest philosophers and theoreticians. Another group, Swimmers, are deep-rangers, developed to work in the ocean depths, mostly around sea mounts and vents where mining occurs. Some Swimmers have chosen to become a quasi-police force known as the Deep-Range Syndicate established since the arrival of the Susuru. Another group of Variants, the Micros, are pixies in body form. They are the pilots and operators of craft where mass or volume are at a premium. Micros have keen eyesight, faster than normal reflexes, and greater tolerances of G-loading and pressure. Discord's population of Variants who call themselves Freefolk numbered 1,135,262 at Kirk's visit. Freefolk are given to bold gaudy colors of clothing often cut to minimize coverage from the sun. Most disregard modesty and nudity is acceptable. Each individual is allowed freedom of choice when it comes to shaping his/her humanoid body. The Freefolk are gene engineered to optimize survival on Discord. Most can survive in the ocean without need of life support. Among the Variants, no single entity or person has the authority to speak for the entire planet for there is no single governing body. Four centers occupy the northern hemisphere and three smaller settlements are located in the southern hemisphere. Individual communities, cities, and ranches exist harmoniously together. Each is mindful of their environment and are extremely carful to treat it well. Multi-level floating population centers vary and are built with landing mats of woven sea-green fiber. Levels are connected by stairways and all metal structure are generally covered with matting to reduce burns. Some centers have a large central plaza with a pool surrounded by homes and shops. All are equipped with gyros and computerized ballast management to dampen the impact from waves and all are capable of submerging when necessary. Centers sport various names. The largest is called Discord. Others are Seventeen, Storm, Harmony, Rakatau, Serendip, Exile, and Qara-Qitay, a "loose and sprawling collection of metal structures anodized in shades of gold and yellow" according to one *Enterprise* crewman report. Harmony produces insulation matting from seaweed and has a large central square. Its residents have few weapons though they do indulge in philosophical discourse that often dissolves into shouting matches. This center was destroyed by a thermonuclear bomb transported there by Commissioner Wayne. Rakatau, built with one section for homes and another for ships, drifts in the Sea of Smokes noted for its sulfuric fumes from nearby sea mounts. Residents mine the sea mounts and vents for a variety of minerals and ores. Serendip, which sits at 20 degrees north and is the closest center to the equator, has a distinct Indian flavor in music and food. Storm, a center known for its looming metal sculptures, artistic competitions, and discordant electronic music is a surface plant where minerals are extracted from seawater. Exile is a mining platform but supports no habitable homes and shops. Smaller residential centers exist. Kirk spent time at Waverider Ranch, one of several multi-level floating cylindrical communities using thermal power and equipped with gyros and computerized ballast management that dampens the impact from waves. It is capable of submerging. Sitting at 40 degrees latitude north, its radar and communications are made possible by tethered balloons. The Ranch is equipped with supersonic Koman ship-killer missiles. Each level provides multiple viewing ports. Transportation on Discord employed by the Variants includes atmosphere vehicles as well as marine and offers movement between centers and out-lying settlements for pleasure or business-related activities. One such vehicle is a scooter with a cockpit fitted with a fragment-proof canopy, form-fitting seat, communications, and electric impellers that cycle water through tubes running the length of the craft. A second sentient population identified as the Susuru came to the attention of the Federation when they requested the Federation remove all humans from Discord. History kept by this group and by the Variants revealed the Susuru came many years after the arrival of the Variants. The Susuru claimed the 3% land mass and for a while lived in peace with the Variants. That is until the arrival of the Klingons who wanted the planet's resources. Susuru are described in reports from various *Enterprise* crew as standing 1 and ½ meters tall, slender in form with long forelegs and short narrow hind legs attached to a short but narrow torso, slim hands, a long narrow shaped head, huge amber eyes above a muzzle of honey-colored fur, and wide sensitive nostrils. Their crested skulls are accented with long pointed ears that track in all directions. Human-like hands and teeth that are "broad chisel-shaped incisors" complete the description. Following the Susuru/Klingon incident resolved by *Enterprise's* efforts, Kirk's report included the information that the Susuru had indeed come later to the planet. Their people began as "mainly agrarian people" who over many centuries developed a technical civilization, including spaceflight. Then came the invasion that sought to exterminate all intelligent life in the universe. The Susuru were forced three separate times to begin life anew but each time were discovered by the exterminators. COMPARE entry Kh!lict. Following the development of warp drive, a few hundred Susuru wandered until the drive broke down. They located a marginally habitable world and took it as home. They disliked the watery world they named Okeanos, but had no choice but stay, living a hand-to-mouth existence until they discovered they shared the world with the Variants. Having lived in fear for so many centuries, they went to war with the Variants. Anatomical studies and their history reveal the Susuru were veldt-loving people who naturally hated water. They hated the Klingons who discovered the planet and them but accepted their help to be rid of the Variants. When they requested Federation help in re-moving the Variants, the Federation soon learned the truth of the situation. Once the animosity between the two races and the resolution of the Klingon problem, Kirk offered Federation help in locating a more suitable planet for them. They accepted.

Discord City Service Corporate (FD)–A security association formed by the Variants for the protection of themselves and their property from the Susuru. It organized in Discord City and those who agreed to serve became known as professional warriors. SEE Aileea dinAthos.

Distress Signal (GSR)–For the Great Starship Race, the distress signal frequency was set at 5,000 megacycles. Any ship tuned to this frequency would be emitting an SOS.

Djelifa (WLW)–A planet recently joined with the Federation. Its strong matriarchal society, the strongest in the Federation, prohibited full interaction with off-worlders. The *Enterprise* hosted Tailka Nyra, its representative included in the archeology team to Careta IV.

Djelifan (WLW)–Native to the high-gravity planet Djelifa. When a female reaches adulthood, she chooses her own unique personal name. The initial survey report mentioned that males and children not "yet worthy carry their class and group designation." A long nose is a thing of beauty on Djelifa.

DLO ports (BD)–Shorthand for "dispatch and loading only."

Dodge, Kenneth (GSR)–Described as having short black hair, this Commanding officer of the *Hood* when it made first contact with Gullrey, was a former field soldier with no Academy training but who had advanced through the rank. Highly revered on Gullrey because of his having answered Gullrey's message. A member of the Great Starship Race and a participating member of the ceremony marking Gullrey's entry into UFP.

Dohama (S)–SEE Sanctuary.

Dominion of Proxima (GSR)–Ship entrant for Proxima Beta commanded by Hunter.

Don Juan (BD)–Character created in Spanish literature and called Don Giovanni by Italian writers. He's become synonymous for womanizer. Many novels and plays have been written based on this character. The term is often applied to James Kirk.

doubloon (GSR)–Spanish term meaning double. Thirty-two reales comprise a doubloon minted in Mexico. A single gold Spanish doubloon recovered from the *El Sol* was the prize for the winner of the Great Starship Race. SEE *El Sol*.

Dozadi worlds (P)–Located in Romulan territory. Attempts to evacuate their population had been made but the released data is suspect.

Drachenfels (GSR)–This ship, entrant of the Great Race and commanded by Helmut Appefeller, ran under the flag of the Colony Drachenfels. Its name translates as "where the dragon fell."

dragonflies (FD)–Kirk reported this life form native to Discord as reaching the adult stage of three meters in length with "six wings that shimmer in the sun" and adults whose armor "is blue tiger -striped over dull scarlet bellies."

Dream-time (WLW)–Australian aborigines subscribe to this mythological period of time that had a beginning but no foreseeable end. All natural environment was shaped and humanized by mythic beings who established local order and its "law." Dreaming includes a close relationship of man to nature, with both sharing a common life force. That which man inhabits is the dreaming; that which man occupies is dream-time supposedly limited only by a man's lifetime. SEE Bendilon.

drone (SG)–Late 20th century Terran space packet sent into the void beyond the solar system. *Enterprise* discovered and retrieved it, bringing it on board. It was described as a mechanical eggplant shape mechanism with skewed antenna. Nothing could be obtained from its logs.

"Drunken Irishman, The" (P)–An operetta written by Andrew Penalt that the critics panned. SEE Andrew Penalt.

Dulcipher star cluster (WLW)–*Enterprise* was sent here to help a team of archeologists study this once densely populated region. Careta IV is located in this cluster. SEE Careta IV.

Duerring, Constance (DC)–This physicist/engineer declared the "use of transporter electrodynamics clearly states that energy is generated whenever a transporter beam encounters a force field...[this] energy [is] absorbed by random arrangement of molecules within transported objects" and concluded that Haslen's anode device could not be useful.

Dumeric (FF)–Klingon uncle to Captain Vheled and a member of the High Council. He was a member of the Gevish'rae, an area located on Qo'noS. By the end of the mission detailed in *Faces of Fire*, he had lost considerable power on the Council.

Dympna (IT)–Daughter of a pagan Irish chief and his Christian wife who lived in the Terran 7th century and was declared a saint of the Catholic Church. The daughter's feast day is May 15. She is considered the saint of those suffering mental illness and nervous system disorders. SEE Risa.

dyna-carrier (BD)–Ocean-going merchant marine ship employed on Discord. The hull was designed to be adjusted to fit the requirements of the cargo. Most often employed to carry harvested sea hatcheries. It had telescoping masts with deckwing stabilizers that folded back when the ship was in harbor but expanded outward when on the open sea. Robotics did most of the work on ship with antigravs used to load and unload cargo in the harbor.

8747.6 (DC)–Stardate for the breach of *Kongo's* containment field. SEE *USS Kongo*.

Earthers (ST)–Slang term as translated from a Klingon term.

Ebahn (FF)–Native Manteil of the planet Alpha Maluria Six and a member of the party who took Kirk, McCoy, Scotty, and Ambassador Farquhar to view the cubaya herd.

Edinburgh (SG)–A museum located in this Terran Scottish city displays an oil painting of Captain Beppe.

Edris pulsar (P)–A pulsar is a star emitting radio pulses in regular intervals that can be timed. When Spock entered the first set of coordinates discovered in the crystal taken from the Exodus Hall on Termais Four, this is what was identified. SEE Exodus Hall.

Edwards (GSR)–*Enterprise's* Process Control Chief came close to refusing Kirk's order to put the earth science staff to monitoring the reactor loop. Scotty convinced him to obey the order.

Eisman, Jak (Di)–Aide to the administrative head of the Gamma Xaridian colony who wore his hair long and tied in a pony tail and was engaged to marry L'rita. The colony was destroyed by hired mercenaries. SEE Parathu'ul.

Elani (SG)–Dr. Rinagh's Romulan wife. SEE Rinagh.

El Capitan (P; SS)–Mountain located in Yosemite National Park, Terra. Kirk declared the effects of the Probe were acceptable, especially the effect of cleaner air, compared to the air he breathed on top of this mountain he had climbed.

Elder (WKW)–SEE Kh!lict.

El Dorado (S)–Known as the "Lost City of Gold." A legendary kingdom/empire of a golden king who washed himself in gold dust. Many Spanish conquistadores searched for it. McCoy ranked it with Sanctuary; he considered both to be fictional. SEE Sanctuary.

Eliot (ST)–*Enterprise* communication officer. SEE Prufrock's World.

Elizsen (SG)–Romulan bird of prey captained by Telris.

El Sol (GSR)–During a heavy storm at sea, this Spanish galleon sunk off Spanish Wells in the Abaco Islands of the Bahamas, Terra, in less than 40 feet. Although treasure hunters searched for the ship, all that was recovered was a single doubloon. Most likely other plunderers came before or maybe most of its cargo was recovered.

Elysian ale (S)–McCoy tasted the ale served on Sanctuary and compared it to Elysian ale.

Elysian cloud-apple (DC)–Uhura purchased this fruit pastry on Space Station Sigma One and gave it to Sulu.

Emily (BD)–Member of Jimmy Kirk's gang. SEE Jimmy's group.

energy wave (UC)–An energy wave coming from 240 degrees mark 6 alerted *Excelsior* that an explosion had occurred on Praxis, a satellite of Qo'noS.

Endikon (FD)–City located on Axanar where Kirk and Kain had met. SEE Kain.

Endris (Di)–This humanoid native of Rithra was governor during this mission.

Enforcers (WLW)–A Kh!lict equivalent to the Gestapo.

Engath (FF)–Klingon crewman on the *Kadn'ra* who accompanied Captain Vheled to search for the colony children on Beta Canzandia.

English River (BD)–Located close to Riverside, Iowa, Terra, this river could be seen from the Kirks' kitchen.

enra (SG)–Spirits are believed to inhabit deep burial pits on Vindali Five. The screeching howls coming from these pits are believed to be spirits coming to the surface.

Enterprise 1701–This ship bore the registry of NCC-1701 and was one of twelve ships in the Constitution heavy cruiser class assigned to five-year missions. The ships were designed initially as the focal point of StarFleet's arsenal. A total of 93 such cruisers were planned though not completed (Reil). *Enterprise* NCC-1701 was the second cruiser of the Constitution class to be constructed. Its builder is listed as StarFleet Division, San Francisco Yards, Terra. Although its keel was laid on 16 July 2218, it took two years to complete the basic ship and its interior contents. By 04 July 2220 it was launched and commissioned on 05 January 2221. Construction continued with new technology being added or updated almost daily (Reil). The above dates are disputed by Okuda and Okuda (*Encyclopedia* 137-140). According to its specifications *Enterprise* 1701 was the largest man-made object in space to date. At 974 feet long, 417 feet wide, 23 decks tall, and weighing close to 185,000 tons light and 195,000 tons fully loaded, its promise was waiting to be fulfilled. Another source indicates *Enterprise* weighed in at 205,000 tons light and 215,000 fully loaded (Reil). The designer's blueprints noted the structure would weigh 190,000 tons fully loaded (Joseph *Blueprints*). Initially designed to cruise at warp 3, 4, or 5, it could if necessary be pushed to warp 7. Fitted with TSS Warp Celestial Guidance, Daystrom Duotronic II computer system, it also came with four banks of phasers, two tubes for photon firing, and a state-of-the-art Hycor Modular Adaptive force field and deflector. Constructed with a gravity generator, radiation shielding along with synthesizing and regeneration systems, the ship emerged with all the latest technology and materials (Reil). A close study of the blueprints reveal a ship composed of three sections. The saucer-shaped primary hull, 417 feet in diameter and eleven decks tall, contained all elements necessary for independent operations if needed. This hull was designed and built to be detached if the captain determined the need. The cigar-shaped secondary hull, 340 feet long, 112 feet in diameter was attached to the third part, the twin-engine pods, each 504 feet long and 60 feet in diameter. The ship also contained a secondary Bridge that operated the secondary hull should the ship be separated into two parts. Designed for a crew of 430 with supplies to sustain it for eighteen years, it stood ready for duty. Although StarFleet's cruisers were constructed, fitted, and operated as military vessels, none were considered to have this as their primary function. The ships' missions, stated as plans went to the drawing board, were "to explore strange new worlds, to seek out new civilizations," and to open up new vistas for humankind. To carry out this mandate, each ship was fitted with fourteen distinct science laboratories, each capable of doing any task (*OA). Once deployed, the captain of each ship was soon called upon to give assistance in various forms, military, political, and medical, to settled locations, to transport people and goods to various planets, and ferry ambassadors to and from diplomatic meetings. In carrying out these duties, the ship and crew's integrity and courage were tested time and again. To protect itself and its crew as well as establish a show of strength, each ship carried a wide variety of weapons, an issue debated for many months in the Federation General Assembly. Principal weapons on *Enterprise* were enormous versions of the hand phaser. Included in its arsenal was a battery of ship-mounted phasers, three banks each. The photon torpedoes, "energy pods of matter and anti-matter contained and held temporarily separated in a magno-photo force field" were a second type of weapon (Roddenberry *Making* 194). When needed, the ship was capable of utilizing its tractor beam as well as its transporters for duty other than what they were designed to do. Standard individual weapons, hand phasers, work on the same principle as the ship's main banks of phasers. Three types of hand-carried weapons were placed on each ship. The first was small, slightly bigger than the palm of the hand and attached to a belt under the uniform shirt. The second was a combination of a small phaser but mounted onto a pistol and worn hanging from a weapon's belt. The third type was a phaser rifle, generally issued to landing parties. Starships, of which *Enterprise* is an excellent example, were equipped with many devices but none more necessary than its variety of sensors, for sensory equipment that enables a ship to perform its missions while maintaining the crew's safety is of paramount importance. *Enterprise's* deflectors, sometimes called navigational shields, were frequently the ship's best weapons. Designed for constant operation, these shields wrapped the ship in a protective "bubble" but also swept far ahead of the ship's path diverting debris and other objects to avoid collisions and hull penetration. Often these shields gave warning of an approaching object, be it a ship, asteroid, comet or other space debris. Another type of shield was employed at the Bridge Communication Station, manned 24/7. *Enterprise* logs have revealed an approach was detected by the officer at this station even before any of the other deflectors signaled. To operate such a vessel requires a crew. Guidelines for crew have not changed much since the initial design. The number of the crew on *Enterprise* 1701 varied from 430 considered "normal" to more or less depending on the situation and mission. Generally a third of this number was female, with a crew composed of international, multi-racial, and alien. Later ships ignored the ratio and focused on quality of crew and the expertise required for a mission. All the ship's members were the crew. However, a small group were "senior officers" who had varying amounts of authority. The ship had a captain, a first officer, commanders, lieutenants, ensigns, and yeomen. Most of these titles designate levels within a discipline. For example, lieutenants are found in navigation, engineering, and medicine. The crew was divided into three groups: science (blue shirts); engineering and ship's services (red shirts); command (gold shirts). Although a starship, like the *Enterprise*, operated at the outer end of a chain-of-command, the captain, on ship was in absolute control. This did not change through the years. The captain's superior is a Starbase commander and StarFleet Command. Starbase commanders are subject to StarFleet Command, whose main headquarters is located in San Francisco. To service the crew, the starship came equipped with many areas, three of which are most interesting. Included on the *Enterprise* was the ship's library-computer, the most sophisticated of its kind and capable of storing and retrieving vast amounts of information. Its services could be channeled to any station or viewing screen on the ship. In addition to the elaborate computer system, and tied to it, was the ship's galley, making it possible to feed the 430 plus crew almost anything they requested. To provide recreation, a variety of areas were created on Deck 20. Here a crewmember might swim, work out on various equipment, play games of choice, or simply lounge. He/she might also use the giant viewing screen to watch films, the passing stars, or any audio/video selection from the Library. *Enterprise's* Library was enlarged at Captain Kirk's request for he believed the more information available the better one could make decisions. The earliest of starship design included shuttlecraft to facilitate boarding and debarking, although the transporter, once proved workable, became the standard method of boarding or debarking the ship. Shuttlecrafts, designed to carry a crew of seven, did, in an emergency, carry nine or ten. In addition they were employed on limited exploratory patrols. Several two-seater Tyco fighters, several workbees, and a captain's yacht were also included on all StarFleet heavy cruisers. Designed for movement within the ship were turbo-elevators, also called turbo-lifts, tubes. These ran both horizontally and vertically, with each elevator cage moving independently. Ship's computer monitored the usage and provided the power to move the cages so that no collisions occurred, even if the cage were stopped for some reason. Later Blueprints indicated these lifts were to be voice activated. Stairways were also included, placed discretely throughout the ship for emergency use only. Though conceived from the original Constitution-class design, *Enterprise* 1701 was not the ship in those designs, due to alterations made from the moment of conception to the moment of completion. Construction was incomplete during her first run under Captain Robert A. April. Even her crew was not StarFleet Academy trained. All were mainly engineers and technicians on board to help monitor and evaluate both design and its execution. Circumstances forced them to complete construction to many areas. Though armed with laser stream and particle cannons both with gradient settings, the ship was hardly ready for an encounter. Sent on a mission before she could be officially named, she sailed with no name and no registry. Her first officer, George Kirk, suggested the name *Enterprise* and Captain April, convinced of the quality and history of the name, bestowed *Enterprise* upon the ship when she needed identification. Later, most of the crew concurred with the choice, for the name suggested the ship's purpose, scope of vision of its designers and construction crews, its preparedness and strength, and its readiness for venturing on its own initiative. The name also suggested imagination. The *Enterprise* 1701 that James T. Kirk took command of changed during the years he captained it. Much of that change can be directly contributed to First Officer Spock and Chief Engineer Montgomery Scott. In addition, Chief Communication Officer, Lt. Cmdr. Uhura redesigned and invented some of the additions to the Communication Bridge Station. Other Bridge officers, particularly Spock, contributed ideas and designs that improved the capabilities of *Enterprise* 1701. The ship was refitted several times through its years of service, receiving its most extensive refit in 2270 "when virtually every major system was upgraded, a new bridge module was installed, and the warp drive nacelles were replaced" (Okuda and Okuda *Encyclopedia* 135; Johnson *Guide*). The *Enterprise* 1701 was considered, especially by Captain Kirk and his crew, to be the best constructed, manned, and tested of the fleet. The ship's log is a storehouse of information. Among captains and crews of the other StarFleet ships, *Enterprise* 1701 became a living legend. Even before the ship's second five-year mission was completed, stories about its adventures were reaching the public. Most of the major officers of this ship became legends within Star Fleet and beyond, even into the most alien of people. Captain April declared *Enterprise* 1701 "the first of her kind...built for constant thrust...[but he was] not sure how fast she [would] be able to go..." (Carey *Best*). Captain Kirk often reminisced about this ship and his attitude toward her when he was sixteen and forced to accompany his father on a mission: "when I took command." he wondered, "...did she remember?" He recalled that "she [1701] had survived all those dangers, all those storms, all those hands at the helm, all the brand new things no other ship had encountered because no other ship had gone so far...." Captain Kirk believed the ship deserved to die in space, "where she had lived, where she had made it safe for countless millions to live" (Carey *Best*). He sometimes felt he owed an apology to the ship he had sent to its death in the atmosphere of the hostile planet Genesis, especially when *Enterprise* 1701-A was about to be decommissioned. Captain April, speaking to Jim Kirk, a defiant sixteen-year-old, lovingly spoke of the *Enterprise*. His words captured the essence of all starships: "She's a starship...a masterful work...her express purpose is to roam free to untouched stars...she and her kind will hammer through the frontiers of space, approach, and contact faraway civilizations... (Carey *Best*). Captain Kirk often recalled these words. *Enterprise* 1701 had three superb commanders: Robert A. April, Christopher Pike, and James T. Kirk. Her final contribution to the crew occurred at the Genesis planet in 2258. Though Kirk and ship were soon to be retired, Kirk had let it be destroyed to keep it from Klingon hands. However, the name lived on, bestowed upon other worthy ships.

Enterprise 1701-A (BD)–This ship, launched in 2286 under command of James T. Kirk, in appreciation for his role in saving Terra from the alien probe, replaced the one destroyed at Genesis on Kirk's order to keep the Klingons from taking command of it. Kirk and his officers fooled the Klingon vessel in orbit above Genesis into transporting them aboard where they took the ship captive. StarFleet Command took charge of the Klingon ship after its return to Terra with two humpback whales. The Constitution class had been the most versatile of StarFleet's ships and for this reason new developments in spaceflight and weapons were tested for value and compatibility to the ships of that class and to those of the *Enterprise* class. Most of the *Enterprise* class ships were initially produced, especially their superstructures, at Terran shipyards at the rate of four per year. For several years before the construction of *Enterprise* 1701-A, research and development companies were working on a transwarp drive that promised an increase in speed. After *Enterprise* 1701 proved the existence of parallel planes of existence and recorded the demise of USS *Defiant*, the possibility of traveling between dimensional planes took on added significance (*TW). StarFleet accepted the data that a "short cut" did exist and pushed for serious research on creating a transwarp ship. Twelve years and many failures finally resulted in the two-drive system, each produced by a separate facility, each believing their warp field configuration worked best. Both designs combined intricate warp and transporter field matrices to generate a "doorway." Since the artificial "interphase" would be of a short duration, the ship's crew would not suffer from radiation exposure. *Mr. Scott's Guide to the Enterprise*, a publication covering the refit of *Enterprise* 1701 completed in 2270, had indicated that only two transwarp engines were built. One by Shuvinaaligus Warp Technologies which mounted its engines on the *Excelsior* for testing with nacelles that required "twice the mass and...double the length of *Enterprise's* FWG-1." Leeding Engines, Ltd. also developed an engine but though theirs had similar field generation machinery, the engine was smaller. Leeding's successful engine was constructed months after Shuvinaaligus' engine and lost the contest. However, the smaller design found favor with StarFleet's Board of Engineers who ordered the Leeding FTWG-1 be tested on an *Enterprise*-class ship. USS *Ti-Ho*, a ship of the Excelsior class built from keel up, was chosen. The M-6 Mark II computer proved capable of handling the logic system required and was installed on the *Ti-Ho*. With refits complete, *Ti -Ho* was registered as NCC-1798. In addition to the Leeding transwarp and M-6 computer, the ship also had transwarp subspace communications capable of transmitting at transwarp speed. An additional upgrade, long considered necessary, was a rear-firing tube. Control consoles featured smooth solid black "faces" when not working. All switches became touch-active generated. Cosmetic changes in bulkhead and flooring design distinguished the ship from her siblings. Scott's observation when quizzed about the new ship included the declaration that "she is well-equipped to expand the boundaries of human exploration...the UFP" has a ship that will "symbolize the spirit of discovery and adventure that has always driven humanity to seek that which is just beyond its reach." All of the shakedown crew concurred that this ship would take her place at the forefront of the fleet. On September 21, 2222, *Ti-Ho* returned from its trials just as the resolution of the alien probe crisis was settled. Admiral James T. Kirk, busted to rank of Captain, was given the *Ti-Ho* command, re-christened *Enterprise* with hull registry NCC 1701-A (Johnson *Guide* 114). The only negative remark made about her was by Captain Kirk who whispered to Dr. McCoy that he missed the grey doors to the Bridge. Historian Carey writes that *Enterprise* 1701-A was a training vessel set to be decommissioned when the Faramond incident proved the old technology still reliable and valuable (*Best*). According to Okuda and Okuda, *Enterprise 1701*-A had not completed all its trials before being sent to Numbus III to intervene in a hostage situation, and later ordered to escort Klingon Chancellor Gorkon to peace talks on Terra. Kirk, crew, and ship played an important part in establishing peaceful relations with the Klingon Empire at Khitomer (*Encyclopedia* 139). Anticipating retirement was on the horizon, Kirk and his crew were delighted to be called upon for another mission – to Ssan (Friedman *Shadows*). StarFleet has not released the logic behind its decision to decommission this ship nor has Command issued a date.

Enterprise **auditors** (DC)–Four auditors John Taylor, Chaiken, Roberta Gendron, and Aaron Kelly, sent by the Federation Office of General Accounting boarded ship at Space Station Sigma One to conduct efficiency test and collect data. Auditor General ordered Kirk to take the four even though Kirk already had an assigned mission.

Enterprise **bomb** (DC)–An alert message on his monitor sent Chekov with a bomb kit to Deck 6, Sector 39 (crew quarters for Sulu, Uhura, and 50 other crew). He discovered the bomb in Sector 38, cabin 8, hidden in a small white carton labeled Gendron in Craiken's quarters. By building a blast cage around it, he was able to contain some of the explosive damage which caused power outages and minor structural damage on Deck 7 and left Decks 5 and 8 with limited power. Deck 6 lost its main power circuit that ran the entire length of the deck, and a portion of its space side was completely blown away. All crew quarters on Deck 6 were vacuumed with the loss of three cabins worth of hull.

Enterprise **deck damage** (DC)–A saboteur's bomb exploded on Deck 6, Sector 39, cabin 8, causing power outages, loss of intercom, and power for circuits to the turbo lift.The vacuum resulted in the loss of 3 cabins located on the outer hull and exposure of all cabins on Deck 6. Part of the damage, Engineering reported, was "a long rippled impact scar [that] ran the length of the secondary hull, level with the shuttle bay" caused by a phaser overload set on the *Clarke* which had exploded a few hundred meters from the *Enterprise*.

Enterprise **guards** (WLW)–Kirk posted eleven officers from Security to Site J3 on Careta IV.

Enterprise **landing party** (P)–According to the Romulan request concerning the joint efforts of Romulan and Federation personnel to work together on the ruins on Termais Four, the *Enterprise* party was composed of Kirk, Spock, Sulu, Riley, and Dr. Benar. SEE Romulan landing party.

Enterprise **malfunctions** (SG)–Several ship reports indicated *Enterprise* faced unexplained problems with anti-grav units in the gymnasium, unresponsive turbo lifts, and doors, as well as food dispensers following their discovery of the Romulan space station *Reltah*. SEE *Reltah*.

Enterprise **naming** (BD)–George Kirk was given the honor of bestowing a name upon the ship Captain April was given to command. Kirk chose *Enterprise*.

Enterprise **repairs** (GSR)–Following the "bust a gut" run to prevent the Romulan *Scorah* from destroying Gullrey, *Enterprise* was strained beyond her limits because Kirk kept ordering warp increases reaching warp 9.3 and 9.5. Kirk's report and in part echoed by Scotty "was the fear of the ship tearing apart. The structural integrity field was compromised; risk of a core meltdown due to channeling power to a pin-point phaser...even some of the life support machinery broke down. All over the ship conduits snapped and on the Bridge most of its safety systems were blown...automatic shutdown of all systems not essential were ordered...the inertial dampening fields were compromised." Two months of 24/7 repairs at Starbase 16 were required to put the ship into space-worthy shape. Kirk requested Scotty supervise the repairs and ordered nothing replaced if not necessary because "the spine, frame assembly and exostructure turned out to be a lot stronger than was thought." Kirk didn't want "her strength repaired out of her."

Entrath (FF)–Native of Alpha Maluria Six; one of four Manteil governing ministers.

environment suit (DC)–StarFleet issued clothing is utilized when an enclosed atmosphere is required. Separate sleeves, pant legs, torso, gloves, boots, and helmets are designed to fit together to provide a comfortable suit for nearly every human physical shape. Communications, breathable air, and a distress signal are included as well as a signal light: all can sustain life for several hours. Several suits and their parts are kept in every shuttlecraft and at various locations on all decks and hangar bay.

Enyart (ST)–Well-known catering service employed by Commodore Favere for his dinner party. SEE Favere.

Epala (Di)–Terran cousin to Uhura. Born deaf and was taught to sign. She taught Uhura.

Erehwon (ST)–Terran novel by Samuel Butler is identified as utopian set in the 1870s in England. Published in 1872, the novel told of the adventures of Higgs who went to Erewhon where the diseased are punished, no machinery is allowed, people are educated in trivial studies, and earning money is a duty: a novel of confusion.

Erehwon (ST)–Dr. Omen's "home." This identifies his specifically designed asteroid/space ship/laboratory. He took the name from Samuel Butler's book of the same title. The asteroid was covered with sensor dishes, warp cylinders, weapon bays, and various spikes, plates, and bumps. The entire globular object, some five kilometers across was composed of iron and nickel with traces of lead and fitted with manufactured equipment. Within this asteroid he placed warp engines, tractor beams, an accelerator, and other machinery necessary for sustaining life and power to his Aleph machinery. His asteroid/ship/laboratory, fitted with a hyper-anchor, powerful tractor beams, and deflectors, was impervious to phaser fire. Part of Kirk's report to StarFleet Command contained a description of the areas he visited. He wrote that Erehwon had a central circular command station with a large view screen capable of showing multiple images in three-dimensions, three steps down from this circular platform was the main floor decorated with "delicate trees with silver leaves (that) extended to the walls," free standing in "odd-shaped plots of open soil." Kirk also noted that small creatures flew from tree to tree, delighting in song. A long hallway led off the main chamber and served as an art gallery displaying "intricate sculptures of light and wire," on wooden tables. In addition to these, Kirk noted "paintings of aliens" decorating the walls, all executed by Omen's daughter Barbara. Omen had displayed in a prominent place a hologram of a smiling blond woman holding a speckled blue flower.

Eric (GSR)–Crewman on the *Ransom Castle* killed by boarding Romulans.

Ericksen (S)–One of *Enterprise's* shuttlecraft. Kirk, Spock, and McCoy used it to reach Sanctuary where it was stripped by the Senites and then put in the Graveyard of Ships where it temporarily served as their home. SEE Senites.

Eris (FD)–Star for the planetary group of which Discord is the only inhabited planet of seven. The human settlers so named the star because the name refers to the goddess of Greek mythology who disrupted a banquet held by the other gods when she tossed a golden apple inscribed "for the Fairest" into the room. SEE Joan-Marie's star; Discord.

Erisi, Dr. Antonin (P)–Terran archeologist who published several papers pointing out a parallel between the Erisian Ascendancy and Australian aborigines. He based his argument on patterns discerned in Erisian cities already excavated, declaring the cities "were designed and built using principles that appear to underlie certain aspects of the music of many cultures, including Terra." Dr. Benar and Dr. Erisi believed these patterns connected Ascendancy worlds.

Erisian crystal (P)–Data crystal found in the untouched Exodus Hall and taken to the *Enterprise* for study. SEE crystals; Probe.

Erisians (P)–Ancient, now extinct, people who designed their cities using the principle "that appears to underlie certain aspects of music," Dr. Erisi wrote in one of his papers. Termais Four is believed to be one of their worlds. Six other sites are known to be in the Neutral Zone. The site on Termais Four was discovered to be quite extensive in size and information from the Termais Four crystal indicated several coordinates. Dr. Benar believed an earlier space-faring race may have destroyed the home of the Erisians, creators of the Probe. All known and located Erisian worlds are believed to have been evacuated at about the same time, 100,000 years before the Romulan/Federation expedition. They left no record of their physical appearances though those discovered inside the Probe as holograms were identified as superdolphins. SEE Termaris Four.

Errico (S)–An albino humanoid who escaped from the Reborning center along with Kirk, Spock, and McCoy and led them to the settlement at the Graveyard of Lost Ships.

escrima (FD)–The term is thought to have originated from the Spanish word "escrime," meaning to fence with a sword. The sport was created during the Spanish occupation of the Philippine Islands, Terra. Known as Filipino Kaili, this dynamic, fast, hard hitting combat sport requires players adorn themselves with pads and protective gear for head, hands, elbows, chest, and knees. Its only item of equipment is two plain skinless sticks (escrima). The sticks are generally made of bamboo and are used to strike and defend. Various aspects of the sport call for using heavy escrima sticks for training and real combat while skinless rattan sticks are mainly used during training combat. These are also employed during stick on stick practice. This sport bears some resemblance to boxing in that the sticks are used to strike the opponent. The sport was one Sulu practiced with Captain Kirk

escrimador (FD)–One who plays the game of *escrima*.

Eskimos (S)–After ordering a steak at a Sanctuary restaurant, McCoy mentioned this Terran tribe whose entire diet was blubber from whales and seals.

Espinoza, Carmen (P)–Principal conductor at the Lincoln Center Philharmonic during the time Dr. Benar worked there.

Estano (SG)–*Enterprise* ensign put in charge of Security by Chekov while Chekov was off ship. On Kirk's orders Estano put two Security guards on a shuttle and sent them to rescue the landing party from the Romulan space station. SEE *Reltah*.

e-suit (SG)–Shortly after entering the Romulan space station, the landing party began experiencing loss of body heat. McCoy located Romulan environmental suits and ordered everyone to put one on to conserve body heart. The suits were made of soft smooth clinging material similar to suits employed by Terran Alpine skiers and deep sea divers.

Eugenics War (FD)–Historian Trimble (256) writes that this group of wars were the last major world wars to take place on Terra. CONSULT *Star Trek Reader's Reference to the Novels*:1988-1989.

Evanston (P)–Noted 23rd century musician and composer whose music McCoy considered for inclusion in *Enterprise's* musical library.

Excelsior-class (BD; UC)–Registry number given as NX-2000 for it was the first of the class to be built. Captain Styles commanded it during the testing of its transwarp drive (Okuda and Okuda *Encyclopedia* 144). When given operational status her registry number changed to NCC-2000, and she began her three-year research mission. Sulu became her captain three years after her initial series of tests and missions under Captain Styles. The ship played a critical part at the Khitomer Peace Conference in 2293 with Sulu coming to the aid of Kirk and the *Enterprise*.

Exile (FD)–Floating city located on Discord whose inhabitants are mostly deep-sea miners. SEE Discord.

Exodus Hall (P)–The central room in all known Erisians ruins that have been excavated to date. Information gleaned from each had led to dozens of burned out worlds. Dr. Benar named the room housed in a squat low-domed building always found on an Erisian Ascendancy world. Dome fragments appeared to contain a star map with highlighted stars. Also always in the Hall was a crystalline memory device that contained a definite lattice structure and fields suggesting encoded information. On Termais Four this Hall's floor was smooth and untouched but covered in dust. Low benches of unknown material lined 90% of the circular wall. In the exact center stood an intact crystal with stored information intended to be read as a tutorial. Spock and his team extrapolated the data to learn that much of it was a catalog of exploded stars. Material from the crystal discovered in the Termais Four Exodus Hall appeared to have the same basic structure as the central crystal of the Probe. SEE Probe.

external moorings (BD)–Ships connected to drydocks, loading docks, etc. are tied to the dock's structure to keep the ship stationary. At times minor adjustments must be made by firing station-keeping thrusters.

Eyes Only (ST)–Highly secret priority message. To receive such a message, the designated person must submit his private security code and allow a retinal scan. In ST, Kirk received one from Admiral Nogura's assistant.

552-4 (GSR)–This Tholius flag ship, an entrant in the Great Starship Race and captained by Kmmuta, collided with *Irimlo Si*. Yet it won second place in the race and a trophy which was accepted by the Andorian ambassador Yeshmal since none of the ship's crew could safely leave the ship.

F 9 (WLW)–Star classification. SEE Appendix D.

Fabrini (BD)–Humanoids from the system Fabrina. They had constructed a massive ark inside an asteroid just before their star went nova in the hopes that enough people would survive the journey to another habitable planet (*FW). In their journey the Fabrini discovered Faramond and left it intact. Logs left behind confirmed their discoveries on Faramond. SEE Faramond.

Faces of Fire–Novel by Michael Jan Friedman. *Enterprise* escorted Ambassador Farquhar to Alpha Malurian Six to settle a religious dispute, but stopped first at the terraforming colony on Beta Canzandia to conduct medical tests and receive progress updates. Though Carol Marcus, who had her son David with her, was one of the scientists on Beta, she and Kirk did not have a pleasant meeting, though he learned later that David was his son and agreed to let Carol decide when to tell David who his father was. During a brief meeting to determine the colony's needs, Spock was given permission to remain on Beta while Kirk and *Enterprise* continued on to Alpha Maluria Six. Ambassador Farquhar, at odds with Kirk about the unscheduled stop, ignored Kirk's suggestions. So, in an attempt to learn the Obirrhat side of the religious issue, Kirk and Scotty went "native," were taken captive, and were given the Obirrhat Holy Books to read. After being returned to the Manteil, Kirk believed he had a solution. With careful reading of the texts, Kirk, who interpreted the scriptures as accepting the use of flowers, suggested the unpleasant odor of Klingon fireblossoms would prohibit the cubaya from crossing sacred grounds. With the dispute settled, Kirk returned to Beta, to learn the Klingons had attempted to steal Dr. Boudreau's G-Seven unit, a technology that increases plant growth and thereby increases oxygen levels. When the Klingons landed, Spock took the unit and fled into the hills where he discovered David Marcus had led himself and three other children to caves. Together they thwarted the Klingon plans, but were unaware of the Klingon agenda that called for the killing of Captain Vheled. Alerted to the colony's situation, Kirk arrived to find the Klingons had burned the settlement's main buildings, but everyone was unharmed. The Klingons left without the unit.

Faramond (BD)–A deserted planet in the Rosette Nebula whose two suns orbit a neutron star. The planet's chemical make-up consists of helium, hydrogen cyanide, nitrogen, sulfur, among other elements. The neutron star had gone through its supernova stage and sucked off matter from the other suns, one yellow-orange, the other scarlet red. Depth scans revealed the neutron star is nearly a billion years old. Four planets orbit the trinary stars of which Faramond is one. None are capable of sustaining life. No volcanic activity had occurred on Faramond for ten million years, and it was too far from its neutron sun to receive much warmth. Once ancient ruins were discovered, five huge domes were built over several sites and served as both a home and a working environment. Each was ten miles long and three miles wide with interior caverns to hold equipment and residents. Archeologists considered it a Mecca. One of their earliest discoveries was a power core that lay 160 miles down toward the planet's center. Evidence they uncovered at the site suggested it had once been the home of an advanced, now extinct race which did not die out but migrated, taking everyone and all essential equipment. An ancient transporter discovered at the planet's core suggested this action. Part of one report, which Captain April quoted to George Kirk, declared no discovery of "vessel residue, technological droppings, dock casualties, no fuel film — nothing." Evidence also discovered led to the conclusion that other space-faring races had visited Faramond. According to Spock's report the computer discovered on the planet still worked but it was a computer "with no software. The old culture took the important parts with them in case they should want to move again, or to prevent others from following...[the machinery] will never work as a long-distance transporter." When Roy Moss attempted to activate it, the planet collapsed in on itself in an explosion of antimatter.

Farquhar, Marlin (FF)–Federation ambassador described as being 6 feet tall with a tendency to stoop, sand-colored hair with a cowlick, blue eyes, a thin-lined mouth that drooped at the corners, a melodious voice, and appeared to be somewhere in age from 45 to 60 years old. He had developed a habit of being brusque to ship captains but gracious to those he negotiated with. Following the conclusion of this mission, Farquhar learned from Kirk to never underestimate ship captains.

Fariss (SS)–Crewman on the *Enterprise* and the most experienced transporter operator after Scotty. He wore his hair in a ponytail.

Favere (ST)–This thin, muscular human male, commodore of Starbase 12, had close cropped blond hair and spoke in a folksy drawl. He came from a long line of family members with careers in military/government service. He was fascinated by the old U.S. Cavalry, especially its systems of forts that were built across the U.S. western territory. He read widely, and took the interest as far as decorating most of the Starbase office areas with replicated items of that period. Hazel Payton and he were lovers and married at a later time. When Kirk requested back-up ships during this mission, he complied.

Favere's base decorations (ST)–Starbase 12 was decorated according to the personal taste of Commodore Favere. At nearly every corridor interval, some 19th century memento could be found such as an old calendar and paintings of horse soldiers and native Americans.

Favere's dinner menu (ST)–Most of his selected items would have been available during the development of the west of the U.S. Items included bison meat and items made from replicated corn or other North American plants. Dessert included ice cream and chocolate sauce.

Favere's office (ST)–SEE Favere. His love for the period of the 1830s through 1880s in the old west of the U.S. revealed itself in his decorations of his office with Cavalry uniforms, spurs, yellow braid and insignia buttons, sabers, a saddle slung across a hitching rack, and a large poster of John Wayne in a production title "She Wore A Yellow Ribbon." On his desk he kept a 3-horned skull and empty rifle cartridges. In a prominent place was a uniformed mannequin.

Favere's table seating arrangement (ST)–Commodore Favere of Starbase 12 held a dinner party in the officer's mess to honor his guests, particularly Conrad Franklin Kent and Hazel Payton. Of course Kirk and selected officers were invited. A pre-arranged seating had been laid out. On one side of Kirk was an elderly civilian woman who introduced herself as Dr. Kroeber. On the other side was a pretty lieutenant name Goshalf assigned to the starbase. Dr. McCoy sat next to a young woman. Spock sat between two women. Across from Kirk sat Conrad Kent. Commodore Favere sat at the head of the table with Hazel Payton to his right. Several other *Enterprise* and Starbase 12 personnel completed the party. SEE Favere's dinner menu.

Faz'rahn (FF)–A Klingon clan group of the Kamorh'dag district. SEE Vheled.

F'deraxt'la (DC)–Orion term for anyone who is a member of the UFP.

Federation– SEE United Federation of Planets.

Federation Astrophysics (BD)–Scientists from this bureau had studied the trinary system that included Faramond and reached the conclusion that the equipment left behind worked but could not be implemented as it had no software to run it. SEE Faramond.

Federation Auditor General (DC)–Division of StarFleet Command and answerable to it and the Federation Council. The Division is subdivided into sections which include teaching, auditing, accounting, etc. CONSULT Joseph *Star Trek Starfleet Technical Manual.*

Federation Council–In the beginning this Council consisted of the five major governments, Terra, Vulcan, Andor, Tellar, Rigel, and Alpha Centauri. Together these created the Federation at the first Babel conference dated 2087 (Goldsteins 98). By the time the Articles of Federation were written and presented to those wishing to become members, the Council was declared to consist of eleven members. Permanent members are: the United Nations of Terra; the Planetary Confederation of 40 Eridani; the United Planets of 61 Cygni; the Star Empire of Epsilon Indii; and the Alpha Centauri Concordium of Planets. CONSULT Chapter V of "The Articles of Federation" in Joseph (*Technical* 1:16).

Federation Interstellar Maritime Collision Regulations (GSR)–Nancy Ransom, captain of the *Ransom Castle*, quoted from Rule 38, Paragraph Two which stated that all space anomaly encounters be reported to the nearest StarFleet vessel. She reported to Kirk about her encounter with the gravity well.

Federation Medical Facility One (SS)–Identifies the operating facility established on Ssan to provide medical teams and services to those wounded by assassin attacks. As one of the trainees, McCoy served here. SEE five doctors.

Federation-*tska* (WLW)–Derogatory term employed by Talika Nyar toward Chekov. Implies childish or one not a Federation adult.

Feinberger attachment (Di)–This small circular device, which has multiple uses, is electronically connected to the main tricorder and provides additional detailed readings.

Feleree (S)–A Senite who answered Captain Pilenna's request to speak with Sanctuary's keepers.

Feric (P)–Romulan subcommander to Captain Hiran of the *Galtizh*, having served four years as Hiran's First Officer. He was noted for answering questions succinctly and for supporting Hiran when Jenyu took control of the ship. Feric released Hiran and Tiam from the brig after cutting power to the ship's weapons. SEE Hiran; Jenyu; Tiam.

Festux (SS)–An assassin killed the master governor of this city-state.

File Pavel-One (Di)–Chekvo's program that consisted of a graphics breakdown of the sensor scans taken during the Rithrim warriors attack on the *Enterprise*. The report led to an understanding of how the raider ships achieved fast maneuvering.

fireblossoms (FF)–These plants native to a Klingon world tend to destroy all nearby plants. Their strong root system gives them advantage over other plants as does their long deep-blue petals and grey-blue pollen dust that fastens to anything brushing against it. Having acquired several plants from the captain's quarters of a wrecked Klingon ship, terraformers on Beta Canzandia employed them for their oxygen-producing abilities. Carol Marcus presented a plant to Kirk who had it planted in *Enterprise's* botany lab of the ship. SEE Amagh.

First Federation (P; Di) The initial reference to the First Federation can be found in Captain Kirk's ship logs that detail first contact in 2266 with the *Fesarius*, a ship captained by an entity calling himself Balok (Okuda and Okuda *Encyclopedia* 155). Crewman Lt. Bailey was given permission to stay aboard Balok's ship as a cultural envoy (*CMn).

first Klingon search party (FF)–Klingons Gidris, Loutek, Aoras, Iglat, Shrof, Dirat, and Rogh were sent to locate the Beta Canzandia colony children.

first landing party to Rithra (Di)–Commodore Wesley, Samuels, Baila, Dr. Coss, and Uhura.

Firth of Tay (SG)–Located on the western side of Scotland, approximately at 56 N and 2W. The Earn River empties into this Firth. The abandoned pirate ship *Stephanie Emilia* was brought here where it caught fire and burned to the waterline.

five doctors (SS)–StarFleet doctors who trained together, attended classes together, and shipped out together to Ssan: Merlin Carver; Janice Taylor; Warren Huang; Paco Jiminey; and Leonard McCoy, all about age 26.

Flags and Pennants Code (GSR)–In Terra's sailing days, ships signaled each other using flags whose colors and forms of presentation were coded. Ships also employed visual signals such as running lights. Generally both of these methods are impossible in space. Most of the communications between ships is conducted via the ships' communication centers, although ships could employ the code by using their running lights in conjunction with high frequency bursts. When the high frequency noise jamming communications coming from the Romulan ship made it impossible for *Enterprise* to communicate with other ships, Kirk ordered Uhura to employ the Flags and Pennants Code by using *Enterprise's* running lights to do the signaling. The message sent was: coming into danger.

Flaming Desert (WLW)–Located on Vulcan; known for its beautiful colors, especially at sunset.

fleiar (FF)–Animal native to Alpha Maluria Six. It is tall with spindle-legs, long droopy ears, doglike snouts, and a good disposition, allowing it to be trained as a mounted beast.

Florida, Carlos (BD)–Helmsman on April's *Enterprise* and on the Liaison Cutter 4 accompanied by April, George and Jimmy Kirk, along with Veronica Hall and two engineers, Thorvaldson and Bennings. He survived the pirate attack.

flushback (BD)–Core-invasive dampening effect at the matter/antimatter mix level that left unchecked creates a negative warp field that results in an explosion. SEE anti-proton flushback.

Fogelstein, Helen (GSR)–Starbase 16 magistrate who allowed the Romulans to dock at the base rather than employing her power as commander of the starbase and refuse their request.

Force fields (ST)–SEE phased field generators.

Forrest, Cal (FF)–Old med school buddy of McCoy's who had sent McCoy an elegant decanter that McCoy used on ship.

Forrester, C. S. (BD)–Name is spelled Forester. Terran British writer born in Cairo, Egypt. Best known for his character creation Horatio Hornblower.

Foss (ST)–A tall thin, nervous Historian on this *Enterprise* mission. Kirk ordered him to research Dr. Omen.

Fragh'ka (FF)–Klingon battlecruiser whose first officer was Kernod, grandson of Emperor Kapronek, and whose second officer Kell was the son of Karradh. SEE Karradh.

Frarey, Mike (GSR)–A large man descended from colonists from Arkansas, Terra. His home port was Port Apt in the Alpha Centauri system. As First mate of the *Ransom Castle* he kept an eye on the guest host from Gullrey and soon developed feelings for Turry. He survived the Romulan boarding party

free-fall gymnastics (DC)–Sulu planned to organize an *Enterprise* group.

Fredericks (FF)–School teacher to the children of the colony on Beta Canzandia.

Frederickson (SS)–*Enterprise* nurse in McCoy's Sick Bay during this mission.

frequency focus travel (BD)–Phrase to identify long-distance transporter. All reports about Faramond indicated that its civilization had employed one.

Friedman, Michael J.—Author of the novels *Faces of Fire* and *Shadows on the Sun*.

From the Depths – Novel by Victor Milan. The Susuru who occupied a water world requested the Federation remove all human colonists. Commissioner Mariah Wayne, transported by the *Enterprise*, was sent to determine the situation, but Kirk and crew soon discovered the situation was different than the Susuru had revealed. Human colonists who called themselves Variants, genetically altered descendants of Khan's laboratory experiments, had occupied the planet many years before the Susuru arrived and were befriended by a Klingon detachment group. Kirk established peace by determining who owned the planet by first colonist settlement. To do so, he visited both groups, was caught in a battle between them, experienced a nuclear destruction of a Variant's city, and struggled to understand Commissioner Wayne's negative attitude. When finally the Klingons revealed their plans for destroying Kirk and the *Enterprise*, Kirk was forced into a fight to save his ship and crew, the planet, and its alien Susuru and Variants. He could not save Moriah Wayne who was killed by Kain.

Gabler (Di)–Member of Scotty's engineering crew. Scotty sent him with crewman Stanley to double check the impulse integration relays to ensure they were in top condition for the coming encounter with Rithrim raiders.

Gale, Dorothy (SG)–Character in the Terran novel *The Wizard of Oz*. McCoy reported thinking as he stepped aboard the Romulan space station that he felt like Dorothy must have felt being "plopped down in the center of Munchkinland."

Gallagher (FF)–Young brawny *Enterprise* security officer whom McCoy wrestled with in the gym.

Galliulin, Irina (UC)–She and Chekov had served on *Enterprise* thirty years before the incident with Chang. Chekov had thoughts of retiring and rekindling their romance, but a note from her indicated she was involved with another and relocating to Rigel.

Galtizh (P)–Romulan bird of prey sent to carry a group of scientists and musicians to Termais Four. Captain: Hiran; First Officer: Feric.

Galvin, Bud (SS)–StarFleet medical officer on Ssan who replaced Dr. Vincent Bando. SEE Bando.

Gamma (Di)–Milky Way galaxy is divided into roughly four quadrants: Alpha; Beta; Delta; Gamma (Mandel *Star Charts*).

Gamma Caius Seven (SS)–Maldinium, a type of rock found here was also found on Ssan.

Gamma Philuria Six (FF)–The last posting for Ambassador Marlin Farquhar before Alpha Maluria Six.

Gamma Theridian Twelve (FF)–Location of a drinking establishment Scotty remembered fondly; a river-side café with beautiful barmaids and birds.

gamma ray (S)–A build up of these rays indicated the Senites were arming their deflectors.

Gamma Xaridian (Di)–Classed as an M planet, it is one of eight in the system that supported a Federation colony. Rithrim destroyed the colony and all eighty-three scientific groups conducting a variety of research projects. The attack occurred following attacks on Alpha and Beta Xaridian.

Gamma Xaridian Two (Di)–*Enterprise* was on its way here when diverted by a distress signal from the Xaridian system. Following the settlement of the trouble in the Xaridian system, *Enterprise* continued to Gamma Two.

Gamma Xaridian Eight (Di)–Planet in the same system as planet twelve; both had settlements that were attacked by Rithrim.

Gamma Xaridian Twelve (Di)–The outermost planet and its two moons in the Xaridian system.

Garcia, Irma (FF)–Colonist on Beta Canzandia and mother to Roberto Garcia.

Garcia, Roberto (FF)–Human male with a dark narrow face and jug-handle ears about age 10 or 12 who was a member of the Beta Canzandia terraforming colony. He followed his friend David Marcus into the hills to avoid capture by the Klingons.

Garvak (S)–A thin faced Klingon commander with tangled grey hair. His command of the cruiser *Rak'hon* had placed him on duty at Sanctuary intercepting ships coming to the planet. After several years of duty, Klingon High Command recalled him to regular patrol duty after deciding Sanctuary made a very effective prison.

Gaston (P)–SEE Alphonse and Gaston.

Gatherers (Di)–One of five castes on the planet Rithrim. At birth these members, identified by voice pitch, are segregated and separately educated. SEE Rithrim.

Gavelan Star (GSR)–A privately owned ship entrant in the Great Starship Race commanded by Ben Shamirian.

Gelb, Jeff (Di)–Human administrator of Alpha Xaridian Two.

Gendron, Roberta (DC)–As one of four auditors assigned to the *Enterprise* to determine ship and crew efficiency, her task was to check dispatch records. She shared quarters with auditor Chaiken. She and Sweeney were killed at Deck 7's transporter room. SEE Sweeney.

General Order No. 7 (P)–Mandel (*Manual* 8) identifies this to read: "No Federation vessel, under any conditions, emergency or otherwise, is to be permitted to visit Talos IV. To do so carries a mandatory death penalty." In spite of StarFleet's enforced order it is rumored that someone recovered artifacts from the star group and likely from the planet itself. SEE Talos.

Genesis (UC)–This research project's goal was to create a process to turn uninhabitable planets into re-formed worlds suitable for life. The process involved a massive explosion to reduce a planet to its subatomic particles and then reassemble them to a preprogrammed matrix (Okuda and Okuda *Encyclopedia* 328). Dr. Carol Marcus and her team had a successful first attempt inside a Regula asteroid. An unintended second attempt caused by Khan resulted in the birth of an unstable planet called Genesis, created from unstable protomatter. CONSULT *The Wrath of Khan* and *The Search for Spock*.

Genrah (UC)–One of several operators at the Klingon Mortagh Outpost Three. SEE Kesla.

George and Gracie (P)–Male and female humpback whales Kirk and group recovered from Terra's past. When Terra was threatened by an alien probe, Kirk and his group discovered the Probe was looking for whales. They went back into time, located two being held in the San Francisco aquarium, retrieved them, and returned to the present timeline. When Spock mindmelded with Gracie and learned she was pregnant, he also received impressions of a form of mental energy and beings similar to George and Gracie. These impressions suggested whales may be descendants of the creators of the Probe though not enough data clearly support this thesis. Presently the two whales are part of the New Cetacean Institute located at Australia's Great Barrier Reef. CONSULT *The Voyage Home* by Vonda McIntyre.

Germany, 1938 (UC)– Terran historians considered this a pivotal year for Nazi Germany. The year included the following: Germany invaded Austria and expelled all Jews; Invaded Czechoslovokia; Concentration camp at Flossenburg opened; Confiscated "degenerate" art; Identity cards distributed for all Jews; Graf Zeppelin II made its maiden flight; and Jewish lawyers were forbidden to practice in Germany. During a meeting with General Chang, Chang declared the Klingon Empire needed "breathing room." Both Kirk and Spock caught the allusion as it related it to Germany in 1938.

gettrex (FF)–Native to Alpha Maluria Six, and feline in general appearance, it is the natural predator of the cubaya. SEE cubaya.

gettrxin (FF)–Plural form for *gettrex*.

Gevish'rae (FF)–Occupants of the southern continent of Qo'noS. Term translates from the Klingon as "Thristing Knives," a group gaining power on the General Council but who lost power when the *Kadn'ra* failed its mission to Beta Canzandia and Councilman Dumeric was ejected from the Council. SEE *Kadn'ra*; Dumeric.

Gezary (S)–One of several ships orbiting Sanctuary, it was captained by Pilenna who conned Scotty into making repairs to her ship. Later Scotty was forced to fire on it to keep it from destroying the balloon believed to be carrying Kirk, Spock, and McCoy. The ship fell into Sanctuary's atmosphere, and its entire crew became part of the Sanctuary population. SEE Pilenna; balloon.

ghost stories (SG)–Scott's reading of ghost stories were part of *Enterprise's* evening entertainment.

Ghyl (IT)–Nordstral native Kitka and member of the Chinit Clan. This aged, yellow-faced grandmother to Nhym had bone-white eyes. Determined to meet her god, she traveled to a lonely sea-cliff shelter and while waiting gave hospitality to Chekov's group who were pursued by Alion. By throwing herself into the sea, she called the kraken who ate Alion and thereby saved Chekov's group.

giant alien (UC)–A silver-scaled alien with horny growths from temple to chin and a brilliant red scar on the left side of his face. As a prisoner on Rura Penthe he had demanded Kirk's coat and Kirk's obedience to the Brotherhood of Aliens.

Gidris (FF)–First officer of the Klingon ship *Kadn'ra* captained by Vheled considered efficient and dedicated. He and six men searched for the colonists' children who were believed to have taken the G-Seven unit. He and fellow officer Aoras fell into a pit dug by Spock and the children. Both men were killed by Vheled. SEE G-Seven Unit.

Gilden, Mark–Author of *The Starship Trap*.

Giotta (Di)–Security chief on the *Enterprise* during this mission.

Girin Gatha (Di)–An important Rithramen procreation facility threatened by approaching lava flow. Crews from Commodore Wesley's *Lexington* erected triple strength shields to protect the area.

Girl Scouts (BD)–Terran group founded in1910 by the British as response to the Boy Scouts. The group is dedicated to good citizenship, good conduct, and outdoor activities. In BD, Jimmy Kirk and his group crossed the Skunk River on a rope walkway used on outings by both Boy and Girl Scout troops.

Glasnost (P)–Russian term that loosely translates as "openness" or "publicity." CONSULT the *Oxford English Dictionary* for other meanings.

G'lops (ST)–Native to the geologically active planet Pegsus IV, this intelligent life form has the appearance of brightly colored mud. Dr. Brewster, a Horta, led a team to study them.

Glover, Miles (GSR)–Commander of *New Pride of Baltimore*, a ship entrant in the Great Starship Race that ran under the flag of Baltimore, MD, Terra. The ship took first place.

God's Kiss (IT)–Translation of a Kitka term that refers to a poison made from Nordstral's native kraken. SEE kraken.

Gogine, Christoff (GSR)–General and commander of the hospital ship *Brother's Keeper*, a UFP ship and entrant in the Great Starship Race.

Golden Gate Park (P)–Located in San Francisco; Kirk took a stroll here before reporting to Admiral Cartwright.

Goldstein (DC)–*Enterprise* crewman at Bridge communications who alerted Kirk to the signal loss from two suit locators on the *Hawking*. He also alerted Kirk to messages from Sulu and Uhura.

Goliardh Seven (SS)–When he overheard their negative remarks about Dr. McCoy, Chekov threatened Dennehy and Christiano with duty on a very boring run to this planet.

Goodyear IX, Charles (GSR)–Captain of the *Blimp*, an entrant in the Great Starship Race.

Gorkon (UC)–Chancellor of the Klingon High Council. A neatly trimmed beard streaked with silver and a cultivated speech hid a quick mind. He accepted Spock's overture of talks in 2293. His flag ship met *Enterprise* and Kirk conducted a tour of the *Enterprise* and held a banquet in his honor. Devoted to peace between the Empire and the Federation, he knew his chance of surviving the peace conference was slim. He was phased by two *Enterprise* ensigns in his stateroom and died later though McCoy attempted to save his life. His daughter Atzebur became Chancellor on his death as he had stipulated.

Gorkon's initiative (UC)–Spock opened talks with Gorkon and then Gorkon proposed negotiations begin between the Empire and the Federation. Some members of both sides opposed the talks and tried to stop them.

Gorkon's quarters (UC)–On his flag ship *Kronos One*, a designated secure area was equipped with security devices and guards at the door. Here he studied Federation's proposals and made notes for the peace conference.

Gorn (Di)–Historian Shane Johnson writes that Gorns are native to the planet Gorner whose star is Tau Lacertae, a red giant supporting nine planets, of which Gorner is the ninth (*Worlds* 146). This cold-blooded race inhabits a warm hot planet with jungle-like areas. At full growth, an adult will stand over seven feet with a deep-green-grey skin coloring. The Gorn eye, which Johnson writes "is multifaceted with a hard outer covering that protects the inner lenses...[with] ears [that] are quite sensitive and can detect a wider range of frequencies than humanoid ears" (*Worlds* 146), is described by Trimble as being iridescent (165). Physiological studies reveal Gorns devote much brain area to conscious thought and speech, with little mass given to body control (Johnson *Worlds* 146). Their slow and deliberate movements often hide true power. Gorns are an intelligent race although they resemble bipedal lizards. Initial contact left Kirk with the impression that a Gorn was similar to an ancient Terran tyrannosaurus rex. Skilled Gorn engineers have produced space-warp capabilities with sophisticated weapons. Observations reveal that Gorns did not have a large space territory although they frequently raided Federation areas. An encounter with the *Enterprise* at Cestus III (*Ar) soon led to other encounters until the establishment of peaceful relations between Gorner and the Federation resulted in extended Federation influence in Gorn-controlled areas. Within a half dozen years Gorner entered into a treaty with the Federation and now Gorns attend the Academy. Some serve on StarFleet ships. Kirk noted that several Gorns were stranded on Sanctuary (S).

Goshalk (ST)–A red-headed female StarFleet lieutenant who did duty at Starbase 12. She was included in Commander Favere's dinner party, seated next to McCoy.

Gowan (BD)–Crew member of the *Shark*. SEE *Shark*.

Grael (FF)–This Klingon crewman of the *Kadn'ra* who wore his hair in long braids was a member of the Gavish'rae group and the clan Nik'nash. Kiruc hired him to kill Captain Vheled.

Graf, L. A. –Author of the novels *Death Count* and *Ice Trap*.

Grand National (GSR)–Grand National Handicap Steeplechase is an annual Terran British horse race challenging skills and spirit of horse and rider over an irregular triangular course dotted with spectacular hazardous jumps.

Grand Prix (GSR)–A Terran automobile race that began in 1906 and became an international race controlled by automobile manufacturers who set specifications for each entry.

Graveyard of Lost Ships (S)–Junkyard for all ships landing on Sanctuary and the last resting place for dismantled ships. Senites transported stripped ships here but never bothered to visit. The ships became residences for a variety of races who refused to accept Senite hospitality. A town council granted resident status based on the most needy cases. The village, which employed gas-thermal energy to run steam turbines that provided electricity, became a "testament to the ingenuity, spirit, and cooperation" among the variety of species stranded on Sanctuary.

gravity well (GSR)–This space phenomena created by a collection of a great number of gravitons over millions of years is believed to have established a spin that pulled the gravitons into a "well" much like a typhoon. Over time it became self perpetuating; *Enterprise* and *Ransom Castle* were caught by a gravity well that appeared on their view screens as funnel-shaped and rifled. *Enterprise* was caught in the trap as it went to rescue *Ransom Castle*. *Hiawatha* which had been stationed near the well to warn all race entrants was not in the same vicinity as *Enterprise* and *Ransom Castle*. *Enterprise's* sensors had, as discovered when sensor logs were studied in detail after the race, captured evidence of the Romulans using their tractor beam to exert extreme pull then ceased, causing *Enterprise* to "bounce" into the well. Romulan torpedoes also helped push *Enterprise* into the well. *Enterprise* fired torpedoes into the well just ahead of the "falling" ship, causing a disruption to the magnetic current and flinging the ship clear of the well.

Great Hall (FF)–Translation of Klingon term for the location of the meeting room of the Klingon High Council.

Great Lakes (GSR)–StarFleet frigate and an entrant in the Great Starship Race. Commanded by Haus Fahl.

Great Starship Race — Novel by Diane Carey. Captain Kenneth Dodge of the USS *Hood* answered a signal and made first contact with the Rey, of the planet Gullrey. For nearly 100 of their years, the Rey had searched for intelligent life beyond their system. Fortune smiled on them when Dodge made contact. Twelve years later, the Rey government, with help from StarFleet's First Contact office, determined to meet other sentient life. To promote their planet, they initiated a starship race, inviting anyone to participate. Romulus sent a ship captained by Valdus who years earlier had a brief contact with the Rey and came to believe they were an unknown weapon. The Rey who have strong telepathic senses and employ them when frightened were taken aboard the Romulan ship. They defended themselves by projecting their fears into the crew. Only Valdus escaped and in time become a captain. He saw the starship race and his participation in it as a way to destroy the people and their planet. Valdus intended to employ one of the entrants as a Trojan horse bearing a planet-busting bomb. *Enterprise*, sent as an entrant to keep an eye on events, distrusted the Romulans. Over the course of the race, Kirk learned about Valdus's attempt and stopped it but not before he was forced to destroy Valdus's ship.

Great Starship Race (GSR)–At Starbase 10, John Orland informed the gathering of ship captains that the residents of Gullrey had established the race to signify goodwill. The race was to be a public relation event, as well as an entertaining one, and a way to draw attention to Gullrey. It also commemorated first contact between Gullrey and UFP. The race would be a strict competition, Orland informed each entrant and reminded them that each captain had received a packet of race information establishing specific gross tonnage and thrust brackets. Each packet also carried information on Gullrey, established restrictions on carrying cargo, and the statement that "when there is any vessel dead ahead, the following vessel must either alter course or power back to adjust for ahead reach." The rules of the race would be those based on Maritime Standard. One communication channel was designated available to all and was considered an SOS, only. In case of an emergency only a fellow entrant could respond to another ship's trouble. He noted to the gathered group that Federation laws would not apply since the area was not yet officially UFP territory. One rule strongly stressed prohibited the disabling of another ship. Beacon and buoys placed throughout the sector marked all routes and dangerous spots. On the course map, gravitational anomalies were identified with a globe, electrical storms with a diamond, sensor blind spots with triangles, and flashers marked storms. StarFleet vessels were handicapped by being deprived of hardware advantage and forced to establish a power reduction. Some entrants were non-Federation members such as the Tholian and Romulan ships. Although Kirk saw the contest as a test of smarts as much as of ships, he expected trouble from the Romulans and only learned later they were determined to destroy Gullrey, believing the inhabitants were weapons to be used against them. Though a Romulan crew boarded the *Ransom Castle*, Kirk sent a Security team who intervened and learned of their intent. Kirk, realizing what was intended, nearly destroyed his ship attempting to stop them from destroying the planet. *Enterprise* required extensive repairs.

Great Starship Race Ceremonies (GSR)–Closing ceremonies were held at Monn Oren on Gullrey with a thirty-meter screen showing the replay of the parade of ships from the day before. Kirk and members of his officers sat in the first ten rows of seats in a huge auditorium. The recently elected Federation president presented the First Place Platinum Plaque and the *El Sol* gold doubloon to Captain Miles Glover and his crew of *New Pride of Baltimore*. A trophy for second place went to Captain Kmmuta and the crew of *552-4* with Ambassador Yeshmal, Federation representative to the Tholian Assembly, accepting the prize. Third place went to Captain Sucice Miller and her crew of the *Ozcice*, the host entry. The Spacermanship and Sportsmanship Award, a large platinum medal, created the night before the final ceremonies by the Race Committee at the request of Captain Nancy Ransom and her crew, was presented to Captain Kirk and his crew with the President concluding his remarks by saying that "from this day forward [when we] remember the true definition of sportsmanship...we remember the *Enterprise*." The Federation president concluded the ceremony by placing a gold star on the UFP banned that already had a background of silver stars and star charts. The additional star represented Gullrey.

Great Starship Race Manifest (GSR)–SEE Appendix E.

Great Starship Race Prizes (GSR)–The winner received a plaque and the gold *El Sol* doubloon while second and third places were given trophies. A special prize went to the *Enterprise*. SEE Great Starship Race Ceremonies.

Great Starship Race winners (GSR)–SEE Great Starship Race Ceremonies.

Great Tea Race (GSR)–This was a competition among the fastest Chinese clipper ships of the tea trade to deliver tea to London at the best speed. Initially run in 1866. In his remarks to the participants of the Great Starship Race, John Orland mentioned this race. SEE John Orland.

Green (Di)– Historian Trimble (165) writes that he was a "military man who led a genocidal war on Earth in the early 20th century...notorious for striking at enemies during treaty negotiations." He held to the motto "overwhelm and devastate." The war he fought could have been WWIII or the wars many "supermen" like Khan created. Kirk was presented with an image of Colonel Green by the Excalbians in 2269 during their study of humans' concept of "good and evil" (*SC). In Di, during a discussion with Commodore Wesley, Kirk pointed out that the Parathu'ul "would make even Colonel Green lose his lunch."

grey market (BD)–Space-borne black market run by a mixture of peoples from various races. Stolen or illegally obtained salvaged parts taken from wrecks went to the highest bidder. The term "grey market" came into existence because at times those dealing in illegal items dealt in legal circles. StarFleet hasn't been able to shut down the operation due to insufficient evidence.

Gridley (SG)–Spock and McCoy were part of the team that transferred to *Reltah*, the Romulan space station found drifting in space. McCoy accompanied Spock who was searching for a computer connection from which to access the ship's log. When he said they would have to search for another, McCoy's reply was "Ready when you are, Gridley." The Gridley he was referring to was one of Admiral Dewey's seamen. During the Battle of Manila Bay, May 1898, Dewey pronounced the order, "You may fire when you are ready, Gridley." The phrase immortalized both men and became a part of Terra's general culture surrounding Terra's sailing vessels. Undoubtedly, McCoy was familiar with the source.

Grokh (UC)–Middle-aged Klingon general and one of Gorkon's advisors.

Grunt (FD)–A distinct Variant and native to Discord. They were developed on Terra and then bred for heavy labor by giving them great strength, endurance, low volition and low intelligence. Once settled on Discord, Grunts were free to reclaim their intelligence, but chose to retain their body styles. They now perform physical tasks, often performing them while their brains engage in thinking. SEE Discord.

G-Seven unit (FF)–A technological innovation, developed by Yves Boudreau, and employed on Beta Canzandia in a trial test, was designed to accelerate plant cell growth by increasing oxygen. The prototype was about a meter long and half that in diameter with a flawless reflective surface. Best effective in a tenth of a kilometer radius with indications of effects to three kilometers radius. Spock took the prototype to keep it from Klingon hands.

Guarnerius (P)–A First Federation vessel tracking the Probe. It sent word the Probe had crossed into the Neutral Zone.

Gullrey (GSR)–Home planet for a population of 5 billion extremely friendly people who had never met space-faring people though they dreamed of the day. They had established colonies in their system to search for other peoples beyond their system. They seeded their immediate area with Whistling Posts in the expectation of receiving signals from intelligent life. Ninety years passed and no signal came. Funding and hope faded and all but one Whistling Post was closed. That one post was manned by Beneon and Vorry. The day before the post was scheduled to be closed, they made contact. Unexpectedly the USS *Hood* captained by Kenneth Dodge answered their call. Beneon was later quoted as saying: "We had hope...we wanted to find someone to be neighbors with the galaxy. We wanted to find out we weren't the only intelligent life in the galaxy." Gullrey had no established interstellar laws and following contact requested Federation membership. Initially only diplomats, natural and medical scientists, and cultural transition teams had interaction with the citizens. Twelve years from the first contact, Gullrey initiated the Great Starship Race as a means of meeting more space-faring peoples. When UFP formally accepted Gullrey as a member, their space increased by 18% and pushed the Federation's boundaries outward. Their planet according to Spock is pronounced as Gullrey but the word in the English equivalent and in the western alphabet is "dguibbealeaichaiereuw." SEE Rey.

Gurg (FD)–A big ugly Klingon who was a member of the boarding party that took control of the *Enterprise*. Kirk stunned him first as he and his group retook control.

Haastra (FF)–As Klingon security officer on the *Kadn'ra* during this incident, he discovered someone had sabotaged the ship's warp drive with an explosive.

Hag mask (WLW)–A particularly ugly mask, according to Chekov, that was employed in the Creation Play presented on Deveron 5.

Hall, Pete (GSR)–This dark bearded human hailed from Virginia, had a deep heavy southern drawl, and was captain of the *Alexandria* flying the flag of Alexandria, Virginia, Terra. Kirk called him "kind and capable... [with] a lot of promise." SEE *Alexandria*.

Hall, Veronica (BD)–Blond blue-eyed female StarFleet ensign, about age twenty at the time of this mission, who wore her hair pulled into a knot on the top of her head. She earned her degree in astrotelemetry and communications and served under Captain April's leadership on *Enterprise 1701*. She accompanied April's group to LC4. In her youth, a canoeing injury got infected and led to the amputation of her right hand. She was fitted with a prosthetic. Eager to be a part of StarFleet she learned to use her hand to good advantage. During the pirate attack she was badly injured from coolant spray, losing her right eye, a leg, and her right arm to the shoulder. She also suffered supercool burns, and some of her blood cells crystallized. To ensure her survival, Captain April and George Kirk put her into a pressure suit and administered blood coagulants, antibiotics, and pain killers. Her recovery was assured, though she could never again serve on a starship. In spite of her injuries, she never lost her desire to remain in StarFleet.

haluski (IT)–Russian term denoting a cabbage dish.

Hagbard's Select (FD)–A distilled whiskey from the planet Discord. While Kirk and McCoy were enjoying a drink, Kirk wondered what could grow on Discord that "could be distilled into a fine shipping whiskey." McCoy replied: "Some things a man isn't meant to know."

haggis (P; DC)–One of Scotty's favorite dishes consists of a mixture of the minced heart, lungs, and liver of a sheep or calf. Mixed with suet, onions, oatmeal, and seasonings, it is then boiled in the stomach of the animal. In DC, Scotty told Kirk and McCoy that this was the Scottish national dish.

Haidar (FD)–Native of Discord described as short with a brown complexion and long black hair. He was one of several stockholders in the Waverider Ranch run by Aagard dinAthos.

Haight-Ashbury (P)–One of several areas of San Francisco that Kirk periodically visited when time permitted for it held good memories.

Haklev, Muav (DC)–Andorian physicist, recognizable by his blue face, flaxen hair, and vinegar smell, who left Andor with top-secret technology, taking it to Orion. Then fleeing the Orions, he stowed away on the *Enterprise*, learned of the bomb set on Deck 6, and alerted Chekov. He was apprehended, and Kirk chose to send him to Sigma One aboard the *Hawking*, but an attempt on his life by an overloaded phaser led to his being taken on board the *Shras* along with Sulu and Uhura. Following the resolution of the situation between Andor and Orion, only with *Enterprise* intervention, he was taken to Sigma One and eventually returned to Andorian jurisdiction. The secret technology he had attempted to sell was a trans-shield anode which others had studied, experimented with, and concluded didn't work.

Halkan fire-lilies (DC)–Translucent lilies that produce phosphorescent pollen and require water chameleons to fertilize them. Sulu purchased a few for his lily pond.

Halkan water chameleons (DC)–Very small gold-speckled lizards whose resting position is a curled up ball. They sing when contented. Chekov, given the task of guarding Sulu's purchase, kept them in his quarters.

Hall of Governance (SS)–Headquarters for the Ssan government. Here the second and third governors along with advisors and security officers, including their staffs, occupy the building.

Hallie, Suzanne (SG)–This petite female ensign, known for her gregariousness, was a member of *Enterprise's* Security with the landing party to the Romulan space station. Her duty was to protect McCoy. When confronted by the creature, she suffered cardiac arrest. SEE *Reltah*.

Hall of Columns (P)–Large imposing government building on Romulus. The Praetor's body lay in state in the Central Septum.

Hanashiro (GSR)–Chief of *Enterprise* Security was sent on Kirk's order to take control of the *Alexandria*, establish a security blockade, and check every ship for Romulans who might be on board.

Handler, Ryan (P)–This tall thin, nervous fellow with corn-silk hair was a StarFleet ensign assigned to aid Ambassador Riley. Though quite near-sighted he took a booster shot of Retenax every six months which helped his eyesight. He participated in the talks between Riley and the Romulan ambassador Tiam and handled the defection of the Romulans Jandra and Dajan while Riley was in Sick Bay.

Hannes (FD)–Native of Discord who lived in the city called Storm. His cousin Sonny Puleomua lived in Harmony. SEE Sonny Puleomua.

Harcum (FF)–Member of the Beta Canzandia terraforming colony who declared Klingon fireblossoms would be quite hardy. SEE fireblossoms.

Hardee, Sue (GSR)–Captain of the race entrant *Thomas Jefferson*.

Hardona's Wall (ST)–Location identified by Captain Iola. Reference may be to the Aleph edge as the Wall is said to be at the "end of the universe." SEE Iola.

Harmony (FD)–One of Discord's cities whose chief export was insulating matting made from seaweed. Moriah Wayne destroyed the city by beaming a half-megaton nuclear bomb into its energy core.

Harrakas (S)–This family unit in the village of the Graveyard of Lost Ships donated tripolymer sheeting for the balloon. SEE balloon.

Harrisburg, AR (GSR)–Located in the United States, Terra. Some of *Ransom Castle's* crew's ancestors came from here.

Haunted Forest (GSR)–Private entrant in the Great Starship Race captained by Buck Ames.

Have-Nots (Di)–Translation of a Parath'aa term that refers to an unhappy minority opposed to the government which is designated as the Haves.

Hawking (DC)–One of *Enterprise's* shuttlecraft. Sulu, Uhura, and Chekov planned to use this shuttle to take Muav Haslev to Sigma One, but its containment field was compromised by an exploding phaser. Sulu employed the shuttle, set it to explode, and lured the Orion ship *Mecufi* close to the *Hawking* which exploded and destroyed the *Mecufi*.

headwall (BD)–Curved dry dock stall that allows the bow of most vessels to fit snugly into it with the forward nose of the ship barely touching the wall.

Hector (P)–In Greek legend Hector was Troy's greatest hero and credited with the founding of the Italian state. Kirk used the name in a statement referring to misinformation often issuing from the Romulan Empire about the Praetor's death. Kirk declared that he'd heard the same news "since Hector was a pup."

heebie-jeebies (SG)–Kirk's phrase he used to tease Scotty about telling ghost stories.

hedgehogs (BD)–Spacedock personnel gave nicknames to one-and two-man work vehicles. SEE potatoes; sandbaggers.

Hellsgate Rift (FD)–Located on Discord in the deepest part of Discord's ocean. Mona Arkazha took Spock to this location where he discovered a colony of microscopic sentient life.

"Henry the Fifth" (ST)–Drama by Shakespeare

Hensu (P)–This Romulan ship followed the Probe while it was in Romulan territory. When the ship fired on the Probe, the Probe destroyed the *Hensu* and a cargo ship that had dropped out of warp in close vicinity.

Hernandez, Nadia (WLW)–A small woman with an aggressive manner. As a language expert she was included in Dr. Kaul's archeology team to Careta IV.

Hernan de Soto (FD)–United Exploratory Ship that conducted part of the First General Survey of Federation territory in 2092. The ship discovered a population one star, an Oort Cloud, and seven planets. The ship's navigator named the star Joan-Marie after herself. SEE Joan-Marie.

Herring (FD)–*Enterprise* crewman in Sulu's group who beamed into *Dagger's* engine room and took its engineers captive. He was injured in the fight to gain control of the room. SEE *Dagger*.

Hiawatha (GSR)–StarFleet frigate placed near the gravity well to warn race entrants.

High Assassin (SS)–Leader of the Ssan assassins was usually chosen by the previous leader and schooled in the cult's beliefs and stories, before being tested. Leadership was assumed after death of the previous High Assassin.

Highland Games (SG)–These games are of Scottish origin. They celebrate Scottish and Celtic culture and are believed to have begun with King Malcom III of Scotland in the 11th century. He introduced a contest to determine the fastest runner of the kingdom. When England gained the rule of Scotland, it forbade the Scots from military training. The story goes that to keep the men in shape, the introduction of training included implements not associated with war. These became a passion with the Scots and soon events evolved into athletic and sport competitions. Today these games include a caber toss (throwing a long pole or log), stone-put (similar to the shot-put of the Olympic games), and sheaf tossing (throwing a bundle of straw weighing 20 pounds over a raised bar with a pitchfork). The games have been held annually since the end of WW II with opening ceremonies attended by the ruling monarch of Great Britain, Terra.

Hii-dou-rai (FD)–Andorian ceremonial stones which are bits of "petrified wood hand-rubbed into glossy-smooth round shapes" which are much admired throughout the galaxy.

Hightower (FD)–Federation commissioner for Interspecies Affairs Bureau. Some of those who worked with him were convinced he disliked StarFleet, believed he increased his power by capitalizing on the so-called human "cultural imperialism," and noted his violent outbursts. He called Federation Councillor Cornelius Wayne a close friend and befriended his daughter Moriah Wayne when she entered diplomatic service. Following the incident told in *From the Depths*, an investigation began revealing many irregularities in his office.

Hillios (SS)–Commanding officer of the StarFleet's ship *Horizon* who delivered McCoy and the other medical trainees, supplies, and staff to Ssan and then retrieved three of them, including McCoy, and delivered them to Beta Aurelon Three for medical duty.

Hindenburg (S)–This 1930s' Terran dirigible filled with hydrogen blew up after striking its landing tower. Renna reminded Kirk and McCoy of the ship as they prepared to lift off Sanctuary in a home-made balloon. SEE Renna.

hinds (FD)–Native Discord marine life. The adults are described as having six red three-meter wings and resembling Terran dragonflies. They have an armor-like outer skeleton that is blue tiger-striping over scarlet bellies. A high-energy metabolic rate requires them to eat frequently. The respiratory exhaust, pumped out through designed spiracles, was recorded as "slightly cooler than live steam." The native humanoid population carry guns for self-protection from these animals.

Hiran (P)–Romulan captain of the *Galtizh* who came from a military family proud of its seven generations of service originating with a matrilineal grandsire. His family forced him into service to maintain the tradition though he preferred attending the university as his sister had done. Even without special social connections, Hiran was promoted to the *Galtizh* after spending some time in the Provinces where he put down a rebellion with only one casualty– his wife. Accepting the command was his way out of the Provinces. His military record indicated there were few instances of blood-letting among his officers and crew. He was sent to the peace conference at

Termais Four, and Kirk, who declared him "a straight-shooter," was impressed when Hiran made the initial overture to develop friendly relations with him by offering a tour of his ship. Kirk reciprocated by escorting Hiran on an *Enterprise* tour. Hiran was impressed with the botanical gardens, walking on the grass with Kirk, and the bowling alley. Hiran told Kirk about his sister, appending his remarks by saying that "if I had been an engineer, I might never have met humans," adding that Kirk and colleagues were the first he had met. Jutak made an unsuccessful attempt on his life. In addition to this problem, Hiran learned from Tiam that experiments had been conducted on intelligent sea creatures in the hopes of perfecting results to be used on the rebel Variizt worlds. Captured by Kital and his aides, he was held prisoner in his own quarters until released by Feric. SEE Kital.

Hitler (WLW)–Terran dictator of the early 20th century infamous for his attempts to extinguish the Jewish People. Kirk thought of the terrible destruction that would befall the galaxy if the technology of the Kh!lict fell into the hands of such a man. For that reason Kirk sought a quarantine for Careta IV.

Hobbes, Thomas (FD)–Reference is to a Terran Englishman who lived from 1588 to 1679 and was known for his political philosophy, especially his book *Leviathan* (1651) which expresses his philosophy on social contract theory. Native Discordian Aileea dinAthos mentioned him in a conversation with Captain Kirk.

Hobbits (FD)–Native Discordians named after characters in the Terran series *Lord of the Rings* by J. R. R. Tolkien. Similar in body form to a Micro but "chunky and round faced" with a tendency to be thick around the middle. Suleyman piloted Mona Arkazha and Spock to Hellsgate Rift. SEE Suleyman.

Holarnis, Zar (SS)–Very thin Ssan master governor of the city-state Larol and highest ranking official on Ssan. He was assassinated in a hover car accident that destroyed all seven state cars at once.

Holmes, Sherlock (BD)–Fictitious detective created by Terran Arthur Conan Doyle. John Roy Moss called Jimmy Kirk a Sherlock because Jimmy questioned his actions. SEE John Roy Moss.

Holy War (SS)–A wave of wholesale Ssan assassinations led by High Assassin Li Moboron began a long bloody conflict precipitated by the enactment of laws banning birth control and assassinations and dissolving the assassin cult. When he called for a Holy War and increased assassinations against those who had supported the laws, the planet was subjected to chaos until he was killed in a raid. The deaths ceased and the planet enjoyed nearly 40 years of peace and induction into the UFP. Renegade assassins lacked a leader until Andrachis became High Assassin and the assassinations began again. As a result of this civil unrest, both sides formed secret cults to preserve the concept of the assassin with the government hiring assassins to fight renegade assassins. With the intervention of Kirk and the *Enterprise*, the cycles were broken and the assassin cult destroyed.

Homeaway station (SG)–StarFleet vessel *Tandarich* docked at this Federation space station.

Home for Old Spacers (SG)–Residence established by StarFleet to accommodate those people who had served in the Fleet, retired, and were too old to take care of themselves.

Homesward (FD)–Main island of the Susuru archipelago on Discord. Cape Sorrow is located here.

Hood (GSR)– SEE USS *Hood*.

Hornblower, Horatio (FD)–In FD, this is the name the Gorn, whom Sulu called a friend, had adopted because his was unpronounceable. He chose this name because he learned it had belonged to a great Terran hero whose adventures were detailed in a series of novels written by Forester. Horatio was a science officer on a Gorn exploratory vessel drydocked at Starbase 23. He gave Sulu a chiropractic treatment of "a rough and ready nature." At least according to Sulu.

Horta (P)–A silicon-based life form discovered on Janus VI. Its natural environment is underground. To enable it to move easily through rock, it secretes a powerful corrosive acid. The adult is about "seven feet long by three feet wide by three feet covered with mottled russet-orange asbestos plating...multiple tentacles or legs on the ventral surface" (Trimble 169). They live to be thousands of years old, then all die except one individual who is chosen to guard the nest and its eggs and to rear the next generation. Miners on Janus VI discovered the creature and with help from Kirk, Spock, and McCoy along with the science labs on the *Enterprise* contact was made and understanding began. Spock, in a mindmeld, discovered the Horta are sentient, thus beginning a new relationship between the Horta and the Federation. The miners and Horta developed a working relationship following the hatching of the eggs (*DD). Some few years later several Hortas graduated from StarFleet Academy and became ship personnel; others became scientists. SEE Dr. Brewster.

host observers (GSR)–Every entrant in the Great Starship Race carried at least one Rey on board as specified by the Federation diplomatic corps. The purpose was to allow the Reys to observe the workings of the ship and crew so that they could convey their knowledge and feelings back to their planet's council to help the council reach a decision about joining UFP. Kirk carried three – Royenne, Osso, and Tom. *Ransom Castle* carried one – Turry – whom the Romulans captured and killed.

hovercraft (BD)–Water vehicle used by Terran Port Authority.

Howard (DC)–*Enterprise* Security guard at the Bridge station.

Howard, Michael (IT)–Young brown-bearded *Enterprise* ensign on Chekov's security team to Nordstral. Chekov reset his shoulder dislocated when he hit a wall of ice in an attempt to cross an ice bridge. When Chekov suffered from kraken poison, Uhura put Howard and Chekov in a sleeping bag together so that Howard could share his body heat with Chekov.

Hrdina (DC)–*Enterprise* Security guard under Lt. Lemieux's command on Deck 6.

Huang, Warren (SS)–One of the five doctor/trainees sent to Ssan. SEE five doctors.

Huck (S)–Huckleberry Finn. McCoy made reference to this character from Mark Twain's novel of the same name when Kirk suggested building a raft and traveling a Sanctuary river.

Huerta's Emperor Syndrome (BD)–McCoy identified the adult Roy Moss as suffering this. Roy Moss lacked the ability to see any weakness in himself and saw "no value in knowledge itself...only in knowledge that leads to power." Quite possibly a study was conducted on the Mexican dictator Adolfo de la Huerta whose rule lasted not quite two years (February 1913 to July 1913). He believed himself superior to everyone else and became a brutal and repressive dictator ("Huerta" *Britannica* 2000).

humpback whales (P)–Terran sea mammal known for its elaborate courtship songs and displays. It creates a variety of sounds from moans to groans and snores strung together to form "songs" which may vary in style and length from region to region. This huge mammal was hunted to extinction in the late 20th and early 21st century. Terra almost paid a very dear price for this. SEE George and Gracie.

Hunter (GSR)–Captain of the entrant ship *Dominion of Proxima.*

Hunters of Stars (IT)–Translated term of Kitka greeting used by Ghyl when she met Uhura.

Hydrohaul (BD)–A long ugly blue grey Federation ship carrying supplies to colonies; capable of transporting nearly anything considered cargo.

Hyper-anchor (ST)–An exceedingly strong tractor beam attached to the fabric of space-time continuum.

Ia'Kriiah (FF)–Series of Klingon campaigns in which Dumeric was awarded two-red metal blades for bravery. SEE Dumeric.

Ice Trap–Novel by L. A. Graf. When the Federation company, Nordstral Pharmaceuticals, reported some of their personnel were missing and other were suffering hallucinations, StarFleet Command sent *Enterprise* to investigate. On a planet nearly 90% covered in ice, Kirk and crew faced unusual circumstances. Uhura and Chekov, ordered to determine what had happened to the missing people, discovered their lives in danger from Alion, self-appointed terrorist leader determined to kill them. They were befriended by a group of Kitha and for a few days shared their "buried" village. Chased across a frozen landscape by Alion who backed them up against the open sea, they saw no way to escape. An old woman of the Kitha village, having gone to the open ocean to give herself to her god, a sea kraken, provided their salvation. The kraken refused to kill them but took her and Alion. At the same time these events were occurring, Kirk and McCoy searched for the cause of the outbreak of mental illness. They joined a harvester group and battled for their lives when a huge kraken attacked the submerged vessel. In the meantime, Spock on board *Enterprise* completed a series of planet scans and concluded from his data that the planet's magnetic poles were shifting. His data led him to the conclusion that the depletion of ocean plankton was the second cause of the poles shift and contributed to the planet's tectonic problems. Once all the evidence came together, Spock told Kirk that to replenish the magnetic biota would require trillions of metric tons of plankton. McCoy suggested *Enterprise's* botany lab clone the plankton and the cargo holds be flooded for breeding space. Spock agreed this would work by employing magnatomic decelerators to provide magnetic energy. When all the data was presented to Nordstral Phamaceuticals, they agreed to work out a plan for harvesting plankton that would not interfere with the planet's natural magnetic fields.

IDIC (SG; FF)–Vulcan concept of infinite diversity in infinite combinations.

idiot savants (P)–People who are far below average in most abilities but have a single ability to instantly learn and reproduce that learning. They have remarkable talents generally in one field. SEE Jandra.

Iglat (FF)–Klingon crew of the *Kadn'ra* and member of the first group sent to search for the Beta Canzandia colony children.

Ike (BD)–SEE Isaac Soulian.

Ilimon (FF)–One of four governing Menikki ministers of Alpha Maluria Six; the two Obirrhat had resigned.

Imea (UC)–Vulcan housekeeper for Valeris' family who lived on Zorakis. SEE Zorakis.

***Im'pac* tree** (FF)–Tree native to Qo'noS, the Klingon home world.

Interim Committee (P)–Governing group between formal elected governments. Romulus had such a group following the Praetor's death.

Interspecies Affairs (FD)–Bureau of the Federation First Contact Bureau. It looks after the affairs relating to sentient beings that compose the Federation. Hightower was its chief commissioner.

Interstellar Maritime Law (BD)–StarFleet academy graduates are required to take a course in these laws, a complicated set of laws established by the Federation to govern space trade and travel.

Interstellar Olympics (GSR)–The concept of Olympics began in Terra's ancient Greek lands. The Second Olympiad, begun in April 1896, Terran reckoning, included many new games. The Olympic games continued even through the Eugenics War and were exported into space. Suggestions from alien cultures led to the organization of the Interstellar Olympics and its inter-galactic committee which selected the games to include, many of them from alien worlds and all highly competitive.

Iola (ST)–A Klingee captain in the Klingee Association who was dressed in a costume of thin pastel green flowing material that laced across one shoulder suspended by a fringe of gemlike teardrops. He phrased his orders with a "thank you." SEE Klingee.

Iola's cabin (ST)–Kirk told Iola about "a soft lumpy thing with a blue circle on its top" that Iola kept in his cabin. Kirk knew this because he had seen it while staring into the Aleph.

Iotian crystals (DC)–One of Sulu's hobbies was carving replicas of famous starships using Iotian crystal.

Iowa (P)–Birthplace of James T. Kirk located in the midwest of the U. S., a Terran nation.

"I'll Take You Home Again, Kathleen" (P)– A Terran love song written in 1875 by Thomas Westendorf for his wife. By the following year it was quite popular. Though not an Irish song, Kevin Riley, who considered himself quite Irish certainly enjoyed singing this song. So much so that he delivered all its verses hundreds of times to "the long-suffering crew" while he was under the influence the virus Psi 200. (*NT; Trimble 216).

Irimlo (GSR)–Entrant in the Great Starship Race captained by Loracon, representing Zeon. This ship and *554-2* had a minor collision near the first race beacon. SEE *554-2*.

Ito (Di)–Stocky, dark-eyed navigator on Commodore Wesley's *Lexington*.

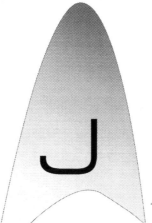

Jacobs (WLW)–This *Enterprise* Security guard who went through the transit-frame with Kirk suffered a broken leg. SEE transit-frame.

jackel-mastiffs (UC)–Huge dog-like creatures used at Rura Penthe to harass the prisoners.

Jaffe (SG)–*Enterprise* ensign from Security along with Corey on a shuttle to rescue the landing party from the Romulan space station. SEE Corey.

Jagr (DC)–Member of Chekov's security contingency on this mission.

Jamaica (BD)–Nickname given to Drake Reed. SEE Trinidad; Drake Reed.

Jancree (S)–A Senite proprietor of a small restaurant on Khyming. He informed Kellen when beginners' philosophy classes were forming. SEE Kellen.

Jandra (P)–This Romulan female had a twin brother Dajan, who was six minutes her junior. As a young child she was drawn to music. With no tutoring, she attempted to play her mother's *tra'am* kept just for show. Once when guests were at the home, she hid behind the drapes and listened to the music, and after all had gone she went to the *tra'am* and played every piece she had heard that evening. Once discovered, she was recognized as a prodigy. Soon tutors, lessons, travel, and concerts occupied her life, and at age eight she gave her first recital. She mastered a number of instruments, becoming proficient in all of them. Nothing mattered except her music which she played for herself though frequently she was required to perform at state functions. When the Romulan Praetor lost his hearing and forbade all keyboard instruments, she turned to strings, mastering most of them. The family suffered disgrace when her brother Keelan, in charge of prisoners, allowed one to escape. This led to the entire family being sent to the Provinces. Later her parents were forced to commit suicide. During her time in the Provinces, she discovered a piano and a musician who introduced her to Bach, Mozart, and Beethoven. While she grew more talented in music, her twin was earning fame as an archeologist. He soon ran afoul of the government position on the Erisian culture and was sent to a correction institute for a time before being declared Orthodox. Jandra married Tiam who became an ambassador, achieving that rank when Jandra was "requested" to play at the Praetor's funeral. When a musical connection was discovered on Termais Four, she, with several other musicians, and her brother, as lead archeologist, were included in the Romulan delegation. On the first night both groups were together, her husband forced her to perform at the evening's festivities. As tensions grew between the two groups, she and her brother, in a bold move, defected to the Federation, and were given asylum. Her study of the Probe's music led her to recognize patterns and from these patterns she created a symphony with Dr. Benar's input based on the "music" of the Erisians. Months later it was performed at the Lincoln Center. SEE Dr. Benar; Dajan; Erisians; Probe, Tiam.

Janus VI (P)–Johnson writing in *Worlds* (110) reports that Janus VI, a class M planet, is sixth of ten planets orbiting a moderate sized star. The initial survey indicated no life forms until the discovery of the Horta. The same survey indicated the world rich in pergium and other heavy elements used by Federation colonies for various purposes. The hostile and uninhabitable surface led to an underground facility that made mining relative easy. After opening a new lower-level cavern in early 2267, miners began dying. *Enterprise's* investigation led to the discovery of the Horta (*DD). SEE Horta.

Japanese banquet (WLW)–Stuck in the body of a Kh!lict, Kirk suffered from hunger. To pass the time he recalled a ten-course banquet he had attended when called to StarFleet Command: clear soup, sashimi, a dozen kinds of sushi, tempura vegetables, chicken teriyaki, steamed rice, sukiyaki with more vegetables than he could recognize, shrimp custard, and lemon-soy tofu salad.

Jarvis, Sharon (Di)–Colony administrator for Beta Xaridian Four. She was a stocky, solidly built, muscular female with short greying hair who enjoyed a cherotta. She refused Kirk's suggestion of evacuation by the *Enterprise*. But when the colony came under attack *Enterprise* saved nearly everyone.

Jasmine, Mina (FD)–A brown-haired, brow-skinned middled aged native of Discord known as a Swimmer. She was a stockholder in the Waverider Ranch run by Aagard dinAthos. SEE Variants.

Jennings (BD)–SEE Dennings.

Jenyu (P)–This former Romulan commander of the *Shulyar* was placed aboard the *Galtizh* as Kital, aide to Ambassador Tiam. His original mission was to derail the peace initiative and ensure the downfall of the Interim Government. Events escalated so quickly that he was forced to take control of the *Galtizh* from Captain Hiran and attempt to destroy the Probe, hoping to discredit the Romulan/Federation mission. His plans failed. SEE Kital; Hiran.

Jefferies (FD)–Engineer Walter Matthew Jefferies of the 20th century designed these accesses into his blueprints for Constitution class ships. Writing about the construction of *Enterprise* 1701, Trimble (173) notes these were "crawlspaces located in various sections of the ship" which gave access to various engineering and communications control circuits. Described as small vertical or horizontal corridors or tunnels they access critical areas of a ship by forming a network allowing travel throughout the ship. Often having access to such a tube has given *Enterprise's* crew an edge when boarded by enemies. In FD, Kirk slide through a Jefferies tube to gain access to the Klingon controlled *Enterprise* bridge.

Jimenez, Emilio (IT)–One of the young men, age 19, who was assigned to Steno's search team. With Uhura's help he monitored communication control and contacted *Enterprise* by sending and receiving reports between Uhura and the ship. Probably the only surviving member of Steno's group. SEE Steno.

Jiminez, Paco (SS)–One of five StarFleet trainee doctors sent to Ssan when the Assassin Wars were in full bloom. SEE five doctors.

Jimmy's group (BD)–Teenagers who followed Jim Kirk: Tom Beauvais; Zack Malkin; Lucy Pogue; Emily; Quentin Monroe.

Joan-Marie's star (FD)–While conducting the first general survey of the area some 300ly from Terra, the USS *Hernan de Soto* while mapping star population discovered a Population One star close to the outer boundaries of Federation space. The survey numbered the star 1123-537 and recorded its name as Joan-Marie after the *de Soto* navigator. The ship's log gave its spectral classification as FO, yellow-white with a diameter 1.72 x 10 ^{6} power, a mass 1.92 Sol, luminosity 9.80 Sol and a surface of 7500C. The report also mentioned an Oort Cloud of comets and seven planets. Two outer planets were identified as gas giants and the other five varied in characteristics. SEE Okeanos; Eris.

Joanna (UC)–Daughter of Leonard and Jocelyn McCoy.

John Lilly (IT)–One of three submarine plankton harvesters employed on Nordstral. Captained by Davis.

Jones (BD)–Science intern who served on April's *Enterprise*. Lorna Simon sent him to get arthritic pills and water for her. SEE Lorna Simon.

Jonesboro (GSR)–Terran city located in the northeastern section of Arkansas and northwest of Memphis, Tennessee. Some of its residents emigrated as colonists to Port Apt near Alpha Centauri.

Jonesy (SS)–*Potemkin* transporter operator who delivered diplomats Clay and Jocelyn Treadway to *Enterprise*.

Jotunheim (FD)–This planet, whose gravity is 10% greater than Terra's, has no atmosphere and no life forms, only large deposits of metal-bearing ores and other materials. Domed habitation centers allow for human settlements. The planet was home to Cornelius Wayne, a member of the Federation Council, and his daughter Moriah Wayne. SEE Cornelius Wayne; Moriah Wayne.

Jovanovich (SS)–StarFleet admiral in charge of the Ssan mission.

Juk (FD)–Young Klingon ensign under Kain's command. He sought permission to commit suicide for his failure to complete a mission. Kain refused permission and assigned him 10 minutes in the *Qighpej* (agonizer booth).

Jutak (P)–This young subcenturion Romulan male was supposed to kill Kirk and Hiran and make it look like Kirk had killed Hiran. Jutak stunned them but was killed by Kital to cover up his part in the action.

Juuxa (S)–The female of the two-person crew who attempted to fly off Sanctuary and died when the ship exploded at 30,000 kilometers.

Jylor (WLW)–*Enterprise* lieutenant in Biology whom Kirk recommended to McCoy as an assistant on the autopsy of the Kh!lict.

K

Kadn'ra (FF)–Klingon ship sent by Dumeric to obtain the G-Seven unit was captained by Vheled until he was killed by Grael. The ship's Second Officer Kruge became captain. SEE G-Seven unit; Dumeric.

Kahless (WLW; FF; FD)– In Kirk's mind he is the Unforgettable, a tyrant who dictated to those he ruled. Other sources identify Kahless as Klingon and is credited with bringing various warring factions together to form the Klingon Empire. Much of his philosophy may be found in the _Ramen'aa_. SEE _Ramen'aa_.

Kain (FD)–This Klingon's father was Krodan, a diplomat. As senior lieutenant on _Fist of Retribution_ sent to Axaner, he hoped that by stealing a valuable holy relic and blaming the StarFleet group, his Empire would gain control of Axaner. Kirk, as a young lieutenant member of the Federation group, learned of the plan and notified the local authorities who caught Kain in the act. To atone for his disgrace at being captured at Endikon, his commander allowed him to put his own eye out with a red-hot dagger. Kain carried the shame of that failure and the pain of the mutilation as well as hatred toward Kirk in particular. Years of dedicated work led to his position as Captain of the First Rank and earned him the position as commander of the _Dagger_. A description entered into _Enterprise's_ records noted a tall Klingon adult, broad in the chest and shoulders and narrow in the hips, wearing a shaven chin and full mustache. A black patch on the right eye was accented by a scar running from the high forehead across the right eye into the cheek. He was given to wearing a Klingon jerkin of silver mesh with a gold sash befitting his rank and concealing a multiple-bladed knife. Resolution of the trouble at Discord revealed he came to Discord to enslave the Susuru and gain access to the planet's resources. Hidden in the deepest part of the ocean, until Kirk called his hand, was an untested prototype ship. Kain killed one of his Bridge officers who had attempted to kill the young ensign Juk, and he manipulated Moriah Wayne into beaming a nuclear device into Harmony's reactor, totally destroying the city. In a battle with the _Enterprise_, Kain lost his left leg just below the knee, but lived long enough to kill Commissioner Wayne and attempt to destroy the _Enterprise_. The destruction of the _Leviathan_ by the _Enterprise_ led to his death. SEE Harmony.

Kalastra (FF)–Klingon father of Kiruc.

Kalgorian combat engine (P)–A type of military weapon; unknown.

Kalin (P)–Romulan governess for Jandra and Dajan.

Kalis Three (P)–Dr. Benar and his archeology team were excavating on this planet when captured by Romulan forces led by Reelan. They were held prisoners and tortured. SEE Reelan; Dr. Benar.

Kamerg (UC)–Middled-aged Klingon Bridadier.

Kamarag (UC)–Klingon ambassador who appealed to Interstellar Law and presented a logical argument for Kirk and McCoy's arrest and trial for the assassination of Counselor Gorkon. He was present at the Khitomer Peace Conference and though he was quite able to argue for peace, Chancellor Azetbur considered him merely an actor with no opinions.

Kamorh'dag (FF)–National group of Klingons who had ruled for ten generations until opposed by the Gevish'rae.

Kane, Maxine (IT)–*Curie* station physician for Nordstral Pharmaceuticals. A short, dark-haired woman with green eyes who called for StarFleet assistance when too many personnel began exhibiting insanity.

Kanin, Pov (DC)–Tall, bony-faced Andorian captain of the *Shras*.

Kapronek (FF)–Klingon emperor with pale green eyes and a large imposing figure. His grandson Kenrod had been First Officer on the *Fragh'ka* until he was assassinated.

Karradh (FF)–Klingon and owner of a typical Kamorh'dag residence in the foothills outside the imperial city. Part of the estate was considered a traditional house with wooden walls draped with weapons and free-form metal sculptures filling every corner of the main room. The estate had a water garden laid out in the classical Klingon style with varying levels and appropriate shrubbery. Karradh, a large man with graying whiskers and a booming voice, and a friend of the Kiruc family, had once been Master of the Second Fleet. He suggested to Kiruc, captain of *Fragh'ka*, that Kenrod meet with an "accident" so that Kell, Karradh's son, could move into the First Officer position.

Kashi (SG)–Young Romulan commander of the Romulan space station *Reltak*. He and Dr. Rinagh, the station's doctor, were friends. Everyone, including Kashi, was killed by the creature. SEE *Reltah* creature.

Kasserites (SS)–Aliens who have black skin, sliver eyes, and long necks. Dr Vincent Bando, as a trainee doctor, administered to several of these people.

Katris (UC)–Klingon guard at Azetbur's quarters.

Kaul, Dr. Abdul Ramesh (WLW)–He was described as short and wiry with teak-colored complexion darkened by weeks of fieldwork and balding except for a fringe of silver-grey hair. His eyes carried an impish twinkle. On leave from the University of Nexqualy, he was included in the mission to Careta IV as the foremost authority on Meztorien culture, having spent more than fifty years studying it. After studying planet scans, he selected Site J3 as the first location to begin the team's on-site study of the ruins. Exposure to suldanic gas left him somewhat weak. He objected to Kirk's proposal of recommendation that Careta IV be quarantined, for he believed it should be thoroughly studied.

Kebo (ST)–A beverage with active ingredients; similar somewhat to alcohol.

Keeler, Edith (SS)–Dr. McCoy, feeling sorry himself, bemoaned the failures he perceived his life to have been. When feeling depressed, one failure he often regretted was the death of Edith Keeler. Trimble (176) identified her as a social worker of the 1930s whom Captain Kirk had met and loved, but allowed to die to reinstate the timeline changed by McCoy (*CEF).

Kell (FF)–Klingon son of Karradh and second officer on the battle cruiser *Fragh'ka* became First Officer after Kenrod was killed.

Kellen (S)–Fair-haired human female who came as a child with her parents to Sanctuary. She informed Zicree of the actions of Kirk in their attempt to learn about the Senite machinery. SEE Zicree; Sanctuary.

Kelly, Aaron (DC)–This trim, black-complexioned man was one of four Federation auditors assigned to the *Enterprise* to conduct efficiency tests on equipment and crew. He researched Chekov's shift duty roster. Wanting to see how quickly Security would respond, he initiated an unauthorized intruder alert. Chekov placed him in the Brig because setting off a security alert without cause is a criminal offense. Impressed with Chekov's actions, he wrote a favorable report when the incident was over.

Kelvas (WLW)–A people whose rigid stylized abstract art, according to historian V. E. Mitchell, "required detailed knowledge of Denaya 4's culture and history in order to interpret the multiple layers of symbols incorporated in each design" and if that "wasn't enough, different combinations of symbols or different colors used together changed the meaning of the basic pattern." Kirk recalled a visit to Denaya 4 and his attempt to learn just enough about their art not to embarrass himself.

Kennedy Drive (P)–This street located in San Francisco runs through Golden Gate Park and houses the Conservatory of Flowers and the DeYoung museum. Whenever time allowed, Kirk enjoyed walking the street.

Kent, Conrad Franklin (ST)–This large human was an ambitious senior member of the Federation Council who wanted to be the Federation President though he believed and preached that StarFleet was "an outmoded, war-mongering, self-serving institution full of half-bright egomaniacs." Hazel Payton served for a time as his assistant. Following the incident with Dr. Omen, he changed his mind regarding StarFleet and its usefulness, especially after reading Payton's complete report.

Ker Dajan (P)–SEE Dajan.

Kerla (UC)–Tall with dark hair and broad powerful shoulders, he had a youthful appearance for his rank of Klingon Brigadier. He loved Atzebur and swore to protect her, but he was given more to passion than reason.

Kernod (FF)–Grandson of Emperor Kapronek and Klingon First Officer on *Fragh'ka* until he was assassinated so that Kell could have his position.

Kesla (UC)–Former Klingon gunner now posted to Mortagh Outpost Three. He had been in one battle, aboard the *Beria*, against Romulans and escaped with slight injuries and a determination to live. He took the Outpost Three position as one requiring the least amount of exposure to action and unknowingly allowed the *Enterprise* to slip past because he believed it was a smuggler.

Khachaturian, Aram (P)–A Terran Russian-Armenian composer (1903-1978) influenced by both Armenian music and American folk music. His "Piano Concerto" (1936) and his ballet "Gayane" (1942) are considered his best. In 1959 he was awarded the Lenin Prize. In P, Dr. McCoy, at Chekov's suggestion, considered Khachaturian as one of several composers whose music might be included in the ship's musical library.

Khan (ST; UC)–SEE Khan Noonian-Singh.

Khan's Stepchildren Resolution (FD)–UN Resolution 51 passed in 2038 came to be known by this title. The Resolution determined "that no Terran citizen could be held liable for the acts of their ancestors" and it also "confirmed the human status of certain human-variant strains" created in genetic laboratories controlled by Khan and others.

Kh!lict (WLW)–This extinct race, gone more than 500,000 years, were briefly resurrected on Careta IV when Kirk, six Security guards, Ensign Chekov and Dr. Talika Nyar were transformed into Kh!lict. The following is a composite of information taken directly from the reports of those who were on Careta IV. The Kh!lict were eight-legged crablike sentient beings with each appendage ending in pincers and retractable claws. When walking, the pincers were closed tightly into a fist. Open, they could manipulate tools or engage in fighting. Binocular eyes appeared on extendable stalks that swivelled independently. Skeletal bracing and tendon linkages enabled the Kh!lict considerable striking power as well as endurance when walking. External ornamentation was used in communication. In places on the carapace, the exoskeleton was quite heavy and thick with triangular spikes. A retractable proboscis identified the specie as requiring liquid nourishment. Three hollow serrated teeth were employed for piercing the flesh and secreting, from ducts in the teeth, fast acting neurotoxins and digestive enzymes. As the flesh dissolved, it was sucked up through the proboscis. Sediment filters were used when drinking liquids such as water. Captain Kirk verified Dr. McCoy's autopsy findings that the Kh!lict were not vegetarians nor omnivores but carnivores, for while he occupied a Kh!lict body, he shared a memory of eating a *nanthken*, a rabbit-like creature bred for its delectable flesh and docile nature. Part of that experience included the image of a hungry Kh!lict visiting a *nanthken* pen, selecting a juicy plump live meal, impaling it on a pincer, snapping its spinal column, and then injecting digestive enzymes before sucking up the liquid flesh. Kirk was also able to tell Dr. McCoy that the Kh!lict identified inferior species by the fact they ate plant material. Further revelations supported the conclusion that this creature continually molted, shedding its outer skeleton several times until maturity. Two autopsies, the only ones conducted, revealed the Kh!lict had two brains. One was the ancient animal brain evolved from primitive creatures. Here was stored the involuntary actions and information needed for everyday maintenance as a distasteful primal memory in the lower brain and seldom directly accessed. The higher brain portion handled information such as caste rules, language, and specialized motor skills, personality, talents, and abilities as determined by the ruling Elders. The Kh!lict persona appeared to be a house-keeping program while some rudimentary elements resided in the higher brain. Thus the Kh!lict separated instinct and intelligence. Captain Kirk's report also included the notation that the Kh!lict bicameral brains did not contain the idea of survival at any cost. However, *Enterprise* sensor logs captured two Kh!lict in a fight. The victor displayed a ritualistic action ending in cannibalism and disfiguration of the defeated one. Additional information came from the two autopsies and Kirk's full report carried the conclusion that this ancient race evolved in warm seas and had retained their need for warmth indicated by full day activity but lessened night activity. They slept only when their back and appendages were protected. Dr. McCoy concluded from his autopsies that the bio-parameters of the Kh!lict were similar to dominate forms in the Selevaii system, offering speculation that the Kh!lict diverged millions of years ago from this group. A genetic relationship or kinship may no longer exist. Evidence also revealed the Kh!lict developed in total isolation from other sentient races, leaving them fiercely xenophobic and fanatically closed-minded, believing they were the <u>only</u> intelligent race in the universe! The species had two sexes with females being dominant and larger than males which were considered juveniles. Kh!lict society was a matriarchal order governed by the oldest and most knowledgeable females called Elders. Most females ignored males unless the need to procreate was activated according to society's needs. In this highly complex and stratified society, males were considered inferior and were employed for most menial tasks and for fertilizing females. It was deduced that the mating drive overcame all other needs and desires, especially in the male. After fertilization a pre-determined quota of females whose clutches had proved fertile were allowed to mature and hatch. When the need arose, some males could become females and rise to dominance. Since the culture did not contain a template for a dominate male, some males were selected as convicted felons with justice meted out by males called Enforcers who determined terms of punishment and ensured the criminal knew his crime, its punishment, and the rules governing the punishment. The Enforcers also executed the punishment. For a serious offense the offender was transported to a deserted location and hunted to death by Enforcers specifically trained for the task. Education consisted of passing information from generation to generation through a complex coming-of-age rite that imprinted crucial knowledge on the lower brain of the adolescent. In time the ritual became so elaborate that most of the knowledge required was directly programmed into the young when they were admitted into the adult world. Machines transcribed the young into faithfull copies of anything the rulers wanted. It also allowed the rulers to entrench themselves through their control of what they taught the young. Communications between Kh!lict, who had no vocal apparatus though it did have external tympanic membranes capable of detecting sounds, depended on flashing colors and patterns across its translucent carapace. For example, a study revealed that carapace zigzags of black and red were symbols of rejection and denial. Each Kh!lict from birth was capable of effecting coloration change and camouflage, sometimes effecting the colors of its immediate environment. Kirk learned he could create words on the carapace in patterns of interwoven blues and greens. The ruins on Careta IV suggested the Kh!lict may have lived on or controlled, at one time, as many as 100 worlds, some similar to their homeworld which may or may not have been Careta IV. Worlds too different from their own were changed to fit the requirement of the Kh!lict which included terraforming the land and extinguishing the native life. Considering themselves to be the pinnacle of life, they could not accept that anyone else might also be sentient. By refusing this concept they exterminated all life forms they came into contact with. This belief emerged early in their spaceflight days for they did not encounter other sentient life when the discovery might have changed the Kh!lict development. Evolution in such isolation led to their complete xenophobic attitude and to the ruthless savagery unequaled by any other culture discovered. Speculation by the archeology group suggested the Kh!lict began dying even before their planet's geothermal resources were depleted. As the sun in their home system began cooling, climate changes, disruption of food supply, infertile hatches, and the heavy suppression of the individual led to the downward spiral into extinction. Many of the cities, more than 30 sites were identified by *Enterprise* on Careta IV, were discovered. All lay in ruins, destroyed by natural means or by other races who deemed the Kh!lict technology too dangerous for anyone. Spock's report offered an understanding of why someone would attempt to erase all signs that the Kh!lict ever existed. He concluded from the beginnings of their space travel they had exterminated every alien race encountered. How fitting that they too were extinguished. Much of what became known about other sentient races in the Dulciphar star cluster was gleaned from the pictorial murals Spock and his team discovered in the Central Control Chamber. Pyar-runes presented a graphic image of just how brutal the Kh!lict were to themselves and to others. One section of Spock's report about the Control Chamber stated he saw carved panels of violent and brutal scenes that "depicted mass sacrifices" of several "races recognized only from a few isolated artifacts." Even interior walls were decorated with scenes of ritual torture and sacrifice. Much of what Spock's team found was recorded for later study. In their investigation of the complex, they discovered an arena believed to be the location where each Kh!lict was programmed, made possible by the bicameral brain. Furthermore, information indicated this place was frequented only by powerful female Elders. For males to be here was a capital offense. The only time a male was allowed into the arena was when he was being programmed or was to be changed into a female. Following the recovery of all personnel from Careta IV and after collecting and sealing all personnel briefings and reports, Captain Kirk, in a meeting with department heads and the archeologists, declared his intention of recommending Careta IV be quarantined by StarFleet indefinitely and all records suppressed from study by anyone. According to him, the brutality of the Kh!lict coupled with their indestructible and irresponsible self-centered technology made the knowledge of their existence a threat to the galaxy. All but one of those present accepted his decision. SEE Kaul.

Kh!lict changlings (WLW)—Seven people (Kirk, Timmons, Bovray, Jacobs, Chekov, Nyar, and Nairobi) were transformed into Kh!lict when they went through transit-frames. Kirk and Security guards, Timmons, Bovray and Jacobs, were changed when under Kirk's orders the three went through to search for Chekov and Talika Nyar who had stumbled through a transit-frame. Bradford Nairobi was accidently pushed into a transit frame and died in a battle with another Kh!lict. Bovray, while in a Kh!lict body died when the Kh!lict died of fright after being transported to the *Enterprise*. Autopsies of the Kh!lict bodies determined which *Enterprise* crewman inhabited which body.

Khitomer (UC)–Sparsely populated agricultural Klingon planet near the Romulan border served as the setting for the peace conference led by Atzetbur.

Khitomer Accord (UC)–Historic peace treaty bringing peace between the Klingon Empire and UFP was framed at Camp Khitomer in 2293. This was the first step to peace and understanding between the two entities.

Khyming (S)–SEE Sanctuary.

Kinshaian (SS)–A Ssan master governor killed by assassins led by Andrachis.

Kirk, James T.–StarFleet serial number SC 937-0176 CEC. Kirk, the second son of George and Winona and brother to Samuel, was born in Riverside, Iowa, a farming region in the old United States, Terra. His birthday is disputed. Mandel (*Manual* 17) records it as sd1277.1 or 26 March 2229 while Okuda and Okuda (*Chronology* 29) record it as 22 March 2232. As a child Kirk believed his middle initial "T" stood for "Tank" which he reinforced by telling all his classmates. When older he inquired from his parents what it stood for. His father promised to tell him the significance of the "T" on his tenth birthday. George Kirk never got around to doing this. Kirk's strong personality and dogged determination revealed itself quiet early. Historian Mitchell had a glimpse of Kirk's childhood from a story Kirk told of vacationing with his brother Sam at their grandparents' home in Vermont. Kirk, Sam, and three McLaughlin boys of the area spent the month building talking drums and playing settlers and Indians (*Windows*). His mother seemed to believe the lack of a father figure at an impressive age created the rebellion that surfaced (Carey *Best*). By his early teen years, Kirk was on the path to delinquency. Winona Kirk, hoping a few days with her husband would help, took fourteen-year-old Jim and his brother Sam and journeyed to Tarsus IV where they were caught up in the turmoil of a strict quarantine against incoming or outgoing ships until relief came from StarFleet. The planet's agencies were overwhelmed with demands for supplies. Food and medicine ran out. Determined to save some of the population, the governor, at the expense of others, began killing selected people. Kirk, being a curious teenager, followed a group of civilians escorted by military personnel. When chased, Kirk, along with a woman and her four-year-old son, hid in an alley. Confronted by authorities and fearing for herself and her child, she forced the child into Kirk's hands and ran off, pursued by armed militia. Kirk and the child eluded pursuit. From his hiding place he witnessed the execution of the group including the child's mother. The child, age four, was Kevin Riley (Ferguson *Flag*). With help from Kirk's mother, the child was spared. Many years later Kirk relieved those memories when he met actor Anton Karidian, whom he believed to be Governor Kodos, infamously known as the Executioner (*CK). The incident on Tarsus IV and Kirk's perception that his father had no time for him led him to embrace a gang of like members. In one incident, Kirk, age sixteen, and five others obtained fake identifies and gained employment on an ocean-going dynacarrrier that ran a Pacific route. Concerned that his son was facing a criminal career, George Kirk had his son's juvenile record sealed and then took him to space, hoping to correct his bad habits and change his attitude. That journey forever changed Kirk's life, though the trip didn't begin well. Kirk didn't want to go and shortly after embarking on a utility stratotractor taking them to spacedock, he stole a work bee, planning to return to Terra. His father foiled the attempt. Together they boarded *Enterprise* under Captain April's command. During the trip April, George, and Kirk, along with several others, hoping to observe space phenomenon, transferred from *Enterprise* to a LC4 cargo craft taking supplies to an outpost with stops for a few scientific observations along the way. Attacked by the pirate ship *Shark*, George put his son in a life pod and cast it off, hoping the momentum would carry the pod beyond *Shark's* attention. Kirk decided to help and crashed the pod into the *Shark*. His attacks of sabotage to the *Shark* bought time for his father and Captain April to resolve the situation. Though he hated to admit it, Kirk learned a lesson and was better able to understand why his father kept returning to space. Kirk returned to Terra with a new resolution. His father who continued to serve on other missions never returned to see the change in his son. He died while on a space mission. After learning of his father's death, Kirk sought out the history of his middle name and came to appreciate his father's choice of Tiberius. CONSULT *Best Destiny*. Aside from his father whom he came to greatly admire, he discovered two other men. Captain Garth of Izar's logs, which Kirk had a complete set, became daily reading (*WGD), and he studied the time period and writings of President Abraham Lincoln who became a personal hero (*SC). His extensive list of readings also included the Battles of Igga (Ecklar *Maru*). The incident on the *Shark* helped Kirk find focus for his life. He put himself to earning good grades which by age seventeen helped him pass the entrance exams for StarFleet Academy. R. Mallory, father of a future *Enterprise* crewmember (Okuda and Okuda *Chronology* 32) and Admiral LaFarge (Gerrold *Whirlpool*) sponsored his entrance. Kirk majored in Interplanetary Relations under the tutelage of John Gill but soon switched to the Starship Training Program finishing in the top 5% of his graduating class with a steady 3.8 grade average (Rostler 28). His years at the Academy were dedicated to education and physical training. Success in various training exercises led to the discovery that he had a natural ability to perceive and understand the problems and views of aliens, and "he gained a respect for the myriad duties of a starship captain" (Thompson "Kirk" 128). He faced his duties with enthusiasm and gained experience and endured daily "torturing" from his first day at the Academy until a bully upperclassman graduated. Finnegan, known for practical jokes, constantly harassed Kirk (Okuda and Okuda *Encyclopedia* 241). After Finnegan graduated, Kirk, who had been a consistent runner-up in the Academy's middle-weight boxing division, took the championship in his senior year (Milan *Depths*). Kirk's legendary reputation for refusing to accept defeat began with his "winning" the *Kobayashi Maru* in his final year at the Academy. He took the *Maru* scenario and failed it twice, and with permission attempted a third time. A chance remark made by Lt. Cmdr. Constrew, an Academy instructor, led to Kirk's reprogramming the test computer and his passing the test (Ecklar *Maru*). Though Kirk was given a commendation for original thinking, cadets, cautioned every year not to attempt anything like it, continue to retell the tale. To date only one other cadet has shown a similar initiative (Carey *Dreadnought; Battlestations*).

For a few months Kirk taught Academy classes. During this time he met Gary Mitchell destined to become a close friend. Mitchell set Kirk up for a date with a lab technician whom Kirk came close to marrying. Later, when they served together on a cadet mission, Mitchell took a poisonous dart on Dimorus meant for Kirk (Okuda and Okuda *Encyclopedia* 305). Following graduation, Kirk began rising through the ranks, showing courage, quick wit, intelligence, a degree of stubborness, and a large amount of intuition and bluff. Ensign Kirk was assigned to the training vessel USS *Republic* along with his friend Ben Finney whose daughter was named after Kirk and whom Kirk later adopted. Kirk prevented a near-fatal explosion aboard ship caused by a mistake Finney made. For many years Finney blamed Kirk for his failure to advance in StarFleet (*CM; Morwood *Rules*). Finney's smoldering resentment erupted when he faked his death and caused Kirk to be court martialed. Finney left the service but returned to serve under Captain Carmondy who breached the Prime Directive. Kirk faced Finney again (DeWeese *Renegade*). While on the *Republic*, Kirk visited the planet Axanar on a peace mission. The operation led by Captain Garth succeeded when Kirk foiled an attempt by the Klingons to steal a holy relic. Kirk took the relic and alerted the authorities, leaving the Klingons led by Kain to be humiliated. Axanar's government wanted to reward Kirk, so on the captain's recommendation StarFleet allowed him to accept the Palm Leaf of Axanar. Others on the mission also received awards. For a short while Kirk was Second Officer on *Aeolus*, but on a suggestion from its captain, who learned of Kirk's involvement with Cecilia Simons, Kirk requested a transfer (Mitchell *Enemy*). Kirk was promoted to lieutenant and assigned to the USS *Farragut* under the captaincy of Garrovick who understood Kirk's deep longing to be in space. He took him "under his wing, becoming a second father..." (Thompson "Kirk" 128). Kirk participated in the initial planetary survey of Neural and a survey mission to Tyree's planet in 2254. He returned to Tyree's planet as captain of the *Enterprise* (*PLW). Shortly after coming to the *Farragut*, one of the older hands on the crew cautioned Kirk not to mix Argelian ale with <u>anything</u> else. He failed to heed the warning (Mitchell *Windows*). Kirk frequently recalled an incident on the *Farragut* when the ship's refrigeration units malfunctioned and the captain traded stores with an Orion freighter carrying *demma*, a food substance considered by Orions as a potent aphrodisiac (Carter *Dreams*). During the mission to Tyco IV, half of the crew and the captain were killed by a vampire cloud creature (*Ob). Kirk, being the most senior officer, took command of the ship. For years Kirk blamed himself because of his inexperience and his fear that kept him from firing on the creature. He learned the truth during a second encounter with the creature and proved to himself that even had he fired, his phaser would not have destroyed it (*Ob). For a brief time Kirk served on the *Excalibur* along with his friend Mike Walsh who later became captain of the *Constellation* (Duane *My Enemy*). According to a novelization of one of Kirk's missions, the historian writes that Kirk served under Captain Schang on the *Thresher* (Eklund *Devil*). At age 27, writes one historian, Kirk was on the *Alexander*, a destroyer-class starship, as a lieutenant and was assigned as its Executive Officer (Mandel *Manual* 17). In a battle with Klingons, the captain was killed, forcing Kirk to take command.

For his bravery and leadership, he was awarded the Medal of Honor and promoted to captain and given the command of the *Lydia Sutherland* (McIntyre *First*). He chose Gary Mitchell as his first officer. During the battle at Ghioghe, led by Commander Sieren of the Federation, Kirk and Mitchell were severely injured. Sieren and many others died and the ship was left to drift in space. Kirk, wounded and nearly incoherent, rescued the remaining crew and himself by dragging them into an escape pod and ejecting from the ship. Most of what Kirk recalled about this incident was his futile attempt to stop Mitchell from bleeding to death. He, Mitchell, and the crew spent months in rehab where Kirk and Mitchell received the attention of Dr. Leonard McCoy. Kirk and McCoy had met previously when Kirk was recovering from wounds received battling pirates under Captain Garrovick's command (McIntyre *First*). Kirk was barely thirty years old when Captain Pike announced his retirement. StarFleet Command considered several men for the captaincy but always returned to reconsider Kirk. Commodore Robert Wesley, one of several on the review board, was the only one to consistently veto Kirk. He considered him too young and wrote in his dissent that "despite all the education StarFleet can provide, the greatest single teacher that our officers can learn from is experience. And in that respect...Kirk is sorely deficient." Yet when the decision was made, Wesley requested the task of informing Kirk of his promotion. His words to Kirk were always remembered: "We are a fraternity. A brotherhood. Brothers can disagree with each other, but the bottom line is that we have to trust each other..." (David *Disinherited*). In 2264, Command delivered the news of his selection to take effect when *Enterprise* completed her refit (Okuda and Okuda *Chronology* 38). Two years later, *Enterprise* 1701 welcomed the youngest captain in the Fleet. Kirk requested Spock of Vulcan to be First Officer and gave the position of Second Officer to Gary Mitchell. Spock, who had always felt Pike took first place with him, soon learned that Kirk was just as dedicated, honest, reliable, and steady. The two men formed a bond that went deeper than the mere mind touch they shared: they built an unbreakable mutual trust. The third man Kirk recruited became *Enterprise's* Chief Surgeon. Dr. Leonard McCoy and Kirk became close friends and dependable colleagues (Ferguson *Centaurus*). For other positions, Kirk relied on these men and his superiors to make good recommendations. Fully crewed and provisioned, the ship, under his command embarked on the first of many missions under his guiding hand. Within a few years, many of the ship's logs were opened to historians who chose to offer the public, via novels and videos some of the adventures of the ship, its captain, and its valiant crew. Kirk's official position was Starship Commander, which, on occasion, he used. As a starship captain he had broad powers over the lives and welfare of his crew, even over people and activities he encountered during his missions. At times he was required to function as Terra's and the Federation's ambassador to known and unknown aliens. Because the captaincy of a starship demanded total commitment, Kirk never married. From the moment he knew a starship command was within his grasp, he ruled out marriage. His first love, Carol Marcus, who bore him his only son, was put aside for the captain's chair. Besides Carol, three other women touched his heart. With Ruth, Kirk found intense satisfaction but a space mission thwarted the romance (*SL). A relationship with Lt. Areel Shaw broke apart over differing life philosophies (*Cml). With the third love, Dr. Janet Wallace, Kirk discussed marriage, but neither could give up a promising career (*TI). An incident involving Dr. McCoy led to Kirk's meeting with the one woman who took all of his heart. Kirk told McCoy and Spock that he met his one great love through the portals of the Guardian of Forever. To save the integrity of the timeline, Kirk let her die (*CEF). For a brief time he was married to Vice-Admiral Ciani who was killed in a transporter malfunction (Roddenberry *Picture*). During the many episodes of the initial five-year mission, Kirk met many women to whom he felt attracted. For those brief days or months he loved deeply. But during those moments he never forgot the love he always returned to – *Enterprise*. His enthusiasm for *Enterprise* expressed itself to McCoy at the beginning of the Great StarShip Race when with pride he exclaimed: "Look at her, Bones. Only twelve of these in the fleet, only twelve people in the galaxy who get to drive them... and this time I get a chance to show her off" (Carey *Great*). He was so attached to the ship that he found no place satisfying, not even his mountain retreat on Centaurus. The land was purchased in haste and enjoyed in leisure. Over the years he enlarged his holdings, upgraded his cabin facilities, and dreamed of retiring there (Ferguson *Crisis*). As the sensitive idealist Kirk was, he exhibited a complex personality. He always understood himself and his responsibility to the ship and the crew, working himself beyond fatigue but always ready to ask more of himself than he asked of others. Kirk understood the power that lay in his hands, yet he solicited information and advice, sometimes on order, but all the while knowing the final decision was his to make. Seeking always to be ready, to live up to his own standards, he often found himself alone. Two men, Spock and McCoy, knew him well, suffered with him, and attempted to protect him while giving guidance and consolation when they thought he required it. During the mission that led to the discovery of the drifting Romulan space station, Kirk exhibited his concern for his crew, especially those on the boarding party. To offer as much protection as possible he ordered Sulu to tractor the station and monitor its every minute. As he gave the order, his words uttered during one of Scotty's ghost tales in the Rec Room came back to him. Kirk had casually declared, referring to those who explored space, that "whatever their goal, they evidently thought it's worth the risk...it's the same risk you make in taking an active part in life...or becoming a StarFleet officer." He understood the risk each crewmember made when signing on board and what they faced when so ordered by him (Crandall *Shell*). Following the completion of the initial five-year missions, *Enterprise* 1701 was drydocked for a complete refit. In 2265 Captain Kirk was promoted three grades to Admiral on the insistence of Heihachiro Nogura, Supreme Commanding Admiral. Nogura assigned Kirk to StarFleet Headquarters, Terra, as Chief of Operations, "a desk command," according to Kirk. During his months on Nogura's staff, Kirk continued his interest in Jamie Finney and helped his mother in raising Peter, the son of Sam and Aurelan who were killed in a planetary disaster (*OA). As a relief from constant "paper pushing," Kirk infrequently conducted training missions beginning on sd7412.3 (Mandel *Manual* 17). It was, however, the encounter with Vejur that showed StarFleet how desperate Kirk was to return to starship command (Roddenberry *Picture*). He and *Enterprise* were on a training mission when ordered to Regulus I Laboratory Space Station. With a ship of cadets in training and Spock, McCoy, Sulu, and Uhura, he bested Khan a second time (McIntyre *Khan*). His record packet mentions his having contracted vegan choriomeningitis as a youth and carrying the microorganism until his death (*MG). He suffered from Dramian plague (sd5257) and Rigellian fever (sd5843) among other illnesses Dr. McCoy cured. His regular medical reports verify his good health, though they indicate he was a bit overweight. After assuming the rank of admiral, a routine medical exam revealed he was suffering a particular eye problem that could not be treated with surgery. When allergies to the prescribed medicine proved to be a continuing problem, he began using reading glasses (McIntyre *Khan*). The packet also reports his Authority Quotient as +97. The final entry declares that "his chief psychological problem is expressing normal human emotions, which he found almost "impossible due to the barriers he...constructed between himself and his crew" (Mandel *Manual*18). James T. Kirk distinguished himself in action in space and on strange worlds. His commendations include these: Palm Leaf of Axanar; Grankite Order of Tactic, Class of Excellence; and Prentaries Ribbon of Commendations, Classes First and Second. Awards of Valor include: Medal of Honor, Silver Palm with Cluster; StarFleet Citation for Gallantry; and Karagite Order of Heroism for winning a battle against two Klingon ships by some fancy maneuvering that led them to destroy each other (Mandel *Manual* 18; Thompson "Kirk" 130). His initial biographers have chosen not to record all his awards (Roddenberry *Making* 214-218; Trimble 177-178). However, biographer William Rostler lists nine Commendations, eight Awards of Valor, and nine Academy demerits (29). If asked about missions that directly effected him, he might have identified the following: allowing Sargon the use of his body while Sargon attempted to create an android body (*RT); being surprised by Janet Lester who switched *katras*, placing hers in his body and his in her body; and finding his *katra* wandering in *Enterprise's* computer before effecting means of putting body and *katra* back together (*TI). Historian V. E. Mitchell would choose the mission to Careta IV where Kirk and six others became Kh!lict (*Windows*). The one mission that Kirk seldom discussed involved traveling back in time via the Guardian of Forever (*CEF). In two separate interviews Kirk waxed philosophicall about his choice of career. Historian Mitchell asked Kirk how he felt about setting foot on the planet Careta IV. Kirk's reply could be addressed to any first planet landings. He stated the feelings that ran through him for the first few seconds were not easy to describe but may have been caused by knowing there was hidden potential on the planet. The feelings didn't come because he "was the first human on a particular world, " he said, because he had experienced the same feeling even on long established human colony worlds he visited. Maybe, he added, it was the "brief charged excitement just after" he materialized "because it was the first time that...James T. Kirk... had stepped onto the world" (*Windows*). Helen Gordon, a member of one of his missions, recorded a conversation with him in which he admitted in a quiet moment that he went to space for its freedom, though, as he said, "It isn't freedom, really. If it was freedom, I think I'd have become one of the free-traders, the planet-hoppers...And I don't think it's power, exactly. I have absolute power over [some] 420 people, but when you think about it, that's not very much...Just to go to those places, to see them...to be where no one has ever heard of... (Hambly *Ghostwalker*). Most of the captains of StarFleet ships have just as much difficulty explaining why they too worked so hard to win a starship captaincy. In a moment of contemplation, Kirk confessed to Dr. McCoy that he could not foresee the day when he would no longer command. Kirk's many adventures are part of StarFleet Command files. Many have been made public, which accounts for the many novels now on the market. All who served with him for any length of time spoke of his unshakeable belief in StarFleet standards. Dr. McCoy, in particular, mentioned his uncanny knack of intuition that made him the "lucky" man he was. By the end of his life, Kirk remained surprised that he was a legend within StarFleet and with the general public. He remained well known and respected on Vulcan, in the Romulan Empire as well as among Klingon spaceship commanders, and many aliens he encountered.

Kirk/Kh!lict (WLW)–Determined to find the two missing people, Captain Kirk took three security guards, and together they stepped into a transit frame, emerging as Kh!lict trapped inside the bodies with no way to communicate to anyone from the *Enterprise*. With some effort, Kirk gained a measure of control over the actions and minds of his host to effect limited communications with Spock. Together they reversed the transformation and restored all but two people who went through the transit frame. SEE Kh!lict changelings.

Kirk, George (BD; GSR)–Married to Winona and father of Sam and James. He served in StarFleet Security several years with April. Discovered in George Kirk's personal records by the novelist for *Best Destiny* are his impressions of the *Enterprise*: " She is the future. She seems to know it too. Her diagnostics and subsystems monitors twittered and chirped and pulsed in beautiful but seemingly senseless patterns, like jungle birds singing. Little squares of red and blue, white and yellow lights and colored bands of black backgrounds patched the circle of black computer control boards all the way around the middle of the bridge in a big headband, flashing in happy nonsynchrony. Each pattern is reporting some remote part of the ship, blinking diligently and waiting to be needed. Above them, mounted on the blue matte walls under soft ceiling lights, are displayed sectors of the known galaxy, known star systems, and nebulae, anomalies and gas giants, maps and charts, prettier than any art. There are shadows too...there will be a lot of thought going on here over the next few decades...it is a fitting place where these decision happen...." George often told his sons stories about the ancient ship *Alexandria*. On demand he often related the story that during his teen-age years he served as a deck hand on the ship included in the Great Starship Race. The family believed George died on a secret mission.

Kirk, Winona (BD)–Wife of George Kirk; mother of Sam and James.

Kirk, Samuel (BD)–George Samuel Kirk son of George and Winona Kirk and older brother to James T. Kirk. Sam attended the Science Academy, majoring in biosciences. As kids Sam and Kirk dug a pond behind the barn for a swimming pool. One time Sam and Kirk spent a vacation in Vermont with their grandparents. They and the three McLaughlin boys from the next farm spent an entire month pretending they were Indians invading white settlements. They built a set of talking drums from a blueprint obtained from the computer network and learned to send messages which they didn't know their parents could decipher (WLW).

Kirk's gang (BD)–By age sixteen Jim Kirk was on the road to becoming a juvenile delinquent. He led a group composed of Zack Malkin, Lucy Pogue, Tom Beauvais, Quentin Monroe, and Emily.

Kirk's mission (UC)–When Chancellor Gorkon requested Kirk escort him and his ship to a peace conference, Admiral Smillie ordered Kirk to afford the Chancellor full diplomatic courtesy.

Kirk and McCoy's sentence (UC)–Following the Klingon trial, they were declared guilty of having assassinated Chancellor Gorkon. Their sentence read in part: "...without possibility of reprieve or parole...to be taken...to the dilithium mines on... Rura Penthe, there to spend the rest of [their] natural lives."

Kiruc (FF)–Son of Kaalastra and Klingon captain of the battle cruiser *Fragh'ka* . His family was close friends to Karradh, a retired Security Master of the Second Fleet who told Kiruc that Grael might carry out an assassination. The Emperor called for Kiruc's death because he had participated in the death of Kenrod, grandson of the Emperor and member of the Faz'rahn clan.

Kisal (Di)–Aunt to Jerome Baila. When his parents refused to acknowledge him after he ran away from home, she took him in and raised him. SEE Jerome Baila.

Kital (P)–Former Romulan captain of the ship *Shulyar* was sent as aide to Ambassador Tiam. Described as old and skeletally thin, he was given the name of Jenyu and the task of ensuring the peace between the Romulan and Federation teams failed. Hating the current government as much as he hated the Federation and wishing to see both fail, he planned to have Kirk kill Hiran so that the talks would fail. To carry out his plan, he had Jutak hide a phaser rifle in the ruins and set up Kirk. Though Jutak did as ordered, Kital had to kill him to cover up his own involvement making a pretense of saving them from Jutak. When the assassinations failed, he informed Ambassador Tiam of who he was and what his purpose had been. Then he took control of the imprisoned Hiran and Tiam, and attempted to destroy the Probe. SEE Jenyu.

Kitka (IT)–Native sentient life on Nordstral consists of clans living along the equatorial belt and in the arctic regions who are short, square, and squat with heavy bones and yellow complexions. Their high flattened cheek bones rest beneath "eyes that sparkle like fish scales," are blue or green though as they age turn white, according to Clare Mandeville, captain of the *Soroya*. The Kitka are nomadic people who follow schools of fish and create safe shelters by burrowing beneath the ice. A "village" may consist of mounded hills of ice with doorways that lead into and down to low-ceiling tunnels with side rooms for family habitats lighted and heated with fish oil. The seas offer food, material for shelters and weapons, and the basis for their religious beliefs. When taking fish the fisherman asks for forgiveness before killing it and when death is approaching, the Kitka will go to the sea and call for their god to come for them. By performing ritual suicide which consists of three deep cuts, made from left to right, on the arms, the dying Kitka summons their god, who appears as a huge kraken. Each Kitka believes he or she can talk to their god who consumes the body, thus returning a protein-rich source, to the seas. Traditional stories tell of heroes returning as pieces of god sent as punishment to wrong doers. Their oral history includes information about sacred grounds. Kitka generally do not have elected leaders and are known for their honesty. Their language is difficult to translate because its words are distinguished by pitch. The Kitka are believed to be a remnant of an pre-ice age culture.

Kittay (P)–*Enterprise* lieutenant at Communications for most of this mission. Kirk commended her efforts to keep the traffic flowing normally.

Klaa (UC)–This captain of the *Okrona* was broad shouldered, stocky, and quite muscular. He earned his captaincy for heroic action on the Romulan border during a short skirmish. As a gunner, he had destroyed three Orion vessels and saved his ship. During a mission detailed by J. M. Dillard (*Final Frontier: Movie*), Klaa itched for a change to show how heroic he was. After following *Enterprise* to the center of the galaxy, he would have killed Kirk, but General Korrd stopped him. Being a peaceful hero had far more possible rewards as he discovered when he served as translator at the trial of Kirk and McCoy for the assassination of Chancellor Gorkon. Kirk recalled the time Klaa had been a guest on board *Enterprise* (UC).

Kledon (FD)–Klingon grandfather to the female Klingon lieutenant Lui Kak Tok.

Klein (BD)–He was of German descent, spoke with an accent, and was first mate of the *Cockerell*, a dynacarrier Jimmy Kirk and friends tried to board.

kligat (FD)–A throwing weapon created by the Capellans. Kain carried such a knife. SEE Kain.

Klingee (ST)–Klingon-like people whom Kirk met in the second Aleph. SEE Aleph.

Klingee Association (ST)–This governmental entity, quite similar to the Klingon Empire, claimed the earth-like planet Kirk's *Enterprise* encountered in the second Aleph. SEE Aleph; Iola.

Klingee Fleet (ST)–Fifteen space ships that are part of the military arm of the Klingee Association. SEE Klingee; Ruko.

Klingee ship (ST)–According to Kirk's report a Klingee ship is "similar to a Klingon ship," yet he estimated that it had a 10% norm for Kreege-class ships. When first seen, Kirk assumed it was the Klingons he was familiar with, but their disrupter cannon had a different shape. The Klingee ship's main sensor was painted a dusty rose, but no triform symbol was seen on the warp pylons. Instead there was a single circling dot that could represent a planet or a hydrogen atom.

Klingons–One of many aliens encountered by humans when they ventured beyond their solar system. Immediately following first contact, historians began to write about them, basing their articles and books upon unreliable well-documented sources. Much of it is now believed to have been acquired through word of mouth and a few ship logs released after considerable public pressure. A StarFleet publication credits the USS *Sentry*, captained by Francis Benoit, with first contact with the Klingons in 2151 (Goldsteins 142). Captain Benoit's logs do not mention a visual contact. Another historian dates the first contact as occurring in 2218 (Okuda and Okuda *Chronology* 27). Although both dates suggest a Terran year, it is possible that one date is a Terran year and the other is a stardate. It cannot be determined which is which, and thus possibly as Thompson asserts, the *Exeter* was the first contact, both visually and in battle ("Klingons" 10). One of the earliest articles about these people is by Leslie Thompson who in his first few paragraphs quotes an earlier source, Roddenberry and Whitfield, who write that Klingons believed that "their only rule of life is that rules are only made to be broken by shrewdness, deceit, or power. Cruelty is something to admire; honor is a despicable trait...[their] society is totally devoted to personal gain by the cleverest, strongest, or most treacherous" (qtd by Thompson "Klingons" 5). This may have been true a few years after Federation contact, but repeated contacts have effected the Klingon Empire, particularly those meetings with StarFleet captains. Much of what was initially thought to be true about Klingons has been shown to be erroneous. More ship logs are being released to historians who are presenting the information to the public in various manners, from videos, to novels, to tomes stuffed with documentation. Extrapolation about an entire people on the basis of the actions of a few encounters is begging for misinformation. Thompson, in his article, writes that the Klingon home world is called Kazh, translated as "earth" ("Klingons" 5). A later historian writes the home world is, in the Klingon language, called Klinzhai (Dvorkin *Timetrap*). Another historian declares the home world took its name from the dominant group, the Klinzhai (Reeves-Stevens *Memory*). Historian Shane Johnson writes the home world is known as Kling (*Worlds* 115). Both Thompson and Johnson write that the planet is second in orbit, but Johnson declares the sun is a binary one. Both men agree the planet is one and a half times the size of Terra, almost entirely land mass with some salty shallow seas and sparse vegetation. Johnson mentions the planet is a class M world that tilts very little on its axis, thus producing a planet with a climate the same everywhere except the poles (quite cooler) and the equator (much warmer). Johnson adds to his description that the planet has "a high dense layer of carbon dioxide in the upper atmosphere" that retains heat (*Worlds* 114). Thompson speculates the environment encouraged the Klingons to venture into space seeking resource-rich planets to conquer ("Klingons" 5). A third highly qualified source insists the planet has one huge land mass, a vast ocean, and a severely tilted axis that causes violent seasonal changes and a turbulent atmosphere ("Klingons" Internet). Thompson speculates on the form of government, calling it "quite communistic" and saying the home world and all conquered peoples are ruled by a council of thirteen men 'whose order and influence is in direct proportion to their power in the empire" ("Klingons" 5). Chief of state is called a Senator-in-Chief and the other twelve men are called Senators. Territorial governors are appointed. Thompson declares that orders and edicts made by the Senator-in-Chief can be overruled or superseded by the rest of the Council. Later discovered documents show that the Klingon Empire was organized under a construct similar to Terra's ancient countries of England and France. The present-day government is considered an oligarchy with a High Council and a figurehead Emperor ("Klingons" Internet). Any description of a typical Klingon is subject to the viewer. One of the first historians to study the people was Leslie Thompson, a graduate of StarFleet Academy's Cadet School of Liberal Arts and its College of Science. He wrote in an early monograph that "Klingons are all of one race...due in a large part to the similarity of climate all over" the planet ("Klingons" 7). Later historians, particularly Vonda McIntyre (*First*) and Diane Carey (*Battlestations*), had access to records unavailable to Thompson. In fact, Thompson was writing about aspects of Klingons and their culture with few records to consult. Both women declare Klingons are considered humanoid and have two sexes. Klingons are composed of five groups: Klinzhai; Rumaiym, Wijngan, Daqawly, and Kumburanya (Carey *First*). These strains exhibit a variety of skin coloring, size, body height and hair, and ethnic customs. All appear to share the trait of bifurcated eyebrows that curl upwards. A second source identifies four groups and distinguishes them according to appearance ("Klingons" Internet). One group lacks forehead ridges and generally have pale complexion. A second group is tall and thin with a single crested ridge extending over their partially bald heads with an occipital bun on the rear of the skull. The third group has a slightly ridged center forehead with no side ridges and are largely hairless except for a small patch at the back of the skull. Some sport a small goatee. The final group has a triple-ridged forehead that bears clan-based ridge patterns ranging from slightly "webbed" ridge pattern to craggy triple ridges. An explanation as to why these two sources have both similar and dissimilar data is put forth as follows. The true Klingon, the Imperial Klingon, is native to the planet of origin, Qo'noS, and bears the ridged forehead among other visual traits. Once they moved into space and began conquering other planets they began interbreeding with them and an amalgamation of races was born. Another explanation might be put forth that as is considered "normal" for planets on which sentient life developed, Klingon development took place along the lines of its natural environment. This natural evolution might account for the physical variety of Klingons. Consider Terra whose population is humanoid but exhibits several varying evolutionary development. The physical appearance of Klingons that entered StarFleet ship logs varies according to the captain and crew and the Klingons they met. Some logs indicate the Klingons StarFleet ships met "wore long manes of luxuriant hair and beards" ("Klingons" Internet). This affectation may be culture and a sign of masculinity. Other logs record the Klingons were smooth faced with thin strands of a beard decorating either side of the mouth. And yet other logs mention Klingons with brow ridges and without. Consensus is that genetic evolution favored the ridged forehead and bony patterns seen on the back, along the spinal column, and tops of the feet. Some have suggested these patterns appear to follow family lines. Mixed species definitely show the ridges and back patterns are dominant. Skin coloring also varies, from very dark to light bronze as does the strength of both sexes. StarFleet records suggest that StarFleet captains have met representatives from all five strains and have constantly updated their computer files with the latest Klingon information, thus providing much information for historians as these files are opened to them. Most of the strains of Klingons exhibit boney foreheads that resemble the back of a Terran turtle as well as redundant body organs and systems. Their general anatomy resembles the humanoid in that they walk upright, have symmetrical body structure, and are mammals. Their three-chambered heart likens to a reptile's but their 23 rib latticework structure, a characteristic known as "brak'ul," makes the body resilient. Teeth are typically serrated with multiple edges and ridges suggesting a carnivore past. One StarFleet officer noted the Klingons lack tear ducts but that may be true for only one of the groups (Movie: *Voyage*). Life span measures from 100 to 150 Klingon years though many die before they reach 40 due to the militaristic life they lead. Pregnancy runs to 30 Klingon weeks with labor lasting for several days. Interbreeding is possible with other species and Betazoid, humanoid, Romulan, and Trill children have been reported. However, breeding with a Trill requires a full thirty-week medical intervention. Always the Klingon traits are dominant. Reproduction procedures are said to be violent. Whether this is foreplay or to stimulate the production of sperm and egg is not known. Physical injuries suffered during this time range from severe to a few bruises. All five strains have violet blood and their DNA contains erythrocytes unlike human DNA. A suggestion has been advanced that Klingons are the result of a "seeding" program by humanoids who mixed their DNA with that of evolving sentient life to give it a "boost." ("Klingons" Internet). The term identifying their language has been rendered into Federation Standard as Klingonese. Both the spoken and the written attest to its guttural nature. The first few encounters left both sides frustrated with their inability to communicate. StarFleet ship captains began compiling samples of the language each time they met Klingons. Within a few months after the captains began this and also began exchanging lists, the Federation Scientific Research Council called for in-depth research to begin focusing on recording, analyzing, and studying vocabulary, grammar, and definitions with the intent to opening a dialogue. With the aid of the Universal Translator this became possible. The project was placed under the direction of the Federation Interlanguage Institute whose ruling council members voted to place the entire project in the fully capable hands of Marc Okrand, the foremost noted Klingonese expert. The first effort of the study group produced a helpful dictionary with limited scope with many of the first words identified pertaining to the military. Much of the unscientific terminology remains missing, especially words relating to the home world's environment. A sub-study group lamented the limited number of food words and attributed the lack of some areas being studied to the problems of recruiting staff who are interested in the study of Klingonese. A second but major problem faced was the fact that Klingonese has a number of dialects, but so far only the Imperial dialect has been studied. An added burden is that this dialect will change with the next Emperor. Most Klingons attempt to be fluent in several dialects. Their writing system, called *pIqaD*, is well suited to the dialects but remains difficult for non-Klingons to produce (Okrand *Dictionary* 11). The few Klingons who have been engaged in a discussion of their language are proud "to speak of its expressiveness and beauty" but have difficultly conveying this (Okrand *Dictionary* 10). Some Klingon starship captains brag that the quadrant is learning their language because they realize that soon Klingons will rule the galaxy (Okuda and Okuda *Encyclopedia* 246). The evolution of a governing force, Thompson writes, might be attributed to a Klingon giant, seven feet tall and weighing over 300 pounds with strength to crush an enemy's head between his hands, as the one who created the Empire. No other source mentions this giant. In addition to this giant story, Thompson credits Klingon civilization–government and culture–to have begun with Kling. Suspicion is that Thompson was told this tale of Kling as a joke and having no access to Klingon history, he accepted it ("Klingons" 8-9). It was, however, accepted by at least one other historian who later used the giant's name to identify the home world (Johnson *Worlds* 114). Later studies reveal that Klingons, particularly the Klinzhai, identify Kahless as their founder and credit him with many noble deeds. An accepted source notes the home world in Klingon is Qo'noS though sometimes referred to as Klinzhai or Kling, which is also a district on Qo'noS (Okuda and Okuda *Encyclopedia* 243). The Empire's structure resembles the 15th and 16th century Terran nations England and France and suggest to some historians a history of having been a vassal state ("Klingons" Internet). At the present time, the Empire is ruled by a High Council with one member being elected as the Head of the Empire. The Emperor is a figurehead with no power. Within this Council a constant power struggle goes on with the waxing and waning of a Councilman's degree of power and influence. A history of the Empire has been put forward by one historian who, in one mission she developed into a novel, relates the Karsid, now an extinct race, conquered the Klingon home world and influenced its rapid technological development. According to her, the Karsid first conquered the Klingons and then were in turn conquered and/or assimilated by the Klingons, whom they lifted from a feudal to a space-flight society. Her history also tells that the Karsid conquest occurred six hundred years before the events recorded in her novel. As she reported, the Karsid arrived on Klinzhai in the "year of the Gashrikith in the reign of Khorad son of H'gar in the five hundredth cycle of Algol." The Karsid quickly established economic influence and within one generation, had control of the people and the planet. Vulcan historian Thae, consulted by the historian, stated full Karsid control occurred "as soon as the majority of the population had never known a time without...new weapons, new luxury goods...." Soon cultural unity was imposed thus uniting all peoples of Klinzhai. A few years later all "recalcitrant minorities, dissidents, and splinter groups were wiped out." In the Karsid Imperial year 930, Klinzhai was adopted into full Karsid "tributary status." Klinzhai life under Karsid rule proved to be "physically healthier and more puritanical" than under former Klinzhai rulers. Records consulted but not identified by the historian suggest the Karsid may have used drugs in specific incidents to hasten their occupation. However, an earlier accepted history, according to Vulcan Karsid scholar Thae, maintains the Karsid preferred to operate on the theory that no people "will willingly forego its source of machine guns to return to the use of bows and arrows." Other sources of Klingon history also consulted by the historian/novelist declare that following a revolt and seizure of power from the Karsid, Klingons, after years of warring among themselves, began to expand into space. Because Klingons are warlike people, their leadership frequently changed as a result of political assassinations. Also because their planet is resource poor, expansion outward to other resource rich planets became acceptable (Hambly *Ishmael*). A later historian studying the origin of Klingons declares the Empire was founded circa 900AD on Qo'noS by Kahless followed by several dynastic rulers with two or three periods between these that came to be known as the "Dark Times" as they were experiments in democracy. The planet was invaded by Hur'q who stole the Sword of Kahless. After years of warring, the Klingons expelled the Hur'q but kept the technology they brought to the planet and employed it to enslave and conquer other planets. Some historians suggest much of their early technology was stolen for Klingon technology did not seem to advance in equipment or sophistication. This may explain why an anti-intellectual civilization could develop warp drive and become a warlike race and why the warrior class developed ("Klingons" Internet). A few sources indicate that by the end of 22nd century the warrior class was exerting so much influence on their worlds that they believed themselves invincible. They even attempted to alter the timeline in 2151 ("Klingons" Internet). Their radical altering of concepts of honor and glory and the gutting of their legal systems was the beginning of the slide toward chaos. Relationships between the Federation and Qo'noS deteriorated and by 2219 relationships were hostile until 2267 when war was imminent. The Organians put a stop to it and by the following year Klingons and Romulans had forged a military alliance (Okuda and Okuda *Encyclopedia* 341; "Klingons" Internet). The destruction of their moon Praxis forever changed the Klingon Empire/Federation relationship. The destruction was so intense that the home world became uninhabitable. All of the residents, along with the government, were removed to another planet which was quickly re-named Qo'noS. The Federation President in a speech at Khitomer mentioned the evacuation of the planet would be completed in fifty-years and stated Phase One: Preparation for Evacuation had begun ("Klingons" Internet; Movie: *Country*). Limited data about their culture is beginning to surface. The earliest article about Klingon culture declares the average Klingon is considered to be owned by the state and that "rank is achieved by assassination and treachery." Most males were raised to be warriors and taught to cheat, betray, steal, and lie with prestige and power on an ascending route to the top. To lose power often results in loss of life. Females frequently become scientists, computer technicians, factory laborers, and providers of the next generation, though a few do rise to power in this militaristic society. Life is a constant struggle and is tied to the environment. The government encourages parents to place their children in state-run facilities (Thompson "Klingons" 5-6). A later document reveals Klingon parents to be loving and kind to their children, preferring to raise them without government influence. Additional information supports the facts that males and females have some freedom of career choice (Lorrah *IDIC*). An interesting and little known fact, which may be a culture adaptation, concerns the Klingon life-disc, an identification badge created at birth that accompanies the person through his/her life. When the badge is removed from the body, at death, its color fades. Historian McIntyre does not indicate if this practice has continued, if it is a cultural affectation, a parental choice, or a family action declared by the head of the House line. Nor does she indicate that all Klingons carry such a disc. The carrying of a disc may be confined to a particular group of Klingons but not by all five strains (McIntyre *First*). It appears that all Klingons follow the ritual of *R'ustia*, a bonding ceremony between individuals joining themselves and their families similar to a ritual marriage between families (Okuda and Okuda *Encyclopedia* 247). Most of the Klingons adhere to the Age of Ascension ritual which subjects the initiate to an endurance of physical suffering administered by his/her peers via Klingon painstiks (Okuda and Okuda *Encyclopedia* 344). Klingons adhere strictly to their home districts and family lines. Some ruling families have established Houses that had become over the years dynastic lines of descent and by doing so have become quite powerful in the Empire. Children who have no known ancestors often are formed into Lineless Houses and become trained pieces in The Game. CONSULT *Star Trek Reader's Reference to the Novels: 1984-1985*. Most historians have ignored the issue of Klingon religion. Xeonhistorians question this conclusion. Historian Jack Haldeman II, writing his novelization of a mission that he titled *Perry's Planet*, declares the Klingon ship commanded by Koral, who had sworn a blood oath against Kirk and the *Enterprise*, carried a priest. However, Haldeman does not explain the purpose or need for the priest to be aboard. No additional information is related except that the priest, identified as Kiel, disapproved of Captain Koral's actions. Klingons' mythological stories, millennium old, often tell of the gods who created the Klingons and of the Klingons who warred with their gods and killed them. (Okuda and Okuda *Encyclopedia* 248). Their greatest mythological hero is Kahless. Stories about him form the cornerstone of their mythology and religion. A legendary story relates a battle fought for honor against the tyrant Molor. Kahless designed and created the *bat'leth* in order to kill Molor. Another legend tells of Kahless using the *bat'leth* to conquer Fek'lhri and to skin the serpent of Xol. Probably the greatest story of them all tells of Kahless and his wife Lukara defending the Great Hall at Qam-Chee against the attack of 500 warriors. Those who study religions have concluded Klingons have no equivalent of a "devil" though Fek'lhri comes close. He is considered the guardian of Gre'thor, a place similar to hell in other religions (Okuda and Okuda *Encyclopedia* 149). Klingons treat death and the disposal of the body in a different way. A warrior who dies honorably in battle is not mourned. The freeing of the spirit from the body is celebrated with horrendous screams meant to inform the residents of Sto Vo Kor of the arrival of a warrior. Though they believe in an after life "there is no burial of the corpse;" it is efficiently disposed of (Okuda and Okuda *Encyclopedia* 247). However, a Klingon who dies by his own hand cannot enter Sto Vo Kor. The striking of one warrior by another with the back of the hand is interpreted as a challenge to the death. Whispering is taboo and considered an insult perpetuated by one on another. Tradition holds that "the son of a Klingon is a man the day he can first hold a blade" (Okuda and Okuda *Encyclopedia* 247). From the very first encounter, Klingons have held a fascination for humans and for this continued study reveals new and interesting details about this race of people.

Klingon assassin (UC)—Male Klingon member of the delegation to Camp Khitomer was provided with a specially designed weapon that had four times the range and double the accuracy but was mistaken by its disassembled components to be a datapad. He hid in overhead alcove to wait until President Ra-ghoratrei had finished his remarks.

Had Kirk and his group entered the hall a few minutes later, he would have already killed the President and Klingon Counselor Atzebur. Scotty spotted his hiding place and shot at it, killing him just before he could shoot. Later he was discovered to be Admiral Cartwright's aid, Colonel West.

Klingon Empire (P; UC)–An entity founded by Kahless the Unforgettable some 1,500 years before the events chronicled in UD. He is credited with uniting the people by winning a battle against the tyrant Molar (Okuda and Okuda *Encyclopedia* 244). Since then the Klingons have been at war with their neighbors. This entity includes the home worlds and others that have been annexed to Klingon control. Since its earliest days, the Empire has been ruled by a High Council. Many years passed before the Empire chose to have an Emperor. In 2369, a second Kahless took the throne (Okuda and Okuda *Encyclopedia* 244). During the incident with the Probe, the Federation conducted a series of negotiations with the Klingons that led to the establishment of a date to meet with Chancellor Gorgon. In UC, Admiral Smillie told Kirk and crew at a briefing that the Empire had less than 50 years of life left as a result of the Praxis explosion.

Klingon/Federation negotiations (UC)–Spock, at Sarek's urging, had contacted Chancellor Gorkon who eagerly began the process of clearing the way for negotiations. He even suggested the dismantling of both the Federation and Klingon space stations and starbases along Klingon space, thus ending more than 70 years of unremitting hostilities.

Klingon Headquarters (FD)–Bunkers whose interior offered atmospheric conditions similar to Qo'noS had been blasted into lava cliffs on the coast not far from the Susuru capital city located on Discord.

Klingon Neutral Zone (UC)–A joint agreement established by treaty identified a specified area as a "no man's land" between the Federation and the Klingon Empire "into which neither side would send ships." The zone was abolished at the Khitomer Accords in 2203 (Okuda and Okuda *Encyclopedia* 245).

Klingon Peace Conference (UC)–Delegates from the Federation, Klingon Empire, and Romulan Empire met at Camp Khitomer to discuss peace between the Federation and the Empire. Chancellor Azetbur and President Ra-ghoratrei sat on the dias for opening ceremonies. Delegates entered in groups led by Ambassador Kamarag with his aid Colonel Worf. Nanclus with his aid, a young man named Pardek, led the Romulan delegation. Ambassador Sarek led the Vulcan delegation. Each group was identified by banners and colored sashes: yellow for Vulcans, red for Klingons, blue for Romulans, and green for humans. President Ra-ghoratrei delivered the opening remarks.

Kmmuta (GSR)–Captain Kmmuta and crew of the Tholian ship *554-2* flying the Tholus flag won second place trophy in the Great Starship Race. SEE Yeshmal.

Knealayz, Temren (WLW)–This female ensign, an expert on alien technology, was a member of Spock's party which discovered the Central Control Chamber of the Kh!lict. SEE Kh!lict.

knifeweed (SG)–A native grass of Romulus known for its sharp edges. Compare to Terran saw grass of the Everglades. SEE Aifor.

Kofirlar (FD)–Variant term for Klingon. SEE Variant.

Kolker (Di)–A person or deity to whom Delacourt referred. SEE Delacourt.

Komack (WLW)–The inflexible head of StarFleet Command in Sector 9. He was a sharp-minded man with a narrow tanned face, blue eyes, and white hair. Evidence suggests that Komack served in the intelligence section of StarFleet (Dillard *Mindshadow*). While in StarFleet Command Intelligence Bureau, he assigned Kirk to Juram Five to deal with the Onlies (Klass *Cry*). He ordered *Enterprise* to Altair IV, but Kirk ignored his order and took a very ill Spock to Vulcan (*AT). On a mission to Sarpaidon's past, Kirk requested backup support and Komack immediately sent ships. He kept Spock's return to Sarpaidon's past a secret (Crispin *Son*). During one mission his office tracked the progress of the search for an antidote to the substance released from the alien boxes recovered from a Romulan ship, and kept the Federation Council fully informed (Clowes *Pandora*). Following Kirk's initial report about the discovery of archeology ruins on Careta IV, Komack contacted him for more information (Mitchell *Windows*).

Koman ship-killer missiles (FD)–Tube-shaped with a sharp nose cone, these supersonic weapons have a hundred-kilometer range and are capable of sinking the biggest Stilter ship. Developed and built by the Discordians for such use. SEE Stilter; Variants.

Korax (FD)–Klingon aide to Captain Koloth but had none of Koloth's charm. His insults directed at Kirk and the *Enterprise* caused a "magnelephant fight on Space Station K-7 (Trimble 180; *TT). A few years later he became First Officer to Captain Koloth on the *Devisor* (*MTT/a).

Kormak (ST)–Klingon warship captained by Torm.

Kordes, Amtov (WLW)–This chunky dark-haired specialist in determining ages of archeology ruins spoke with a thick Dindraed, broad on the vowels and burred on the consonants. Assistant to Dr. Meredith Lassiter and supporter of Dr. Abdul Kaul's theories about the ages of "orphan" cultures and the Kh!lict ruins as well, confirming their carvings to be upwards of 300,000 year old. During a briefing conducted by Kirk and Spock, Kordes declared "so-called 'orphan' cultures are sensationalist media reports created by publicity seekers who use improper excavation techniques and careless data analysis." Spock included him on the team to investigate the Kh!lict Central Control Complex, but when he ignored Spock's decision and acted on his own, Spock returned him to the *Enterprise*.

Korrd (UC)–This Klingon general had a distinguishable career in the Klingon Defense Force until he fell out of favor and was sent to Nimbus III as the Klingon diplomat. He saved Kirk's life in the incident dealing with Sybok (Dillard *Final*). His actions in the incident led to his regaining power and position on Gorkon's Council, and though injured in the assassination attempt on Gorkon's life, he survived his injuries. His military strategies are required reading at the Academy.

kraken (IT)–The word is a Norwegian term for a sea monster from Norway (Terra) legend. It is also the translation for a Kitkan word denoting its huge sea monster considered their god, and the planet's largest predator which hunts mostly under the ice pack. Its color varies from green to gray to brown though some have been noted to have a milky pale skin. A First Contact description reveals that it is native to Nordstral's seas, can and does grow to an enormous size, and has a small head and double-hinged jaws suspended on a long graceful neck. A portion of the description of the animal taken from Dr. McCoy's briefing report reads: "Its eyes are large, iridescent set close together on the front of the head, above two slitted nostrils and in front of what appeared to be gill-like membranes of brilliant white that resemble stiff, water- buoyed feathers. The four limbs [are] short and broad, but [are] tipped with claws." It had a short broad flat tail that "sat perpendicular to the body's orientation." Dr. McCoy included information on an interesting feature. He wrote about the kraken's ability, for short periods, to breath air, especially when feasting on Kitka who have come to the edge of the ice pack to commit ritual suicide. The young are carried in the female's body and are born live and independent from birth. They have four to six hours to find their strength and swim away from the female before being subjected to being eaten. They will "spend the majority of their lives as asexual, androgynous, until the mating rapture strikes when they met in pairs and battle to the death. The victor becomes female and eats the other's yellow sack of nutrients first then the rest of the body" [taken from Captain Mandeville's notes]. Although the kraken consumes the native Kitka, it refuses to consume any off-worlder. Nearly all of the kraken is recycled into various items by the Kitka who also produce a poison from it that is capable of causing sleep in the Kitka but kills off-worlders.

Kras (FD)–Trimble (180) describes this person as a Klingon spy with a "dark complexioned... sneering round face and a low hairline." Sent to Capella IV to prevent the Federation from gaining mining concessions for topaline, he was killed by one of the planet's natives. His brother Kain blamed Kirk for his death. CONSULT *"Friday's Child." SEE Krodan.

Kreege-class ships (ST)–SEE Klingee ship.

Krodan (FD)–Klingon name: QoDang. Once this Klingon was one of four or five most powerful men in the Empire and a noted diplomat. He had two sons: Kain and Kras.

Kroeber, Dr. (ST)–Elderly female civilian present on Starbase 12 during this mission, possibly a counselor. She enjoyed off-color jokes.

Kronos (UC)–Standard Federation spelling for the Klingon term for its home world: Qo'noS.

Kronos One (UC)–Flag ship of the Klingon High Command and Gorkon's transportation to the peace talks. The cruiser, badly damaged in an unprovoked attack believed to be caused by the *Enterprise*, lost its gravity generators. Sickbay along with other areas was destroyed. The confusion allowed two StarFleet men to board and kill Gorkon.

Kruge (FF; UC)–Known to have been born in S'zlack in the hinterlands of Qo'noS, he was described as having large protuberant eyes and big shoulders and known to speak quite slowly. In FF, he was the tallest of the Klingon crew of *Kadn'ra* captained by Vheled. Kruge was Third Officer to Captain Vheled and had told him that he was going to assassinate First Officer Gidris. When Vheled killed Gidris for failure of duty, Kruge moved up in rank. Grael killed Vheled, and Kruge moved into the captain's chair. In

UC, Kirk remembered Kruge as the commander of a bird of prey who had learned of the Genesis device. Securing the information for the location of the newly created planet, Kruge went there and confronted David Marcus, Lt. Saavik, and the physical form of Spock. When Kruge demanded the information and Kirk, Kruge killed David Marcus. Kirk transported to Genesis and confronted Kruge. In a fight, Kirk killed Kruge (* *The Search for Spock*; Okuda and Okuda *Encyclopedia* 253).

Kruzaak's World (P)–A dozen Romulan scout ships had been on a training exercise in the vicinity of this world when the Probe appeared. Two ships were able to fire before the Probe drained the power from all the ships.

Krysztof (FD)–This native Discordian, a stockholder in the Waverider Ranch, was described as having a craggy sharp-nosed face with blond hair and beard, but showed no outward indication of genetic manipulation.

Kudao (UC)–Planet located near the Klingon Neutral Zone had been attacked by Klingons who killed hundreds for political reasons.

kudzu (SG)–An oriental vine native to Terra imported into the United States in the late 1920s as a possible way to cover the eroded lands of the South. McCoy remembered this plant over- running his grandmother's garden.

Kyle (ST; Di; FD; FF)–StarFleet serial number: TE818-617 (Mandel *Manual* 15). A tall lanky blond officer with a British accent though he came from Australia. Though his Academy training focused on the helmsman position, he included training in operating the transporter. He preferred the helmsman position but took the transporter position with comfort after Kirk's assertion that Kyle was one of the best on the ship. His continued study of the transport system under the supervision of Lt. Cmdr. Scott led him to being at the station during most of the demanding times Kirk required the use of the transporter. Kirk showed his faith in Kyle by calling upon his ability during the accident on Careta IV (Mitchell *Windows*). Kyle furthered his education and expertise by taking training at the Bridge/Library Computer Station where he sometimes worked the scanners (Trimble 181). Sometimes he worked double duty between the helm and the transporter. His ship record reveals that during his four years with Kirk on the *Enterprise*, he received only one reprimand. Kirk reprimanded him for leaving his post to go to the ceramics lab to sculpt (Vardeman *Gambit*). The record also carries the notation that he was under an outside influence. For a short while he served on the *Reliant* as its transporter chief which could have been a training session for new transporter crew (Okuda and Okuda *Encyclopedia* 255). Everyone on *Enterprise* knew of his passion for the game "Quaester," especially when he was one game shy of being declared a master player. That one game was beyond his reach when the ship's computer continued to refuse to acknowledge his request and substituted a game called "Captain's Square" (Vardeman *Gambit*; Murdock *Web*). Though it took some time, he achieved that rank (Reeves-Stevens *Memory*). As was the desire of every crewman on Kirk's *Enterprise*, Kyle longed to be on a landing party. Kirk included him during a trip to Sherman's Planet (Larson *Pawns*). For a short time, he returned to the helmsman's seat when Kirk sent Chekov to the Klingon *Falchion* (Carter *Dreams*). He received commendation from Kirk and Scotty for his work with

Scotty on the ship's transtators following the Talin IV incident (Reeves-Stevens *Prime*). Sometimes during conversations with fellow officers and talk turns to remembered incidents, Kyle has spoken of the time Kirk, Spock, and diplomat Moriah Wayne were in a heated debate. Realizing the discussion was taking place before the Bridge crew, Kirk put Kyle in command of the ship and the three retired to a briefing room (Milan *Depths*). In 2285 he accepted promotion to commander, grew a moustache, and served as communication officer aboard the *Reliant* (*BFS/a; Okuda and Okuda *Encyclopedia* 255). He always recalled his years under Kirk's command as the best of his career, citing them as the prod that led him to excel as helmsman and transporter and communication chief.

Lady (SG)–Reference is to the Romulan proconsul who approved the crew selection for the *Reltah*. SEE *Reltah*.

Lakandir, Cor (SS)–Very young male assassin whom Andrachis believed could become the next High Assassin with guidance and education. Cor urged the death of off-worlders (StarFleet personnel) and thought at one time to kill Andrachis and take control but then decided he was not leadership material and the perpetuation of the cult was more important. Born in a sea-coast town, he hated the mountain retreat the assassins used for their headquarters. When Andrachis was wounded, Cor killed him according to the tradition that to preserve a master's life was wrong.

Lamb (FF)–Carol Marcus called her son David by this pet name.

lancefish (S)–Marine animal native to Sanctuary; considered dangerous, though edible.

Landing Party Kirk (FD)–Title bestowed on Kirk because he almost always led landing parties.

landing party to Beta Canzandia (FF)–Kirk, Spock, McCoy, and Nurse Chapel.

landing party to Parath'aa (Di)–Kirk, McCoy, Sulu, and Giotto.

landing party to Rithra (Di)–Commodore Wesley, Wynn Samuels, Jerome Balia of the *Lexington*, and Lt. Uhura of *Enterprise*.

landing party to Xaridian II (Di)–Kirk, Spock, McCoy, Chekov.

Landon, Martha (Di)–*Enterprise* yeoman on this mission. She had blond hair worn in a tight weave, had bright eyes, and was quite young. She and Chekov become very good friends (*Ap).

Landorian (Di)–StarFleet is familiar with these pirates.

language of the flitting birds (Di)–Descriptive term for sign language that employs hand movements. Uhura, as a child, began learning sign language from her cousin Epala who was a year older and born deaf.

Larol (SS)–A Ssan city-state governed by Zar Holarnis.

Lassiter, Dr. Meredith (WLW)–Described as a delicate, willowy woman with luminous white-blond hair and sea-green eyes who was raised in low-gravity, was a native of Bendilon. She tended to avoid eye contact when speaking to another and often nibbled on her hair when nervous. Her Fleet record indicated she was able to perceive subliminal perceptions, dream messages, and certain forms of extrasensory perceptions. As one of two chief assistants to Dr. Abdul Kaul, she accompanied him to the surface and was able to sense Kh!lict hatred toward all intelligent creatures. Once inside the Kh!lict Control Chamber she had flashes of insight that led to the resolution of the mission. She concurred with Kirk that Careta IV should be quarantined.

Laughran, Captain (SG)–In the Terran 1600s the *St. Brendan*, captained by Laughran, discovered the abandoned pirate ship *Stephanie Emilia*.

Laurudite (FF)–Blue-skinned race of people the Klingons conquered.

LBR complex (BD)–Loading port of a space dry-dock; also refers to repair facility.

LC4 (BD)–Liaison Cutter 4. A few years later shuttlecraft would replace the class. *Enterprise* Captain April, George Kirk and his son James along with Veronica Hall and Carlos Florida as well as engineers Thorvaldsen and Dennings were on board. The craft was described as having a blunt bow, sextagonal body with detachable freight hold, a sensor pod attached to the top, an impulse engine, and 2 low-warp engines mounted on either side. Pirates of the *Shark* attempted to take it.

Lead Walker (FD)–Susuru known as Swift, the leader for the Susuru. SEE Swift.

Lefarnus (SS)–A Ssan city-state master governor killed by Shil Andrachis' assassins.

Legarratlinya (GSR)–Captain of the *Ytaho* representing the Orion Union in the Great Starship Race.

Lemieux (DC; IT)–After the bomb explosion, this *Enterprise* female member of Chekov's security was second in command of a team to Deck 6.

Leno, Christina (SG)–*Enterprise* ensign was described as pale-skinned with violet eyes and an Amazonian build. Selected as one officer in the landing party to the Romulan space station, her main duty was to guard Spock, giving him time to devote his attention to the station. She also carried the generator for him. Caught in the turbo car when its power went off, she climbed out the car via the roof and then down the turbo shaft. When confronted by the Romulan Orrien in the Engineering room she disarmed him, and finding Spock unconscious, carried him from Engineering to a safe place.

Lerma requiem (P)–Romulan musical composition that ranks high on the Orthodox list. Most think it is too bland. Lerma was one of three composers whose music was played at the Praetor's funeral. The other two were Talet and Mektium.

Leslie (Di; FF)–Member of the *Enterprise* crew. His Serial Number is HC 205-787 (Mandel 15). He had curly hair and sturdy features. Sometimes he served at the Bridge Engineering and Environmental Station and as relief helmsman (*CL; *AF). Head of a Security team on the mission in FF.

Lev (FD)–Native of Discord and a stockholder in the Waverider Ranch. SEE Waverider Ranch.

leviathan (P)–Huge ocean-dwelling mammal identified as builders of the Probe as no other name was discovered. The Terran word describes what Kirk and his group initially saw.

Leviathan (FD)–The Klingon term *bIQa'a'veqlarg'a'* translates as Great Demon of the Ocean. This gigantic blocky arrowhead-like ship, a prototype built over a span of five years in a secret dockyard, had a truncated nose and wingtips, meter thick metal walls, and a powerful fluxing magnetic field. It weighed in at more than a quarter million ton mass. On completion of the ship, Kain became its captain, took it to Discord, and concealed it in the Hellsgate Rift. Damaged in the initial encounter with *Enterprise*, it was later destroyed by *Enterprise* when Kirk ordered "all weapons fire" for a proton spread. One hit the centerline, destroying the central warp drive tube and in-board impellers. A secondary explosion killed one fourth of the crew. One photon hit the ship's photon torpedo tubes setting off a chain reaction that ripped the ship apart. Kirk destroyed the remaining debris.

Lexington (SG; Di)–SEE USS *Lexington*.

Liaison Cutter 4 (BD)–SEE LC4.

Liberace Bernstein (P)–Reference is to a musician whose style of composed music and execution of music was influenced by these two Terran men who lived in the 20ᵗʰ century. Liberace was a noted entertainer and pianist who had great flair for showmanship and mixed classical music with folk music. Bernstein, also a composer, conductor, and pianist gained a reputation during his years with the New York Philharmonic Symphony. He too produced both classical music and mainstream music.

Lift Seven (UC)–Elevator on Rura Penthe where Kirk and McCoy met Martia and escaped from the prison.

Lihalla (P)–Romulan name for Temaris Four. SEE Termaris Four.

Lincoln Center's Philharmonic Hall (P)–Included in a sixteen-acre area in New York City, Terra, its construction began in 1960. Included with the Philharmonic Hall are museums devoted to music and classical schools such as Julliard for talented musicians. Andrea Benar served as a rehearsal conductor under the guidance of Carmen Espinosa, maestro and chief conductor. Following the success of the Probe mission, Dr. Benar and Romulan Jandra presented a highly successful concert based on whales songs at the Hall.

Lincress (S)–Chubby Senite who ran an inn in Dohama, Sanctuary. He provided clothes for Kirk, Spock, and McCoy.

Ling (Di)–*Lexington* junior officer at the Communication station on this mission.

lithium hydride (GSR)–SEE Romulan bomb.

Littlejon (SG)–Many *Enterprise* crew enjoyed this game that employed quarter staves.

lizards (DC)–SEE Halkan water chameleons.

L-Langon Mts. (WLW)–Located on Vulcan.

longitudinal antigravity pontoons (BD)–One section of each constructed dry dock is much longer than the others and always lines up with the longitudes of the planet's surface to accommodate extra-large ships.

Lonteen's Light (BD)–Captain Roth employed part of this old code to send a distress message. SEE Roth.

Loracon (GSR)–Captain of the *Irimlo*.

Lost Ones (S)–Wild child-size humanoid creatures not native to Sanctuary. A group attacked Kirk, Spock, McCoy, Renna, and Billiwog. SEE Renna; Billiwog.

Loutak (FF)–Klingon crewman on the *Kadn'ra* and member of the first group sent to find the Beta Canzandia settlement's children. Together Spock and the children rendered him unconscious.

L'rita (Di)–Trained in quantum astrophysics, she was a vital member of the Gamma Xaridian colony. She started shaving her head after coming to the colony. Jak Eisman and L'rita were engaged to be married, but they and everyone else in the colony were killed when the colony was attacked by Rithrim pirates.

Lu Kok Tak (FD)–Young female Klingon senior lieutenant under Kain's command described as being tall with a straight nose and high slanting cheekbones. Her grandmother always called her Lu, which she considered a pet name. Her full name translates as "they killed him" and refers to a glorious episode in the history of her clan. Her grandfather was Kain's first captain.

Lujexter (S)–A cobbled together slim-nosed ship built by the technics at the Graveyard of Lost Ships. After launch it disappeared when it reached 30 kilometers in Sanctuary's atmosphere, destroyed by the Senite shields that prevented any metal object leaving the planet's influence.

Luke (GSR)–Crewman on the *Ransom Castle*; likely killed by boarding Romulans.

Lungo (ST)–This very thin human whose bush of black hair covered his head and forehead delivered Admiral Nogura's message to Kirk.

lunks (S)–Giant sea mollusk native to Sanctuary. Smaller version is edible.

lunkjuice (S)–A sealant made from the lunk. Billiwog employed it to make his ships watertight.

M-113 (SS)–Planet excavated by Robert and Nancy Crater (*MT).

Magda (FD)–Native of Discord. A waverider who monitored robot wranglers.

Magellan, Ferdinand (FD)–A Terran Portuguese-born explorer of the late 14th century credited with circumnavigation of Terra even though he personally did not complete the journey. In a conversation with Sulu, Kirk pointed out that he and Magellan were in the same line of work and Sulu told Kirk that Kirk was "nicer to work with."

Magistan Seven (SS; FF)–One of several planets McCoy had visited. Its healing arts are symbolized by *phornicia* shells.

Mahaska County, Iowa (BD)–Oskaloosa, named for an Indian chief of the Iowa tribe, is the county seat. A rope foot bridge once spanned the North Skunk River. Jim Kirk and his gang's crossing caused it to collapse.

maldinium (SS)–A mineral found in heavy deposits on Ssan prohibits the use of transporters. The same mineral is found on Gamma Caius Seven.

Malkin, Zack (BD)–As a member of Jim Kirk's gang, he created fake IDs for each. George Kirk told Jim that Zack had a police record. A descendant of Zack's could have been a member of Riley's landing party (P).

Malik (P)–Died in a landing party detail led by Riley who had trouble living with the memory.

Mallot (FF)–Klingon crew on the *Kadn'ra* who accessed the computers on Beta Canzandra and discovered the G-Seven unit was missing. SEE G-Seven unit.

Maltusian maze (Di)–Academy test for all cadets. Chekov told Sulu that "to find your way through the maze...It's all in how you handle the third fork on the fifth level."

Malurians (FF)–Native people of Alpha Maluria Six and members of UFP. Two religious groups, Manteil and Obirrhat had engaged in a religious quarrel resolved with Kirk's help. SEE Manteil/Obbirhat quarrel.

Malurian Hall of Government (FF)–Seat of planetary-wide government. The building is hexagonal with six long windows, alternately tinged green and violet. The walls are of a variety of dark stone with threads of silver running through. In the middle of the room, a gray-polished metal ring with six spires hangs suspended from the ceiling. Beneath it is a round table and six chairs.

mainstage flux-chiller (P)–A necessary component in the coolant container.

Manarba, Dur (SS)–Ssan master governor of Orthun. As a member of the government he met with Kirk and diplomats Clay and Jocelyn Treadway.

Mandelbrot Set (P)–In mathematics it is a set of complex dynamic points in a complex plane whose boundary forms a fractal. When computed and graphed, the set is seen to have an elaborate boundary which does not simplify at any magnification. First pictures of such a Set were drawn in 1978. McCoy's experience inside the Probe's internal crystal bubble reminded him of a Mandelbrot Set.

Mandeville, Clara (IT)–This short human female, who had lots of long multi-braided hair and was described as having a strong handshake, hailed from Jamaica, Terra. She was captain of the *Soroya*. She and several crew were killed when an icequake shook the ship, damaging the Bridge and sheering off the top three levels.

Mandris, Hardin (SS)–Native of Ssan and an assassin ordered to kill his own parents because they had questioned the actions of the governor of Orthun who had increased his personal wealth over the needs of the city-state. Mandris then killed the governor. Andrachis often told this story to his followers to instill the understanding that an assassin had to be loyal to his calling. Mandris had shown that loyalty and had honored his parents and the administrator. SEE Andrachis.

Mansur (FD)–Native of Discord; a giant Grunt cook for the Waverider Ranch. SEE Grunt.

Manteil (FF)–Alpha Maluria Six has two main religious groups, the Manteil and the Abirrhat. The Manteil are humanoid in general appearance with black skin. In adulthood, weblike patterns emerge around the mouth and chin. Pale-silver eyes set in deep sockets give them an unusual appearance. The twitching of the face reveals internal conflict. SEE Manteil/Abbirhat quarrel.

Manteil/Obbirhat quarrel (FF)–The differences between these two religious groups escalated into a civil war focused on a large herd of cubaya, held sacred by the Manteil, whose migration trail led through the Obirrhat's sacred city. The Manteil, who believed each animal in the herd carried the soul of a long-deceased holy man, insisted the herds could not be destroyed or moved from their migratory path but must be allowed access anywhere and everywhere, even ancient cities held sacred by the Obirrahat. The other side of the quarrel responded that their sacred places were being blasphemed by the cubaya. For many years both groups had lived with the cubaya issue unresolved because the cubaya were slowing dying out. When the planet joined UFP, veterinarians discovered the cause and effected a cure. Their action led to an increase in the numbers which threatened sacred places. *Enterprise* delivered Ambassador Marlin Farquhar to settle the issue, but Kirk solved the problem after reading the Obirrahat's sacred texts: he suggested planting the foul smelling Klingon fireblossoms along the migratory route.

Manwaring, Skippy (SS)–Boyhood friend of McCoy's who collected butterflies.

Marcus, Carol (UC; SS; FF)–Mother of David Marcus. CONSULT *The Wrath of Khan* and *The Search for Spock*. In UC She had been injured in a Klingon raid on the Themis project. In SS, Kirk planned, following this mission to Ssan, to retire so that he and Carol could be together. In FF, she was a member of the terraforming colonists on Beta Canzandia.

Marcus, David (UC; FF)–Only son of James T. Kirk; mother Carol Marcus. CONSULT *The Wrath of Khan* and *The Search for Spock*. In FF, he was about ten-years-old when he led the other Beta Canzandia colony children to safety in the hills, protecting them from Klingons. He also helped Spock capture several Klingons. In UC, Kirk recalled his death at the hands of Klingons.

Marcuslabs (UC)–Research facility established by Carol Marcus and her son David.

Maritime Standard Race Rules (GSR)–As soon as sailors began competing against one another, rules were set up to ensure fair play. Over the years and in many Terra nations that had naval power, civilian sailors established races. One particular race organized in December 2000, was non-stop, no-rules, and no limits to be raced around the world. Its purpose then seemed quite similar to the purpose established by the Reys: to unite space entities; gather the best ships and racers; promote competition; create the most spectacular and prestigious fleet of racers. SEE Appendix E for list of entrants.

Maritza (FD)–Native of Discord; a surgeon living in Serendip; aunt to Aileea dinAthos.

Mark IV Defense Com (DC)–A navigation device that enhances the Bridge Communication Center. Quite an item on the black market.

Markson, Daniel (SG)–Born on Vendali 5 and raised there, this human male strongly believed in enra and ghosts. He served aboard the *Enterprise* in Security and was a member of the boarding party to the Romulan space station. His beliefs in the supernatural effected him so much that when confronted by what he thought was a ghost, he lost all sense of himself and died in a fall down a turbo-lift shaft. SEE enra.

Martia (UC)–Dark-skinned female chameloid with gold eyes and an addiction to hand-rolled cigarettes who called Arc her home planet. She was a prisoner on Rura Penthe and was tempted by a pardon if she would lure Kirk and McCoy beyond the shield barrier so they could be killed "attempting to escape." Her ability to morph into various creatures enabled her to convince them she could get them out. Her first morph was into a hideous seven-foot tall simian with orange hair. Her second morph was a young human girl who showed Kirk and McCoy a passage leading to the outside. Her third morph was into a huge furry brute with wide sharp-fanged jaws and talons. When Kirk and McCoy questioned how she was able to escape and find heavy furs and heat flares waiting she morphed into a Kirk-like mimic. Prison guards killed her while she was in the Kirk disguise.

Martians (SG)–Reference is to Scotty's storytelling about Martians and their attempt to invade Terrra as related in the Terran novel *War of the Worlds* by H. G. Wells.

Martine, Angela (Di)–She was commander of the phaser crew on the *Enterprise* and considered one of the top weapons specialist in the Fleet. A few months before this mission, she was ready to marry Robert Tomlinson, but the ceremony was interrupted by a Romulan attack. He was the only casualty (*BT). In Di, she favored the Meteors in the championship magno-ball game against the Pipers. During this mission she and Chekov ran simulations against the Rithrim ships beginning with routing patterns and working toward creative responses.

Marvick, Larry (BD)–Chief warp drive engineer on April's *Enterprise* mission to Faramond.

Mary Celeste (SG)–Terran sea-going vessel built in 1868. The history of this ship tells that she left Staten Island, N. Y., on November 7, 1872 under the captaincy of Benjamin Spooner Briggs. The vessel carried a full crew along with the captain's wife and their two-year-old daughter. A month later, on December 4, the ship was sighted by Captain David Reed Morehouse who declared the ship was under short sail and moving erratically. After boarding her, Captain Morehouse reported in his ship's log that no one was aboard. Consensus of the facts arrived at by an investigations board held that an explosion aboard caused by the load of alcohol caused all aboard to take to the lifeboats. No evidence of the missing lifeboats or passengers were ever found. Several of the *Enterprise* boarding crew to the *Reltah* the Romulan space station recalled the *Mary Celeste* incident, comparing it to what they had discovered. SEE *Reltah*.

Master Dominion Pandect for Martial Crisis (P)–Evoking this Romulan military order declares martial law anywhere in the Empire and places in action any and all of the current laws. Declaration in this case, established by Jenyu aboard the *Galtizh*, governs only the ship and its passengers. SEE Jenyu.

Master Governors (SS)–Term identifies elected Ssan rulers of city-states. At the time of this mission, thirteen had been assassinated. They included Thur Canbralos of Petur; Kimm Dathrabin of Tanul; Zar Holarnis of Larol; Lefarnus; Kinshaian; and Dur Manarba of Orthun.

Masters (Di)–This tall slender black complexioned female was an *Enterprise* engineer who supervised the team working to repair a number of circuit boards in Engineering following an attack by Rithrim ships.

Mathulsa (S)–One of many ships dumped in Sanctuary's Graveyard of Lost Ships. Some of its tanks were used to store hydrogen. SEE balloon.

Mattie (FD)–This native of Discord was a young Micro female whose cropped orange hair was beginning to grey. SEE Micro.

M'Benga, Geoffrey (Di; WLW)–StarFleet serial number: M324-004 (Mandel *Manual* 17). Described as a "tall, slender, elegant African with a cultured voice" who was trained as a doctor/surgeon (Trimble 190), M'Benga was also well-learned and well-trained in Vulcan medical practices, and having served several years in a Vulcan ward, he was granted his request to serve aboard a StarFleet vessel, being assigned to *Enterprise*. He often was called to treat Spock, once slapping him into consciousness. In Di, Commodore Wesley expressed to Kirk that M'Benga was gaining a reputation "as the new McCoy." In WLW, Spock called him to the briefing room to administer to the group exposed to suldanic gas.

McCoy, David (IT)–Dr. McCoy's young cousin who drowned in a river close by a park where the McCoy family was holding a reunion. The incident stayed with Dr. McCoy for years because he had been just a child then.

McCoy, Leonard Horatio –StarFleet serial number: S-357-977. McCoy was born to David and Eleanor in Georgia, Terra, in 2227, according to Okuda and Okuda (*Chronology* 28) and on January 20, 2218 according to Mandel (*Manual* 21). Records made available to historians may not be as accurate as they should be. However, records do agree that McCoy attended grammar school and high school in Georgia and entered medical training upon graduation from high school, completing his requirements and earning a doctorate from John Hopkins in 2240 (Mandel *Manual* 18). Sources and historians do not agree on the dates for much of McCoy's career during the years between graduation from medical school and assignment to the *Enterprise*. Two separate sources offer conflicting information. He entered medical school, writes Okuda and Okuda (*Chronology* 35; 152), in 2245 and graduated in 2253 and may have worked as a general practitioner at the University of Georgia and then, according to Mandel (*Manual* 18), he returned to Atlanta where he worked at the Atlanta General Hospital for two years and served as staff physician for three years. During these years, he met and married Jocelyn Darnell and they had a child, a girl they named Joanna (Friedman *Shadows*). When the unhappy marriage led to divorce, he enrolled in extensive courses in space medicine. Though his studies and duty left him little time, he never let them and his work interfere with continued contact with his daughter whom he helped become a nurse. Mandel (*Manual* 21) writes that upon completion of his duties at Atlanta General, and his medical studies, he volunteered for StarFleet and was soon dispatched with four other young doctors to the planet Ssan where he met and tended to a young assassin who changed McCoy's views about himself and his chosen work. CONSULT *Shadows on the Sun*. His record indicates he interned in the Federation assistance medical program and was responsible for the inoculation teams on Hydra III and Dramia II (Mandel *Manual* 21). For a time he was stationed on Capella IV as part of a mission (Okuda and Okuda *Chronology* 152). Writing in his report, McCoy noted that the Capelians "were totally uninterested in medical aid or hospitals because of a cultural belief that only the strong should survive" (*FC; Trimble 137). He served on the USS *Hood*, probably his first ship tour of duty, for two years as a surgeon-trainee and then was assigned, by request, to StarFleet's Surgeon General Office (Mandel *Manual* 21). After some time, he sought ship duty and in 2266 was assigned at Kirk's request to be Chief Surgeon on the *Enterprise*, replacing Mark Piper who retired (Mandel *Manual* 22; Okuda and Okuda *Chronology* 40). Kirk gave him the nickname "Bones," which generally was used only by Kirk. McCoy and Kirk had become close friends following McCoy's special care to Kirk and other survivors of Ghioghe (McIntyre *First*). As *Enterprise's* chief medical officer, he served the full five years of missions under the command of Kirk. As the Chief Medical Officer on ship, he had, by StarFleet regulations, broad areas of medical responsibilities, including the right to demand physical as well as psychological examinations for any crew member, even the captain. These responsibilities also extended to any guests traveling on the ship. He was also the "counselor-at-large" to the crew "who [consulted] him about many problems" (Roddenberry *Making* 261). McCoy, who enjoyed his ship duty, and found much of it challenging, always knew he wanted to be a doctor. He prided himself on

being "an old-fashioned general practitioner" who believed a little suffering [was] good
for the soul" (Trimble 191). It took some time to reach this decision, something he
decided during the mission to Ssan when he nearly traded ethics for unforgiving logic
and honor for expedience by allowing the individuals he was treating to become part
of an equation. He had put the life of an assassin above his own desires to play a part
in breaking the assassin code on Ssan (Friedman *Shadows*). It was, however, the events
on Ssan and his role in them that reinforced his belief that to kill is against nature.
He also believed that everyone has a right to exist. Life, to him, was sacred, anywhere.
His attitude toward the Prime Directive stemmed from this belief. Though it declared
no intervention should be taken, McCoy wouldn't accept that "we have to condone
everything that happens in [a] culture or say it's right" (Friedman *Shadows*). A
combination of events convinced him to accept that there are reasons doctors don't
meddle in things beyond medicine. Over the years he became known as a technophobe,
especially regarding anything that removed, for even a short period of time, self-
control from himself, yet he was grateful for medical advances brought about by
technology. His excessive reaction against technology, however, bordered on the
humorous, leading to the assessment that his attitude may be typical of the medical
profession, having emerged in the middle of the 20th century on Terra. No evidence
exists to suggest that this belief ever effected patient care. One historian remarked that
McCoy was "a twenty-second century H. L. Mencken" because he was highly cynical
and used his acid wit (Roddenberry *Making* 239). In reality Dr. McCoy was a bleeding
heart humanist who believed in the dignity and individuality of man. He was the least
militaristic of the crew, yet its most idiosyncratic. His dislike for the transporter was
known ship-wide as "the damnedest way for a man to travel, having his atoms scattered
across the universe." He sincerely believed he was subjected to severe reactions when
being transported and noted that he suffered "a tremor of disorientation [that] started
at the tips of [my] extremities and thrummed inward through [my] discorporeating
body...[my] vision swam...and darkened...as if [I] had been confined to a depravation
tank" (Crandall *Shell*). Often complaining that "microseconds [in the transporter] can
seem like years," he worried Spock with the idea that the McCoy which emerged from
the transporter was not the McCoy that entered (Crandall *Shell*). Spock could not
convince him of the opposite. Though much of his time was spent in Sick Bay or on
some research project, McCoy did enjoy interacting with *Enterprise's* officers and crew.
He and Chekov, from time to time, reviewed the ship's musical library and updated
the holdings (Bonanno *Probe*). Kirk often enticed him to play games, though Kirk
refused to learn the game sheepshead, which McCoy recommended, and when Kirk
introduced him to Riseaway, an anti-gravity game played in the ship's gymnasium, he
soon came to regret it because McCoy consistently beat him (Crandall *Shell*). An early
"game" played with fellow interns which involved discovering how much information
they could learn about a patient from merely silent observation soon had the entire
staff involved. All deductions arrived at were recorded and compared to the final
medical report to be corroborated or refuted. His classmates took to calling him
Sherlock Holmes because he was good at observation. What had begun as a game

suggested by a remark made by a Native-American professor who suggested the doctor should "be where [the patient is] looking," became a life-long habit. McCoy realized his understanding of his observations of a patient helped in determining the illness or injury and treating it accordingly (Crandall *Shell*). A "game" Dr. McCoy always enjoyed for reasons only he could say involved baiting his fellow officer, Spock, in verbal battles. During the mission written about by Victor Milan (*From the Depths*), after Spock completed the analysis of Okeanos' orbit, detailing it in a string of numbers, McCoy declared that Spock came "close to a textbook case of numerolalia." When Spock corrected him, saying the Federation Psychiatric Union did not recognize numerolalia as a syndrome, McCoy's answer was: "It will be...once I publish my paper on you." Regardless of what their bantering did or did not reveal, Spock respected Dr. McCoy and relied upon him to preserve his *katra* until it could be taken to Vulcan (McIntyre *Search*). Medical records reveal McCoy suffered from the rare and once fatal disease, xenopolycythemia (sd5476) and was the first patient to fully recover but only after the application of ancient Fabrini medical techniques (*FW). While on the planet Miri sd2713, he contracted a virus (Mandel *Manual* 22) and on Dramia (sd5276), he was a victim of an auroral plague while on a supply call to that planet (*A/y; Trimble 151). His isolation of a vaccine in both cases resulted in StarFleet Medical awards. While on Minara II, he suffered severe injuries inflicted by the Vians but fully recovered with the aid of a natural empath (*EM). An overdose of cordrazine (sd3234) caused him to enter a state of wild paranoia and led to his fleeing through a time portal to Terra's past (*CEF). After years of acute hay fever, McCoy suffered a severe attack (sd2713) and was treated, successfully eliminating the disease (Mandel *Manual* 22). One item of interest from his psychological records has been noted. It indicates he "reacts quickly and decisively" though his "regard for life often results in hasty and emotionally-charged actions" (Mandel *Manual* 22). He had several interests, one of which was research, which he saw as being similar to what a detective does. He played an important part in a mission to Vulcan when Vulcan had called the question of whether or not to secede from the Federation. He, almost single-handedly, broke the question wide open. Using his detective skills and strong curiosity about who or what would benefit from secession, he uncovered T'Pring as the mastermind of the issue (Duane *World*). StarFleet records show that his father, who was suffering from pyrrhoeuritis, repeatedly requested McCoy remove the life support sustaining him. McCoy did indeed end his father's suffering. Some months later a cure was discovered. The horror of what he had done haunted him for many years until he met Sybok who helped ease him past the pain (Dillard *Final*). Various records reveal a surprising number of involvements with the opposite sex, including several marriages and a few medical problems. Okuda and Okuda (*Encyclopedia* 283) mention his romantic involvement with Emony Dax who was attending a gymnastic competition on Terra around 2245. This was confirmed in later years. Mandel (*Manual* 21-22) reveals he was married to Jocelyn Darnell with whom he had a child. After a few years they divorced. A second marriage to Natira, high priestess of Yonada (sd5476), in a native ceremony was annulled when the Instrument of Obedience was removed (*FW).

McCoy also had been involved with archeologist Nancy Carter (*MT) and Yeoman Tonia Barrows who served for a short time on the *Enterprise* (*SL). "Bones" found himself, many times over, being involved on ship and off in continuing *Enterprise* missions. On one mission he and Spock worked together to identify the cause of hallucinations and fluctuating magnetic pole changes on Nordstral (Graf *Ice*). At the conclusion of that mission he declared to Kirk that the next time Kirk expected him "to go swimming around some planet with millions of tons of freezing water on top of my head, I'm gonna pretend to be a Vulcan. That way, you'll leave me at home." For all of his protestations, he wouldn't have wanted to be left on the ship. The Nordstral mission led him to memories of being a child and spending time in the northern climes of Terra with an uncle and visiting Alaska which he didn't like because of the cold (Bonanno *Probe*) He also recalled that at age seven or eight he attended a McCoy family reunion where he and other boys his age built a raft and went sailing on the river. When the raft broke apart, McCoy, who couldn't swim, was rescued but his cousin David drowned. McCoy never learned to swim and always had a fear of being in water over his head (Graf *Ice*) . Interesting tidbits about Dr. Leonard McCoy reveal he once described Lt. Cmdr. Uhura as being as "delicate as ten-penny tails and as defenseless as a cornered tiger" (Graf *Ice*). He kept, in his quarters, an original set of matched *phornicia* shells symbolizing the healing arts of Magistor Seven. When *Enterprise* 1701 plunged into Genesis' atmosphere they were lost but replaced with a synthetic set (Friedman *Shadows*). He kept a well-stocked liquor supply in his quarters including Saurian brandy. He never liked to drink alone, generally preferring Kirk or Scotty to accompany him. When he drank brandy, he liked it at room temperature and his favorite food was chicken fried steak, one of very few dishes Jocelyn could make (Friedman *Shadows*). His outstanding service to StarFleet and his dedication to the medical field brought him recognition which includes five awards of Valor and six Federation commendations with 14 StarFleet commendations (Rostler 56). Honors also include the Legion of Honor awarded by StarFleet Medical in 2267 and a Resolution of Distinction for his ground-breaking work in a radical new neurosurgical technique to repair damaged cerebral cortex (Okuda and Okuda *Encyclopedia* 293-294). Convicted of murdering Chancellor Gorgon in 2293 and sentenced to the Rura Penthe dilithium mines, McCoy, along with Kirk, was rescued by Spock who discovered the truth of the incident. StarFleet and Klingon records cleared both men of all charges. One of McCoy's StarFleet awards may have been for his part in the solution of this incident. Over the years Dr. McCoy had written many articles. One in particular grew from the incident of the testing of the Intergalactic Inversion Drive. He wrote a particularly interesting article published in the *Journal of the Interstellar College of Xenomedicine* titled "Somatic, Hypersomatic, Psychological, Effects of Exposure to Entropy Loss and 'Secondary Creation Syndrome' in Terrans, Sulamids, Vulcans, Sadrao, and Hamalki" (Duane *Sky*). Close friends and colleagues swear that McCoy could help any patient given the opportunity. They cite his unorthodox treatments that in the end do the job. One such patient involved a Horta. McCoy never ceased to remind his colleagues of his saving the Horta by plastering it with cement (*DD).

Comments from fellow crew reveal a man who always felt he had to know but hated asking for help and felt shamed if he let a patient die because the patient wanted to die (Friedman *Shadows*). John Griffin, writing about *Enterprise's* voyages interviewed Dr. McCoy and recorded him saying: "I'm the man on the spot. I must make, all too often, guesses...But I cannot have the luxury of operating on an unlimited time frame... lives depend upon my decisions" (Rostler 63). In a letter to Captain Kirk on his selection of McCoy as Chief Surgeon, Dr. Joseph Boyce stated: "He's a good man... you can rely on him. Listen to him" (Rostler 60).

McCoy's Pharaoh Syndrome (BD)–Dr. McCoy's suggested dissertation he could have written about Roy Moss whom McCoy considered a very disturbed individual.

McGaven (WLW)–*Enterprise* security guard who accompanied Spock to explore the Kh!lict Control Chamber.

McKelvic (BD)–Member of the pirate ship *Shark*; human.

McLaughlin boys (WLW)–Three youngsters with whom Kirk played during a summer vacation at Kirk's grandparents' Vermont farm.

McLaughlin, Tommy (WLW)–One of three boys with whom Kirk played during a summer vacation in Vermont. Tommy enjoyed creating a set of talking drums, taking their patterns from the Network.

Meahlavion mountain ants (FF)–McCoy indicated his dislike of ambassadors in general by mentioning these tiny insidious insects in a comment about ambassadors.

Mecufi (DC)–Orion police cruiser docked at Sigma One looking for the Andorian physicist Muav Heslev. It attacked the Andorian ship *Shras* believing Heslev was aboard. The *Mecufi* was destroyed when it came too close to the *Hawking* whose containment field had collapsed. SEE *Hawking*.

Medford, Dr. (FF)–Member of the terraforming colony on Beta Canzandia. He attempted to create a casserole of chondrikos. SEE chondrikos.

Medford, Keena (FF)–Daughter of Dr. Medford, a member of the terraforming colony on Beta Canzandia. She followed David Marcus and the other children into the hills above the settlement to keep out of reach of the Klingons.

Mektius (P)–Romulan musician, one of three whose music was considered Orthodox. Several of his compositions were played at the Praetor's funeral as were compositions by Lermas and Talet.

Meladion (SS)–Ssan who replaced assassinated Holarnis as governor of Larol.

Mellon, Cindy (SS)–High school classmate of Kirk's who remembered her as a better dancer than he.

Melville, Herman (BD)–Terran author of the 19th century novel *Moby Dick*. Captain April's words reminded George Kirk of a quote, and he asked if it came from Melville. SEE Quotations.

memoboard (ST)– Similar to a stylo-pad though closer to being a notebook bearing a single message. Memoboard and stylo-pad may refer to the same object though a stylopad employs a stylus to mark the pad while the memoboard might just carry retrievable information.

memory-augmentation/carinal interface (ST)–Directly wired to the wearer's brain, it allows a memory chip to be plugged into the brain, giving immediate access to a foreign language, higher mathematics, rules of various games such as 3-d chess, and other needed information. An entire library of chips are available. The manufacturer of the interface does not guarantee the wearer will understand the supplied information. SEE Hazel Payton. Kirk employed an intradermal transponder and Dr. McCoy chose a Vulcan RNA language series, both similar devices, during their stay on Vulcan (Duane *World*).

Menikki (FF)–Native of Alpha Maluria Six and a member of the Obirrhat religious group. Kirk met with him and Omalas when attempting to settle the dispute between the religious groups. SEE Omalas.

Messenger (P)–One of many titles attached to the Probe; considered as the one who brings a message. In this case the Probe delivered information from its creators to developing life forms on various planets. SEE Probe.

Meteors (Di)–Contending sport team that lost to the Pipers in a magno-ball championship.

Meztorien culture (WLW)–Extinct race whom Dr. Abdul Kaul had studied for more than thirty years. Earliest known sites declared to be Meztorien have been dated to more than 172,500 years old, and Meztorien expansion of that era is well documented. Additional evidence suggests they had space flight and a high level of civilization over 200,000 years before this mission. Studies of this culture have revealed that it often placed orbiting habitats in remote sections of systems they didn't occupy. Studies also support the theory that the culture is believed to have been extinguished by the Darneel invasions. Some of the patterns of jamming fields discovered on Careta IV suggested Meztorien field generators. Some of their devices lacking appropriate power sources were restored to working order for a short time. *Enterprise's* study of Careta IV suggested the Meztoriens explored the system, discovered the Kh!lict artifacts, experienced their danger, and concealed them, placing shielding and jamming devices around the transit frames. SEE Kh!lict.

Miaskovsky (P)–Russian Terran musician considered a significant composer. The Russians referred to him as the "father of the Soviet symphony." One of several Russians Chekov suggested that Dr. McCoy add to *Enterprise's* musical library.

Michaelson (GSR)–*Enterprise* ensign whom Kirk ordered to take Lt. Boles' place because Boles "froze" at his station. SEE Boles.

Micros (FD)–Natives of Discord genetically developed by Eugenicists as pilots of crafts where mass and/or volume are at a premium. Though never more than a meter tall, they have faster than normal reflexes, greater tolerance for g-forces, and keen eyesight. Another name for them is Pixies. SEE Mattie; Discord.

microsteering verniers (ST)–Engineering term for graduated ship thrusters generally used for maneuvering in and around spacedock. Control is accessible on a different system than the general thrusters.

Milan, Victor (FD)–Author of *From the Depths*.

Milky Way Galaxy (P)–Terran identification for the galaxy they inhabit. By the beginning of the 20th century, Terran scientists were agreeing that the galaxy was a spiral galaxy with "arms." As instruments became better and allowed for better images, opinions about the structure changed. In early 2010, scientists were agreeing on the number of "arms" and had named them. To date nine "arms" have been identified: Sagittarius; Scutum; 3KPC; Norma; Crux; Carina; Orion; Perseus; and Outer (Johnson *Star Charts*).

Miller, Sucici (GSR)–Captain of the *Ozcice*, a host entrant in the Great Starship Race whose ship won the third place trophy.

Milton, John (ST)–Terran English poet considered by many to be the greatest poet of the English language. He was also a historian, scholar, pamphleteer, and civil servant. His best known work, and the one Khan often quoted from, is "Paradise Lost" (1667).

Min (FD)–Human female proprietress of the "Min and Bill Pub." Her husband is an Atarakian. SEE Bill.

"Min and Bill Pub" (FD)–This Starbase 23 pub is owned and managed by Min, a Terran female, and her Atarakian husband Bill. SEE Bill.

Miraskin (ST)–*Enterprise* ensign on duty when the message came through from Admiral Nogura. He informed Kirk it was "Eyes Only," meaning it was a private message for Captain Kirk.

Miri (SS)–A young woman who, along with other children, survived a biological experiment that wiped out all the adults and killed each child maturing into adulthood, even though childhood lasted many years. Although some of the *Enterprise* crew were infected, McCoy developed an antitoxin for the virus (*Mi). In SS, McCoy told a young doctor in Sickbay about the virus and the antitoxin during their discussion about the assassins.

missing starships (ST)–A number of ships – Klingon, Romulan, Federation – went missing. No debris or warp trail remained to indicate what could have happened. Spock, who had studied the number of disappearances, concluded to Kirk and Commodore Favere that the Federation would be without a fleet in two Terran solar years if the disappearances continued. Only after his conversation with Dr. Omen could Kirk confirm what happened. Dr. Omen admitted he sent them through an Aleph. SEE Aleph.

Mitachrosian (FF)–Alien group noted for its height, pale-blue eyes and pale white skin that emerges at adulthood. Two tendrils protrude from beneath the jaw line on either side of the face. Klingon Kiruc encountered one in a bar; she probably owned it. SEE Kiruc.

Mitch (GSR)–Crewman on the *Ransom Castle* who was trapped with other crew when Romulans boarded the ship.

Mitchell, Gary (P)–A good friend of Kirk's from their Academy days. He was Kirk's Second Officer and chief navigator until contact with an extragalactic energy barrier increased his psionic abilities and he threatened the *Enterprise*. Kirk was forced to kill him (*WNM). In P, Kirk reminisced about his days at the Academy in San Francisco and the good times he and Gary had.

Mitchell, V. E.–Author of *Enemy Unseen* and *Windows on a Lost World*.

mites (P)–Term the Probe employed to identify what it considered a nuisance.

Moboron, Li (SS)–Native of Ssan who became High Assassin on the death of the former. Li was described as having long, bulbous earlobes and tiny indigo eyes that stared out from beneath bony brows. His successor described him as a "poet [with] remarkable sensitivity and bountiful expression [that] combined two disparate traits into a single, superior intellect." After the government passed a law outlawing assassination, Ki began viewing himself as the agent of his culture and began killing individuals before moving to mass executions to force the government to reinstate or to recognize the right of assassination. One target was the police barracks in the capital city and another was the medical facility where McCoy and four other trainees were stationed. He was killed in a government raid during the Assassin Wars and succeeded by Andrachis.

Moguru (S)–Large red-skinned humanoid whom Kirk, Spock, and McCoy approached to inquire about their missing shuttlecraft grounded on Sanctuary.

Monfarr City (SS)–Located on Beta Aurelon Three. McCoy was here on assignment when he received the news of Merlin Carver's death. SEE Merlin Carver.

Monfarran Union (SS)–Collection of towns and cities of which Monfarra City is the capital located on Beta Aurelon Three. Dr. Janice Taylor sent McCoy a message from here.

Monn Oren City (GSR)–Gullrey city where closing ceremonies for the Great Starship Race were held.

Monroe, Quentin (BD)–A frail ten-year-old brown freckled-faced boy with black hair who was a member of Jim Kirk's gang. His fear of heights caused him to "freeze" up and he would have died attempting to cross a rope walkway, had Kirk not saved him.

Montoya (SS)–StarFleet commodore of Starbase Twelve. This petite woman with strong cheekbones wore her long raven-black hair braided in a long club. She briefed Kirk, Spock, McCoy, and Scotty on the Ssan situation, then delivered StarFleet orders that they were to make contact with the assassin renegades and negotiate a peaceful settlement. She included the diplomat team of Clay and Jocelyn Treadway to the negotiating group.

Moog, Robert (P)–In the early days of 1960 on Terra, attention was being given to electronic music. Moog is credited with the first design types of compact synthesizers that supplied an extended range of possibilities for sound manipulation. Once the design was in place, composers wrote pieces just for synthesizers.

Mora, Donald (S)–As one of StarFleet's oldest captains at age eighty, and a foremost expert on oceanography, he was assigned the captaincy of the *Neptune*, an oceanic research ship sent to Sanctuary by StarFleet. He hoped to open discussion with Sanctuary about their aquatic life. Whey they refused to respond, he and Scotty beamed one million irradiated Regulan locusts larvae into Sanctuary's oceans. They got a response.

Morehouse, David Reed (SG)–Captain of the *Dei Gratia* and discoverer of the abandoned *Mary Celeste*. SEE *Mary Celeste*.

Morse Code (BD; WLW)– A Terran code invented in the early 20th century composed of character encoding that transmits telegraphic information using long and short bursts of sound. In BD, Captain Alma Roth of the *Bill of Rights* sent a distress message using this code and some of Lonteen's Light, another code. In WLW, the Kirk/Kh!lict created a Morse Code by flashing long and short bursts of different colors across its carapace to signal to Spock.

Morison, Rory Dall (IT)–Well known native Terran Scottish Highland Harper who died in 1713. SEE Bracken.

Mortagh Outpost Three (UC)–This understaffed and underfunded decaying Klingon post on the far edge of Klingon-controlled space was the least sought after post because of its isolation and near lack of equipment. Personnel used outdated scanners with no visual display. Smugglers creeping across the border were generally ignored. Even *Enterprise* under Spock's command passed this station and was mistaken for a smuggler.

Morvain (P)–Romulan subcommander on the *Galtigh*. Captain Hiran felt sure of his intelligence and allegiance. SEE Hiran.

Moss, Big Rex (BD)–A 300+ pound human father to Roy Moss and a pirate member of the *Shark*. He killed Captain Angus Burgoyne and took command and even admitted to his son he'd killed the boy's mother. He was electrocuted in the cargo hold of the *Shark* as Jim Kirk and Roy Moss watched.

moss rose (DC)–One of many plant forms Sulu had in his collection, destroyed when someone searched his cabin.

Moss, Roy John (BD)–Human. Son of Rex Moss. He wore his long hair in a ponytail. Roy at nineteen and Kirk at sixteen met when he was a member of the *Shark* crew and Kirk was its captive. Roy admitted the crew had discovered technology at the ruins on Faramond. One application allowed the *Shark* to enter the Blue Zone around a neutron star. Roy was probably responsible for his father's death. After seven years at a rehab colony he was released. He chose to return to Faramond. He wanted to do something great, spending 45 years at that effort and believing all those years that the Federation had stolen ideas from him. During his time at Faramond, he discovered a long-distance transporter but failed to consider the machinery that allowed for its use was gone. In his attempt to activate the machinery, he destroyed Faramond. He lived the rest of his life with the thought that he'd destroyed Faramond and all the knowledge it could have provided. Dr. McCoy considered that he suffered from Huetra's Emperor Syndrome. Kirk's final words to him were that he'd be famous as "the biggest buffoon of all time."

Mother City (FF)–Term used to identify the main city and its government location on Alpha Maluria Six.

Mount Rushmore (BD)–A national memorial park located in Keystone, North Dakota, USA. A colossal granite sculpture by Gutzon Borglum commemorates four U. S. Presidents: George Washington, Thomas Jefferson, Abraham Lincoln, and Theodore Roosevelt. When dealing with his wayward son, George Kirk often felt as stiff and stoney as one of these men.

Mozart's *Twenty-third* (P)–Famous musical composition by Wolfgang Amadeus Mozart, Austrian composer who lived in 18th century. In P, Andrew Penalt concluded his *Enterprise* concert with this piece. SEE Andrew Penalt.

Mr. Highpockets (GSR)–One of several derogatory titles Nancy Ransom called Kirk.

muguto (FD)–Alternate spellings: mugatu; mugato. According to Trimble, who spells it as mugato, this is a Nerualese great ape with red face, hands, and feet and a large horn projecting from the forehead (198). Its bite is poisonous unless countered by a mako root (*PLW). In FD, provoked by Moriah Wayne who insisted Federation law prohibited the keeping of dangerous life-forms in personal quarters, Kirk asked Sulu, in jest, if he had a mugatu or a Denebian slime devil in his cabin.

Muhanti (IT)–Of Indian descent, this member of the *Soroya's* crew had been doing his duty as the ship's doctor until he began suffering, though he never knew it, from the effects of the magnetic fields on Nordstral. The effects led him to believe he had discovered a new science he called phrenology. McCoy did not appear to believe him and in an attack on McCoy, he slashed McCoy's hand. When the *Soroya* suffered damage to its Bridge during a seaquake, it was believed Muhanti had died, but he survived and locked McCoy and Nuie in the ship's medical lab. He tried to kill McCoy a second time, attacking him in the engine room as McCoy stood watch over the oxygen generator. Kirk fought with Muhanti who died as a result of a fall against a bulkhead. SEE Nuie.

Mullen (DC)–*Enterprise* ensign stationed at the Bridge phaser station.

Munchkinland (SG)–McCoy likened his reactions to his experiences aboard the *Reltah* to Dorothy's on her arrival in Munchkinland. His reference is to the diminutive inhabitants encountered by Dorothy, a character from the Terran novel *The Wizard of Oz* by Frank Baum.

Munkwhite (BD)–The large dirty male member of the *Shark* was rendered unconscious by George Kirk with a hypodermic and put in a storage unit.

Muta (S)–This doctor, trapped on Sanctuary along with others, practiced holistic medicine for those in need. McCoy watched him employ his seven fingers on one hand and eight on the other to repair wounds sustained in a brawl.

mycelium (FD)–A vegetative portion of a fungus consisting of a mass of branching thread-like filaments. Sulu kept one in his quarters for a while. SEE walking slime mold.

mylezan (WLW)–Dr. McCoy treated those crew exposed to suldanic gas with this.

Nanclus (UC)– Romulan ambassador to the UFP and part of the conspiracy along with StarFleet Admiral Cartwright and Klingon General Chang to disrupt Gorkon's peace initiative. All three were captured at Khitomer along with others.

nanthken (WLW)–A rabbit-like creature domesticated as food for the Kh!lict.

Nairobi, Bradford (WLW)–*Enterprise* security guard who was pushed through a transit frame and emerged as a Kh!lict. He was killed by another Kh!lict. Dr. McCoy's autopsy determined the dead Kh!lict had contained Nairobi's persona.

Natira (SS)–High priestess of the Fabrini people on their space ship Yonada. For a while she and McCoy, who believed he was dying of an uncurable disease, were married. When he was healed, she helped gain his release from the Yonada computer. In SS, Jocelyn, McCoy's former wife, told Kirk she knew about Natira and several others.

Naval Construction Contract 1701-A (BD)–Reference is to *Enterprise* 1701-A.

Naval Exploration Extension 2010 (BD)–In 2010, new guidelines were adopted for UFP's extension of exploration. SEE USS *Bill of Rights*; Alma Roth.

navigational shields (Di)–According to Okuda and Okuda (*Encyclopedia* 317), these shields are created by "a powerful forward-looking directional force-beam generator [that is] used to push aside debris, meteoroids, microscopic particulates, and other objects that might collide with the ship." Starship captains have employed these shields for a variety of purposes. In Di, Chekov suggested using these shields to protect the Beta Xaridian Four colony. After Spock calibrated and re-aligned them, Kirk told Chekov to handle the activation. Their application created a narrow but very effective barrier spread along the perimeter of the colony.

N–dimension (ST)–Mathematics surrounding n–dimension "postulates the universe extends in many directions beyond the three of space and one of time...dimensions eleven through twenty-seven are...small dimensions...[that] do not extend...," Spock related this in reply to Kirk's inquiry of what n–dimensions were.

Network (WLW)–Planet-wide internet service available to everyone.

New Malurians (GSR)–The ship, *Unpardonable*, from New Malura and captained by Lauria ifan Ta, had unfamiliar engine emissions.

New Pride of Baltimore (GSR)–Captain Miles Glover X ran this ship under the flag of Baltimore, US, Terra. It won first prize for the Great Starship Race. SEE *El Sol;* Great Starship Race.

Neptune (S)–StarFleet science vessel that specialized in studying ocean worlds; captained by Donald Mora.

New Cetacean Institute (P)–This 23rd century marine biology study center is located in the Coral Sea off the coast of northern Australia. After George and Gracie, two humpback whales were retrieved from Terra's 1980s, the institution became the center for care and sturdy of the two mammals. CONSULT *The Voyage Home* by Vonda McIntyre.

Neutral Zone (P)–An area approximately one light year across that divides the Romulan Empire territory from Federation territory. Frequently identified as the Romulan Neutral Zone by the Federation and the Federation Neutral Zone by the Romulans. Following a conflict between these two entities in 2160, fought with primitive atomic weapons, a peace treaty was reached, negotiated by subspace with no visuals (Okuda and Okuda *Encyclopedia* 427). The main provision declared that neither side would enter the designated area for to do so would constitute an act of war. SEE Romulan/Federation War.

neutron radiation (UC)–Spock detected high amounts of this radiation coming from the *Enterprise* shortly after Gorkon's ship was fired upon. He informed Kirk of two possibilities why this radiation would be noted: breach in the matter-antimatter reactor unit or the ship's photon torpedoes were armed and locked on target. Thorough investigation by Spock led him to conclude the radiation came from a cloaked ship hiding beneath the *Enterprise*. It had fired on *Kronos One*.

neutron star (BD)–Formed when a massive sun having passed through its supernova phase quite rapidly collapsed into a ball a few kilometers across. Though it continues to acquire matter due to its intense gravity, it is expected to eventually collapse into a black hole. Its sphere of influence is projected as a blue color on the sensor scans, hence the term Blue Zone. SEE Blue Zone.

Nhym (IT)–Young native Kitka whom Uhura befriended. She called Uhura "Kraken Eyes" because the first time she saw Uhura, Uhura was wearing protective goggles. She invited Uhura to her home. Nhym probably was killed in an icequake that demolished her village.

Nik'nash (FF)–A Klingon clan. SEE Grael.

Niles, Dara (WLW)–This *Enterprise* lieutenant was a biologist who accompanied Spock to investigate the Kh!lict Control Chamber.

Noel, Doctor (Di)–*Enterprise* medical personnel whom Commodore Wesley actively recruited.

Nogura (ST)–This slight silver-haired Oriental with dark eyes and a calm demeanor was a Commander Fleet Admiral who came to the post a few years before Kirk completed his first five-year mission. Upon taking the post, Nogura immediately erased all references to his age and birth from both the private and public memory banks of the Federation. Through the years he insulted many officers, ordered a few to duty they believed was beneath them, and assigned ships to missions only on his word, but in all he had guided StarFleet to its golden heights. A few years into his position, those under his immediate command began referring to him as "the old Man" (SW; LY). Kirk's orders for the initial mission in ST came from Nogura's office but were delivered by an aide.

Nonnatus (IT)–This Terran Spanish saint, who lived from 1204-1240, was born by Caesarean section in the region of Catalonia, Spain. His sainthood made him liked by pregnant women giving birth and midwives ("Nonnatus" Wikipedia). SEE Risa; Nordstral.

Noonien-Singh, Khan (FD)–A human product of genetic engineering in the early Terran 20th century who became one of the "selective bred supermen" (Trimble 117). At the height of his career, he ruled a fourth of Terra from 1992-1996 which included the area from South Asia to the Middle East and influenced other areas. Overthrown near the end of the century, he and 897 of his followers, also "selective bred supermen," escaped in a "sleeper" ship called the *Botany Bay*. Evidence suggests that before Khan left Terra, he exploded several nuclear devices in the Middle East in the area known as Iran (Ferguson *Flag*). Some hundreds of years later, on stardate 3192.1, *Enterprise* discovered the "sleeper" ship drifting in space. Dr. McCoy was able to awaken about 80 of the inhabitants, including Khan who almost immediately set about gaining control of the ship. Lt. Marla McGivers, a member of *Enterprise's* Historical section, fell in love with Khan but helped Kirk outwit him. To avoid potential future trouble with Khan, Kirk enacted an administrative ruling, in the year 2267, and settled Khan, McGivers, who chose to go with him, and the other 80 "supermen and superwomen" on Ceti Alpha V (Okuda and Okuda *Chronology* 49, 73). Kirk did not anticipate the resilience of the group. With all the abilities the group had, they managed to survive the devastation to the system when Ceti Alpha VI exploded, causing a shift in the orbits of the remaining planets. Khan and his survivors were released from the "hell" of Alpha V when Captain Terrell of the *Reliant* came to the planet believing it was Alpha VI to determine if it was devoid of all life and could be used by Drs. Carol and David Marcus for their Genesis project. Through the use of Cetic eels, Khan gained control of Captain Terrell and his officer Pavel Chekov and learned of the Genesis project and that Kirk still lived. With the *Reliant* in his control, Khan stranded most of its crew on Alpha V and went in search of the Genesis device and Kirk. He went to Regula I space station and took the device, leaving a frustrated Kirk in the bowels of an asteroid. In a second confrontation, Kirk, knowing Khan did not fully understand maneuvering in space, was able to destroy the *Reliant* and all aboard (McIntyre *Khan*). At his death, Khan released the destruction of the Genesis device. With considerable irony, the Variants of Discord owe their existence to Khan and those who created him (FD). SEE Variants; Discord. CONSULT Geoffrey Mandel's *Officer's Manual* for two articles about eugenic experimentation.

Nordstral (IT)–On discovering this ice-bound planet and noting its population was sentient, StarFleet released much of their collected data. It included the statement that the planet was an extremely cold place with iceberg-dotted oceans. Another item of data noted at first contact revealed the planet had no axial tilt and exhibited no seasons. The varied lifeforms were tied directly to the conditions of the seas, and the largest predator was a sea animal likened to a kraken. Noted also was the fact that the natives could leave the surface of their planet only for a brief time. Of much interest to various companies was rich plankton flourishing in the seas. The Nordstral Pharmaceutical Company won rights to harvest the plankton, shipping tons of it off planet. When too many of its employees began exhibiting signs of insanity, the company contacted StarFleet Command which sent *Enterprise* to investigate. On arriving, *Enterprise* learned that off-worlders had to wear insulated clothing and protective goggles against the harsh temperatures and strong sunlight. *Enterprise* also collected data on the constantly shifting transient magnetic fields, brutal boreal winds especially in northern latitudes, periods of magnetic calm, pole reversals, and tectonic disturbances (earthquakes and seaquakes) linked to pole reversals. Kirk assigned Spock to study Nordstral's problems. Spock soon concluded that other magnetic components had to be involved in the magnetic fields shocks, that the pole reversals were happening every 30 hours with a progressive decrease in calm periods, and that auroral intensity was increasing at all latitudes. He also concluded that the oceans of plankton which provided oxygen for the planet were also contributing to the planet's magnetic fields. The drastic problems had begun soon after the harvesting of the plankton began. His studies also led him to declare that the absence of much of the magnetic bioto were causing the storm conditions. At McCoy's suggestion, and with Spock's help, they cloned trillions of tons of the plankton and re-seeded the oceans, estimating the planet's magnetic fields would stabilize in 14 days from the beginning of the seeding. McCoy decided the illness that effected those humans who had worked on the harvesters was caused by the fluctuation in the magnetic fields. They recovered, as did the planet, once the fields were restored. With the help of StarFleet's Environmental Bureau, Nordstral developed a method of extracting plankton, but maintaining a healthy supply in the oceans. SEE kraken.

Nordstral Pharmaceutical (IT)–Privately owned company developed the medical/food benefits from the Nordstral plankton. Shortly after the discovery, the company erected their orbital space station *Curie* to process the material for shipping. It also built and employed two shuttles and three ocean harvesters. Until the arrival of the station and the harvesting of the plankton, the planet had no drastic magnetic changes. When Spock, with help from *Enterprise's* Science Department, discovered the causes of the swift magnetic changes, the cure was implemented by seeding the oceans with millions of plankton. The scientists on the *Curie* began initiating ways to obtain the plankton *and* maintain the stability of the planet. SEE Nordstral.

Nordstral landing party equipment (IT)–Kirk assigned Chief of *Enterprise* Security Chekov to conduct the rescue of the stranded Nordstral Pharmaceuticals' planetary research team. The following items, along with others, were part of Chekov's equipment required for his five-man team: Chekov, Uhura, Howard, Publicker, and Tenzing. The items were: shielded packs, lanterns, insulation suits with close fitting inner body slips, a garment that conserves body heat, emergency medikit for each person, powered winch, phasers, suit breather filters, reflective goggles, food packets, and two tents.

Norm (FD)–Shortened term for Normal; referring to a non-altered human being. SEE Variants.

North Skunk River (BD)–Located in Mahaska County, Iowa, north of Rubia, Iowa. A jute rope footbridge spanning the river collapsed from the weight of Jim Kirk and his gang.

not-under command light (BD)–While a ship is in port its exterior lights flash a blue light between the flash of two red lights which are vertical to the ship's lines. This indicates the ship is temporarily out of service.

Nuie (IT)–This male native Kitka of Nordstral with heavy cheek bones, green eyes, and copper-colored complexion was a crewmember of the harvester *Soroya*. Following the kraken attack, he aided McCoy in the ship's sick bay and saved his life. Deeming death imminent, he would have committed suicide, but McCoy convinced him to live. His knowledge and expertise of the ocean and of the harvester *Soroya* may have led to his taking command of it sometime after its captain's death.

Nurturer (P)–A title given to the Probe by those who knew it had "seeded" several planets.

Nyar, Talika (WLW)–She exhibited sturdy bones and powerful muscles of her native high-gravity planet Djelifa, a matriarchal society which had recently joined the Federation. She was described as short and wide with mousey-brown hair, a large beak-like nose, and a low gravelly voice. Dr. Abdul Kaul selected her to be an assistant on this mission as she was a post-doctoral research student. Sent to the surface of Careta IV, she teamed with Chekov to survey several site ruins. An accident forced her through a transit frame, and she was transformed into a Kh!lict. The Kirk/Kh!lict communicated the Nyar/Kh!lict and she entered the proper code to ensure the *Enterprise*/Kh!lict crewmen were transformed back to their original form and person. Her experiences convinced her to agree with Kirk that Careta IV should be quarantined.

Nyssay (SG)–*Enterprise* ensign at Bridge Communications when the *Reltah* was sighted.

Oates, Sam (GSR)–This young crewman on the *Ransom Castle* helped McCoy treat several injured crew and helped capture boarding Romulans.

O'Boyle, Andy (GSR)–Crewman on the *Ransom Castle*.

Obirrhat (FF)–One of two religious groups native to Alpha Maluria Six. SEE Manteil/Obirrhat quarrel.

Obirrhat Holy Book (FF)–Three religious books containing tenets of belief held by the Obirrhat. Kirk and Scotty were allowed to read them and Kirk found in them the solution to the quarrel between the Obirrhat and the Manteil. SEE Manteil/Obirrhat quarrel.

Obirrhat sacred precincts (FF)–The Obirrhat hold certain cities sacred. These cities have narrow winding cobblestoned paths between two or three story buildings with an inner open-air market. Many of the cities have ruined statuary of women and children carrying arms full of flowers. Kirk and Scotty devised a plan to save the sacred cities from the sacred cubaya. SEE Manteil/Obirrhat quarrel; fireblossoms.

Ocean of Discord (FD)–Since less than 3% of Discord is surface land, the 97% water is considered a single ocean.

Officer's Mess (ST)–On Starbase 12, this mess was decorated much the same as the rest of the base, in the U.S. western motif. Cavalry flags in shreds hung across the front walls and other similar items according to the wishes of Commodore Favere. SEE Favere.

Oghir (FF)–This large powerfully built Klingon was one of two personal guards for Kruge. SEE Kruge.

Okeanos (FD)–Planet name given by the Susuru to the same planet the Variants named Discord.

Okeanians (FD)–Designation employed by StarFleet to identify those sentient beings believed to be native to the planet they called Okeanos. SEE Discord..

Okenga (BD)–Andorian engineer on the *Shark* was killed when the LC4 rammed it, and it lost its gravity compensator. SEE *Shark*.

Okrona (UC)–Ship captained by Klaa.

Old Culture (BD)–Identifies the race which once occupied Faramond. Evidence suggested the entire civilization went someplace else via a massive transporter system whose power source apparently went with them.

Old Hemcree (S)–A lunk native to Sanctuary's waters; it lived in the waters around the island of Khyming. Kirk, Spock, and McCoy had a near fatal encounter with this creature. SEE lunk.

Old Ironsides (FD)–Nickname given to the Terran USS *Constitution* launched in 1787 as a three-masted heavy sailing frigate. The name was won during battles with the British because the cannon balls bounced off her sides. The history of the ship is on display along with the ship berthed at Peir 1, Charlestown Naval Yard, Boston. Kirk displayed a model of the ship in his quarters behind which he kept a bottle of Saurian whiskey.

Old Lucy (FD)–At around 200 years old, this ancient 200 hundred ton, 50 meter long prawn-like animal is a native to Discord. Though considered nonaggressive, she is kept away from Discord cities and ranches by sonics. To identify her, an identifying waverider crest had been laser burned into her back, thick as battle plate armor.

Omaha (BD)–Major city of Nebraska, USA, Terra. Jimmy Kirk and his gang planned to hop a dynacarrier here to take them to South America.

Omalas (FF)–This hunched and aged native of Alpha Maluria Six was a member of the Obirrhat religious group, representing the Obirrhat on the government council. He allowed Kirk and Scotty to read the Obirrhat sacred texts. SEE Manteil/Obirrhat quarrel.

Omen, Barbara (ST)–Daughter of Professor Omen, She was a crew member of the scout ship *Crocket* and was killed in the battle with Klingons.

Omen, Professor (ST)–This brilliant scientist was described as little taller than medium with a cultured voice, a muscular build, black eyes, and a pleasant smile partially hidden by a black beard that framed his face. His only daughter, Barbara, was killed aboard a starship in a small battle skirmish. Omen brooded over her death even as he helped develop the latest generation of weapons for StarFleet ships, and though most of his staff considered him the chief designer of phasers and photon torpedoes, they did not know his attitude was becoming anti-military. Since he had no close friends, no one questioned him periodically disappearing for months at a time. Several years after his oddly announced disappearances, he revealed a new phase shield generator. With the help of Conrad Franklin Kent, arrangements were made for the tests to take place at StarBase 12. Following the initial test, he lured the *Enterprise* away from the base and sent it into an Aleph. When the *Enterprise* returned, Kirk and a small landing party went aboard the asteroid that hid Omen's machinery. In a discussion with Kirk, Omen declared he'd "designed a weapon of peace," and believed he had killed no one when he sent ships through the Aleph. Refusing to be captured, Omen opened an Aleph and entered it. His legacy to StarFleet included the perfection of the phaser and photon torpedo, an augmented tractor, phased deflectors, and the Aleph. SEE *Erehwon*.

Omen's inventions (ST)–SEE Omen.

Omicron Delta (SS)–While listening to Jocelyn Treadway tell the story of how she and McCoy met, married, and then divorced, Kirk remembered the adventures on the shore-leave amusement planet (*OUP/a; SL).

Ondarken (DC)–Orion commander of the *Umyfymu*.

Operation Retrieve (UC)–Admirals Smillie and Cartwright's plan, designated by this title and formulated to rescue Kirk and McCoy from Rura Penthe, was presented by Colonel West to Federation President Ra-ghoratrei. SEE Colonel West.

Ophane star cluster (P)–Home to silicon-based creatures who have very little metabolic rate.

Orchestra (P)–Group composed of various Federation musicians conducted by Andrew Penalt. Comparable to a group on the Romulan. Both groups were part of a peace initiative being conducted at Termais Four.

Orders for Peace Initiative (P)–This began with a Romulan message to the Federation. It had six parts offered by the Romulans. SEE Romulan agenda.

Oregon Trail (BD)–One of the main overland migration routes across the northern section of the U.S. The years from 1841-1869 saw the most travelers. The route generally ran from Missouri to Oregon. During Kirk's youth, an above-ground tube train, called the Stampede, traveling close to 900 kmp, followed the original trail. Jim Kirk had plans for his gang to travel a portion of this trail to the coast on this train.

Organia (UC)– Home world to a powerful species who are non-corporeal. They put a stop to the Klingon/Federation conflict and imposed a peace treaty between them (*EM).

Organians (UC)–Non-corporeal beings discovered on a planet both the Klingon Empire and the UFP claimed imposed the Organian Peace Treaty, but in a few years the Klingons tested the treaty by killing settlers at Kudao. It was theorized that the Klingon actions were linked to the disappearances of the Organians, and though StarFleet attempted to contact them concerning the Klingon violation, it got no response (UC).

Organian Peace Treaty (FD)–Imposed by Organians and effecting both the Federation and the Klingon Empire, it settled the question of how a planet could be claimed: it would go to whichever one showed it could develop it efficiently. An additional section noted that forces of each side could take shore leave at the other's bases (*TT).

Orions (DC)–An occupied region in the vicinity of Rigel VIII with a government and a military. The Federation considers them mainly pirates. Their blood is a rusty orange in color.

Orion Chrome-5 (FD)–A form of Orion music humans consider a jarring unstable series of sounds.

Orion dance-fighting (FD)–A form of martial arts similar to Brazilian *capoeira* but employs elaborate movements often described as dancing. SEE *capoeira*.

Orion ship (S)–One of several ships that patrolled above Sanctuary. Scotty destroyed it when it fired on the balloon carrying Kirk, Spock, and McCoy.

Orion T-class destroyer (DC)–A type of military vessel. SEE *Umyfymu*.

Orion Trapezium (BD)–Term StarFleet uses to identify the trapezoidal shape of Orion claimed space.

Orion Union (GSR)–Area of space claimed by Orions consisting of planets and systems governed and patrolled by Orion ships. They entered their ship *Ytaho*, commanded by Legarratlinya in the Great StarShip Race.

Orland, John (GSR)–Broad chested, about 40, with black hair and salt and pepper mustache. A chemist by trade, he ran a youth rally on Rigel 12 before being appointed chairman of the Race Committee through the efforts of his brother-in-law, a UFP diplomat. Orland spoke to the assembled group at Starbase 10, outlining the purpose and rules of the Race. Knowing he couldn't deal with the Romulans, he requested Kirk do so.

Orphan cultures (WLW)–The quadrant where the Dulcipher star cluster is located contains "an anomalously high number of 'orphan' archaeological sites that have no context," according to Spock's report. Spock also considered "orphan" cultures in this area could be explained by the violent encounters with the Kh!lict. At the conclusion of the mission, Dr. Meredith Lassiter included in her report the statement that by using "references Mr. Spock discovered in his computer search and the evidence of carvings, it is clear that the Kh!lict exterminated every intelligent race they ever encountered. [This] accounts for 73% of 'orphan' cultures [indicated] by direct reference to Kh!lict carvings that show these people being killed."

Orrien (SG)–This Romulan was the only survivor of a beaming party to the *Reltah*. He told his commander Telris about the creature, his attempt to trick the *Enterprise* boarding party, and the likelihood that no one survived the creature. SEE *Reltah* creature.

Orthodoxy (P)–Translation of a Romulan term that identifies anything acceptable to the ruling Praetor and the present government.

Orthun (SS)–A city-state once represented by Zar Holarnis. After his assassination, Meladion became master governor. Orthun was represented by Dur Manarba in the initial talks with Kirk and the Federation diplomats.

Osso (GSR)–One of three Rey who were on board *Enterprise* during the Great Starship Race. He stayed the entire time in his assigned quarters. SEE Rey; Tom; Royenne.

Otello (P)–During her visit to the Lincoln Center, Uhura saw some of the stage sets for this Shakespearean play being prepared for presentation. The plot of the play centers on Iago who is angered that he had been ignored in favor of Otello who was given the higher military position. Iago plans to ruin Otello by leading him to believe his wife Desdemona is unfaithful. Otello is led to believe it so and kills her but when he discovers she was faithful commits suicide.

Ouija board (Di)–Considered a spirit board or talking board, it is a flat board marked with letters, numbers, and symbols used to communicate with spirits. A small-heart shaped moveable object known as a planchette is used to spell out messages. Participants place their fingertips on the planchette which then moves about the board hitting on individual letters that eventually spell out words. Kirk told Commodore Wesley that the *Enterprise* was going to Parathu'ul to prove the link to the raiders. If his plan didn't work, then he might have to consult a Ouija board.

Oxford (BD)–Noted university town located in England, Terra. Captain April came from the area around the town.

Ozcice (GSR)–Host entrant in the Great Starship Race. Captained by Sucice Miller under the Gullrey Flag, the ship won the third place trophy.

Paek (DC)–Female *Enterprise* ensign of Korean ancestry. Member of Chekov's Security team.

Pajwl (FD)–Klingon vessel lost during a skirmish between it and several Variant vessels. SEE Varient.

Palmer (Di: WLW)–Second officer in *Enterprise's* Communication section. She served on the *Trudeau*, a smaller ship than the *Enterprise*, and had asked to be transferred to the *Enterprise* because of its reputation. She told Chekov that "everyone makes mistakes. But we're supposed to learn and prosper by the learning. At least that's what Mr. Spock tells me whenever I screw up."

palm reader (FD)–Used by the native of Discord, this hand-held computer is similar to a 21st century Terran blackberry.

pandree (WLW)–A python-like Vulcan animal that creates a pseudo-random pattern to attract prey into its sand traps.

panic channel (BD)–Any signal coming over the lowest grad signal capacity is considered a "last resort." An academy student gave it this term signifying that all other out-going signals could not be sent or had already been sent.

Pantazian (SG)–A type of silk considered by to be the finest known.

Paragran (S)–A ship in the Graveyard of Lost Ships whose insulation was used in McCoy's balloon. SEE balloon.

Parath'aa (Di)–Humanoid race native to Parathu'ul. Initial contact described the people as having thin skin, nearly translucent with shadows and hints of their inner workings quite visible. The skin on their faces is tightly drawn with eyes that seem to float in their sockets. Mouth and teeth are set in a permanent grin. Their appearance gave rise to the nickname Dead Heads. Parath'aa dislike being touched and when meeting an outsider they bow at the waist which seem to sit just below the armpit. Though the government is totalitarian, most of the people are orderly and mannerly and occupy clean cities. When they applied to become a member of the Federation, the team sent to review their application reported the government declared it allowed no dissent, easily killing dissenters rather than torturing them first, believing a quick death more "merciful." Their application was denied when it became evident they sought membership solely for access to more advanced technology. At the time of the initial review, their space vessels employed conventional warp with standard phaser arrays and photon torpedoes. Denied membership, the Parath'aa hired mercenaries to raid nearby Federation colonies, stealing equipment which went to their paid Federation scientists to build into weapons. One such weapon was a plasma cannon. Defeated in their attempt to subjugate the Cygni Maxima system, Kirk forced them to return everything stolen, destroy all weapon designs, and cease hostilities.

Parathu'ul (Di)–Planet designated by StarFleet as Aleph Xaridian Five. The natives of the planet call it Parathu'ul which translates as "our world."

Pardek (UC)–Romulan assistant to Ambassador Nanclus. See Nanclus.

Parnell (P)–*Enterprise* lieutenant who often served at the Bridge Science Station. He notified Spock that three Romulans had beamed to the inside cavern on the Probe. SEE Probe.

Parness Planet (FF)–Ambassador Farquahr negotiated a successful treaty here. SEE Farquahr.

particle accelerator (ST)–Early in Terra's 20th century when particle accelerators were being built, they were described as a device used in electric fields to propel ions to high speeds and contain them in well-defined beams. The definition seemed to be accurate into the 23rd century. Kirk informed Captain Iola that his cyclor had a microscopic defect in the accelerator. SEE Iola.

passion bloom (FD)–Orange-colored flower native to Discord. Jason Strick gave one to Uhura. SEE Jason Strick.

Payton's recordings (ST)–Hazel Payton, aide to Conrad Franklin Kent, had recorded everything she was a witness to during the Aleph incident, beginning with her arrival on the *Enterprise* at Pegasus IV to the final meeting between Kirk and Kent. She edited all the materials for a complete report submitted to Kent along with her resignation.

Payton's sensor (ST)–SEE memory augmentation.

Payton, Hazel (ST)–A stunning, dark-haired human female known as "the woman who gets the job done." She served for several years as Conrad Franklin Kent's aide. Engaged to Commodore Favere of Starbase 12, she married him following the mission detailed in *The Starship Trap*. Her main task, for which Kent hired her, was to collect all images of and materials relating to him, including video-taping him anytime he was in public. To do this with ease and comfort, she wore a sensory enhancer that many mistook as a jewel nestled in her hair, and she had a cranial interface that recorded everything happening in her presence. Material thus collected could be replayed and edited. One of the demands Kent made to Kirk was that he take her on the *Enterprise* so that she could record what happened during the test at Starbase 12. After she signed a release, exempting StarFleet of any responsibility, Kirk allowed her on the *Enterprise* and while she was on board *Enterprise* was engulfed by the Aleph. During the time she was in the first Aleph, she reported to Dr. McCoy that she experienced hallucinations which he concluded were being created by the effects of the Aleph on her equipment. It was her equipment that allowed Spock and Scotty to study the Aleph and devise a means of exiting it. After returning to Starbase 12, she informed Kent he would no longer have her services after she completed her report about the past events. Her experience in the Aleph decided the issue of whether or not to marry Favere.

Pegasus IV (ST)–This planet's daytime temperatures reach 37 Celius with an atmosphere barely breathable for humanoids who require supplemental oxygen in order to work there. It is not a Federation member. The only native form of life is identified as G'lops. Its natural weathering by the corrosive wind and volcanic activity create beautiful sculptures. Neither the sculptures nor the G'lops are sufficient reason for interest. However the 10% daystromite found there is. The *Enterprise*, ordered here by Nogura, picked up civilian passengers. SEE daystromite; G'lops.

Penalt, Andrew (P)–This large broad bearish man with a bone-crushing handshake who liked everyone to call him Andy was a noted Terran conductor and pianist with political connections. He enjoyed being center stage, deliberately making a last minute entrance. Only two of his compositions are ever mentioned, and his "Symphony for the Nine" is the only composition to gain any wide spread recognition. Some critics credit his wife with most of the composing. His operetta called "The Drunken Irishman," which the critics panned, was hardly ever presented though he always managed to force mention of it into the conversation. Included in the Federation group of musicians and archeologists, he deliberately decided he would be the only musician to play the first night the two groups met. His presentation was "considered by some to be a display of extremely loud playing with so much great strength and dexterity that he appeared to hammer the piano keys. His bobbing head and shoulders along with tortured looks that twisted his features repulsed many in the audience" noted one member in a private letter home. After the encounter with the Probe was resolved, he wrote a Probe concert. Agreement is that it will probably not be produced. When Dr. Benar and Jandra presented their concert, he labeled their music "derivative" though he didn't outright accuse them of plagiarism. He did write that their composition was "nothing more than variations on a theme."

Penarthil (SS)–This native Ssan second governor supported Zar Holarnis' decision about keeping his movements secret. SEE Zar Holarnis.

Pentathlon of Alpha Centauri (GSR)–An athletic contest consisting of five events with each athlete participating in every one. John Orland mentioned this race, along with others, to emphasize the fact that the Great Starship Race was a real race, with real rules, and a real winner.

penthorbaline (SS)–A drug in McCoy's medical cabinet used to stabilize security officer Diaz for surgery. SEE Diaz.

perestroika (P)–Russian term translated as "restructuring" and often employed with another Russian term, *glasnost*.

Perils of Space Rescue Response Clause (BD)–A StarFleet command clause that allows emergency actions to be taken by the captain without consulting a superior. Kirk gave Uhura this order when *Enterprise* experienced a flushback. Her entry into the ship's log identified time, stardate, circumstances, and decision to act without headquarter consent. All outgoing communications from the ship were closed until Kirk ordered them open. SEE flushback.

Perren IX (WLW)–Home planet to the University of Nexqualy. SEE Abdul Kaul.

Peterson (Di)–Sulu enjoyed flirting with this auburn-haired lieutenant on the *Enterprise*.

Peterson (SS)–*Enterprise* security officer who accompanied Kirk, Spock, and the Treadways to the surface of Ssan was killed by an assassin. SEE Diaz.

Peterson, Maxwell (DC)–Given a high recommendation for the position of Commodore of Sigma One by Kirk, its was Peterson who ordered *Enterprise* to carry out the *Kongo's* assignment. SEE *USS Kongo*.

petroglyph (P)–A carving or inscription on rock. Dajan discovered several on a newly acquired Romulan colony world. He was removed from the archeology dig before he had time to study them or to take readings of them. SEE Dajan.

Pfeffer, Will (FF)–One of the children of Beta Canzandia colony who chose to follow David Marcus into the hills to avoid capture by the Klingons. He had red curly hair and freckles.

Phartharas (FF)–These natives of Alpha Maluria Six made good alcoholic drinks.

phased force field (ST)–Omen created a method of producing such a field and installed the machinery on his ship. It is believed these shields operated by enveloping a ship, planet, building, etc., and their shield strength was limited by the strength of materials used to build the generators for the starship. Omen strengthened the polarity of the field by modifying the delta hyperdyne allowing for switching the field off and on thousands of times every nano-second.

phased shield generator (ST)–Machinery that enables a ship to protect itself by raising shields around it.

Pheranna (FF)–Klingon name for the planet UFP called Beta Canzandia Three being terraformed by Federation scientists.

***phornicia* shells** (SS; FF)–McCoy kept a matched set of these shells in his personal quarters. They symbolized the healing arts on Magistor Seven similar to Terra's caduceus. McCoy was told when he purchased them that holding one to the ear allowed one to hear the voices of all whose lives had been saved by that listener. McCoy's original set was destroyed along with the original *Enterprise* at Genesis.

photo-imaging (S)–Every StarFleet ship carries a lab that can produce studies of planet images. *Enterprise's* lab informed Scotty of the balloon rising from Sanctuary's surface. SEE balloon.

phrenology (IT)–Shown to be a false medical pursuit as an analytical method based on the fact that certain mental faculties and characters traits are indicated by the contours of the skull. Dr. Muhanti insanely believed in it. SEE Muhanti.

Physics Lab (ST)–Deck 2 on *Enterprise* 1701.

piano (P)–Terran musical keyboard instrument. Romulans had declared it un-Orthodox and forbade anyone playing it. When the government ordered all to be destroyed, one in the back Provinces escaped. Jandra had access to it and learned how to play it. SEE Jandra.

Pike, Christopher (SS)–Captain of the *Enterprise* sent to take charge of Dr. Vincent Bando on charges of murder and to deliver him to Terra for trial. CONSULT *Star Trek Reader's Reference to the Novels: 1990-1991.*

Pilenna (S)–Green-skinned Orion female captain of the *Gezary*. She and Scotty spent some time together, and she got him to clean and repair her ship in exchange for contacting the Senites on Sanctuary.

Pipers (Di)–Champions of the latest magno-ball game, having beaten the Meteors.

Pitharese (Di)–*Enterprise* lieutenant in the astronomy section who had been dating Ensign Berganza.

Pitur (SS)–The third largest city-state on Ssan. Governor Thur Cambralos was assassinated and Sarennor became governor. The city-state's council chambers were destroyed by an assassin's bomb during the time trainee McCoy was there as part of StarFleet's medical corps.

Pixies (FD)–SEE Micros.

Planet Earth (ST)–Inside the second Aleph that delivered *Enterprise* to another dimension, geographical features of the single planet there matched to within 1% those of Terra. Sensor sweeps reported plant life, simple animal forms, a natural magnetic field, no humans, and no chemicals in the atmosphere indicating industrialization.

Planetside Assembly (GSR)–Main governmental body on Gullrey.

plasma cannon (Di)–SEE Parath'aa. StarFleet scientists had developed a plasma cannon to the manufacturing stage and had built a small-scale model whose testing with limited range caused great damage. Scotty called it a "treacherous beastie [using] ionized gas with electrons and positive ions combined...to neutralize the electrical charge and allow it to be controlled through magnetic fields." When this occurred and it contacted a force shield, the result was devastating. StarFleet had no good reason to include the cannon on a starship, especially since it taxed the warp engines beyond their safety limits.

plekt (P)–A twelve-stringed Romulan instrument Jandra was ordered to play at the Praetor's funeral.

Plumtree (ST)–*Enterprise* ensign described as thin with sandy hair and a worried expression. He helped Dr. Omen set up his equipment for the phased field generator tests.

Pogue, Sarah (BD)– Woman with straw-colored blond hair. She was the doctor on April's *Enterprise* and later became his wife.

Pointy Ears (S)–Term Billiwog used to identify Spock. SEE Billiwog.

poker (ST)–A popular card game played by nearly every sentient race encountered. The rules may differ slightly but the intensity is the same. Hundreds of forms that exist differ only in the details. Names generally identify the rules: draw, closed, open, stud, and freak or dealer's choice. Though Spock could hold his own in the game, he much preferred chess for its logical moves.

pon far (SG)–The term is fully understood in the context of the Vulcan marriage ritual. It may be the ritual. CONSULT *Star Trek Reader's Reference to the Novels: 1984-1987* for a fuller explanation.

Population Two Stars (FD)–All stars are classified One or Two. Those of Two are stars that are extremely old and believed to have formed at the creation of the galaxy (Bradley 52-53).

Port Apt (GSR)–Human colony near Alpha Centauri settled by immigrants from Arkansas, U.S. Terra and named for Port Apt, Arkansas, established in 1920. The colony is now 200 times the size of the original namesake which was of the Confederate frame of mind. The colonists enjoy a thriving industrial business and entrepreneurship. The small size of its government allows full participation.

potatoes (BD)–A slang term used by StarFleet drydock workers when referring to small work bees, one-man vessels. The bays where they are kept are called pantries.

Praetor (P)–Romulan ruler at the time of this mission. Considered third in rank, he was first in power. Shortly after he lost his hearing, he established the Orthodoxy, a list of all books, plays, music, instruments, etc., he did not like. No one, short of a penalty, would dare ignore the list ordered posted on all Romulan-controlled worlds. He also had a list of books, plays, music, instruments, etc., which he allowed and a list of musicians who could compose or present. Included in his last set of orders was that Jandra should play at his funeral. He died just before the Romulan and Federation groups met at Termais Four. His body was placed in the Hall of Columns in the Central Septum of the capital city for all to pay their last respects. The funeral lasted for two nights and a day.

prawn (FD)–On Discord these egg-laying marine animals are a major food source for other marine animals. They range in size from infants to a full-grown human male to adults that can reach 200 tons or more. A funnel-shaped mouth sucks microscopic sea life for food. Young prawns give off a waxy substance between the scutes of their belly which is scrapped off and after processing, produces substances used in a number of pharmaceuticals and cosmetics.

Praxis (UC)–This moon of Qo'noS had been used as a key energy production facility until 2293 when a massive explosion ripped the satellite apart, causing severe damage to the homeworld. Insufficient safety precautions and over mining caused the reactor to overload and explode, sending out several high energy waves detected by *Excelsior*. As a result of the explosion, StarFleet determined the Klingon Empire had slightly less than 50 years of life. Qo'noS suffered an instability of its orbit that had to be corrected. Its ozone was polluted and fear rose that it might compromise the health of the planet. Estimates of lost energy was set at 80%. This explosion and its future problems led the Empire to seek peace negotiations with the Federation.

President of the Federation Council (P)–The Council is the governing body of the Federation with main offices located in San Francisco, Terra. It also holds power over StarFleet. The President of the Federation is not President of the Council. The President of the Council is elected from the Council membership while the President of the Federation is elected in a federation-wide election based on popular vote. SEE Federation Council.

Presidio (P)–During Kirk's time this old military installation become part of the Golden Gate Park environment. As a cadet Kirk liked to walk its park-like lawns and enjoy its wind-sculptured stands of trees.

Prester (FD)–German SS general who engineered genetic projects during World War II. Aileea dinAthos mentioned this general to Kirk who had wondered where she got the term "hind" for the giant hinds native to Discord. SEE Aileea dinAthos.

Primus Oran (GSR)–This Romulan captain of the *Scorah*, a large man with sunken eyes and an angular shaped head, had an injured foot and a reputation for ignoring circumstances and blundering in, often with success.

Principles of Exploration (FD)–When Kirk took this StarFleet required course, Douglas Satanta was the lecturer. SEE Douglas Satanta.

Priority One (IT)–One of a series of StarFleet emergency protocols. This one states starship personnel outrank their equivalent planetary authorities. Chekov quoted this rule to Nicholas Steno, commander of the *Curie*. SEE *Curie*; Nicholai Steno.

Probe, The (P)–Novel by Margaret Bonnano. A few months after the alien vessel identified as the Probe left Terra after conversing with the two humpback whales George and Gracie, the Romulan Praetor died. One of the first actions of the Interim Government was to issue an invitation to the Federation to form a joint archeological expedition to an empty world in the Neutral Zone. Their invitation included six provisions the Federation was to agree to. Both parties made arrangements. The *Enterprise* conducted the Federation's scientists and a full orchestra with their instruments to Termais Four. The joint effort began unraveling the ruins discovered there. The venture didn't start well with ill feelings in both camps, caused by an attempt to kill Kirk and the Romulan captain, missing data collected at the site, and the accusation by the Romulan ambassador that Ambassador Riley via the Federation had sent the Probe to attack Romulan worlds. Interest turned from the planet to the Probe, which after reviewing all its data, decided to return and converse again with George and Gracie. The *Enterprise* and the Romulan made contact and both landing parties learned the history of the Probe and met its creators via holograms. Spock with considerable help exchanged information with and devised a new plan for the Probe.

Probe (P)–Alien constructed artifact described as a long dark cylinder-shaped object with a ball-shaped object that protrudes from the bottom and may serve as a communication device. Few ships got a good view of it and none were able to scan it. It threatened Terra. One report made by Spock indicated the oceans were heated "by direct physical acceleration of the water's molecules...capable of effecting trillions of individual molecules simultaneously...[and] capable of reversing polarity thousands of times a second in a...random pattern." The Probe caused much damage until Kirk with Spock's help determined it was seeking to communicate with whales. None existed on Terra, having been hunted to extinction in the late 1990s. To save Terra, Kirk relied on Spock to program the Klingon ship which they had captured at Genesis and slingshot it and his crew around the sun and back in time. They arrived in the 1980s, were able to repair the ship, locate and beam two whales on board, and return to their own Terran timeline. The two whales, though young, were able to effect some degree of communication with the Probe which returned the seas and atmosphere to normal and left the solar system. Spock assured StarFleet Command that the Probe would return to check on the conditions of the whales because he was convinced they and the Probe had communicated. The song of the whales had never been translated and the few efforts made to do so ceased when the population died out. No one had discerned any of the content of the song, knowing only for sure that it was the male who did the singing. To ensure Terra's and the whales survival, the New Cetacean Institute was instructed to study and to care for them, with the hope of reviving the species though a breeding program. CONSULT *The Voyage Home* by Vonda McIntyre. Satisfied with what it learned from George and Gracie, the Probe left the Sol System after reversing the damage it had caused. Its path led it past Starbase Nine and Thirteen in the area of old First Federation-held territory. Eventually its course took it toward Romulan/Federation Neutral Zone and Romulan-held territory. Romulan High Command was informed of the Probe's route but they chose to deny such a thing existed. Its route took it quite close to Termais Four, a planet in the Neutral Zone and then on toward a world whose sentient beings had, in a minor way, communicated with the Probe on a previous journey. What the Probe encountered at the planet determined its actions. It destroyed the "mites" preying on this world known as Wlaariivi by the Romulans, having colonized it. Settlers were in the process of destroying life in its oceans, something the Probe did not allow to continue. When word reached Romulan High Command that the colonies on this world were gone, ships were sent to locate the Probe and destroy it. After confirming the Probe's previous course and its present course, High Command accused the Federation of creating the Probe and programming it to destroy Romulan worlds. *Enterprise* was on a mission to Termais Four when Kirk received word about the destruction at Wlaariivi. When confronted by the Romulan Captain Hiran, Kirk gave him all of *Enterprise's* records about the Probe, including what had happened to Terra. Convinced that the Federation was not involved, Captain Hiran joined with Kirk tracking the Probe and attempting communication. If no communication could be made they would destroy it. Word went to the Romulan ships tracking the Probe to forward all data directly to the *Enterprise*. First Officer Spock was given data from all tracking ships. Masses of data required the combined efforts of crews from both ships to access. After reviewing the record of events at Terra and his own personal notes, Spock recalled an image from his mindmeld with Gracie of beings similar to George and Gracie. After some study, Spock reported that he believed the creators of the Probe were similar to Terran whales and had probably developed telekinetic powers to develop machines to amplify their powers, telling Kirk that communication was "some form of mental energy, analogous to telekinesis." With good evidence, Spock theorized that intelligent beings without opposable thumbs would discover other means of manipulating their world. Some factor might lead to a meaning assigned to a fragment of sound, then to others. Super memories would develop and become the equivalent to written records. As their minds developed, they allowed the storing, retrieving, and manipulating of massive amounts of information, in this case musical. Only, Spock cautioned, after a thorough study of the Probe, would his reasoning be found accurate or not. The patrolling ships, staying just outside of provoking the Probe, continued to send data to the *Enterprise*. In time, various bits of acceptable data were discovered. It was concluded that the Probe employed some form of unknown and undetectable energy. When that energy would be released could not be determined nor could the time between the discharge of energy and the time it hit its target, though the consensus was the energy was a form of tractor beam. Also concluded was its ability to navigate by identifying star positions even if they had changed. Spock with Uhura and Jandra's help studied the sounds. The two women concluded the sounds were a language, citing their musical backgrounds as enabling them to identify patterns. Romulan and StarFleet ships continued to follow the Probe and soon reported it had slowed and reversed course. Its new course would pass Wlariivi, heading toward Terra. Kirk and Hiran agreed it must be stopped and the way to do that was to either communicate with it or board it and seek out its controls. Scotty modified *Enterprise's* tractor beam to function as a "voice" and a message was sent. The Probe reached out to the two ships, *Enterprise* and *Galtizh,* and drew them closer to it, capturing them. Spock employed his time studying the Probe and determined no living being inhabited the Probe, though he detected "much material, including the otherwise metallic shell and the crystalline object it extrudes on occasion,...that in some senses could be organic." His sensors also detected a "ten-meter block of crystalline material in the heart of the Probe, but of a different form of crystal from that which makes up the extruded object....the structure of the material... is similar to the so-called crystal memory [taken] from the Exodus Hall on Temaris Four." Continued study led to the accumulation of massive amounts of data. The following is a very brief summary. After the Probe became "aware" that the "mites" were possibly sentient and might have an inkling of the True Language, the Probe decided it did not have the necessary instructions to deal with the problem. It was a paradox of how the "mites" could speak the Language, yet not speak it. Only by returning to its creators, taking the metallic bubbles (ships) with it would it find an answer. It set its course and traveled at excesses of warp twelve, according to *Enterprise's* sensors, moving through the Orion and Sagittarius arms. After communications were established, it was learned that the Probe had attempted to contact its home world. When no reply came back, the Probe stopped in a position of 120 degrees around the galactic disk almost on the opposite side of the Shapley Center from the Federation. Sensors indicated it stopped at its home world, unsure of its proper move. *Enterprise's* sensors located a domed area with breathable air some meters below ground to which Kirk led an away team that included Spock. The Romulans also sent a team. By some trial and error, the teams learned many things. First, that the Probe had been designed and built to seek out life similar to its creators. If it could not find similar life, it was to prepare the planet for new life. Having found developing life on Terra, the Probe marked it for a revisit which occurred in early 2286 (Okuda and Okuda *Encyclopedia* 388). Second, that some 30,000 parsecs from its home world and 193 millennia after its creation, it lost part of its memory in a confrontation with what later was determined to be the Borg. Third, that the message it received from the "mites" (*Galtizh*) was the message it had sent to every passing world, a greeting, history, and invitation in an attempt to communicate with sentient life. It found no evidence that anything it met spoke the True Language. Together, Romulan and Federation teams learned that at one time a marginally class-M planet existed. Yet all they discovered was a planet with no life signs almost buried in 300,000 year old ice, debris from satellites, and some evidence of an advanced civilization. Geological studies suggested an asteroid impact resulted in the covering of the planet with ash. The same studies revealed an artificial cavern with a crystal identical to the one on the Probe and to the one found in the Exodus Hall on Temaris Four. Fourth, evidence revealed the creators of the Probe were huge leviathan-life creatures, McCoy dubbed "superdolphins," who communicated via sonic holograms. By studying the images, it was learned that some of the creators had chosen to leave their planet in what they called a Winnowing. A second Winnowing came after an attack by Borg-like ships followed by an attempt to recall the Probe. Knowing its Probe could not return in time to save them, the creators built ships, filling and launching them in a hundred different directions. Kirk's landing team, led by Spock achieved limited communication. Kirk had Spock send a message. The Probe detected two phrases, "there is no danger" and "time to talk" and recognizing these established communications with Spock. He was able to expand the creators' definition of intelligence to include technologically advanced "mites." He also modified the creators' goals. The Probe should continue searching for its creators but be aware of life-forms both similar and dissimilar to its creators and be aware that even "mites" had a place in the rightful scheme of things in the universe. Spock, however, could not restore its lost memory. When the re-programming was complete, the Probe returned the *Enterprise* and *Galtizh* to Temaris Four. Spock told Kirk that the Probe had come to be known by many names – Messenger, Wanderer, Traveler, Seeker, Communicator, Protector, Nurturer, Recorder – during its wanderings. The joint operation between Romulans and humans led both to a new level of understanding between them.

Prokofiev, Sergei (P)–Noted 20th century Terran Russian composer, pianist and conductor highly admired during his life. Chekov wanted Dr. McCoy to consider adding his works to *Enterprise's* musical library.

Protector (P)–Title bestowed upon the Probe for it protected creatures that might someday become like its Creator. SEE Probe.

Provinces (P)–Translated from a Romulan term that identifies farthest planets and regions of the Empire. For a military member to be sent here is considered a demotion. Few careers survive duty here.

Proxima Beta (GSR)–The entrant *Dominion of Proxima* in the Great Starship Race flew the flag of this government.

Prufrock's World (ST)–Planet whose main evolutionary level had reached crustaceans. The world was named by Eliot, a communication officer on *Enterprise*, who identified crustaceans as one life form and mistook their claw-clackings as an enemy code. Being familiar with Prufrock, the name of the elderly character in the T. S. Eliot poem by the same title, he thought the title appropriate.

pyrrhoneuritis (SS)–McCoy's father died of complications from this condition.

p'tach (ST)–Klingon noun that may refer to an animal carved and served at meals.

Publicker (IT)–*Enterprise* security officer and a member of Chekov's Nordstral rescue team who was killed while fleeing Alion and his group. Though Chekov had to leave his body behind to save the others of his team, it was retrieved at a later time. SEE Alion.

Puleomua, Sonny (FD)–Native of Discord, citizen of the city Harmony, and a cousin to Hannes who lived in the city Storm. While monitoring the fusion reactor he discovered a nuclear device had been beamed into his office. He died along with all the residents.

purls (F)–Klingon-known herding animal indigenous only to the northern continent of Qo'noS; hates fireblossoms. SEE fireblossoms.

Purviance, Lindsey (DC)–Tall, heavy set man assigned to Commodore Peterson's office. He arrested Chekov on charges of damaging a store and placed him in detention, then released him and accompanied him to the *Enterprise*. On the ship, Purviance became the liaison officer to the efficiency auditors and was believed to have been killed along with Genron and Sweeney, *Enterprise* crewmen. However, it was learned later that Purviance had been killed while still on Sigma One and an Orion searching for the trans-shield anode had taken his place. Failing to find it, he damaged the *Hawking* shuttle by placing an over-loaded phaser near the warp core. He was killed during the battle among Kirk's crew, the Andorian ship, and the Orions.

pyar-**runes** (WLW)–Kh!lict markings discovered on the transit frames. SEE transit frames.

Qara-Qitay (FD)–This Discord city is a "loose sprawling collection of metal structures anodized into shades of gold and yellow," one *Enterprise* crewman noted in his report. It is known as the electronic manufacturing plant of the planet.

Qas (FD)–Klingon; brother to Kain. SEE Kain.

Qighpej (FD)–Klingon term translated as "agonizer booth," device used to both punish a crewman and to extract information. Each Klingon cruiser generally has one on board.

QoDang (FD)–The Klingon name of Kain's father is translated as Krodan.

Q'reygh (FD)–Klingon computer technician whom Captain Kain ordered to break into *Enterprise's* computer core.

qrokhang (UC)–A Catullin liquor highly prized for its fiery taste and enormous effects.

rabbit and briar patch (P)–The President of the Federation informed Kirk and crew that Romulus had suggested the Federation not send Sarek in any capacity to Termais Four. McCoy, on hearing the news, insisted that Sarek should be sent and reminded Spock of the old Terran tale "Brer Rabbit and the Briar Patch." When the rabbit was caught by the fox, he begged the fox not to throw him in the briar patch as that would be a cruel and unusual punishment. Instead the fox should immediately eat him. Wanting the rabbit to suffer, the fox tossed him in the briar patch, failing to realize the patch was protective territory for the rabbit.

radical Romulan reforms (P)–Following the Praetor's death, the Interim Government liberalized the government by simplifying an unwielding bureaucracy, eliminating government corruption, and increasing efficiency of production in industry and agriculture. It also opened prisons and released all political prisoners, established free trade with non-Federation worlds, abolished the Banned Lists, and granted freedom to scientists, artists, writers, etc.

Ra-ghoratrei (UC)–A pale skinned, white-haired male Deltan president of UFP. He and Chancellor Atzebur shared the dias at Camp Khitomer Peace Conference and were the targets for assassination.

Rakatau (FD)–City on Discord located in the Sea of Storms near sea mounts mined for their resources. The residents also built ships and floating habitations.

Rak'hon (S)–Captain Garvak's Klingon cruiser was orbiting Sanctuary per Council order.

Ramen'aa (FF)–Klingon texts written by Kahless. SEE Appendix B: Quotations.

Rand, Janice (SG; Di; UC)–StarFleet serial number: CTE 086-496 (Mandel *Manual* 16). Much of what is known about Janice Rand was uncovered by Vonda McIntyre when she wrote about Kirk's first official mission (*First*). McIntyre revealed that Rand's early life was quite hard. She was orphaned with two younger brothers to raise after the family was caught in a space accident that left her older by three years. The ship carrying them deposited the Rand family on Saweoure. After her parents died, she was forced to accept help even though help came in the form of servitude. Determined to find a way off planet, Rand soon was able to sneak herself and her brothers Ben and

Sirri onto a cargo shuttle where they hid in a crate of relief supplies. The shuttle took them to Faience where they ended up in a refugee camp. Authorities there deemed Rand of age and issued birth certificates for all three and gave her custody of her brothers. Within a few months, she enrolled them in good boarding schools and joined StarFleet service in the quartermaster section. Her experience on Saweoure served her well for when Kirk requested a yeoman, the quartermaster assigned her. She came to *Enterprise* 1701 a fearful child of nearly seventeen although she had passed herself off as being over twenty-one. Her blue eyes and atrociously cut blond hair reinforced her subservient manner to anyone with whom she came in contact. She began her duties as Kirk's yeoman, doing executive paperwork, arranging his schedule, reminding him of changes to it, handling problems or referring them to the proper departments, and registering the ship's log and seeing that Kirk signed it, among other tasks. Unaware that the yeoman position came with an office, Kirk seated her at a desk on the Bridge near the environmental systems station until Dr. McCoy pointed out that a yeoman's cabin was provided, a few doors away from Kirk's quarters on Deck 5. Afraid of nearly everything and everyone, Rand constantly apologized. When Uhura heard Kirk giving Rand a strict talking to about her appearance, she stepped in and talked with Rand. Uhura soon got the story of Rand's early life, how she came to be on the *Enterprise*, and why her uniforms never fitted. Uhura urged Rand to file charges against the Saweoure citizen who had kept her and her brothers as servants. Letting that matter drop, Uhura moved Rand into the yeoman's cabin, helped her get settled, and replicated several quality fitting uniforms. Having learned how Roswind, Rand's cabin mate, treated Rand, Uhura played a trick on Roswind. With Dr. McCoy's help, Uhura placed a large blob of regen culture made to resemble a sentient being in Roswind's quarters after moving Rand to the yeoman's cabin. It took a few days before Roswind understood what she had done to Rand and she apologized. Soon Kirk noticed changes in Rand, came to appreciate her work as his yeoman, and noted the quality of his coffee was the result of her making it fresh each morning. When members of the Worldmind came aboard, Rand was with the group who met them. For a few minutes, Rand interacted with them. All of these events increased her self-confidence, and she determined to let her hair grow and "do something fancy with it." In a few months most of the crew were commenting on her elaborate basket-weave hair arrangement (McIntyre *First Adventure*). During the years of Kirk's first five-year mission, Rand completed medical training and served with Dr. McCoy in Sick Bay, trained for transporter position, and worked on qualifying for StarFleet Academy. She completed her training as an ER nurse and ably assisted Dr. McCoy with the injured (Corey *Abode*). Kirk encouraged her to continue her studies. She sometimes was included on landing teams. As an away-team member to Mercan, a planet in the void between Orion and Sagittarius Arms, she served as the team's historian (DeWeese *Attack*). Her training as a transporter operator resulted in her working that ship position as a back-up member of the team (Mitchell *Enemy*) and eventually being appointed Transporter Chief for Terra (Roddenberry *Picture*). During one mission, she was assigned duty at one of the ship's transporter stations (Crandall *Shell*). By the time of the mission to Rithra,

Janice Rand had already transferred off ship (David *Disinherited*). Rand's training paid off, and Sulu requested she be assigned to his ship *Excelsior* crew. She sat at Communications. On his order she sent Sulu's message that *Excelsior* stood ready to give aid to Qo'noS, but it was rejected. She also sent his message to *Enterprise* that the ship and crew were ready to assist Kirk (Dillard *Country*).

Ranit (FD)–Female native of Discord. A meter-tall Mircro and a member of the Waverider Ranch. She and Yuki work together. SEE Yuki.

Ransom Carnvale Interstellar Mining Company (GSR)–Privately owned family company run by Nancy Ransom; specialized in ore shipping.

Ransom Castle (GSR)–This entrant in the Great Starship Race captained by Nancy Ransom ran under the flag of Ransom Carnvale Interstellar Mining Company. Though boarded by Romulans who attempted to place sheets of lithium hydride about the warp core to create a bomb, she and her crew, with McCoy's help, and a group of *Enterprise* security, led a counter attack and won back the ship. The *Ransom* was a cargo ship with few amenities. It was arranged along its horizontal axis beginning forward with the commons (eating and sleeping alcoves), followed by the kitchen quadrangle with a walkway, above which were kept the dry stores and a solarium above the dry stores area, a lazaret, ore bunker, wet stores, then cargo bunkers, coop stores that were reinforced airtight removable wall sections, and finally the engine room at the stern end.

Ransom, Nancy (GSR)–Those who knew this Captain of the *Ransom Castle* often described her as self-confident, suspicious and refractory, resistant when pushed, hard working, and a believer in the values of the Southern Confederacy. She had a "draft horse work ethic" which was the most infectious trait about her according to Mike Frarey, though she tended to blame others when something failed. She kept the family-built and owned Ransom Carnvale Interstellar Mining Company in the black, having built it to its success without government help. Her family background was U. S. southern military, her ancestors having migrated from Port Apt, Arkansas to Alpha Centauri. To show where her sympathies lay she flew the Stars and Bars on the *Ransom Castle*. During her Academy days, when she had been a member of Kirk's cadet command team in a competition, Kirk berated her for not keeping up her part in the game and entered his impressions into the record. She came to intensely dislike Kirk and eventually blamed him for her being washed out of the Academy. She fought along side her crew to regain control of her ship when Romulans boarded.

Reborning (S)–A Senite developed process, based on their religious beliefs, in which male humanoids were physically and mentally changed into Senites. Male fugitives, thinking they had escaped to paradise, were subjected to a sleep-inducing trance and then transported to a huge cavern located in the mountains close to Dohama. The cavern could hold hundreds of wagons of sedated male captives transported in coffin-like cages by flatbed wagons. As each wagon passed into the cavern, it was subjected to intense radiation that cleansed them. Along the towering walls were hundreds of levels of rooms where the males were kept prior to their surgery. On the floor of the cavern, hundreds of metal operating tables awaited patients. As each sedate captive was removed from a cage, each was checked for life signs, with non-humanoid beings discarded and probably disposed of. Those chosen were placed in the small rooms lining the walls until time to be strapped on tables. The process of Reborning consisted of Seven Holy Steps. <u>Harvesting</u> consisted of a once-a-year selection of male captives from the village of Dohama who were sedated and carried to the Reborning site. <u>Selection</u> consisted of inspecting each male to determine his health and rejecting those deemed unfit and discarding those who had died in route. <u>Cleansing</u> consisted of placing a chosen male on a hospital table, inspecting to see that he had been thoroughly irradiated when passing into the cavern before washing him and removing all his hair. <u>Operation</u> consisted of two parts. One part erased all memories of a previous life and new memories were inserted. Physical surgery performed on each selected candidate removed the genitalia. <u>Hormonal treatments</u> removed all residual traces of gender, and cosmetic surgery employed electrolysis to ensure a uniform and pleasing appearance. <u>Recovery</u> allowed the patient time to recuperate from the surgery and time for each to be eased into the community. Finally, <u>Training</u> completed a total of 70 days to ensure loyal and devoted members of the Senite community.

Recorder (P)–One of many titles given to the Probe for it kept data on all that it encountered during its long journey per its creators' instructions. SEE Probe.

Red (S)–Nickname for one of the stranded survivors who came to Sanctuary. He was a member of a group of eight composed of a Gorn, a Tellarite, an Orion, two Klingons, and three humans who found Kirk, Spock, and McCoy a few hours after they landed.

Red Talon (GSR)–Romulan military battle cruiser captained by Valdus. Hidden in the walls of the Bridge were molded panels of lithium hydride to be fastened to the warp core of a chosen vessel which would be plunged into Gullrey. Valdus' efforts to wrap *Ransom Castle's* warp core were thwarted by Nancy Ransom and her crew. With orders from Valdus, second-in-command Romar took *Red Talon* to Gullrey, intending to destroy it. Kirk's use of a pencil-thin phaser pulse to destroy the ship by igniting the remaining lithium hydride it carried. SEE Valdus.

Reechi (DC)–*Enterprise* ensign in Security.

Reed, Francis Drake (BD)–This friend of George Kirk's spoke with clipped Trinidad English, liked to play poker, and was jokingly referred to as Lt. Jamaica or Lt. Trinidad by his ship mates. He was a Security officer on Captain Robert April's *Enterprise*.

Reelan (P)–Romulan and older brother to Dajan and Jandra. He was given charge of captives taken at Kalis Three. When one escaped, his superiors held him responsible. Shortly thereafter, he was executed, and his parents were forced to commit suicide. His sister and brother Dajan and Jandra were exiled to the Provinces.

reformers (P)–Term Romulan Jenya employed whenever he referred to the present Interim Government. SEE Jenya.

Reggae drum section (BD)–Reggae is a music genre developed in Jamaica, Terra, late 1960s. The term denotes a particular rhythmic style. Included in the instruments used is a selection of drums. Apparently Francis Reed enjoyed the music and playing in a group. SEE Francis Reed.

Regulan locusts (S)–This insect native to a Regulan planet was kept as larvae on board the *Neptune* to be used as food for other marine animals collected by the research vessel. Captain Nora and Scotty sent more than a million to Sanctuary's oceans in the hope that when they hatched they would create a plague and get the attention of the Senites who had refused to talk with Scotty. The adult insect is quite large in comparison to the Terran variety.

Regulan wine (S)–Native alcoholic drink from Regulus. Scotty and Pilenna shared the remains of a bottle. SEE Pilenna.

Regulation 2477.3 (S)–Prohibits deliberately falsifying ship's records. Spock attempted to quote this to Kirk when Kirk agreed to let the ship's records show the pirate Auk-rex died on Sanctuary. SEE Auk-rek.

Regulation 727.9 (S)–A sub-section of Operations Regulations that prohibits endangering a prisoner's life; thus Kirk could not take Renna in the balloon with him, Spock, and McCoy. SEE balloon.

Reichert (FD)– This large-boned man with curly blond hair was a member of *Enterprise's* security personnel. Following Kirk's regaining control of the *Enterprise* from the Klingons, he ordered Reichert to assist Van Pelt and escort the Klingons to the Brig. Kirk included him in the boarding party to the Klingon ship *Dagger.* SEE Van Pelt,

Reltah (SG)–The name of the Romulan space station whose entire personnel were killed by a space creature. Documents found in the central control room stated Kashi was its commander. Also revealed was the indication that the *Reltah* was the first of her kind, a radical move away from the xenophobic attitude to which Romulans steadfastly held. The multi-level station was much larger than the *Enterprise.* Its grey-green hull revealed unusual lines and angles with protrusions at all angles. McCoy's report declared it "looked like an unruly planet" while Spock reported that it had "a striking resemblance to early Klingon prototype stations." Scotty's engineering crew report contained the notation that the outer hull was pocked and scratched with evidence of collisions with space debris. When *Enterprise* detected it, the station was traveling inside Federation territory at impulse speed and drifting. No life signs were detected with the initial scan. This was proven correct after the boarding party searched the station. McCoy, after dealing with a number of dead, deduced that many had died from hypothermia while some died from spinal fractures and concussions. The boarding party's reports gave access to the following information. Stairs and lifts connected the levels while lengths and directions were confusing. Suggestion by one boarding member was that this confusion probably helped security. The corridor leading to the Bridge and Botanical Garden ended in a T. Entrance to the Bridge was gained off a short corridor that was mirrored on the other end of the T and led to a turbo lift. The station's Bridge had wide windows circling the area and could be shielded by heavy panels. Nearby were small lounges with black upholstered furniture. Walls were devoid of decoration. A small botanical garden also occupied the level with the Bridge, its dead withered plants a reminder of life on the station. The large station's central office, probably occupied by the station commander, took up as much space as the Bridge. A large desk sat in the central portion with two computer screens and keyboards embedded flush to its surface. A series of twelve-inch viewscreens allowed observations of various areas of the station, as well as its personnel. These faced the deck across several feet of empty space. A group of lockers created the wall behind the desk. On one level, a large area labeled as a mini-mall had radiating corridors containing shops, bars, and restaurants. An amphitheater with vaulted ceiling was discovered filled with Romulans, all dead from hypothermia. In the mess hall food packs strewn across the floor indicated attempts to utilize the food. The transporter room, to which the boarding team had been beamed, had ten elliptical pods on a deck set flush into the floor. The operator's console was massive, a bulky contraption set behind a transparent protective wall. A number of cross corridors intersected the corridor to the transporter room, but no doors led off from the corridors. Of much interest to all was the Engineering level and its series of lattice-work catwalks suspended above the central energy core. Floor area in Engineering had work stations, computer banks, conduits, and the central core, rising from floor to ceiling, providing energy to run the station. Other areas searched offered nearly bare rooms with minimum furniture and no computer terminals or work consoles. Some rooms displayed furniture in disarray, half-eaten meals, scattered personal belongings. All corpses found had been dead from three to six weeks. SEE *Reltah* creature.

Reltah creature (SG)–Described as pale and diaphanous, almost transparent in places with faint colors of pale pink, green, and lavender that flickered across its surface. Its movement appeared as a series of easy glides. Frequently cilial-like filaments of varying lengths sprouted at irregular intervals. After considered study, the conclusion was that the creature was not sentient and sought only "food" by taking it from the station's warp core. By the time Kirk's landing party encountered the station, it had grown, nearly filling the engine room. While studying it, the party came to realize that it could "suck" energy from one's body. McCoy's observations included the following: "Its vast bulk filled half the central chamber [of the engine room with a] sense of immense weight. It was diaphanous, shimmering with colors and hues like the inside of an abalone shell caught by the sun...Tiny lights played along the gently expanding and contracting surface...Ropes of color that might have been veins and arteries plied the body like colorful streamers around a maypole...giving off sparks of light." Once the creature was removed, it was discovered that it had given birth. McCoy surmised all the energy it had consumed would account for the birth. He also added a personal observation to his report: "it was, unequivocally, the most beautiful thing I had ever seen in my life... and I was overwhelmed with emotion."

removable airlock (BD)–A device that allows transfer of pressure-sensitive cargo from one ship to another. Once the transfer is complete, the airlock is removed and stowed.

Ren (P)–Romulan female and former subcommander under Captain Hiran. They had been friends and conversed on many topics.

Rencree (S)–Senite name Renna assumed in order to help Kirk, Spock, and McCoy to enter the Senite Seminary. SEE Renna.

Renna (S)–Human female with brunette hair whom Kirk thought was about 25 years old. She and her father came to Sanctuary to avoid capture by the *Enterprise*. He died from wounds inflicted when their craft crashed. She helped Kirk, Spock, and McCoy get to the transporter room in the Seminary and when the men were captured she helped them escape. She chose to stay on Sanctuary, revealing to Kirk that she was Auk-rex, the one he had been chasing.

Retinax booster (P)–Alternate spelling Retnax V as given by Okuda and Okuda (*Encyclopedia* 408). Medicine prescribed for certain kinds of nearsightedness. Kirk, who later in life suffered from nearsighted, was allergic to Retinax V. SEE Ryan Handler.

Rey (GSR)–These tall, gangly red-blooded humanoid bipedal natives of the planet Gullrey number about 5 billion. They have a complexion ranging from yellow to copper. Their large wide eyes that have almost no whites, together with flat brows, blunt teeth, black to light brown hair, good hearing, and high metabolic rates, as well as their herbivore habits, suggested to Dr. Leonard McCoy that Reys probably had evolved from antelope-like creatures with intelligence developing from a prey animal. The Rey, who require very little sleep, have high intelligence and though shy are quite social. Studies of their genetics and physiology suggest their ancestors were runners, good at hiding, with interest in the character of others. When under strong emotional stress they tend to emit strong telepathic signals that effects others, though the Rey had believed it effected only themselves and lower life forms. Their society, highly developed in the arts and sciences with a developed literature filled with stories about aliens, had initiated a space program that took nearly 700 Terran years to develop into short warp flights to nearby planets and a series of listening posts called Whistling Posts to search for other intelligent beings. Years of listening and sending robotic probes in the hopes of hearing from others left the Reys concluding that they were alone in the universe. The one ship that could have provided the evidence met a Romulan ship and the meeting ended in disaster. SEE Valdus. At the end of 70 years when no signal had come, the government gave up hope of reaching other life forms and began shutting down the Whistling Post stations. Just before scheduled closure, the one remaining post sent a signal. The received answer that came from the USS *Hood* was a salvation. All Reys were happy to have discovered other intelligent beings. Dr. McCoy's report to Captain Kirk included the observation that when the Reys discovered intelligent "humanoid life that almost looked like them— why hell, they broke down and had a planetwide sob...they're desperate not to miss anything...they're been wrapped up in humanity like some kind of big hobby...they think we're nifty!" In time they came to look upon the StarFleet contact as salvation and Captain Kenneth Dodge as a hero. Within months English was declared mandatory planet-wide and recognized as a Gullrey's second, and international, language. After ten to twelve years sharing their culture with contact teams, the planetary government proposed a Great Starship Race which they hoped would expose them to other sentient beings. Gullrey ran a ship under their planet flag.

Reydovan (UC)–*Excelsior* spent three years mapping this section and discovered 54 relatively lifeless planets and gaseous atmospheric anomalies of little interest to anyone except xenogeologists. Some areas of this sector crossed into Klingon space.

Rigel (WLW)–Also known as Beta Orionis, it is visible from Terra as one of the "legs" in the constellation Orion. Rigel is a quadruple star system that includes a blue-white super giant and a smaller blue-white giant. Together these two stars support thirteen planets, six of which are inhabited. Historian Johnson details the following information. The habitable six planets are attributed to the orbital zone of each and to the Hakel radiation belt surrounding and shielding the planets from excessive radiation emitted by the super giants. Rigel II and Rigel IV are sometimes noted as the Rigel colonies as they were settled by Terrans several hundred years ago. Their combined population has reached more than eight billion. Rigel V, whose population is an off-shoot of the Vulcan race, has approximately one billion and has been a Federation member since 2184. Rigel VI and VII are a double planet in a trojan orbit. Rigel VI offers a trade center that handles much of the cargo transportation among the Rigel planets while Rigel VII's population consists of "belligerent races of Neanderthaloid creatures called the Kalar" who are generally avoided. Their culture is rated D-plus on the Richter scaled. Rigel VIII is noted as having an Orion population of five point 4 billion, all aggressive yellow-skinned warriors. Once they had interstellar travel, they quickly colonized the two planets of Rigel's secondary blue giant and established a pirate empire, building a slave trade and a lucrative business supplying green-skinned females. Rigel XII is identified a class-G desert planet with deposits of dilithium available to the Federation by a small mining colony (*Worlds* 36).

Rigel IV (WLW)–Orbits Rigel also known as Beta Orionis. This planet, settled by humans, was the home world of Hengist, an administrator on Argelius III. Several women were killed on Rigel IV by a malevolent energy creature who occupied the body of Mr. Hengist (Okuda and Okuda *Encyclopedia* 410; *WF). SEE Rigel.

Rigel VIII (DC)–Historians Okuda and Okuda indicate Orion is a constellation near Taurus and contains the stars Rigel and Betelegeuse (*Encyclopedia* 341). According to Johnson (*Worlds* 36) Rigel VIII orbits a quadruple group of stars and is occupied by an Orion group. SEE Rigel.

Rigel XII (SS)–Historian Trimble (216) describes this planet as a "dust-dry planet swept by continual sandstorms" but "rich in dilithium crystals." Population: 6 – three miners and their wives (*MW). SEE Rigel.

Rigel Passage d'Arms (GSR)–A noted sporting race of great importance in the Rigel system.

Rigellian (UC)–A race descended from human stock. Their physiology is similar to that of Vulcans. Both Johnson (*Worlds* 36) and Okuda and Okuda (*Encyclopedia* 410) indicate their primary star is Rigel which supports twelve planets.

Rigellian husk (ST)–Large grey edible bell-shaped husk-covered fruit from the whispering smith, plant native to a Rigel world. One seed properly prepared can serve four for each contains smaller edible pods inside.

Riley, Kevin (P; Di)–Human though he was born on Tarsus IV. At age four he lost both parents to Governor Kodos' orders to kill half the planet's population in order to save the other half. He survived as one of nine witnesses to the massacre (*CK; Trimble 216). Small in stature with a narrow face and red hair, he always believed he was descended from kings. Proud of his Irish ancestry he never missed a change to talk about it. Trained at StarFleet Academy to be a navigator, he accepted a navigator's position on the *Enterprise* when he could no longer endure crew harassment about an incident with a Capellan choir (Gerrold *Whirlpool*). He also served in Engineering and at Helm when needed. During the one year he served under Kirk, he contracted the virus psi2000 (*NT). Under its influence he locked himself in Engineering, shut down the ship's engines, and proceeded to entertain the crew with a horrid and repetitive rendition of "I'll Take You Home Again, Kathleen." Kirk recalled his endless off-key choruses, and McCoy recalled Riley being among the group including Bailey, Styles, and Chekov as navigators who frequently got into trouble (Di). After a year on the *Enterprise*, he accepted a teaching position at StarFleet Academy. At age 26 when he was promoted to Lt. Commander by Kirk who saw great promise in him, he had grown into a witty charming person. He accepted the position as Kirk's secretary while Kirk served at StarFleet Headquarters. During this time, in the hopes of looking older, he grew a beard and frequently told the story about applying for a position in Sarek's office, expecting a secretarial job. During the interview Sarek told him that "humans have a certain– spontaneity– which I have frequently found of value" and proceeded to hire and train him. Years later Riley learned that Kirk had quietly nudged him into the Diplomatic Corps based on his unusual high scores on simulation problems in diplomacy. During one mission he served as the Federation's representative ambassador having tutored under Sarek. He kept his cool when Romulan Ambassador Tiam accused the Federation of having created the Probe as a weapon. It was his uncomfortable feeling about the situation that led him to beam to the planet in search of Kirk and Captain Hiran. He intervened in a phaser fight, was heavily wounded, and lay in a deep coma during which he told Dr. McCoy later that he continually relived the time when his father left their home to comply with Governor Kodos' order, the death of his mother, and his being rescued by the teenage Kirk (Bonanno *Probe*). Resolution of these incidents was the result of being carefully tended by Jandra and Dajan who helped him to understand their significance. One love affair has been documented. During his time as Kirk's adjutant he fell in love with Aned Saed. Although they discussed marriage neither was willing to give up their dreams of StarFleet service. She accepted a position with the *Starhawk*, and he remained with Kirk (Ferguson *Flag*).

Rinagh (SG)–Romulan doctor who had thought himself too old for space service was recruited by Kashi, commander of *Reltah*, Romulan's first space station. From his youth, he had kept a personal diary in his own hand and had continued to do so on the station. After discovering the creature in Engineering, he proceeded to fill his diary with observations and thoughts about it. His records enabled the *Enterprise* to remove the creature from the station with no casualties. Most likely his personal effects along with the diary were returned to his surviving family members.

Rioc (GSR)–Romulan First officer and member of the Bridge crew of the cruiser *Scorah*. In his spare time he built replicas of space craft including StarFleet vessels. Died when the *Scorah* exploded.

Riordan, Dana (FF)–Member of the UFP terraforming colony on Beta Canzandia and mother of Timothy and wife to Martin.

Riordan, Martin (FF)–Member of the UFP terraforming colony on Beta Canzdandia and father of Timothy and husband to Dana.

Riordan, Timothy (FF)–Son of Martin and Dana Martin, members of the terraforming colony on Beta Canzandia. Though he bullied and teased David Marcus, he turned out to be a coward when facing Klingons.

Risa (IT)–Female crewmember of the harvester *John Lilly*. She suffered from Nordstral's strong shifting magnetic fields. During her affliction, she "talked" with Saints John Bosco, Raymund Nonnatus, and Dympna. Once the fields were stabilized, she recovered.

Risa (SS)–Early surveys recorded a class-M planet with beautiful beaches and splendid landscapes. Its inhabitants were once caught in the throes of disputes among themselves with daily pitched battles occurring. Finally its government requested Federation diplomatic help. After two failed attempts, the Federation sent the team of Clay and Jocelyn Treadway who brought peace to the planet. Their report made mention of its natural splendors and hinted at its possibility of offering amenities to tourists. The government, having read the report, hit upon this one item and began developing the planet's beauty and resources into multiple spas spread around the planet to take advantage of its climatic offerings. What had been described as "a rain soaked, geologically unstable planet" with help from StarFleet climate engineers soon developed "a sophisticated weather control system" that could create and maintain perfect weather to allow Risa to become the spot for a vacation (Okuda and Okuda *Encyclopedia* 412).

Riseaway (SG)–A hard and strenuous antigrav game whose equipment consists of tight white suits, protective goggles, rackets, and a ball of spherical colored lights denoting value. Described as a cross between handball and cricket with the logic of chess played in zero gravity. Generally two players contest to see which can hit a "ball" off his racket toward a goal pin, score a hit, and earn points while scaling the walls of the playing area. "Balls," generated by the computer, are presented to the players in prescribed order. Buzzes indicate inaccurate scaling of wall with loss of points with the other player given the play. Kirk found the game so challenging that he had it installed on the *Enterprise* and often played with Dr. McCoy.

Risans (SS)–Native born and naturalized citizens of the planet Risa.

Rithra (Di)–This class M-planet is slightly larger than Terra but has less gravity, atmosphere, and meteorological characteristics. Conditions are within human tolerance. It is quite beautiful when seen from space as "a cloud-wreathed umber-and-aquamarine majesty" so states a StarFleet report.

Rithramen (Di)–Adjective used to describe the language and culture of the Rithrim on the planet Rithra. The language, a mixture of verbal and sign, is considered quite difficult to master.

Rithrim (Di)–Basically humanoid people with pinkish orange complexion, small black eyes, and feathery crests on the head. A rigid five-caste system divides the population "with strict division of responsibilities." The five castes are composed of governors, builders, procreators, gatherers, and warriors, in order of importance. The governor-class are generally bald and slender and reside in an ancient residence Uhura described as having "an ancient-looking courtyard constructed of material that looked much like sandstone. An abundance of frescoed walls, carved corner pillars, and free-standing statuary made of the same material...." A small pool of "squared still water" had a bench on either side. The procreators maintain nurseries and determine who will procreate. According to tradition, or instinctual survival, those born at a particular Center must return to it to produce offspring. One *Enterprise* crewman likened this behavior to Terra's salmon that return to spawn in rivers where they were born. One Center visited by Uhura was described as " simple and boxlike" estimated fifty by fifty meters, two stories high constructed of sandstone-like material. Statuary surrounding the courtyard portrayed Rithramen castes. Uhura theorized during her initial visit that they were being destroyed due to a possible philosophy change. Personnel of all Centers are female, generally short and squat with exaggerated musculature in the area of the hips. A short stiff, almost springy, crest covers the head. The senior female has as much authority as any governor but seldom employs it. A Center is composed of two general areas: a stark unadorned foyer with high ceiling lights set in a double helix pattern. A hallway leads off to the second area, various nursery rooms, one to house each caste births, distinguished by an individual vocalization each its own. An office, provided for the head female, has an entire wall of sixteen viewscreens, each showing a different nursery of children ranging from newborns to those nearly ready to leave the Center. Following contact and extended study by StarFleet's Office of First Contact, it was evident that Rithra would become a Federation member. Following StarFleet's request for the establishment of an outpost in Rithramen space, which was given, the governors signaled their intent to apply for membership and requested a delegation of Federation personnel to help establish the issues and detail the procedures. With unrest in the sector caused by unknown pirate raids, the *Lexington* under command of Commodore Wesley was sent to conduct diplomatic meetings while *Enterprise* was dispatched to determine who was raiding small colonies in the sector. Kirk and crew discovered the Parathu'ul were employing Rithrim, members of the fifth caste: warriors. This fifth caste was slowly being eliminated from society though the members had been a valuable part, enforcing laws, preventing crimes, apprehending and punishing criminals, and generally protecting Rithramen space. Their space experience developed them into extremely battle-capable military as skilled pilots and marksmen with expertise and experience in space fights. With no one to fight or protect, they began fighting among themselves until forced by the governors to take their aggression elsewhere. They became hired mercenaries to the Parathu'ul. By the time Rithra applied for Federation status, the planet had no fifth caste. To keep it secret, the governors ordered all statuary of this caste destroyed. StarFleet representatives learned of this fifth caste when a breeding Center asked for help when an intensive volcanic flow threatened sterilization and extinction from the heat and radiation . Engineers from both the *Enterprise* and *Lexington* erected barriers around the threatened Center and diverted the flow. Once *Enterprise* discovered the involvement of the Parathu'ul, who were angry at being denied Federation status, the situation of the raiding pirates was resolved. It was a matter of time until Rithra became a Federation member.

River of Will (GSR)–This entrant in the Great Starship Race was commanded by Eliior and ran under the flag of Branlian College, Eminiar.

Riverside, Iowa (BD)–Hometown of the George Kirk family. James was born here.

Robinson (DC)–*Enterprise* Security member who preferred third shift duty.

Robison, Sean (FD)–*Enterprise* yeoman at transporter duty whom Commissioner Moriah Wayne sedated.

robot wranglers (FD)–Pod-shaped programmed robotic marine vessels designed to herd the huge prawns native to Discord.

Rogh (FF)–Klingon crew of the *Kadn'ra* and member of the first search team sent to find the Beta Canzandia colony's children.

Romar (GSR)–Romulan First Officer on the *Red Talon* had reddish-brown hair, light brown eyes, and strong shoulders. After suffering from exposure to Rey telepathic fear, he accepted the necessity of destroying all Reys and agreed with Valdus's plan to destroy Gullrey. In command of *Red Talon*, he took the ship to Gullrey to ignite a planet-wide explosion. Kirk destroyed him, his crew, and his ship using a pencil-thin phaser charge. SEE Valdus.

Romulan Agenda (P)–The Romulan peace initiative that came from the discovery of ancient ruins on Termais Four had six parts. First, both sides would agree to meet on an uninhabited world of Romulan choosing (turned out the planet was Termais Four inside the neutral zone). Second, the meeting would be a full-blown cultural and scientific exchange. Third, Romulan and Federation would each provide a full orchestra. Fourth, each orchestra would take turns presenting nightly music recitals on their respective ships. Fifth, the Romulans would not accept Sarek as the Federation's ambassador or as a member of their designated group. Sixth, Romulans requested the Federation archeology group be led by Dr. Audrea Benar whom they acknowledged as also being a great musician.

Romulan ale (UC)–Highly potent light blue liquor illegal in the Federation because of its potency. Valeris suggested Kirk serve it at the evening banquet held for Chancellor Gorkon. Following the disastrous dinner, Kirk made a note in the ship's log that Romulan ale would not be served on his ship and recommended it be banned from other StarFleet ships.

Romulan bomb (GSR)–Valdus attempted to capture *Ransom Castle*, intending to cover its warp core with lithium hydride infused panels and send the ship crashing into Gullrey. SEE Valdus.

Romulan cloaking (UC)–Trimble (141) credits the Romulans with having developed the first practical cloaking device some time after the initial contact between the Romulan Empire and StarFleet. A mechanical device attacked to the warp core enables a ship to be invisible to another ship's sensors. However, the ship can be detected by motion sensors and ion exhaust trails. A cloaked ship crossing into the Neutral Zone alerted StarFleet of the device in 2266 (*BT). An improved version led StarFleet to order Kirk to steal one (*EI). It is assumed the Klingons obtained the technology around 2268. Records show that in 2292, the Klingons had a prototype ship capable of firing its weapons while cloaked (Okuda and Okuda *Encyclopedia* 79). The ship was discovered to have fired on *Kronos One*. SEE *Kronos One*.

Romulan/Federation War–Hostilities between the Romulan and the Federation. Many in the Federation believe the Romulans, intending to extend their control over additional territory, initiated guerrilla attacks. The following information is reported by historians Goldstein and Goldstein. They indicate several events occurred before the declaration of war between the two which were believed to acts committed by Romulans. The year 2094 is cited as the year the Delta VII outpost was confirmed destroyed by Romulans. In 2099 another "pirating" incident was reported. The transport *Diana* was plundered of its cargo and 500 passengers killed. Captain McKenna of the *Intrepid* indicated in his report that something had sliced through the ship's hull with a "precision [of cutting that] seems to indicate some sort of advanced laser drill specially designed for plunder." The Federation mobilized StarFleet to combat the situation. By 2106 war had been declared as the two sides confronted each other again in the vicinity of the Rigel system. Goldsteins include a report filed by Captain Joseph Spadora of the *Patton*. It is now believed his meeting with Romulans was the first confrontation after the declaration of war. He writes his ship had detected a "hostile Romulan War Fleet" in the Tri-Beta Sector in the Rigel Star System: "We have been ambushed by three...ships...fully equipped...with four laser banks per ship...with a faster attitude control response." Employing Warp Advance Maneuver 74, Captain Spadora slipped out of the ambush. With the ship damaged beyond repair, he recorded his last entry: "in fifteen minutes the *Patton* will be reduced to a lifeless hulk with all lives lost. I didn't think it would end this way." In 2107 Romulans penetrated the security of Sector 5B and destroyed the facility there. In the same year, according to the Goldsteins, StarFleet's Sector 7 Wing Fleet was victorious over one entire Romulan armada. However the next year, Romulan ships killed 200,000 people on Alpha Omega B. In 2109 at the Battle of Cheron opposing sides erupted into a decisive battle with Federation forces victorious. StarFleet ships would have pursued the Romulans to inflict more damage, but were forbidden to cross into Romulan territory. Writing in his report of the battle at Cheron, Admiral Alex Hamilton stated he was forbidden to cross the boundary, adding that if "a favorably negotiated peace treaty will accomplish the same goal without further loss of life...I endorse the restraint." In 2109 a shaky peace treaty was signed (Goldsteins 118). Another highly respected source indicates the year 2160 as the signing of peace between the two entities (Okuda and Okuda *Encyclopedia* 417). A copy of the treaty may be seen in Joseph's *Technical Manual*. The agreement to end hostilities was conducted with no actual meeting of diplomats and no visual. Why the two sources disagree on the dates cannot be determined with limited access to records, although the later reference date might be to a later treaty or an addendum to the first.

Romulan History (P)–CONSULT the entry "Rihannsu" in *Star Trek Reader's Reference to the Novels: 1986-1987* for a complete history. In *The Probe*, Bonanno mentions the Praetor had much power and controlled most of the webs of intrigue but with his death, chaos appeared. No one's loyalty was guaranteed. Some familiar faces remained in power though a frightening number were missing. In ancient days of the Empire bodies of the fallen were laid out in the streets as a lesson. Years later their bodies, and families, simply vanished. The Interim Government intended to eliminate this action.

Romulan Interim Committee (P)–Following the death of the Praetor no single group had enough power and support to command control of the government. Agreement was reached that an Interim group be elected to run the government until such time elections could be held or until a group managed a successful coup.

Romulan landing party on Termais Four (P)–Initial group landing on Termais Four according to established protocol included six members: Captain Hiran, Centurion Tiam, Dajan, Subcommander Feric, Jutak, and Kital. SEE *Enterprise* Termais Four landing party.

Romulan Neutral Zone (SG)–Established area agreed upon by both sides that declared that neither would enter.

Romulans (SG)–Humanoid. Call themselves Rihannsu. By choice they split from the original Vulcan stock. For a more complete history CONSULT *Star Trek Reader's Reference to the Novels: 1986-1987.*

Romulan space station (SG)–Found deserted with all its occupants dead, it was boarded by an *Enterprise* party consisting of Spock, McCoy, Chekov, Christina Leno, Daniel Markson, and Suzanna Hallie. SEE *Reltah.*

Rondorrin, Ans (SS)–Native Ssan and the oldest assassin member of Andrachis' group who often stated he had served with the High Assassin Dal Biminoth. Ans killed Thur Cambralos, governor of Pitur.

Roon, Turrice Belliard (GSR)–Female Rey and sister to Tom; often called Turry. He was placed on *Ransom Castle* as a host observer. Kidnapped from the ship by the Romulan Valdus, she was killed when Valdus determined she projected fears to "unhinge" him and his crew. SEE Tom; Valdus.

Rosa's Cantina (FD)–This Starbase 23 bar was a popular place for base personal and visitors.

Rosetta navigational buoy (BD)–SEE Rosetta Nebula Buoy.

Rosetta Nebula Buoy (BD)–Vast cloud of dust and gas that is the nursery of fairly young stars. Interesting data was obtained by Terrans John Herschel, Marta, and Swift in the early 20th century. Different NGC numbers were assigned at different times by different people studying the nebula. Located here is a trinary star cluster whose two suns orbit a neutron star orbited by the planet Faramond. SEE Faramond.

Roth, Alma Anne (BD)–Captain of the *Bill of Rights* whose mission was under the guise of the Naval Exploration Extension 2010. It sent a distress call just before a flushback. Alma had been a cadet on one of Kirk's training missions. This 36-year-old captain, who always wore her brown hair cut quite short, served in engineering for ten years, but at Kirk's insistence and recommendation she attended command school and was promoted to captain. She, her ship, and all its crew were lost in a flushback. SEE flushback.

Rothbauer (GSR)–Doctor who cared for *Enterprise's* injured while McCoy was on *Ransom Castle.*

Royenne (GSR)–Native of Gullrey and one of three hosts placed on the *Enterprise.* SEE Tom; Osso.

Ruko (ST)–Commander of the Klingee Fleet; dressed similarly to Captain Iola. SEE Iola.

Rules of the Great Starship Race (GSR)–The idea for this race grew out of the Reys' desire to become a member of UFP and to entice people to visit their world. The race was viewed as a public relations event to draw attention to Gullrey. Each ship entrant was given a list of participants and rules. Starbase 10 served as the race starting line which concluded at Gullrey. Individual ship information packets included a list of the basic maritime rules which applied to this race and extensive information on Gullrey and its people. One rule stated that the cargo from all participating ships would be stored in security-safe warehouses on Starbase 16. Chairman of the Great Starship Race John Orland imposed the rule that "When there's any vessel dead ahead, the following vessel must either alter course or power back to adjust for ahead reach." It was hoped that this would prohibit one ship plowing into another. Furthermore, Chairman Orland stated: "beacons and buoys have been placed throughout the sector to mark dangerous areas...globe topmarks are for gravitional anomalies, diamonds are for electrical clouds, triangles are sensor blind spots, and flashers mark storms.. the distress signal frequency [set at] five thousand megacycles subspace...equipment on that channel will constitute an SOS."

Rura Penthe (UC; SS)–A nearly inhabitable planetoid located in Klingon space having three suns which do not provide any heat. Its massive deposits of dilithium make it valuable but its extreme Arctic-like weather made mining near impossible until underground caverns were created. The Empire employed this mining facility as a prison, using the prisoners as forced labor. So inhospitable was the place that no guard towers or electronic devices were needed except for area magnetic shields around the underground entrance and several miles beyond. These shields prohibited anyone being beamed off. Guards carried weapons set on kill and leashed jackal-looking mastiffs to intimidate. Huge underground labyrinths of corridors and niches opened onto open yards ringed with crude huts. All prisoners wore leg irons and were given only the rudiment of mining tools to extract the dilithium.

Russhton syndrome (SS)–An infectious medical condition that has no cure.

Russian roulette (DC)–Sulu, on the *Sras*, knowing *Hawking's* containment field will explode, lured the Orion *Mecufi*, totally unaware of *Hawking's* condition, to chase him around and around the *Hawking.* The chase continued until the *Hawking* exploded and destroyed the Orion ship.

7249 (DC)–The first four digits on Chekov's phaser. Chekov suggested the number to replace Sulu's because Sulu's cabin was broken into and its contents destroyed.

Saavik (UC)–Half Vulcan, half Romulan. She was a protegee of Spock's and during her Academy days had been friends with Valeris. She and David Marcus explored the Genesis planet. CONSULT *Star Trek Reader's Reference to the Novels: 1990-1991* for a complete biography.

sabora (ST)–An alcoholic drink served at Commodore Favere's dinner party on Starbase 12.

sabotage (UC)–The Terran term originated with workers throwing their shoes, *sabots*, into machines to stop them. Valeris offered the definition to Uhura and Chekov as a suggestion that they find a way to avoid reporting to StarFleet Headquarters until they knew more about the situation on board *Enterprise*.

Sagittarus Arm (P)–One of the spiral arms of the Milky Way galaxy, it is named after the principal constellation that it contains (Bradley 90). Astronomers have verified the galaxy has 5 arms. From the center outward they are: an inner closer arm; Sagittarius, Orion, Peresus, an outer one beyond Peresus. The Federation, Klingon Empire, Romulan Empire, Vulcan system, and other governing entities occupy the Orion Arm, the most explored. The first three of this group also claim territory in the other arms. It was learned that the Probe journeyed through this area on its way here. As instruments became better and allowed for better images, opinions about the structure changed. In early 2010, scientists were agreeing that the galaxy had four major spiral arms – Perseus, Norma and an outer arm discovered in early 2000 and smaller arms, Sagittarius (two smaller arms) and Orion-Cygnus (location of Sol) ("Milky Way Galaxy" Wikipedia).

Salet (P)–A Vulcan composer of the 23rd century. One of his compositions requiring the use of an obsolete instrument, the *tlakyrr*, was performed at the Terran Lincoln Center Philharmonic. SEE Benar; *tlakyrr*.

Salzburg (P)–One of several metropolitan centers offering frequent live performances of Beethoven.

Samno (UC)–*Enterprise* ensign with an undistinguished service record. He and his friend Burke enjoyed their dislike of Klingons and made negative remarks about them. Valeris killed Samno and Burke, using a stun setting against their skulls causing arrhythmia and instant death.

Samuellsson (DC)–*Enterprise* Security member sent with Hrdina to check all access ladders in a search for the Orion intruder. SEE Purviance.

Samuels, Wynn (Di)–This muscular, athletic looking fellow with dark hair and a reddish-brown beard was First Officer on Commodore Welsey's *Lexington*.

Sanabar (FD)–Deceased wife of Aagard dinAthos and mother of Aileea; described as gentle and resilient.

Sanctuary–Novel by John Vornholt. *Enterprise* had been chasing a pirate vessel, expecting to capture it and its notorious Captain Auk-rex. Chased to a relatively unknown planet, the pirate ship crashed on the planet. Kirk with Spock and Dr. McCoy shuttled down, although they had been warned not to. They found themselves stranded by the Senites who occupy the planet they call Sanctuary. Planetary shields prohibit any mechanical ships from leaving the surface. Faced with getting themselves off planet, the three find themselves helped by other stranded visitors. They were saved from the ritual Reborning by another stranded visitor who it turned out was the pirate they had chased to the surface. Her swift actions saved them from being forever a member of the Senite colony through massive surgical alterations. Together they escaped to an encampment populated by those who refused to live with the Senites. Combining their own knowledge with what the residents had learned about the planet, Kirk and group built a balloon to lift them off. Rising above the shields, they were rescued by Scotty who had ignored StarFleet orders and stayed in orbit.

Sanctuary (S)–This planet located in uncharted Federation space had, over the years, been reported as a fable by StarFleet but included on Klingon charts of the area. Klingons had reported it as a place that accepted anyone, just or unjust, but refused to ever allow anyone to leave. Following Kirk's chase of the pirate Aux Rex, a much better sets of facts emerged. The planet is a member of a system with nine planets. The one that has an atmosphere capable of supporting humanoid life is considered class M with two moons, one small and pinkish and the other a white giant with near neon brightness. The larger moon effects tides on Sanctuary. Many islands dot the landscape. A variety of unrecorded plant life consists of unusually tall orange-flowered bladder trees whose liquid is drinkable. Thick moss covers the ground in areas around tall mountains created by volcanos. Schools of lungfish, scrawney rodent-like mammals, batlike creatures, lunks that are huge mollusks similar to a Terran snail though many times larger, whale-like creatures even bigger than Terran whales, lancefish, bottom dwelling predators, eel-like fish with ferocious jaws, and animals that resemble boulders when resting. These were just a few the *Enterprise* landing party reported. The planet, whose electrical power is generated by wind turbines, supports only two major settlements, Dohama and Khyming. Dohama, surrounded by a low unguarded purely ornamental perimeter wall, offers a variety of two-story buildings with porches and porticos all strung with colored lights. At the center of the village is a large open grassy area where chunks of meat are cooked over large iron braziers and freely distributed to all residents along with drink, rooms, and clothing. Tattoo parlors, a library, gaming establishments, smoke shop and hat store plus museums and a whorehouse comprise a village kept clean by the Senites. Any voiced request is generally met by the Senites. The population is of mixed races; however no females or children live here. When the Senites deem the male population has reached a certain level, they are thinned in an action called Reborning. Khyming, an island with a large inactive mountain volcano in the center, employs wind turbines to generate electricity. The population is composed of only women and children. Located here is the Senite Seminary, hospital, and Senite residents. The only village has a white pavilion anchored in the trees to provide shade for dining and living areas with open-air decks on all buildings. Seen from some distance the village appears to be a giant tree house with several levels. Small shops and vendors offer free items and houses are built along the cliff edges. Rope bridges link houses, pavilions, and pagodas; everything is painted white. Sanctuary government, kept intact by Senite integrity, welcomes anyone to come to Sanctuary and enjoy its freedom but no one is permitted to leave. Senites are the major race and determine the rules which all must obey. No sick, or physically disabled or mentally ill people were reported in the population. Although Sanctuary, on the surface, appeared to be of one race, in reality there were hundreds of species. Kirk's report and those of Spock and McCoy made mention of seeing Gorns, Klingons, Orions, Cheronians, Tellarites, Andorians, Saurians, and humans among other bizarre non-humanoid beings. They witnessed an attempt of two people to leave the surface in a rocket. At 30,000 feet it exploded, hitting the Senites' protective shield that allows atmospheric entry but disables the ships and prohibits anything mechanical from leaving the planet. Senite weaponry includes their planetary shield, a deflector able to reach phasers and other weapons in orbital space and hand weapons that resemble lopsided piccolos but with no discernable trigger. Some individual Senties have implants that allow weapon activation. Included in their arsenal of weapons is an instrument for producing sound waves and a Central Observation Unit for visual and auditory communications among the planet Senites and with anyone in orbit. SEE Senite; Reborning.

Sanctuary landing party (S)–Kirk, Spock, and McCoy.

San Francisco (P)–Terran city location of StarFleet Headquarters and the main campus of StarFleet Academy.

sandbaggers (BD)–The term originated in the 1860s to refer to racing sloops that had big sails and extra-long booms that used sandbags for movable ballast. Workmen at Federation drydocks employ the term to identify a one or two-man work vehicle. SEE potatoes; hedgehogs.

Sarek (UC)–Vulcan ambassador to the peace talks with the Klingons. He could name three humans he trusted without question: Amanda Grayson; Captain James T. Kirk; and Dr. Leonard McCoy. Even with the evidence, though circumstantial, he didn't accept the guilt of Kirk and McCoy for the assassination of Chancellor Gorkon. However, he did agree they were "properly arrested, and the Klingons [were] within their rights to try them." CONSULT *Star Trek Reader's Reference to the Novels: 1990-1991* for a full biography.

Sarennos, Pel (SS)–Native of Ssan and second governor of Pitur. He became master governor when Cambralos was assassinated. As a member of the Ssan delegation he met with Kirk and the Treadway diplomat team.

Sassenach (FD)–A term often used by the Scots to refer to Englishmen; derogatory. Scotty identified the Klingons he and Kirk met at Station K-7 by using this term (*TT).

Satanta, Douglas (FD)–A large man with scarred and pitted face who wore his black hair in long braids. Although he had been a planetary scout and first-contact specialist prior to becoming a captain, he seldom spoke of his exploits in either of these positions. After retiring from StarFleet service he taught at the Academy, lecturing in Principles of Exploration. Kirk received his orders concerning Discord from Satanta as well as orders that a Federation fleet was on its way to Discord to begin evacuation of the Variants.

Satterfield (FD)–*Enterprise* engineer reported to Kirk that the transporter personnel were found drugged and tied up behind the transporter controls. Kirk ordered him to remain in the transporter room until relieved.

Saurian brandy (ST; FD)–A potent alcoholic drink seldom served on the *Enterprise*. However, at the reception to honor Federation Councilman Kent, it was served. SEE Kent.

Saurian jazz (FD)–Native music some Terrans consider jarring and disjointed.

Saurian ship (S)–One of several bounty ships on orbital patrol around Sanctuary.

Schwimmer (FF)–A terraforming project on which Carol Marcus had worked.

Science Assembly (GSR)–Gullrey governmental body in charge of the space program consisting of Whistling Stations. It ceased funding the stations after ninety or more years because there had been no results.

Science Labs (ST)–All StarFleet cruisers maintain a variety of labs devoted to various sciences. Many are equipped on demand while others are manned daily. A variety of studies are being conducted as any given time. CONSULT *Enterprise Blueprints* by Franz Joseph Designs.

Scorah (GSR)–Romulan cruiser captained by Oran was the fleet ship in command of a Swarm. Crewman Valdus destroyed the ship, killing everyone aboard because he believed all were out to kill him. He saved himself in a life pod. SEE Valdus.

scotter (FD)–One-person, twin-machine gunned, marine vehicles used exclusively on Discord with a form-fitting seat designed to the operator's measurements.

Scott, Montgomery –StarFleet serial number: SE 197-514 (Mandel *Manual* 23); SE 19754.T (Okuda and Okuda *Encyclopedia* 432). Mandel identifies his parents as Kathleen Margaret and William Donald Scott of Aberdeen, Scotland, Terra. At least two different birthdates are given: 3 March 2222 (Mandel *Manual* 23) and 31 August 2121 (Rostler 70). Other information differs depending on the biographer. Scott, or Scotty to his friends, became well known in StarFleet as the engineer who "could perform miracles." His mother died when Scotty was age five, leaving brothers and sisters and a grieving father and son who never forgot her. One biographer reports that by age ten he was showing a talent for machinery by repairing the latest-model aquatic pleasure craft and tinkering with land-based vehicles, often at the request of adults who would not pay full price to a child repairman (Krophauser "Scott" 140). By age fifteen he was working at repair for money. Lured by the appeal of space, he had, by age sixteen, signed aboard a private prospecting vessel as a crewman. Soon he was promoted to its assistant engineer. Mandel who provides a short biographical sketch states that Scott's age, 16, at the time did not distract from his expertise and experience when Tri-Planetary Shipping Lanes hired him as an impulse engineer for their Rigel run (*Manual* 23). Another biographer indicates that a short time before he took ship, he submitted an article, "Aberdeen Solution," to the *Encyclopedia of Engineering Development and Design* (Ecklar *Maru*). In it he debunked the current Perera Theory about Klingon ships always running in threes. Although math and theorems seemed to support the Theory, the Theory didn't work in practice which Scotty's article proved. In addition to his proficiency with mechanics he desired knowledge of physics. A series of courses taken from the Durham University in Durham, England, indicated his interests ranged from advanced physics taught by Karen Jenson to aeronautic engineering taught by Christine Rudd, and warp dynamics taught by Debra Jo Martini (Krophauser "Scott" 142). When these "earth-bound studies," as he called them, no longer held his interest, he turned to the stars, finding employment with a variety of vessels. Scotty worked from age sixteen to twenty on a variety of interplanetary liners and cargo vessels before accepting the position as senior engineer on the Deneva-Asteroid Belt run. At age twenty-two he applied for his warp drive papers. His long career in space mechanics applying his knowledge of warp began with his apprenticeship served on the freighter *SS Glasgow* before he entered the merchant marine as a certified tachyon engineer. When the position of second engineer came open on the USS *Deneb Queen*, he accepted it, staying in the position for the next five years (Mandel *Manual* 23). When his tour ended he was offered a position with the Terran-based Cochrane Tachyonics Corporation but declined it to enter StarFleet Academy, first in command and then in engineering when his college commandant discovered his love and talent for mechanics. He stayed two years, one semester as an instructor. The Academy offered him classes with the famous Dr. Kahn Revox of the Deneva Research Station, galactic techtonics with Dr. Granville Weber, and special studies with Commodore Rex Oberman, more famous for his service on the SS *Trithium* than his work in advanced warp-drive modifications (Krophauser "Scott"142). Scotty's senior thesis, the theory and implementation of a compact impulse-drive engine, led to the developing of the Constitution class shuttlecraft. For this work he won the StarFleet Academy Engineering Excellence Award. Some time within these years of work and study, he began writing technical manuals and engineering texts, many of which today are required reading for Academy engineers. Although Scotty attended StarFleet Academy, he promoted the idea that he was not StarFleet educated but rather a graduate of the school of experience. In time he admitted StarFleet Academy had been the most challenging and rewarding period of his educational years. Montgomery Scott's Academy cadet record reveals during his time at the Academy that he accumulated six demerits and one serious blemish. After a drinking bout with friends to celebrate a difficult exam, Scotty and two companions inserted their own program into the navigation control simulator. Cadets taking the tests the following morning discovered that instead of navigating through heavily populated Klingon battle zones, they were navigating through scenic vacation spots on Rigel IV. A senior cadet discovered the culprits had forgotten to remove their access code cards after entering the program. Each received a reprimand that appeared permanently on their records (Krophauser "Scott" 142). Included also in his Academy record is the result of his *Kobayashi Maru* test. Scotty had discovered he did not want to be captain but was in command school because his family wished it. His scheduled test pitted him again Klingons. When three Klingon cruisers appeared, Scotty ordered all phaser bays to fire on command by beginning at the lowest possible frequency then ranging upward to destruction. With these three destroyed, five more appeared. Scotty deployed a cannister of antimatter and let the ships explode it. This destroyed these five but nine more appeared. Finally the computer stopped the scenario when the Klingon ship count reached nineteen and Scotty kept destroying them. He had proved that his "Aberdeen Solution" was correct (Ecklar *Maru*). His actions in his test proved how capable he would be as an engineer. An Academy professor noticed Scotty's drawings of ships and suggested he transfer to the engineering school. Scotty always gave Admiral Winston Cauffield the credit for engaging him in ship engine design. Cauffield , who asked him to assist in the designing of the Marshall class cruiser, had him assigned to developing Constitution class cruisers instead. Scotty took the opportunity to excel in the work he loved. An early biographer, Krophauser, writes that daily breakthroughs in warp-drive mechanics, computer duotronics, and molecular transportation challenged him in new ways ("Scott" 143-144). StarFleet, after studying multiple designs, settled on those submitted by the erratic genius Dr. Franz Joseph IV. Admiral Cauffield's team of engineers were assigned to the project with Scotty given the position of systems supervisor. It took three years for the project to be completed by which time Scotty had earned his lieutenant rank and Cauffield's complete trust. Joseph lost interest in his blueprints, finding the challenge of producing a smaller ship more to his liking. The same biographer insists that Scotty was the strength and "steam" for the hard work and long hours with a crew that worked harder, drank harder, and fought harder than any other crew and got the work done. Comparing the dates when Montgomery Scott served with Captain Kirk on the *Enterprise* to the dates for the construction and trial runs of the Constitution-class ships, the Scott mentioned in those files could not have been the Scott of the *Enterprise*. Regardless of which Scott, the ship proved itself under the capable hands of Captains Robert April and Christopher Pike. Scotty's personal logs reveal he read all the trial reports and used them to begin designing his own small ship with heavy firepower and capable of high warps. He saw it as an answer to the Klingons' deadly Devastator class of ships. It was years before his design saw approval from StarFleet and by then he was on the *Enterprise* doing what he loves best, taking care of engines (Krophauser "Scott" 143). Though his age seemed to suggest he was quite young to have accomplished so much, he found, at age thirty-eight, his place as Chief Engineer of the USS *Enterprise* 1701.

His ship career continued with the USS *Pompey* which had an empty slot for an engineer. Scotty arrived as an ensign but soon earned the rank of lieutenant. He served in an engineering position on the transport ship USS *Thales* and the destroyer USS *Saladin* (Mandel *Manual* 23). Evidence suggests Scotty held a position, for a few months, with the Bureau of Planetary Works, a Federation subdivision (Duane *Sky*). When Lt. Cmdr. Pitcairn, Chief Engineer of the USS *Enterprise*, chose to retire, the in-coming chief lured Scotty to the *Enterprise* at the suggestion of its captain, James T. Kirk. Faced with the opportunity to work and serve on a heavy cruiser, Scotty did not hesitate to accept. The *Enterprise* became the "love of his life" and he served on her until his retirement (Mandel *Manual* 23). At first Scotty though Kirk too young for command, but grew to respect Kirk. And soon Kirk came to ask "a little bit more" from his Chief Engineer, optimistic that Scotty could do anything asked of him and finding Scotty did not disappoint him (Krophauser "Scott" 145). The two men found working together an easy task. It may be that this relationship led to the legend that Scotty was "a miracle worker." What he found on his first inspection of *Enterprise's* engine room, according to him, "almost made me cry." The battles, stress, and general wear and tear of years had left the ship in need of a refit. He undertook the task with Scottish determination and worked until he was satisfied with his "wee brains" (Krophauser "Scott" 146-147). He offered redesign, upgrades, and re-wiring to be included in the installations of the latest in technology, especially in engineering. Over the years he served on *Enterprise*, he completely changed the general design of the engine room, its functions, and much of its general schematics which appeared on demand according to the needs of the missions or the results of a mission. Frequent inspections from Command revealed the extent of the changes. Some were recommended for upgrading to other ships and for future implementation on ships just emerging on the drawing boards. His first passion and love was engineering, for he was an engineer by nature, trade, and schooling. Much of his off-duty time was spent tinkering. To him engineering was "an emotion." He had been heard to say that "beauty is a perfectly maintained, perfectly operating [engine]" (Roddenbery 244). His earliest biographer declares Scotty drew upon that "special relationship [that exists] between the creator and the creation and how no one but the one who designed and built it could get that 'little extra' from it and how he could communicate with the ship on a level inaccessible to anyone else" (Krophauser "Scott" 145). Ensconced aboard his beloved *Enterprise* with a captain and crew he admired and worked with, Scotty came as close to being in heaven as a man could be. Although he was third in command after Kirk and Spock, Scotty had no desire to command because his heart was in the engine room. He repeatedly refused command of his own ship. A varied engineer's career illustrated his life as shown by two sources of Scotty's StarFleet flight record. Okuda and Okuda (*Encyclopedia* 432) show that he served on a total of eleven ships including the *Enterprise* while a second source lists eight (Rostler 71). His resume reveals he served on a variety of vessels – passenger, merchant marine, freighter, and military craft. Those who have served with him declared that he knew more about starship engineering than anyone else and, having penned many papers and books, it appears to be true. *Advanced Astrophysics, The Essence of Warp Drive Mechanics* (co-authored with Admiral Cauffield), *General Starship Engineering: Constitution Class*, and *Applied Astroengineering* are only a few (Krophauser "Scott" 144-145). Few historians reveal much of the personal life of the one about whom they write. For this reason only a few anecdotes are known about Scotty. It is known that he spoke with a Scottish brogue, nearly incomprehensible to the listener, that he enjoyed wearing his tartan colors, and could play skillfully on the bagpipes. He was loyal to Kirk and Spock, but McCoy was his closest friend and drinking buddy. A few items of personal information have come to light. In an early log, written when he was about age fourteen, he declared his love for Maureen Ryan, a classmate, but her parents were not wanting them to become serious. They took themselves and their daughter to Mars for a tour of duty. When she returned, she and Scotty were no longer "in love" (Krophauser "Scott" 141). Scotty did reveal two serious romances. He felt deeply for Lt. Carolyn Palamas, chief anthropologist on the *Enterprise* (*WM), and Lt. Mira Romaine, whose father Jacques Scotty had met when he worked on the *Deneb Queen* (Mandel *Manual* 24). Lt. Romaine served on the *Enterprise* for a short time (*LZ). Scotty never married, finding his excessive love of starships and engines too demanding. His off time was spent in tinkering with engine specs, contributing to StarFleet technical manuals, writing textbooks, and when on shore leave, searching out the most exotic local drinking establishments. He collected rare and exotic alcoholic beverages and was registered as owning one of three bottles of pre-Eugenic Wars Gallo wine. During some down time, Kirk discovered Scotty studying the Klingon language. Scotty reasoned to Kirk that "with the Klingons giving technical assistance to the Romulans...there's a lot of Klingon engineering manuals floating around..." (Milan *Depths*). His enjoyment of reading or telling ghost stories in the Rec Room endeared him to the crew and he enjoyed the time, considering it well spent (Crandall *Shell*). Records of one mission under Kirk's command showed Scotty was killed by Nomad on sd3541, but the machine repaired his internal damages and returned him to life (*Cg). A powerful electric shock by an entity on Pollux IV on sd34368 resulted in minor surgery to replace damaged heart tissue. Exposure to a lethal form of radiation on Gamma Hydra IV on sd3748 caused rapid aging, but the condition was reversed by adrenalin therapy (*DY). A minor concussion received when an explosion threw him against a bulkhead, sd3614, was considered too insignificant to report. Known only to his doctor, Dr. McCoy, Scotty's erratic blood pressure was regulated by an arterial implant (Mandel *Manual* 24). He suffered hypertension aggravated by his self-imposed schedule. Exercise controlled the stress as did his occasional drink enjoyed with Dr. McCoy or Captain Kirk (Mandel *Manual* 24). Lt. Cmdr. Scotty was a hell raiser on shore leave and known to become involved in fist fights over such accusations as the *Enterprise* "is a garbage scow" (*TT). However, these incidents did not prohibit Scotty being decorated several times. He holds five commendations, ten awards of valor, and two awards from the StarFleet Engineering Society (Mandel *Manual 23;* Rostler 70). The only taint to his career occurred on sd3614 when he was arrested by authorities on Argelius II for the murder of three women. His commanding officers

Kirk and Spock, along with Dr. McCoy, acquired the services of a good lawyer and discovered the real murderer was an entity occupying the body of Hengist, a bureaucrat imported from Rigel IV (*WF). Scotty showed his bravery and wit in three encounters. With Kirk, Spock, and McCoy stranded on Sanctuary with no way off, Scotty needed to converse with the authorities but they refused. When Captain Mora of the *Neptune* arrived to replace *Enterprise* on patrol, he and Scotty devised the scheme of seeding the planet's oceans with millions of irradiated Regulan locust larvae. They got their attention (Vornholt *Sanctuary*). He nearly jeopardized his career when he sabotaged *Excelsior* to keep it from pursuing Kirk and group on their way to rescue Spock on Genesis (McIntyre *Search*). At the peace conference on Khitomer, he shot the assassin attempting to kill Chancellor Atzebur and Federation President Ra-ghoratrei (Dillard *Country*). As a Scotsman, Scotty is qualified to wear, on special occasions, his traditional tartan kilt woven in the Scott pattern of green, red, black, and white. Adventure is in his Scottish blood, for Scots may be found having served on Yankee Clipper ships, on early powered flights, in WWI as RAF pilots, engineers in WW II, and on the first settlements on Terra's moon. When Kirk's five-year mission ended, his ranking officers had determined their next career change. Scotty did also. But he returned to serve with Kirk when asked. Only at Kirk's death did Scotty move off the *Enterprise* into another less demanding position. His character has been succinctly captured by his biographer Bill Krophauser who declares Scotty is a "man [with a] healthy, well-rounded personality [that] makes him a good man to have in a crisis" (141).

Sea Dragon's Teeth (FD)–Island member of the Susuru held archipelago on Discord.

Sea of Smokes (FD)–Discord location for the city Rakatau. SEE Rakatau.

Seaside Falls (S)–Sanctuary location where Kirk, Spock, and McCoy launched their river raft.

Second Fleet (FF)– Klingon Karradh had been Master of Security for this Fleet.

Second Klingon search party (FF)–Vheled, Chorrl, Engath, Norgh, Zoragh, Grael were searching for the Beta Canzandia colony children.

second landing party to Rithra (Di)–Commodore Wesley, Baila, Samuels, Dr. Coss, Uhura.

Second Winnowing (P)–Reference to the creators of the Probe leaving their native planet. SEE Winnowing.

Section 504A (FD)–Part of the Federation Environmental Statues Spock quoted to Moriah Wayne who had objected to Sulu's latest pet, a walking slime mold from the Gorn homeworld. Spock reminded her that Paragraph Three provided "an exemption to exploratory and scientific vessels and their crew."

Section Three Security (GSR)–StarFleet regulation governing Federation ships believed to have been boarded by enemies. SEE Hanashiro.

Section 39, Cabin 8 (DC)–Location of the bomb; also the quarters assigned to *Enterprise's* auditors. SEE *Enterprise* auditors.

Sector 412 (ST)–Location of Dr. Omen's asteroid, the *Erehwon*. *Enterprise* went to this sector on Nogura's orders and was attacked by Omen who sent the *Enterprise* into an Aleph.

Sector 918 Mark 3 (DC)–Area along Andorian space that *Enterprise* was scheduled to patrol.

SecuriTeck (FD)–Shortened term for Security Technicians, a Discord organization the human Variants organized because of the increased hostilities between themselves and the Susuru. Ailaee dinAthos represented this group in talks with Kirk and Commissioner Moriah Wayne.

Security Division (BD)–Even as the Academy was being developed, the Federation established a branch of police governed by the Federation Council, but answering directly to StarFleet Command. This division, one of sixteen under StarFleet Command, governs all security officers and personnel at all starbases, space stations, and starships. Trained and assigned by Security Division, all men and women in this section are considered the elite of trained personnel. They are the strong military arm in all phases of the term StarFleet. George Kirk, father of James T. Kirk, was a trained Security officer and served many years under the command of Captain Robert April. CONSULT Joseph *Star Trek Star Fleet Technical Manual.*

See Eleven Planets in Three Days (SG)–One of many tours offered to tourists.

Seeker (P)–One of many names bestowed on the Probe for one of its chief functions was to search for another race like the Probe's creators. SEE Probe.

Selevai system (WLW)–Location of several dominant species similar to the Kh!lict.

Senite (S)–Androgynous humanoids with shaven heads and white robes whose ancestors have occupied the planet for years before developing it as a Sanctuary. They call themselves Keepers of Sanctuary and are the dominate group on the planet. They render all weapons useless and confiscate all crafts that land on the planet, stripping them of anything useful especially machinery. Each Senite has a purpose and a job. Many cook, clean, etc. and keep the two major settlements in good repair. Senite living quarters are located on the island known as Khyming and close to their Seminary. All females arriving on the planet are placed on the island. Whenever the male population of those who have come to Sanctuary become too many, they are rounded up and subjected to massive surgery, turning them into sexless Senites. Indoctrination assures that each Senite will accept his sexlessness, as well as conformity and sacrifice. Though they profess sympathy to those coming to the planet, the Senite tend to treat them like children, by spying on them, and monitoring their activities. Their philosophy is offered as classes to anyone on request and is really indoctrination of their teachings that emphasizes why the planet was chosen and what its function is. SEE Reborning; Sanctuary.

Sequoia National Forest (P)–Located in the southern part of California, Terra, in the Sierra Nevada mountains, this area, consisting of 38 groves of trees, was established in July 1908. Spock spent a few days of R&R here following the mission detailed in Vonda McIntyre's novel *The Voyage Home.*

Seredip (FD)–One of seven Discord cities. It sits at 20 degrees north of the equator and is the closest city to the equator. Has a distinct Indian atmosphere.

Sessl (UC)–Vulcan male married to T'Paal and father to Valeris. He and his wife were members of the Vulcan diplomatic corps stationed on Zorakis, a planet near the

Klingon border. Husband and wife attempted peace talks with the Klingons. After the death of his wife at the hands of Klingons, he questioned Surak's teachings and became so obsessed with his private thoughts and his anti-stance against Surak that his family renounced him. Following a second attack by Klingons, his mind gave out and he died. An autopsy revealed he had a long-term degenerative brain disease. SEE Valeris.

Seventeen (FD)–One of seven Discord cities. SEE Discord.

Shadows on the Sun – Novel by Michael Jan Friedman. Expecting to be retired and *Enterprise* to be scrapped, Kirk and crew were surprised to be called to diplomatic duty and ordered to deliver a diplomat team to the planet Ssan. Kirk and crew were also surprised to learn McCoy already had experience with the assassin cult on Ssan and that his ex-wife was part of the diplomat team. When the peaceful attempt to communicate with the assassins resulted in the death of one security guard and the capture of Kirk and diplomat Jocelyn Treadway, McCoy put aside his feelings toward Clay Treadway and those relating to Jocelyn and helped rescue them. The death of High Assassin Andrachis led to the disintegration of the cult and the beginning of peace for the planet. However, many deaths, including Jocelyn Treadway's, bought that peace.

Shalyar (P)–Romulan ship Jenyu once captained. SEE Kital; Jenyu.

Shamirian, Ben (GSR)–Dark-haired captain of the *Gavelan Star*, a private explorer.

ShanaiKahr (UC)–Vulcan's planetary capital.

Shandaker (DC)–Visual description of this Orion revealed a male heavy with high-gravity bone and muscle, a thick black beard razored off the chin leaving two long plaits braided with silver grommets that hung well below his ears, dark green skin, and bronze eyes. As Orion police commander of the *Mecufi*, he planned to retrieve the trans-shield anode by attacking the *Hawking*. He and his ship were destroyed when the *Hawking* shuttle blew up. SEE *Hawking*.

Sharf (P)–A spindly Andorian assistant to Dr. Benar. He helped organize and pack the musical instruments required by the Federation musicians who accompanied the group of archeologists to Termais Four.

Sharkian (Di)–Kirk relieved Chekov from the Bridge during a tense moment when Chekov questioned Kirk's order. Later in conference with Spock who spoke highly of Chekov's actions during the mission to Sharikan telling Kirk that Chekov "had shown poise under tension," Kirk agreed to give him another chance. Spock added that Chekov's " natural curiosity has stood him in good stead at the science station." With Kirk's consent Spock returned Chekov to navigation duty on the Bridge.

Shark (BD)–Built piecemeal from several designs and utilizing parts from many, this pirate ship's power formula was Andorian. With a gargoylish appearance, special shielding, and crewed by pirates, the ship preyed on any ship that came into its area because its special shielding allowed it to come and go from the Blue Zone. Initially commanded by Angus Burgoyne, he was killed by Rex Moss who took command. Moss died from electrocution.

Shapley Center (P)–Identifies the center of the Milky Way galaxy named for the Terran astronomer Harlow Shapley. The Probe did not cross the center on its way home but skirted around it.

Shenandoah (P)–StarFleet ship assigned to follow the Probe and to sent its reports to the *Enterprise.*

Sheepshead (SG)–A trick-taking card game with elaborate rules and playing strategies related to *skat* and quite popular in the Terran 17th century. Generally requires five players although the game can be played with two to eight players and uses a standard deck of playing cards but only the cards seven through the ace. McCoy tried to teach the game to Kirk, but Kirk quickly concluded it was "incomprehensible" and doubted it was an actual card game.

Shell Game –Novel by Melissa Crandall. While on routine patrol *Enterprise* retrieved an information drone sent out from Terra many years before. During retrieval operations, Spock informed Kirk that an unknown object was approaching. On investigation, it was discovered to be a drifting Romulan space station. A boarding team composed of Spock, McCoy, Chekov, now Chief of Security, and three Security ensigns: Hallie; Markson, and Leno. The team's exploration of the station revealed the occupants died of hyperthermia. Further investigation led to the discovery of an alien creature occupying the engine room and absorbing the station's energy. When the boarding team and the *Enterprise* were effected with electrical malfunctions, Kirk and Spock decided to retreat from the station. Before the boarding crew could beam back to the *Enterprise*, several Romulan ships appeared and demanded Kirk's surrender. Kirk used his wits to avoid killing the creature and starting a war. Only when the Romulans experienced the creature were they convinced of Kirk's story.

Sherfa (S)–Old woman with few teeth who once was a brilliant technician; she befriended Renna. SEE Renna.

Sherwood Forest (FF)–Experimental forested area on Beta Canzandia headed by Dr. Riordan. Specimens here multiplied at seven times the average annual rate.

shiatsu (FD)– Japanese term translated as "fingers," referring to a traditional hands-on-therapy that applies pressure points. Considered a semi-mystical activity performed generally by women or blind men. Kirk, who discovered Sulu having his neck re-aligned by a Gorn, was told that Gorn massages are renowned for their rough-and-ready nature, "but ...wouldn't replace *shiatsu*."

shift regulations (DC)–StarFleet regulations state that no crewman can be made to work a third shift for more than four weeks out of every twelve. Auditor Kelley quoted this regulation to Chekov after learning that Chekov had allowed several of his Security personnel to determine their own shifts. CONSULT "Watch" in *A Reader's Reference to Star Trek Novels: 1990-1991.*

ship distress signal (DC)–Federation rule states that misuse of a universal distress signal is a first-degree violation of space-faring peoples and is punishable by exclusion from all Federation space ports for a standard year.

ship events (DC)–*Enterprise* had barely cleared the docking port at Space Station Sigma One when these events began. The disruption of all computer circuits for a few minutes before all came back on-line was the <u>first</u>. A radiation pulse was discovered to be the cause. The <u>second</u> event was discovered but acted upon later when all alarms were silenced except the screeching intruder alert. It was silenced. Sulu along with Uhura and Chekov found Sulu's quarters had been searched and many of his possessions destroyed. This became the <u>third</u> event. The <u>fourth</u> event was Chekov's reception of a bomb threat on Deck 6, and the <u>fifth</u> was Sulu's discovery of the murders of Auditors Taylor and Gendron in their cabins. The <u>sixth</u> involved the deaths of Ensign Sweeney and Lt. Lindsay Purviance and Engineering's reported loss of cutters, capacitors, and other items. The <u>seventh</u> event involved the apprehension of the Andorian Muav Haslev, his confession that he was running from the Orions, and had been followed on board by a disguised Orion, searching for his trans-shield anode. All of these events created the situation leading to the damage of the *Enterprise*, destruction of the *Hawking* shuttle, and loss of unnecessary lives, Federation, Andoridan, Orion. SEE trans-shield anode.

Shostakovich, Kovich (P)–A 20th century Terran Russian composer whose style was considered a hybrid of "sharp contracts and elements of the grotesque [that] characterize his music" ("Shostakovich" Wikipedia. Internet). Chekov wanted Dr. McCoy to consider adding several of Shostakovich's compositions to *Enterprise's* musical library collection.

Shto bendachnya (DC)–Russian; loose translation: "What the hell happened here?" Chekov's words when he saw the damage to Sulu's quarters.

Shrof (FF)–Klingon crew of the *Kadn'ra* and member of the first search party sent to find the Beta Canzandia colony's children.

shuttlecraft (BD)–A small ship, one of several generally carried by a starship. It is used for going from ship orbit to planet when the transporter is not required. Generally carries ten to twelve passengers. SEE LC 4.

Sibler, Joe (GSR)–Crewman on the *Ransom Castle*.

Sigma One holding cell (DC)–A six-by-four-foot police station cell with a toilet, a bench bed, and a replicator. Chekov was held here for a short time.

Sigma Security (DC)–Police forces for Sigma One wore black uniforms with station identification patch.

Silariot Marn (SS)–Young male assassin who questioned Andrachis' actions as a leader. He probably was part of the group who supported the assassination of Andrachis and any Federation personnel including Kirk and Jocelyn Treadway.

silent running (GSR)–StarFleet order for which all crew trained but seldom was required to execute. Many crew forgot there was such an order. It required all running lights to be turned off, all systems shut down except for thrust, weapons, and life-support. All automatic controls were also shut down including reactor controls, deflector shields, and long-range navigational guidance systems. All personnel were moved to secure inner-ship areas and required to be silent. The temperature of the outer hull was dropped to 4 degrees Kelvin and all exhaust disguised. All sensor emissions were shut down and crew movement kept to a minimum. No electronic equipment could be used. Kirk employed this technique against the Romulan cruiser *Scorah*.

silicon based creatures (P)–Found in the Ophane star cluster. Communication with the Probe gave the Probe its title Traveler.

Silva (Di)–Planetary governor for the Parath'aa.

Simon, Lorna (BD)–This grandmother whom a colleague described as someone on whom everything was round–face, hair, eyes, fingers, etc.– stood hardly five feet tall, wore her white hair in a shag cut, and frequently took medicine for her advancing arthritis. She had refused a captaincy nine times prior to becoming Robert April's first officer. On this *Enterprise* mission, she was left in command to ferry a diplomatic group to Vega 5 arriving just as the message from Faramond announcing the failure of April's group to arrive. She ordered Lt. Reed to get the diplomats off ship before it left to search for April and group.

Sir Christopher Cockerell (BD)–A dynacarrier on which Jim Kirk planned for his gang to work their passage.

Site J 3 (WLW)–This archeological site on Careta IV promised the best ruins in the five largest sites surveyed because it exhibited less weathering and provided shelter for the archeology teams. This site, estimated to be at least 100,000 years old, had immense walls of fissured basalt fractured into columns, nearby cliffs piled with talus collected near the walls, and a two-kilometer river. At first the ruins were believed to be Meztorien, but when a cleverly-buried transit frame was discovered the archeologists began revising their hypothesis.

Site N 4 (WLW)–One of the five largest sites surveyed on Careta IV. A transit frame was also discovered here. SEE transit frame.

slime mold (FD)–Sulu's Gorn friend gave him a specimen of a walking carnivorous slime mold that resembled a yellow and purple carpet and was capable of "walking" nearly a ½ kilometer a day. It had several other attributes, according to Sulu.

Sloan (Di)–This resident of Gamma Xaridian Three stationed at planetary defense station Bravo was killed in a Rithrim raid that destroyed the entire colony.

Slocum, Bahia (ST)–Blond female StarFleet observer for Dr. Omen's experiment with the class-J freighter. She also investigated the effects of the phased deflectors after the tests were complete.

Smillie, William (UC)–The youngest Fleet Commander-in-Chief in StarFleet and a Rear Admiral whose stellar record and past experiences led him to a cautionary approach to the Klingon offer of peace negotiations. Though Admiral Cartwright and Colonel West were held, no evidence linked Smillie to the attempted assassination of Klingon Chancellor Atzebur and Federation President Ra-ghoratrei. SEE Cartwright; West.

Smith (P)–Female ensign on the *Enterprise* assigned by Kirk to show Andrew Penalt to his quarters.

Smith (BD)–Crewmember on the pirate ship *Shark*.

Smithsonian's xeon-archaeology department (P)–One of many departments that came into existence as space exploration expanded beyond Sol's system. Was organized, founded, and mainly funded by the renowned Terran Smithsonian Institute.

sonic hologram (P)–Images created by dolphin-like creatures which Kirk's group identified once they were inside the Probe. The creatures employed a sonic sonar similar to Terran dolphins and whales and utilized it to create images.

Snodgrass (FD)–This female Commodore of Starbase 23 didn't suffer fools gladly. Scotty told Kirk he ought to "give her a piece of my mind," upset that she had ordered him to R & R. Kirk told Scotty that "people who try the commodore on for size usually wind up with more than their minds in pieces."

Sohlar (UC)–Vulcan engineer and member of the Themis research corps. His leg was crushed in a Klingon raid on Themis, and he bled to death. SEE Themis.

Sorenson (SS)–A junior officer on the *Republic*; transporter operator.

Soroya (IT)–Plankton harvester owned by Nordstral Pharmaceuticals and captained by Clara Mandeville.

Soulian, Isaac (BD)–This young skinny Arab or Lebanese was Navigator on this *Enterprise* mission commanded by Captain April.

space amoeba (ST)–McCoy made reference to this creature in an attempt to explain why the ship and crew were suffering fatigue when inside the Aleph. The creature he was referring to had generated a black zone that absorbed all energy inside it, including metabolic energy. SEE Aleph. CONSULT *IS.

Spacedock Control (UC)–Authority responsible for ships entering and leaving spacedock.

Space Haven (WLW)– SEE Bendilon.

spaceman's luck (ST)–General blessing employed between space travelers; compare the Terran phrase "good luck."

Spacemanship and Sportsmanship Award (GSR)–Created by the Great Starship Race Committee at the request of Nancy Ransom and crew of the *Ransom Castle* and awarded to Kirk and crew for their efforts in rescuing the *Castle* and saving Gullrey. This very large medal made of platinum was presented by the Federation President who stated that "those who merely watched the race and were so joyously entertained by it must from this day forward remember the true definition of sportsmanship. Therefore we must remember *Enterprise*...."

Space Station Sigma One (DC)–Located deep in Andorian space, the station has its own commander, Maxwell Peterson, and its own Security force.

Spanish Wells (GSR)–Island located in northern Bahamas, Terra. May have been the final resting place of the ship wrecked *El Sol*.

Spock–StarFleet serial number S 179-276 ST (Okuda and Okuda *Encyclopedia* 458). Mr. Spock was born to the Vulcan Sarek and the human Amanda Grayson at ShiKahr, Sas-A-Shar, Vulcan, on 26 March 2230 or sd1272.7 (Okuda and Okuda *Encyclopedia* 458). Mandel (*Manual* 19) identifies the year of his birth to be 2225. His full name is S'ch T'gai Spock of the House of Surak, Clan Talek-sen-deen (Hambly *Ishmael*). Sarek and Amanda named their son "after the most famous of Sarek's clan, Spock the Uniter, a disciple of Surak's who brought together the two great nations of Vulcan in the final act of the Reformation" (Thompson "Spock's Career" 119). The name Spock suggests a male who communicates, a blended tradition, a founder of dynasties (Mandel *Manual* 20). The name is appropriate since the child was a union of a Vulcan father and a human mother. If the naming was to ensure Spock would follow his father to the Vulcan Academy of Science, through the Diplomatic Corps and back to the Academy, it did not happen. Spock, a product of genetic engineering, combining DNA from both parents, seemed destined for greater things, even to surpassing most of his ancestors. An interesting piece of information about Spock's Vulcan ancestors appeared in a report stating Vulcan genealogy records reveal that Kesh, the first Vulcan recorded having a nictitating membrane, was an ancestor of Spock's (Duane *World*). He inherited characteristics from both parents but growing up on Vulcan, where he had to subdue his human side, gave him feelings of inferiority that took him most of his years in StarFleet service to eradicate. The stronger of the two influences, the Vulcan heritage, was seen in the upswept eyebrows, mildly slanted eyes, yellowish complexion, and enlarged pointed ears. His internal structure was mainly Vulcan— the greenish blood, particularly noticeable, and the location of internal organs. His heart beat 242 times a minute (Terran standard) and was located "where his liver should be" Dr. McCoy often said (*TSP) and his blood was T-negative (Okuda and Okuda *Encyclopedia* 458). Spock, stronger than a Terran male, was resistant to heat and low levels of radiation, but less resistant to cold, had sensory organs better adapted than a Terran's and was known to be able to go for extreme periods of time without food or water. On one particular mission, Dr. McCoy discovered Spock was suffering from hypothermia. His temperature, normally 85 to 91, had dropped to 79. After medication, McCoy insisted he and all the boarding party wear Romulan environmental suits to conserve heat (Crandall *Shell*). Part of his Vulcan heritage equipped him to endure high levels of pain with a stoic temper. He was a vegetarian though he could and did, if necessary, eat meat. He also ate many Terran foods but cared nothing for alcoholic drinks, though on occasion he did indulge. Few childhood facts have emerged. Historian Pamela Rose (177) declares Spock "was a very intelligent child...part of this could have been his hybrid makeup...His curiosity was insatiable...Sarek was well pleased...except for one thing which he deemed a fault...Spock was a dreamer...[and] occasionally strayed from the path of logic to seek answers without facts to base them on." Spock reluctantly admitted that he revered his father, but that at age nine when Spock determined to endure the *kahs-wan*, his father discussed the ritual with him, telling Spock that he expected him to fail but declaring that there was no disgrace if he tried his best. Without letting anyone know, Spock set out alone into the desert. His pet *shelat*, I-Chaya, followed him. In protecting Spock, I-Chaya was severely wounded (*Yy/a). A Vulcan appeared who represented himself as a distant cousin named Selek. He returned Spock home safely and got help from a healer for I-Chaya who soon died. One of Spock's first biographers speculates that this "cousin" enabled "young Spock to make the most difficult decision of his young life, to agree to let the healer put his pet out of its misery, enabling the *shelat* to die with dignity" (Thompson "Spock's Career" 121-123). The story eventually reached Dr. McCoy's ears when Spock's mother mentioned it at a dinner party (*JB). Many years later Spock attempted to trace information about his cousin Selek, but only after traveling back in time and meeting himself as a child, did he come to understand who the cousin really was (*Yy/a). Other childhood incidents have been discovered. One incident that Spock preferred to ignore involved Sekar who with a group of young Vulcans tormented Spock at every opportunity. Another childhood acquaintance, Svoon, along with a group of his friends, once forced Spock to eat sand to determine if Spock were a true Vulcan (Dillard *Lost*). A third incident was related to Dr. McCoy by Spock's mother. She and Spock, age 10, visited her sister Doris and Doris' two sons, Jimmy and Lester, on Terra, for Amanda wanted Spock to experience winter and snow. Out of boredom and curiosity, Spock dismantled the visiphone to learn how it worked. He put it back together, but when Doris discovered it in pieces, she confronted Spock who admitted he had taken it apart but insisted he had reassembled it to its working order. Doris believed her two sons who said Spock had dismantled it when in reality they had. Amanda and Spock soon returned to Vulcan (Haldeman *Judgment*). Amanda has contributed Sarek's lack of compassion as causing misunderstanding and stubbornness on the part of both father and son that kept them separated for many years. Historian Rose writes (177-179) that Spock did attend the Vulcan Science Academy, entering at any early age and rising "to the top of his class, earning the equivalent of a doctorate in mathematics, computer science, and biophysics." Spock, however, "could not help but be intrigued by the possibility of scientific investigation in totally unknown areas." She hints that "some controversy over whether to admit to this trait" in Spock's psychological make-up or an attempt to correct it may have led him to leave the Vulcan Academy and request permission to enter StarFleet Academy. Sarek, though he did not show it, was disappointed when Spock chose StarFleet rather than stay at the Vulcan Academy where Sarek believed Spock would have become a renowned scientist. When he was sixteen (Vulcan years), Spock applied and was accepted by StarFleet Academy. He may have been the first Vulcan to do so. He has never revealed the reasoning behind his decision, not even to his mother. At StarFleet Academy, Spock's first roommate was "a taciturn young Greek who was willing to put up with Spock's grimness in exchange for tutoring in the sciences" and though they never became close friends, Spock was saddened to learn he had been killed on Bellerophon II (Thompson "Spock's Career" 125). Spock majored in the sciences and computer technology, graduating at age nineteen with an A-5 computer rating which he continued to upgrade over the years. His graduation age is disputed by another historian who writes that Spock was twenty-three (Okuda and Okuda *Chronology* 35). The difference may be accounted for by the additional years Spock chose to stay at StarFleet doing post-graduate work in computer science and alien culture (Mandel *Manual* 19) and by the misunderstanding whether or not his age is based on the Terran or Vulcan year. Encouraged by his Vulcan curiosity, he took every opportunity during his Academy days to visit other worlds and meet other life forms. He officially graduated at age 25, receiving the rank of lieutenant senior grade. A photo-video taken for graduation records a tall Vulcan, gaunt almost, with angular features and a shallow complexion, wearing his hair in the Vulcan mode, cut straight across the forehead in short bangs and combed away from the crown of the head. The story about his phenomenal mind began in the Academy where he exhibited "the ability to extract and interpret complex information with great rapidity without voice translation" (Roddenberry *Making* 224). According to one historian, young Spock's ensign days on the *Formalhunt*, captained by Christopher Pike, revealed just such an ability. Spock's assignment on the ship was as assistant navigator, usually the traditional first assignment for Command School graduates (Thompson "Spock's Career" 127). Soon Spock was doing shift duty for others and in this way became more knowledgeable about starships. The same historian records that Spock was a member of the crew that pursued a Klingon ship discovered to be a scout ship for a larger fleet bound for New Federation outpost Berengaria VII. Spock won a commendation for his action on the Bridge by doing double duty at the Science Station and as navigator following the deaths of crewmen assigned those posts. It is believed that Spock went from the *Formalhunt* to an assignment under Captain Daniels, spending two years as Daniels' Third Officer aboard the *Artemis*. Almost two years went by and Spock realized promotion on Daniels' ship might not come for several more years. However, Daniels recommended a promotion for Spock and suggested he accept a posting with the *Enterprise*. Before reporting for duty on Captain Pike's ship, he spent a few days on Kauai, Hawaii, Terra, enjoying its beaches as his mother suggested he should do. He even walked barefoot on the sand, hoping to identify his experience with hers. This experience took place only because Captain Daniels ordered Spock to take time away from his duties (Fontana *Glory*). With the rank of lieutenant senior grade, Spock posted to the *Enterprise* as science officer and Second Officer. For the next few years, Spock served under the direct command of a woman First Officer often referred to as Number One. From her he further learned how to avoid showing emotion. For eleven years and some months, he served with Pike (Mandel *Manual* 19). It is known that he was injured on Rigel VII and participated in the initial Talos IV contact (*Me*). Also during those years, Spock won the Vulcan Scientific Legion of Honor for developing a more efficient method of mining via sonic disintegration (Thompson "Spock's Career" 128). Spock's years with Pike resulted in many missions. One such mission concerned the capture of the *Lisander* by the pirate Hamesaad Dreem. Following Pike's orders, Spock convinced Dreem that Pike wanted to trade dilithium crystals. While Spock kept Dreem occupied, Pike sent Security forces onto his ships, capturing all three with no fighting (Friedman *Legacy*). Another mission note taken from the above source mentions that while he was on Pike's ship, he became curious about why the entire crew of 290 on the *Telemakhos* had died. He searched the ship and found a living virus in the captain's quarters. After being informed that only two known places existed where the virus could be found – Mercenam Four and C'tinaia Seven — and that the C'tinaia were behind the deaths on the *Telemakohs*, Pike sent Spock's data to Admiral Penn. The records of an incident connected to Number One, Pike's First Officer, reveals that Pike sent her and Spock to an Elarnite station to retrieve its computer data. Together they established a link with the *Enterprise* computer and began sending data. When a chain reaction in the station's core reached the critical stage, Number One, instead of beaming off, ordered Spock to monitor the approaching breach and implement back-up life support systems so that she could continue holding the connection. Told the core was reaching maximum overload, she insisted he beam away, but he refused to go without her. They beamed off just as the control panels of the Bridge began breaking up. From this shared moment they began a strong friendship. Even though Spock and Number One had been "thawing" toward each other, when her father died, Spock wrote in his log that he found it difficult to speak to her about it. To let her know he understood her loss, he initiated a game of chess. The same source, Friedman's *Legacy*, relates that Spock, in an effort to socially interact with members of Pike's crew, learned to accept human ribbing when he observed Navigator Jose Tyler take a kidding about his involvement with a princess from Kalajiian. Historians who have read some of his logs reveal that several times while he was on Pike's ship, members of the crew attempted to socialize him. Once, Transporter Chief Abdelnaby and Navigator Jose Tyler took Spock to a saloon for a drink. After that experience Spock resolved to avoid shore leave. Another log from the same source tells of a surprise birthday party for Dr. Boyce. Always willing to do as Pike asked, Spock attended. However, before the celebration could get under way, a thick yellow gas billowed out of the ventilation system, caused by a spill in one of the cargo bays. When Pike was kidnapped by dissidents on Dinamori, Spock along with Yeoman Colt was sent as a two-member landing party to attempt a rescue (Friedman *Legacy*). Another story is found in Spock's logs about the rescue of a survey party during which Pike and Spock engaged in conversation about the simple things of life. From the same historian comes a reference to Spock's report about a planet survey. Spock, along with Yeoman Colt, crewman Sellers, and Jose Tyler, encountered creatures capable of shape-shifting, becoming replicas of any person, and also able to protect themselves by emitting intense radiation when touched. Another story from the same historian reveals a portion of one of Spock's logs about Dr. Boyce whom he accompanied to the chambers of a Horidian prince who had contacted Bendal Fever while attempting to subdue the planet Bendalia. The log records a conversation between Pike and Boyce over the fact that Boyce was angry about treating the prince, declaring to Pike "...it scares the hell out of me. A chief medical officer who lets his feelings get in the way of his duty...is a chief medical officer who should be considering some other line of work." Though few of Spock's logs are open to the public, most of those concerning Pike's *Enterprise* are unavailable to historians. When Captain Kirk took command of the *Enterprise*, he promoted Spock to full commander and placed him as his Second Officer. Early in Kirk's first five-year mission after his First Officer Gary Mitchell was killed, Kirk quickly moved Spock to First Officer position. During that five-year mission with Kirk, Spock engaged in many encounters though most have not been made public through StarFleet initiative or by popular novels. With the rank of Commander, Spock was the number two ranking officer, but he had no desire to command. His position as Science Officer put him in charge of all scientific departments and at the Library/Computer Station when on the Bridge. He served Kirk for many years. To avoid fist fighting, Spock often employed the technique commonly known as the "Spock pinch." It is "applied with the fingers of the right hand to the area on top of the right shoulder near the base of the neck [and] blocks blood and nerve responses to the brain [which] produces instant unconsciousness," writes Roddenberry (*Making*). It is a valuable asset for Spock is peace loving and logical. Spock admitted to Kirk that he had learned the technique as a child during his *kahs-wan* when a cousin saved his life and tried to save his pet. During the few days they spent together, the cousin had him practice the technique. Spock did not marry. At an early age he was bonded to T'Pring, a full-Vulcan, but that bonding was dissolved (*AT). This freedom did not allow him to enjoy encounters with females for he was bound by his Vulcan heritage and training both biologically and culturally. Records from Pike's *Enterprise* reveal that during the incident pertaining to Vulcan's Glory, Spock became involved with T'Pris as they worked together to unravel the true story of the Glory (Fontana *Glory*). Kirk's *Enterprise* missions reveal that during a mission to Omicron Ceti III, sd3417.3, Spock renewed an emotional attachment to Lelia Kalomi brought on by symbiotic spores whose effects were nullified when his emotions of anger were aroused by Kirk (*TSP). Another record (*Cms) suggests that Spock found the young woman Droxine of Stratos City to be quite interesting. Additional searches of ship records may turn up other women. However interesting and fascinating Spock found a woman to be, his life remained based on logic, and he found life aboard ship interesting, fascinating, and challenging, three words he employed frequently when discussing issues. Commander Spock served with StarFleet most of his adult life with many years aboard the *Enterprise* as a Second Science Officer, lieutenant rank under Pike, and as Chief Science Officer under Kirk. He completed five-year missions under both men and continued with Kirk throughout Kirk's career, both as a reliable officer and as a friend. Spock surpassed his parents' hope for him and even his own expectations. He was highly educated, and though widely read in many of the diverse cultures of the galaxy, he especially like Terran poetry, a result of his mother's long hours of reading to him from Shakespeare, Byron, Blake, and Shelley. Music was another art he enjoyed. He could recognize Brahm's handwriting, sight-read music and play several instruments with expertise, including the Vulcan lyre (Trimble 229). His ability also included deciphering musical codes (*Psy). Many evenings aboard *Enterprise* Spock accompanied Uhura's lovely voice in concerts for the crew's enjoyment. In the field of painting he appreciated da Vinci's technique and could discuss it as an expert. As did Captain Kirk, Spock became a legend in the galaxy. This elevation to public notice never restricted him from continuing to study and learn. His re-designed Bridge Science console was for the ease of use and location as well as efficiency. Several of his mathematical calculations have become standard on starships. One in particular allows for the starting of cold starship engines (*NT). Commander Spock has been commended on many occasions and holds a variety of commendation medals. One source lists Spock holding eight commendations, one of which is this Z-Mangre Prize, Tenth Class, and ten Awards of Valor, one awarded posthumously (Rostler 92). Twice he was decorated by StarFleet Command and in 2267 was awarded the Vulcanian Scientific Legion of Honor (Okuda and Okuda *Encyclopedia* 458). Spock remained with Kirk throughout Kirk's missions and continued when Kirk became an Admiral. Many unusual things happened to Spock. He voluntarily became a Kh!lict in order to effect a complete regeneration of those

Enterprise crew who had changed into Kh!lict and to set the machinery so that it could not be used again (Mitchell *Windows*). Dr. McCoy often remarked that he re-inserted Spock's brain in his body and maybe that was a mistake! (*SB). And Spock died saving the *Enterprise* but left his *katra* with McCoy which was restored to his body in refusion (McIntyre *Khan*; *Search*). For all his years in StarFleet and later, his Vulcan estate was administered by an overseer (Duane *World*),

Spock's calculations (ST)–Spock developed the proper formula for re-tuning the warp engines. Though the specifications were bizarre, they were accurate and worked. Kirk called Spock's calculations "unorthodox tune-up specifications." Scotty wasn't too happy about changing the standard warp engine specifications but they were required to get the *Enterprise* out of the second Aleph.

Spock's cabin (UC)–A functional single cabin located on Deck 6. It reflected his mixed heritage in items such as a flickering statue, polished meditation stone, and a Chagall. SEE Chagall.

Spock's theory (P)–The Probe employed "a form of energy...undetectable except for its effects... propagation rate [cannot] be measured...[but] could be duplicated by some form of tractor beam...readings indicate the heating" of the Terran oceans "was accomplished by direct physical acceleration of the water's molecules...computer simulations indicate... the *Enterprise* tractor beams could be used to duplicate the" production of sound waves. "Energy utilized by the Probe is some form of mental energy, analogous to telekinesis...." Portion taken from Spock's thorough report to StarFleet.

Ssan (SS)–This planet had long and time honored traditions, dating from 1,200 years before the mission detailed in SS. It also had a tradition of legal assassination. Once the planet became aware of the Federation, it sought to eliminate the assassin cult. For nearly forty years, the cult was believed to have been eradicated. But new outbreaks of assassinations spoke otherwise. This led to Assassin wars and an attempt by Andrachis to revitalize the cult. It was broken with his death although not until many lives had been lost and property damaged. The heavy deposits of maldinium had prevented the government from locating assassins' hiding places. And until StarFleet's intervention, the planet appeared to be reverting to its old tradition. SEE Andrachis.

Ssana (SS)–Humanoid natives of the planet Ssan. Most adults have long, bulbous earlobes, tiny indigo eyes, and boney brows.

Ssana silk (SS)–A material native to Ssan whose qualities are similar to Terran silk.

Ssanitation Detail (SS)–Title medical trainee Paco Jiminez gave to the group of five doctors. It is a play on the term Ssan and sanitation and referred to a clean-up detail. SEE five doctors.

SS *Butter Cookie* (GSR)–When Kirk teased McCoy about his saying that "there's nothing somebody won't name a ship," McCoy's quick reply was that no one had used this name.

SS *Rest in Peace* (GSR)–Kirk's teasing reply, that no one had used this name, was in response to McCoy's remark about the naming of ships.

stampede Tubetrain (BD)–Considered the fastest train in the U.S. at 900kpm. It runs five centimeters off the rail through a tube. It stopped in Omaha, Nebraska, and Jimmy Kirk had planned for his group to hop aboard. SEE Zack Malkin.

Stanley (Di)–Member of Scotty's *Enterprise* engineering crew. He repaired a forward converter and was sent by Scotty to work with Gabler to check on the impulse integration relays.

Starbase One (P)–Historians Goldstein and Goldstein (116) quote from Commodore Feliz Pjindik's log which declares this first StarFleet-built base to be in Sector 3A, quite near the Romulan Neutral Zone, towed there in 2095 (89). In 2103 seven Romulan birds-of-prey destroyed it. Rebuilt and re-commissioned, it continued to serve StarFleet in that area. In the mission detailed in *Best Destiny*, StarFleet Command ordered Kirk's *Enterprise* 1701-A be saluted with alternating white and gold lights as it left drydock for its final flight that would take it home. Captain Kirk recalled that he left Terra as a cocky young boy with his father aboard the original *Enterprise* under the command of Captain April and now was retiring as Captain of the *Enterprise*.

Starbase Seven (FF)–Ambassador Farquhar wanted Scotty to take him to this base so he could use the *Hood* to reach Alpha Maluria Six. SEE USS *Hood*.

Starbase Nine (P)–The Probe passed this base a few hundred parsecs away as it moved out from Terra and Federation space.

Starbase 10 (GSR)–Someone described it as "a large light-dotted spool floating in the middle of nowhere." The base offered a carpeted sound-proof officers' lounge decorated with cherry moldings, rough-hewn ceiling beams, and walls displaying painting of ships through the ages. A large viewing screen gave access to views outside the ship and for videos and inter-ship information. Located on the outer rim of the station, the lounge offered a 180 degree view, including docking ports. The chairman of the Great Starship Race Committee made the initial announcement about the race at this base.

Starbase 12 (ST; SS: FF)–Commodore of the base at the time of this mission (ST) was Favere. SEE Favere's base decorations. At the time of the SS mission, the base was commanded by Commodore Montoya who passed orders to Kirk for the Ssan mission. In FF *Enterprise* picked up Ambassador Marlin Farquhar and took him to Alpha Maluria Six. The base alerted Kirk that it had lost contact with Beta Canzandia.

Starbase Thirteen (P)–The Probe passed this base a few hundred parsecs away as it moved out from Federation space. When the Probe turned around, the base relayed a message to the *Enterprise* that the Probe was "singing" as it headed for Terra at warp twelve. The base sent updated coordinates of its course and location as it changed.

Starbase 16 (GSR)–Starting line for the Great Starship Race.

Starbase 23 (ST; FD; UC)–The base was carved from a metallic asteroid in the debris belt of a blue giant star, and the reflection from lights upon the metal-content walls is welcome. Rough arched ceilings and passageways provide a hint of the material from which the base was carved. Two general areas, military and civilian, offer many amenities. The civilian section offers taverns, bars, restaurants, cabarets, and a myriad of shops alongside meditation rooms for various faiths and philosophical disciplines. StarFleet crewmembers frequent the pubs, particularly Bill and Rosa's Cantina, for drinks and entertainment. In ST, *Enterprise's* crew had begun their R&R here only to be called away on a mission. In FD, *Enterprise* docked here for a general refit and while engineers were checking and updating the ship, Kirk allowed shore leave. In UC, survivors of the Themis raid by Klingons were taken here for hospitalization.

Starbase 48 (S)–After Scotty notified StarFleet Command of the Sanctuary situation, he was given 48 hours to conclude a rescue mission after which the *Enterprise* was to report to this base for a new assignment. Scotty seemed to have trouble interpreting the orders and remained in Sanctuary orbit far past that time limit.

StarFleet (SG)–Military branch of the Federation. Answerable to the Federation Council.

StarFleet Academy (FD)–Okuda and Okuda (*Encyclopedia* 467) declare this is a four-year training facility to produce trained StarFleet personnel. Its main campus is in the area of the Presidio, San Francisco, Terra. All Federation citizens, generally those who are young though there is no age limit, are allowed to test for positions as cadets. Non-Federation applicants must produce a letter of reference from a command-level StarFleet officer. Generally applicants are referred by others who are graduates or in service somewhere in the StarFleet organization. The motto of the Academy is "Ex astris scientia" (from the stars, knowledge). Divided into two schools, the Cadet School and the Graduate Colleges, it offers the widest variety of training possible in all areas of study. The Cadet School, governed by a vice Commandant, has thirteen discipline areas. The Graduate Colleges are administrated also by a vice-Commandant. Eight colleges comprise the graduate level. Both divisions are responsible to a Board of Regents and a Commander (Joseph *Technical*). Both division receive more than 12,000 applications for admissions.

StarFleet clothing (UC)–Since the inception of StarFleet, its members have endured a constant change of clothing issue. Color and style for each division, each level, each grade differs. Most are considered unisex with the choice being optional. Color indicates branch and level. Cadets are issued uniforms and are expected to wear them at all times while on campus. Fleet vessel uniforms, available at no cost to the person, generally adhere to the suggestions made by StarFleet Command though off-duty dress is left to the choice of the person. All uniforms bear the insignia of StarFleet. All StarFleet issued uniforms are fireproof.

StarFleet Command (P; ST)–This division of the Federation is responsible for recruitment, education, supervision, and control of the personnel who serve in StarFleet. This echelon has a military staff and various committees and answers to the Federation Council (Joseph *Technical*). Its headquarters is located in San Francisco, Terra. On one mission (ST) Kirk had Uhura send a full report by scrambled tight-beam detailing a full account of *Enterprise's* contact with the Klingon ship *Kormak* and requesting a complete report on the disappearance of Klingon vessels.

StarFleet Headquarters (P; UC)–Located in San Francisco, Terra, this complex houses the offices of StarFleet admirals and some commanders, a historical museum, and an alien museum. It also provides several parks and residential areas for personnel and their families as well as the central headquarters for StarFleet Academy. In synchronous orbit above this city is an enormous space station with six starship docks that allow ships to "float" within the docks. Attached are multiple floors with living quarters designed to accommodate most of the representatives to the Federation.

StarFleet Medical Corps (ST)–Division of StarFleet Armed Forces. It is headed by a medical admiral or someone very highly qualified. The division answers directly to StarFleet Command and the Federation Council (Joseph *Technical*). McCoy declared to Councilman Kent that the Corps' "methods of approving new drugs and medical techniques hadn't been updated in twenty-five years" and added that Kent should look into the problem. SEE Conrad Kent.

StarFleet Order 958 (SS)–Spock took command from Clay Treadway and cited Order 758, Article 3, Paragraph 7 & 8 giving him the power to do so. The Order pertains to situations in which the diplomatic envoy has been killed or incapacitated. Spock was justified in doing so because Kirk and Jocelyn Treadway had been taken captive by Ssans after a failed attempt by the Treadways to establish contact with the assassins.

StarFleet Operations (ST)–One of seventeen subdivisions of StarFleet Command. Generally has control over the day to day operations of fleet vessels (Joseph *Technical*). SEE Councilor Carter.

StarFleet Regulation (S)–A sub-section of this regulation requires a search party be deployed if a crewman has been missing for more than 48 hours. The landing party to Sanctuary had been stranded for more than five days. SEE Regulation 927.9; Regulation 2477.3.

StarFleet Security Team (BD)–Three men and two women were sent to get the group of teenagers led by Jimmy Kirk off the *Cockerell*. SEE *Cockerell*.

star orchids (DC)–One of many potted plants Sulu kept in his quarters. It was destroyed along with everything else by an Orion intruder posing as Lt. Lindsay Purviance.

***Starship Trap, The*– Novel by Mel Gilden. Ordered to Pegasus IV to pick up two people whom he knew nothing about, Kirk and *Enterprise* were delayed by a Klingon who told them of the disappearance of Klingon ships. Once the two passengers were on board, Kirk learned one of them was Federation Councilor Kent, definitely anti-Federation, and the other his secretary. Given little information about his mission, Kirk was ordered by Admiral Nogura to proceed to Starbase 12 where they dropped off Councilor Kent and met Dr. Omen. *Enterprise* was to witness the testing of new deflector/tractor beam machinery. Also on Nogura's orders Kirk had to allow Hazel Payton to film the testing. Shortly after the tests, Kirk visited Dr. Omen's asteroid which he had built to his own specifications. Declaring he was ridding the galaxy of war and admitting that he had sent warships into created Alephs, he sent *Enterprise* into one. The field tests were a way to lure the *Enterprise* to Dr. Omen. After several days, Kirk and crew returned to their own space, having implemented Payton's memory augmentation sensor. Realizing that Kirk knew how to defend against the Aleph, Dr. Omen took himself and his ship into an Aleph. Hazel Payton's final report changed Franklin Kent's attitude toward StarFleet.

Staten Island (SG)–This densely populated island, approximately 60 square miles, is part of New York City, Terra. A ferry runs between Manhattan and Staten known as the Staten Island Ferry.

Station K-7 (FD)–Space station K-7. This Federation deep space outpost is near Sherman's planet, one parsec from the nearest Klingon outpost. Most of the station consists of storage areas and industrial fabrication facilities with limited habitation space (*TT; Okuda and Okuda *Encyclopedia* 109).

St. Brendan (SG)–Ancient Terran sailing vessel captained by Loughran who discovered the drifting *Stephanie Emilie*.

Stehle, Vernon (IT)–Head of the planetary rescue team for Nordstral Pharmaceuticals. Chekov and his team discovered Stehle's frozen body and concluded he and his men had been killed by Alion. SEE Alion.

Stein, David (DC)–First Officer on the *USS Kongo* killed attempting to reach the central core via outside. SEE *USS Kongo*.

Steno, Nicholai (IT)–A tall angular man with blond hair. As station manager for the Nordstral orbiting station, he opted to lead the rescue team searching for the missing group led by Stehle. Alion killed Stehle and Steno. SEE Alion.

Stevens, Harry (GSR)–Crewman on the *Ransom Castle*.

Stilters (FD)–Slang term the Variants of Discord gave to the other sentient race on Discord. SEE Susuru.

Stoner (Di)–Resident of Gamma Xaridian Three stationed at the planetary defense station Bravo. He and the entire colony were destroyed by Rithra raiders.

Storm (FD)–One of seven cities on Discord. Though the residents are known for their maintenance of a surface plant where minerals are extracted from sea water, the city is better known for its annual artistic competitions featuring metal sculptures and discordant electronic music. SEE Hannes.

Strick, Jason (FD)–Light-skinned black complexioned native to Discord had pronounced epicanthic folds to his eyes but no other indication of any genetic manipulation. By trade he was an arbiter. He found Uhura attractive and they spent time together.

STD formula (BD)–Equation employed in navigation. Refers to speed, time, and distance. With known numbers for two, the third can be discovered. Jim Kirk impressed his gang with knowing how to navigate employing this formula.

Strato-838 (BD)–A vessel described as " a chunky squared-off utility crawler" that could function in space. It transported George, Jimmy Kirk, and Captain April to the drydocked *Enterprise*.

stratotractor (BD)–SEE Strato-838.

Steinway (P)–Musical instrument known as a piano. Many improvements were made to the piano beginning in 1856 by Henry Steinway who produced the grand piano in 1856 that quickly became a favorite of concert pianists. His company improved the mechanics, redesigned the iron frame and case, increased string tension, and strengthened the soundboard. A Steinway was specifically requested by the Romulans. SEE Romulan agenda; Jandra.

Stephanie Emilie (SG)–Ancient Terran sailing vessel captained by Marco Beppe was found floundering on the high seas completely deserted except for the dead captain.

Strauss (P)–The reference may be to Johann Strauss Jr. A 20th century composer of over 500 waltzes, polkas, quadrilles in addition to ballets and an opera. One of many whose music McCoy considered adding to the ship's musical library.

Styles (Di; UC)–StarFleet serial number: OC978-497 (Mandel *Manual* 15). A sandy-haired, pompous human. He and Kirk served for a time together on the *Farragut*. In the mission detailed in *Prime Directive* he was a lieutenant. When he didn't get command of the refitted *Enterprise*, he accepted Admiral Hammersmith's assignment to ferry the Orion ship *Queen Mary* to Starbase 29 following the Talin IV incident. Chekov sabotaged the ship's gravity units by setting them on 3-g (Reeves-Stevens). In Di, he was heavily recruited by Commodore Wesley prior to taking a position on the *Lexington*. After a period of time at the Bridge navigation console he shifted to transporter. According to McCoy, Styles was one of several navigators who got into trouble with Kirk but eventually proved a capable crewmember. In the mission detailed in *Search for Spock*, Styles, commander of the *Excelsior* during its trial runs in 2285, faced the humiliation of having his ship "die" before he could order it into warp and chase *Enterprise*. In UC, he was promoted to StarFleet Headquarters and had thoughts of retiring, but postponed his retirement and his actions postponed Sulu's captaincy of *Excelsior*.

Suarez, Kwan-mei (UC)–Straight chin-length black hair streaked with auburn and brown eyes flecked with green gave this female mathematician on the Themis project a noticeable characteristic. Unharmed by the Klingon attack though her lover Jackson Dahl was severely injured.

subcutaneous transponders (UC)–A small device that emits a signal for locating a landing party or an away team member in an emergency. Made of rubidium cyrstals in micro size, the transponder can be injected under the skin, generally on the back of the hand (Okuda and Okuda *Encyclopedia* 518). SEE virdium patches.

suldanic gas (WLW)–Highly corrosive air-borne gas protecting transit frames on Careta IV.

Suleyman (FD)–A curly-haired, red-cheeked native of Discord known as a Micro. He piloted a deep submersible carrying Spock and Mona Arkazha to Hellsgate Rift. SEE Mirco.

Sulfur Island (FD)–One of several islands of the Susuru-claimed archipelago on Discord; its name denotes its character.

Sulu, Hikaru–StarFleet Serial Number: CHC 173-950 (Mandel *Manual* 25); SH 203-622 (Rostler 119). With dispute over his serial number, the dispute continues as related to facts of his biography, including his first name which one historian gives as Hikaru and another gives as Itaka (Rotsler; Mandel *Manual* 25). All who write about Sulu indicate he is an Oriental of mixed ancestry, Japanese dominate. Historians and novelists disagree on both his birthplace and his birthdate. Historian Colleen Arima (106) writes that Sulu, the only child of Kenjo and Sumiko, was born in the Pacific Northwest of U.S.A., Terra. Historian Geoffrey Mandel (*Manual* 25) insists Sulu was born on Alpha Mensa Five and believes him to be a descendant of the Golden People of Hawaii. Okuda and Okuda (*Encyclopedia* 482) identifies the place as San Francisco,

Terra. Rostler indicates the birthplace is Wailuku, Maui of Hawaii (120). Historical novelists Theodore R. Cogswell and Charles A. Spano, Jr. agree with Mandel that Sulu was born on Alpha Mensa Five (*Messiah*). If his birthplace is confusing so is his birthdate. Mandel (*Manual* 25) gives it as 24 June 2230 and Okuda and Okuda (*Chronology* 30) as 2237. Rostler, who has compiled many StarFleet officers' biographies, records it as 3 July 2141. Rostler also records his parents as Liholiho Sulu and Graef Hatoyama and that they had two other children. McIntyre (*First*) includes the notation that sometime before his tenth birthday, he and his parents migrated to the frontier world Ganjitsu. Here they enjoyed the unspoiled wilderness of a planet settled by conservationists who controlled how much and how fast change would effect their world. Shortly after arrival, the Sulu began hearing about Klingon pirate raids bent on driving off the settlers. Sulu supposed the stories were just stories until he and his friend Kumiko experienced first hand the destruction and death these pirates rained upon the settlers. Although he tried to seek help for his friends the Weisels, who operated a local grocery, the help he found came too late to save them. Even as young as he was, Sulu remembered the incident and carried the wound for many years, suffering guilt because he did not bring help soon enough. The guilt continued into his adult life until he met Sybok who helped him face the reality of that situation and understand that nothing could have been done to save the Weisels (Dillard *Movie*). Sulu and family returned to Terra, settling in the area of supra-Tokyo, Terra. Several visits to Hawaii and areas of Japan led Sulu to study his ancestors' native language, customs, and history. Early in his youth his imagination was captured by the romantic concept of the samurai, and research revealed to him a samurai ancestor (Arima106). Shortly after learning of his ancestor, he commenced his study of *bushido*, the samurai code of ethics based on virtues of rectitude, endurance, frugality, courage, politeness, veracity, and loyalty, especially to ruler and/or country. This study lasted a lifetime (Arima 106). Years later Sulu experienced the life of a samurai when on an *Enterprise* mission he met a powerful entity who sent him back in time to Japan of the 1600s (Kramer-Rolls *Home*). At sixteen StarFleet beckoned him and he applied and by the following year he was ready to enter (Mandel *Manual* 25). For his seventeenth birthday his grandfather Tetuso folded 1,000 cranes, telling Sulu that the act would create a miracle (Ecklar *Maru*). Sulu considered his grandfather's present the best he ever received. On entering the Academy he selected spatial navigation as his major (Mandel *Manual* 25). According to one historian, Sulu's first student day at the Academy had him role playing, assigned to Cadet Bloc W, one of 25 students under the command of Commodore Rachel Coan. The game of Galactic Politics allowed Sulu to exercise his imagination. Delegated as ambassador to Menak II, a planet without warp technology and with no way of contacting the Federation, he was forced to create a means of communicating directly with the Federation ambassador when his communication line would not allow him to do so. His solution earned him credit with Commodore Coan. Also on that first day he met his roommate Kevin Riley, an Irishman with whom he would serve duty on the *Enterprise* 1701. His days at the Academy kept him busy with classes in Terran and alien biology, botany, xeonbiology, biophysics, and physiology as well as a variety of classes devoted to navigation and piloting. He became such an enthusiastic lover of botany that it became his chief hobby. A second hobby grew from a birthday gift of an ancient Terran revolver which he restored and had bullets made for (Arima 109). Throughout their Academy days, cadets are put to tests to determine strengths and weaknesses. Sulu participated in an open-air navigation/orientation exercise in which he was given command. The squad of cadets, dropped off in the Allegheny Mountains and provided with limited food, water, and warm clothing, were to make their way to a predetermined base camp. Sulu's squad was in the top group to finish early (Ecklar *Maru*). Every graduating command-track cadet is required to take the *Kobayhashi Maru* test. Sulu's test results indicate the notation that he chose to allow the passengers and crew of the *Maru* to die rather than surrender to Klingon demands. In spite of this, one of his teachers, Commodore Timothy Emmett, once commander of the *Hood*, noted in his record that Sulu was one of the best students he had at the Academy (Arima 110). Mandel (*Manual* 25) records that upon graduation in 2250, he enrolled at Tufts College of Military Science, specializing in astrophysics and tactical weaponry and earning his degree in 2254 (Mandel *Manual* 25). Sulu was captain of the Academy fencing team three years running. One source indicates his first ship was *Sacajawea* (Rostler 121), but another records the *Paul Revere*, under the command of Captain Trenton Forbes who recommended Sulu for Command School (Arima 110). Following Forbes' advice, Sulu enrolled and showed an aptitude in astronomy, chemistry, electronics, and math (Arima 114; Rostler 121). At age 25 he was ordered to duty on USS *Essex*, a heavy cruiser, to serve as relief Helmsman. Though by now he had earned the rank of lieutenant junior grade, he chose to leave StarFleet in 2256 and take a position at the Daystrom Duotronics Corp (Mandel *Manual* 25). However, in 2261, he returned to StarFleet (Mandel *Manual* 25) and in 2266 was assigned to the *Enterprise* 1701 as staff physicist in the Astronomy Section (Okuda and Okuda *Chronology* 40) under the supervision of the chief helmsman. Within a few months he earned the rank of lieutenant senior grade. When Lee Kelso transferred from the helm, Sulu became senior Helmsman on sd1313 and then was promoted to Chief Helmsman on sd7318 with the rank of Lt. Cmdr (Mandel *Manual* 25). As a career officer, he was given opportunities to be in command for Kirk often left the con in his hands, and over the years of service on *Enterprise* 1701, Sulu gained experience in many capacities, particularly in command. As a helmsman he handled the firing of phases and torpedoes. His ability with ship weapons is nearly legendary as is his marksmanship. His piloting, when Kirk gave him free rein, saved the *Enterprise* many times. Mandel mentions that his secondary duty while on the *Enterprise* was Weapons Officer, a position for which Spock recommended him. Under Spock's supervision, he developed the Romulan plasma weapon into standard photon torpedoes for use by StarFleet ships (*Manual* 25). He was considered an expert with all kinds of weapons, a distinction unparalleled in StarFleet and became known Fleet-wide for his superb reflexes in handling a starship. Sulu's years with Kirk provided him with opportunities to learn the art of command as well as the ability to take orders. On his StarFleet application forms, he revealed his belief that he was a mixture of Japanese, Filipino, Hawaiian, and Americanglo with a philosophical outlook on life largely drawn from the samurai class of feudal Japan (Mandel *Manual* 25). Although he was considered a Renaissance man adapted to his century but drawn to the samurai concept as a philosophy, he used this belief to become an expert in *Katana-to-ashi*, the modern martial art which combines ancient Terra-European fencing with karate. One biographer described him as a "'hip' character with an excellent sense of humor" (Robbenberry *Making* 247). He was always remembered by his crew mates as an enthusiastic lover of exercise and chocolate – "the chocolate gives me the pep, and exercise keeps me trim" (David *Disinherited*). Most recalled he integrated well with the crew. Although his fellow crewmen teased him for his variety of short-term interests, his consistent interests included botany. Close friends during his *Enterprise* days often recalled the time he grew a carnivorous plant he named Filbert (Ecklar *Maru*) and kept a temperamental plant he named Beauregard (David *Disinherited*). Chekov, in particular, remembered Sulu's difficulty in remembering the code for his quarters. He changed it frequently, once even selecting star coordinates but couldn't recall which ones he had chosen (Graf *Death*). He also excelled in fencing, martial arts, and ancient weaponry, of which he had a varied collection. Dr. Leonard McCoy, a close friend, called his collection "Sulu's vegetable slicers" (Yep *Shadow*). Sulu constantly tried to get Uhura to engage him in fencing and attempted to recruit other crew members to help him in his botany interests and once tried to organize a musical theater group (David *Disinherited*). Sulu's StarFleet record holds much interesting information. As helmsman, he was known as "the driver" of the ship. In a partial interview in his record is the note that his fellow Bridge officers concluded he was always the first to "feel" impending trouble though he enjoyed being the first to catch sight of the unexpected and "particularly" enjoyed " a good view of each cosmic event" (David *Disinherited*). He admitted to Uhura that he "felt challenged guiding the massive starship through the heavens and from star to star" (David *Disinherited*). Uhura's impression of him was that he "was too irrepressible, too full of energy, to work at any speed slower than fast" (David *Disinherited*). She also recalled that he told her "that the feeling of finding the unknown [is] what led [me] to StarFleet and [keeps] me tied to the helm" (David *Disinherited*). All who knew him and worked with him remembered he integrated well with the crew. Only one historian speaks of any relationship with a woman. Arima (111) mentions Lynn Mihara, of Japanese descent and the *Revere's* navigator. It developed to the point where they began discussing options but a mission brought them to a brief halt. Soon afterwards she fell ill with a rare disease and died. Captain Forbes helped Sulu through the period of mourning by reminding him that to give up would tarnish her memory (Arima 113). His medical record shows that on sd1672 he suffered severe frostbite on the planet Alfa (*EW). On planet PSI 2000, he came in contact with a virus that tends to relax one's inhibitions and bring out one's basic nature. It caused Sulu to roam the corridors of *Enterprise* with a fencing foil, challenging anyone he met (*NT). A brief exposure to spores on Omicron Ceti III caused the fencing scar on his face to disappear (Mandel *Manual* 25). In an accident on the planet Phylos, he was bitten by a retlaw plant and would have died had a native not saved his life (*IV/a). The Dramen Auroral plague and Rigellian fever both caused him pain and lost duty time (Mandel *Manual* 25). His service record indicates he received the Legion of Honor and was decorated twice by StarFleet Ordnance Division (Bonanno *Dwellers*). Rostler lists four commendations, seven Awards of Valor, and identifies ten ships he served on, generally as helmsman. In addition Rostler includes 21 Academy demerits (120-121). Some three years after the end of the final five-year mission on *Enterprise* 1701 under Kirk's command, Sulu made captain, but when he learned Kirk was coming back to active duty, requested permission to pilot the shuttle carrying Kirk, McCoy, and Uhura to Kirk's new command. Also on granted request, Sulu was given permission to serve as helmsman with Kirk, thereby postponing his commission (McIntyre *Khan*). He participated in the destruction of Khan, the refusion of Spock and his *katra* and the retrieval of humpback whales. Okuda and Okuda (*Chronology* 76) record that he received his captaincy of *Excelsior* in 2290 sometime after his debriefing concerning the destruction of *Enterprise* 1701 and the facts in the case of the search for Spock. When asked to identify a memorable mission, Sulu chose to identify two. One involved his time in disguise as a Romulan Records Clerk (Bonanno *Dwellers*). Another revealed the time spent on Direidi gave him the opportunity to sing and dance (Ford *How Much*). He might have also included mention of Kirk leading a small group into Terra' past, circa 1980s, to capture two humpback whales. He definitely should include mention of being allowed to fly a Huey helicopter (McIntyre *Voyage*). Some of his *Excelsior* Bridge crew expected he would be demoted for his actions during the Klingon/Federation peace talks held at Khitomer. When Kirk, after escaping from Rura Penthe, requested the conference location, Sulu gave no thought to putting his career on line by giving Kirk the location and time. Sulu arrived just as the situation came under control. StarFleet Command never learned from his ship log nor his officers just what he had done.

Sulu's access code (DC)–Each crew member of each StarFleet vessel has a personal code for his/her quarters which can be locked, accessible only by Security or through the code. Sulu often forgot his and needed Security to open the door. When he and Chekov discovered his quarters demolished, Chekov suggested the code 7249, the first four digits of his phaser serial number. Sulu patiently told Chekov that he couldn't remember the one he had chosen and wouldn't remember this one. He had tried a code based on star coordinates but couldn't remember which one he chose.

Sulu's quarters (DC)–Deck 6, Corridor C, Sector 39. The bomb planted on this deck in the auditors' quarters caused a hull breach that destroyed Sulu's cabin and exposed all his plants and animals to space.

superdolphins (P)–Term McCoy used to identify images of leviathans displayed in the hologram emitted by the Probe's crystal. So named because dolphin "see" with their sonar and also because the physical appearance was similar to dolphins.

Susuru (FD)–This sentient agrarian race evolved on a veldt-type world and shortly after developing warp drive were discovered by an alien race who attempted to eradicate them. Forced to flee their home world, they were discovered three separate times by

Alva Underwood

the same alien race before a small remnant reached the world known by the Variants as Discord. *Enterprise* logs described the Susuru as having a short-narrow torso with attached slender hind legs whose toes are tipped with thick pads, slim human-like hands, a muzzle covered in soft honey-colored fur, wide nostrils, chisel-shaped incisors that line a narrow mouth, and long pointed ears that trace in all directions sit on crested skulls. The Susuru have a complicated greeting ritual part pounce, part genuflection. Their common greeting is, "Our browse and water are yours." A five-member Council of Elders called the Vanguard Walkers govern the people. According to their records and those of the Variants who named the Susuru Stilters, the Susuru came to the planet and named it Okeanos, some forty years before the Federation became involved. The two races, one on land, the other on the ocean, lived in relative peace until the Klingons arrived, promising the Susuru to eliminate the Variants. SEE Variants.

Swarm (GSR)–Translation of a Romulan term that refers to the six small scout ships (a Swarm) carried in a "mothership" known as a Bird-of-Prey. CONSULT Diane Carey *The Final Frontier.*

Sweeney, Dennis (DC)–Blond-haired Security member killed in the transporter room along with Robert Gendron and Lindsay Purviance.

Swift (FD)–Susuru leader whose body was covered in golden fur with white fur on the belly and a ruff of dark fur and black ear tips. The fur around his mouth was hoary with age, his hands were bony knuckled and sparsely furred, and his front teeth, broad chisel-shaped incisors, were yellow and worn. He was the representative speaker of the Council of Elders of the Vanguard Walkers.

Swimmers (FD)–SEE Variants.

Sybok (SS)–Spock's half brother by Sarek's marriage to T'Rea. CONSULT J. M. Dillard's *The Final Frontier: Movie.*

Sydney (P)–Terran city located on the Australian continent and one of many cities holding live Beethoven festivals each year.

symbiotic virus (SS)–A Ssan virus that when injected into a Ssan renders him an assassin. The virus lives comfortably in the Ssan blood stream.

"Symphony for the Nine" (P)–Only composition of Andrew Penalt that ever gained any widespread recognition. Some critics consider it having been composed by his wife at the time. SEE Andrew Penalt.

S'zlach hinterlands (FF)–Area of Qo'noS where Kruge was born. SEE Kruge.

Szlar'it (FF)–Place to which Klingon Teshrin had traveled for a secret meeting with Nik'nash elders and where Grael had planned to have him killed. SEE Grael.

192

3-d chess (ST)–Until Spock helped to develop 4-d chess, 3-d chess was considered the most complex form of the game. Generally played only by a true master of chess, for it utilizes three levels of a game board, one for initial board set-up and two for moveable attack positions. Number of playing pieces are determined before the game begins. "The game is exactly the same as in conventional chess except that such moves have tridimensional freedom to the extent of available consecutive squares," declares Franz Joseph in *StarFleet Technical Manual*. Spock preferred 3-d chess over poker because poker relied on chance while 3-d chess relied on logic and skill.

Tahl, Hans (GSR)–Captain of the StarFleet frigate *Great Lakes*.

Ta, Lauru ifan (GSR)–Captain of the *Unpardonable* representing New Malura in the Great Starship Race.

Talet (P)–Orthodox Romulan musician whose works were played at the Praetor's funeral. SEE Lerma; Mektius.

Tallieur (WLW)–*Enterprise* assistant historian and member of Spock's team investigating the Kh!lict Central Chamber. He discovered how to enter the headquarters.

Tallyrand, Charles (FD)–Noted Terran French diplomat in the governments of Louis XVI, Napoleon, Louis XVIII, and Charles X. History regards him as the most versatile and influential diplomat in European history, able to "flow with the current" ("Tallyrand." Wikepedia). Kirk compared some of Moriah Wayne's actions to those of Talleyrand.

Talos (P)–Relatively little is known about this system whose number four planet is under strict quarantine. According to Mandel (*Star Charts*) the system consists of five planets. However, Johnson (*Worlds* 132-133) and Trimble (235) declare Talos is a red giant supporting eleven planets. No two planets lie in the same orbital plane. Some scientists believed this may be due to planetary engineering though no evidence exists to prove or disprove their theory. Five inner worlds have eccentric orbits. The six outer planets are gas giants with conventional orbits. Talos IV is the only one of the planets to have any life. It is home to the Talosians (*Me).

Talos IV (P; WLW)–Known by its natives as Clesik, Talos IV is classed as a M world with a oxygen-nitrogen atmosphere, an orbital period of 194 days, and a rotation of 49 days and 31 minutes. It has traces of heavy metals, but no oceans or open bodies of water were noted in the initial survey though intelligent humanoid life was discovered. This humanoid race (Homo Talosii), forced by an atomic war that devastated the surface, are telepaths who live underground in shielded complexes (Johnson *Worlds* 132-133). SEE Talosians. The Federation imposed Order No. 7 following Captain Pike's recommendation that the planet be placed under "immediate and unconditional quarantine, with severe penalties established for any contact or communication with its inhabitants" (Mandel *Manual* 98-99). When differing archeology groups from various governments began a systemic surveying of planets with possible ruins of ancient civilizations, rumors rose that some artifacts had supposedly been recovered from Talos. Dr. Benar could not confirm such rumors (P). In WLW, Kirk decided to recommend an absolute quarantine on Careta IV to be included under the same order as Talos IV. According to StarFleet records, Talos IV and Careta IV are, to date, the only planets that bear such a designation. SEE General Order No. 7; Dr. Benar.

Talosians (P)–Historians and anthropologists declare Talosians (Homo Talosii) are a dying race of humanoid beings who once had a space-faring civilization, but nearly destroyed themselves in an atomic war and were forced to live in shielded underground complexes due to the intense radiation (Johnson *Worlds* 132-133). In time they lost the knowledge and ability to repair or rebuild much of their machinery. Survivors were described as "pale-skinned [with a] slight build" with extremely "large cranial structures, a result of their developing" telepathic powers. They have sophisticated machinery to enhance their skills which they use to create and maintain "sensory illusions indistinguishable from reality," and "can create, select, modify, any memory or fantasy" (Mandel *Manual* 94). They are also able to make "others see, hear, and feel, anything they wish with powers that extend deep into space," Johnson writes (*Worlds* 132). As a dying race, they sought to live in others' memories by luring people to Talos IV and since they could not reproduce, they sought out "breeding stock" in an attempt to repopulate their planet (Johnson *Worlds* 132-133). Following Captain Pike's encounter with the Talosians and his complete report to StarFleet Command, StarFleet declared their technology "more sophisticated than anything currently known" become "a dangerous and wide spread narcotic if [the information were] released to the public." Following Pike's recommendation that Talos IV be quarantined and "placed under ...unconditional quarantine with severe penalties" to anyone making contact, the Federation enacted General Order Seven (Johnson *Worlds* 132). SEE Talos.

Talulu, Beecah (Di)–A native-born African who preached primitive values were the best. Entire villages embrace her teachings and remain on primitive levels. This self-styled prophetess who claimed to be descended from the great kings of the region, de-valued education and declared that going to the stars in ships was wrong for it insulted the soil from which one sprang. She strongly influenced the parents of Jerome Baila.

Tandarich (SG)–StarFleet vessel docked at Homeaway Station just as *Enterprise* left on a duty run and became involved with *Reltah*. SEE *Reltah*.

Tanul (SS)–Ssan city-state governed by Kimm Dathrabin until his assassination. Nem Antronic replaced him.

Tarn (GSR)–Romulan centurion on the *Scorah*.

Tarsus IV (P; BD)– Kevin Riley's parents were among those citizens killed on orders from Governor Kodos. Captain Kirk often relived his ordeal on this planet.

Tate (DC)–*Enterprise* security personnel on night duty with Davidson. The Orion intruder posing as Purviance killed him.

Tau Ceti (SG)–Location of a graveyard for derelict ships.

Taylor, Janice (SS)–One of the trainee doctors dispatched to Ssan along with McCoy, Huang, Jiminex, and Carver. She requested to stay with the medical team on Ssan after the assassin cult was broken. She sent McCoy the message telling him about Merlin Carver's death.

Taylor, John (DC)–Head of the auditor team performing efficiency tests on *Enterprise* and crew.

Tellarities (FD)–Members of UFP. CONSULT *Star Trek Reader's Reference to the Novels: 1990-1991*.

Tellarite bloodworm (FF)–Animal native to Tellar.

Tellurian nickel (DC)–Phrase used by the shop keeper on Space Station Sigma One to influence Sulu to accept a marble epoxy pond for his Halkan water chameleons. Compare the Terran expression "a wooden nickel." SEE trans-shield anode.

Telris (SG)–Romulan commander of the *Elizsen* who accused Kirk of abducting the Romulan space station and murdering its occupants, but then discovered Kirk's story about the alien creature aboard the station was correct.

Tenuda (FF)–One of two colonists on Beta Canzandia who had worked with Klingon fireblossoms, believing them to be tenacious in most any environment. SEE fireblossoms.

Tenney (FD)– One of the transporter crew discovered drugged and taped up in *Enterprise's* transporter station. SEE Zellich.

Tenzing (IT)–Female *Enterprise* security member of Chekov's team to Nordstral. Her Sherpa ancestry and training made her a good choice. She died during a Nordstral icequake, when the interior ceiling of a Kitka village collapsed around her.

Termais Four (P)–Planet located in the Romulan/Federation Neutral Zone. Romulans identified it as Lihalla, the Federation as Termais Four. An archeological site of much importance to both groups was discovered here. The initial survey group declared it to be "a decaying grey world with a feeble sun" though it had an atmosphere within tolerances for humanoids. Also included in the first report was the location of a possible intact Erisian city for no right angles were discovered nor straight lines except for brief interruptions. The report suggested an excavation of the site would shed light on the Erisian Ascendancy. War between the Romulans and the Federation kept the door closed on the site for 100 years until the Romulan Interim Government contacted the Federation and suggested a possible excavation as a joint endeavor and offered a plan. SEE Romulan agenda.

Terransen (WLW)–*Enterprise* engineering technician and a member of the initial crew who opened the first buried transit frame. SEE transit frame.

Terran wolverine (FF)–One of several animal scents Kirk proposed to Minister Traphid as a way to protect the sacred cities from the herds of cubaya, animals noted for their strong sense of smell and aggressive nature.

Terrik (FF)–Klingon crewman of *Kadn'ra* and sensor officer who discovered five signatures, indicating other Beta Canzandia children were on the planet.

Terror of the Red Tape Mansion (FD)–McCoy's allusion to a short story made to Kirk.

Teshrim (FF)–Klingon head of the Nik'nash clan. SEE Grael.

Tetracite mudpack (FF)–Tetracite mud is famous for its microscopic parasites that inflict terrible bites. Kirk told McCoy that the prosthesis he'd applied so Kirk would blend with the Obirrahat natives left Kirk feeling like he'd been covered with a Tetracite mudpack.

The Blimp (GSR)– Entrant in the Great Starship Race captained by Charles Goodyear IX.

the'el (P)–A one-stringed instrument Jandar was required to play at the Praetor's funeral. SEE Jandar.

Themis (UC)–Themis had seemed the most secure planet since it was located near a well-protected starbase. Carol Marcus and other researchers chose Themis partly for that reason and partly for the ease of establishing a facility to study mostly agricultural projects. Witnesses to the Klingon attack declared "phaser fire came out of nowhere" with fire that "seemed to originate <u>below</u> the clouds, as if the ship were simply invisible...." Klingon High Council condemned the raid and issued a statement declaring pirates were responsible. Possibly the attack was General Chang testing his ship, *Dakronh*.

They Who Walk in the Vanguard (FD)–The four male Susuru who form the Council of Elders along with the leader to make a perfect number. These are the leaders who consider all actions taken or motioned toward their people.

Third Interstellar Convention for Safety of Life in Space (BD)–Series of safety protocols, laws, and bylaws established by the initial convention, initiated by StarFleet Medical, was held on a regular basis as updating was required.

Thirellian mineral water (P)–Refreshing drink from a Thirellian world. Kirk, Spock, and McCoy enjoyed a round in the space dock officers' lounge while observing the view of San Francisco.

Thlema (UC)–This Andorian female xenopsychologist who specialized in Klingon culture pointed out that Ambassador Kamarag's argument was logical and stated that a quick military strike against the Klingons was acceptable to her: "I think the risks of a quick military strike to retrieve Kirk and McCoy are acceptable."

Thomas Jefferson (GSR)–A Federation museum ship commanded by Sue Hardin ran in the Great Starship Race.

Thorvaldsen, Bill (BD)–Chief impulse engineer on April's *Enterprise* during this mission.

Three Musketeers, The (S)–Novel by Terran Dumas published in 1844. Renna made reference to a "third musketeer" when questioning McCoy about Kirk's absence. SEE Renna.

Thrusting Knives (FF)–Translation of the Klingon term Gevish'rae referring to the sworn enemies of the Kamorh'dag. SEE Gevish'rae; Kamorh'dag.

Tiam (P)–A handsome, but arrogant Romulan male whose face seemed to always carry a self-satisfied expression. His record indicates a distinguished academic record, with degrees in political science and prizes for fencing and gymnastics. Found also in his record are awards of merit for his work in linguistics and etymology. He was married to Jandra at the insistence of her uncle and placed in a mid-level administrator position by the Praetor. The Interim Government approved his appointment as ambassador to the Romulan/Federation peace initiative and assigned him two aides: Kital and Jutak. Though he at first supported the actions of Kital, alias Jenyu, he came to comprehend the situation and offered his help to Captain Hiran by ensuring Hiran regained control of his ship.

Tierenios Four (SS)–Kirk was part of a mission here and picked up a few elaborate curses.

Tiberius (BD)–James T. Kirk's middle name.

Timmons (WLW)–*Enterprise* security guard who helped Kirk retrieve all the crew/Kh!lict from Careta IV.

"tir" (SS)–Title of respect for an elder Ssan. SEE Ssan.

Tisur (FF)–A Klingon pleasure compound where green Orion women perform.

Tithranus (SS)–Ssan security officer in the employ of Master Governor Holaris. Assassins killed him and the governor.

Tiviranisch Island (FF)–Located on the Klingon homeworld, off the coast of the southern continent. Dumeric had an estate here. SEE Dumeric.

T'Noy (GSR)–Vulcan female commander of the StarFleet all-Vulcan crewed *Intrepid* which participated in the Great Starship Race.

Tom (GSR)–Native of Gullrey and one of three host observers placed on the *Enterprise*. He chose his name for its friendliness in sound. Tall and gangly with fair hair and a fair complexion, he told Kirk and the Bridge crew the story of the Rey's search for other beings. When Valdus attempted to breach the Bridge, Tom found the courage to stab Valdus and help Kirk gain control of the *Ransom Castle*.

Tootsie (IT)–A technician working for Nordstral Pharmaceuticals.

Torgis (FF)–Klingon; one of two body guards for Kruge.

Torril (FF)–Located on Alpha Maluria Six. Kirk and Scotty, in disguise, told an Obirrhat they were from here.

T'Paal (UC)–Vulcan female who served in the Vulcan diplomatic corps stationed on Zorakis which bordered Klingon space. Mother to Valeris and wife to Sessl, T'Paal was a devout pacifist, as was her husband. Believing firmly in peace, they attempted to contact the Klingon Empire. She was killed by Klingons as she and her husband attempted talks. SEE Valeris; Sessl.

transit-frames (WLW)–The first one discovered on Careta IV was indicated by sensor readings taken by Chekov and Dr. Talika Nyar. It had to be excavated by heavy equipment during which time the personnel were exposed to deadly suldanic gas. The following was lifted from Kirk's report. Four huge basalt slabs standing on their edges, capped by a fifth hid a "frame two meters high and four meters long and ten centimeters thick. The back side was a metallic blue-gray with no scratches or tarnish to mar the finish. The other side reminded [me] of a pair of plate-glass windows enclosed in a flat black frame. [The front side provided an allusion of a] life-like landscape on the left, showing a rolling plain covered with knee-deep grass." Sensory studies indicated the object emitted a subharmonic frequency that produced feelings of unease in most of the human crewmembers. One study revealed it appeared to "power up" as though anticipating usage. Another hinted at a cooler temperature, near ten degrees different, on one side (deemed the front) than the other. The back side repelled any attempt to penetrate it, being protected by a force field. The front side allowed penetration and radiated warmth and a strong pull. Non-organic objects did not penetrate either side. Accidently discovered to be a form of transportation, seven unlucky crew were passed through to emerge as either male or female Kh!lict, an unforeseen effect. Once a frame was found, others were soon identified. All were controlled from a Central Chamber buried beneath tons of rubble. Kirk added to his report that following the conclusion to this incident, he was recommending Careta IV be quarantined.

trans-shield anode (DC)–Term applies to a device capable of transporting objects through shields. The term anode refers to the "collecting of energy being sent." When the device is activated it disrupts a multitude of circuitry be it computer, sensors, etc. The radiation impulse created by activation superimposes interference patterns on sensitive equipment. When an object is beamed to the trans-shield anode, a side effect is a burst of subspace radiation. Objects can only be beamed <u>to</u> the anode not away from it. This entire theory and device were proven inoperable by Constance Duerring's work that declared the energy generated whenever a transporter beam encounters a force field is absorbed by the random re-arrangement of molecules within the transported object and that the anode device diverts the energy to the surrounding subspace boson field creating a low-frequency radiation.

Traphia (FF)–Native of Alpha Maluria Six, member of the Manteil religious group, one of six government ministers. He had ebony skin with web-like patterns around his mouth and chin. He sought to stop the conflict with the Obirrhat. SEE Obirrhat.

Treadway, Clay (SS)–Diplomat sent to help bring peace to Ssan. Described as having a reddish-gold mustache neatly trimmed, thick dark hair, and a strong sense of duty though known as a flirt. Married Jocelyn Darnell after her divorce from Leonard McCoy. Jealous and a bit possessive especially towards her. Clay was Jocelyn's high school sweetheart until she met McCoy whom she married after graduation. Twelve years before this mission Clay and Jocelyn were married and became part of the diplomatic corps. Clay followed in the footsteps of his grandfather, father, and two aunts who had also been in the corps. Sent by the Federation's Diplomatic Office, he and Jocelyn were transported by *Enterprise*. On board they met McCoy and tensions ran high. On the first attempt to contact the renegade assassin group, Clay overruled Kirk's intended landing party and insisted that he along with Jocelyn be sent to start the peace negotiations. The first landing party suffered the death of one security guard and the wounding of another before Spock beamed himself and Clay out. Kirk and Jocelyn were taken captive. In an attempt to rescue her, Clay killed one of the assassins and inadvertently caused Jocelyn to be killed.

Treadway, Jocelyn (SS)–See Jocelyn Darnell.

tribbles (FD)–Trimble (242) declares these small furry creatures have no "discernable feet, head, or other appendage, although it has some means of locomotion." They come in a variety of colors, born pregnant, and multiple rapidly where there is food. They have a sweet disposition toward Vulcans and Terrans but not Klingons. Kirk and crew suffered through an outbreak of these animals on Space Station K-7 (*TT). In FD, when Moriah Wayne complained to Kirk about Sulu transporting dangerous animals, Kirk wondered if they were tribbles.

Tribulation (FD)–One of the islands forming the Discord archipelago claimed by the Susuru.

Triple Crown (GSR)–Well-known Terran horse races refers three races: Kentucky Derby, Preakness, and Belmont Stakes. Quite an honor for a horse to win all three the same year. John Orland, Chairman of the Great Starship Race made reference to this and several others in his opening remarks to those participating in the Great Race.

Trojan Horse (GSR)–The allusion is to a Terran military tactic first employed by the Greeks against the Trojans, a story told by Homer. The Greeks placed soldiers inside an enormous horse knowing the Trojans wouldn't suspect trickery. When the Trojans took the horse inside their walled city, the soldiers burst forth and conquered Troy. Romulan commander Valdus planned to employ the *Ransom Castle* loaded with explosives to destroy the planet Gullrey for no one would suspect a Federation ship of carrying a dangerous cargo. SEE *Ransom Castle*.

Trottier (DC)–One of three *Enterprise* security personnel who preferred night duty.

Through the Looking Glass (ST)–Terran novel written by Lewis Carroll is a sequel to his other book – *Alice in Wonderland*. Dr. Omen quoted from this novel. SEE Appendix B: Quotations.

tlakyrr (P)–An obsolete Vulcan instrument required in a composition by Salet. SEE Dr. Benar.

T'lekan (P)–Romulan-held planet on which Dajan had been excavating petroglyphs before being called away. SEE Dajan.

Tocchet (DC)–*Enterprise* security personnel; preferred night duty.

Tokyo (P)–A Terran city that holds live festivals to honor Beethoven.

Tomlinson, Robert (Di)–Phaser crewman killed by escaping phaser-coolant fumes during a Romulan attack that interrupted his marriage to Angela Martine (*BT). SEE Angela Martine.

Torm (ST)–Klingon whose long thin nose and a spot of beard on his chin made him easily recognizable. He believed he had found StarFleet's secret weapon when he located the *Erehwon*. He fired on Omen's asteroid but inflicted no harm. Kirk destroyed the Aleph to prevent the Klingon ship from being caught in it.

tra'am (P)–A Romulan keyboard instrument that is vaguely similar to a piano.

Tramway of the Oregon Trail (BD)–This aerial transportation follows the old Oregon Trail and serves mostly tourists who wish to see the trail.

transit-frame transportees (WLW)–A total of seven *Enterprise* crew were changed from humans to Kh!lict. Chekov and Talika Nyar accidently fell into a frame. Kirk and Security guards Bovray and Timmons, and Spock, willingly walked through. Ensign

Bradford Nairobi was accidently pushed into the frame when a Kh!lict charged at him. Of these seven, two lost their lives. Bovray died of sheer fright after being transported onto the *Enterprise* while still in the Kh!lict body. Nairobi was killed by a Kh!lict in battle.

Traveler (P)–One of many names acquired by the Probe. This one was bestowed by the silicon-based creatures of the Ophane star cluster.

Trindad (BD)–Lt. Reed is often called Trinidad. SEE Francis Drake Reed.

Trudeau (Di)–StarFleet vessel slightly smaller than the *Enterprise*. Lt. Palmer transferred from the *Enterprise* to this ship. SEE Palmer.

True Language (P)–Identified as the language spoken by the creators of the Probe. They believed intelligent life would speak their language. SEE Probe.

Turnaga defense (Di)–Starship maneuver often employed against multiple enemy ships nearly equal in size to the *Enterprise*. When Chekov urged Kirk to employ this maneuver against the Rithra raiders, Kirk relieved him from the Bridge and ordered him confined to his quarters.

Turrice (GSR)–SEE Roon.

Turry (GSR)–SEE Roon.

Tutankhamen (P)–A 14th century BC Terran Egyptian king known chiefly for his intact tomb discovered in 1922 by Howard Carter. Sulu recalled the discovery of this tomb as he watched the Romulans and Federation archeologists working to uncover a portion of a wall they believed defined the Exodus Hall. He suspected this find on Termais Four would be as exciting as that found in the desert of Terra's Egypt. SEE Exodus Hall; Termais Four.

Triumph (P)–Reference is to the attainment of the Probe's creators to use their power of speech to clear mass and create a small breathing arena so they could construct ships to lift them off their dying world.

Tupperman (BD)–Engineer's mate assigned to Scotty on the *Enterprise* 1701-A on this mission.

UES (FD)–United Exploration ship. Before the completion of the organization that led to the United Federation of Planets, Terra had already dispatched ships whose missions were to explore space. One was the *Hernan de Soto*. SEE *Hernan de Soto*.

UFP (FD)–SEE United Federation of Planets.

Uhura, Nyota Upenda–StarFleet Serial Number: CCE 540-621. She was African born of the Bantu Nation of United Africa, Terra, in the small town of Koyo, west of Mombasay, according to one historian (David *Disinherited*) or in the Kitui Province of Kenya (Mandel *Manual* 27). Historians Okuda and Okuda (*Chronology* 30) list the year as 2239 while Mandel (*Manual* 27) gives it as 19 January 2233. She came from a distinguished family both in service and name. In Swahili her entire name means "she who loves freedom." Her mother, M'umbha Majira Nafuu Uhura, which translates as "progression of seasons," was a career diplomat, first for her native region of Kenya, then for U.S. Africa, and then for StarFleet (Mandel *Manual* 27). She was also a talented sculptress (David *Disinherited*). Her father, John Indakwa Uhura, a noted professor of African history, was named for a distinguished and beloved African educator. After many years of teaching and several tours of duty with StarFleet, her father accepted a professorship at the University of Kenya, but his teaching career began in his home village. One historian (David *Disinherited*) declares Uhura was an only child while another writes she had a brother who was a doctor at the University in Kampala (Mandel *Manual* 27). Historian Love (140) writes that she was the oldest of four children and the best known. Her sister Lulua ("pearl of freedom"), brother Shukrani ("he who gives thanks for freedom"), and Mweda ("keeper of freedom") had successful careers. Uhura's mother, from time to time, served as a diplomat and continued to live in the family home on Terra. Her brother David (Mweda) became a doctor at Makere University in Kampala while her brother Shukrami appeared to follow in his father's footsteps, pursuing a life-long commitment to education. John and M'umbha raised their children in John's home village, exposing them to the "unique life" as lived in "many undeveloped regions of Africa." The same writer notes that Uhura "had always been grateful for the foresight of her ancestors who preserved the wilderness and its animal life" (Love 140). From her background came her philosophy that reflected "the warm, nonaggressive man-nature-oneness culture of the 23rd century Bantu nations" which has shown the world how to blend technology and agrarianism (Roddenberry 252-253). Once in an interview, Uhura admitted her unusual childhood led to a deep commitment to StarFleet's Prime Directive (Love 141). From early childhood, her parents encouraged her interest in learning. They arranged for Uhura to attend the Terran Institute for Advanced Mathematics in a program for gifted children. During the time there, she shared a room with T'iana who died at age eleven from wounds caused by a fire. The incident troubled Uhura for some years (Paul *Three*). Her deaf childhood friend Epala taught her sign language which she continued to study and employ to understand alien sign languages (David *Disinherited*). When she discovered the mystery of communicating long distances via technological devices, she knew she had found her vocation. Her father, a starman and explorer of space, as well as an educator, encouraged her to assemble, disassemble, and use most known communication devices. She was seventeen when her father died and at age eighteen she entered Space Service and took training in communications, first at the University of Kenya and later at StarFleet Academy College of Communications. She studied spatial navigation, duotronics, and cryptography under Lt. Benjamin Finney (Mandel *Manual* 27). Following her graduation from the Academy, Uhura was unable to immediately secure a ship post so she accepted a position on the scout *Atlantica* which required every skill she had to help its crew reach Altair 7. The ship suffered every sort of breakdown in the books (Love 143). Nearly eight months at this post honed her various skills. Following the completion of this tour, StarFleet promoted her to full ensign and assigned her to the destroyer *Adad*. When her superior was killed in a skirmish with Klingons, the captain promoted her to lieutenant and posted her at Bridge Communications. Her next assignment was to have been the *Constellation*, captained by Matt Decker. She was to meet the ship at Starbase 3 but during her wait she injured herself in a rescue operation and was in Sick Bay when the ship left port (Love 144). Once healed, she posted to the destroyer USS *Ahriman* and served as its junior communication officer (Mandel *Manual* 27). Though no date is given, Uhura was part of a mission to the planet Wynet V where her captain was killed (Snodgrass *Tears*). Promoted to full lieutenant on sd2260 she received distinction after deciphering a Romulan micropulse code during a border skirmish (Mandel *Manual* 27). Her transfer and assignment to *Enterprise* (sd1514) began a long and illustrious career. After Lt. Alden Chief of Communications was promoted, she assumed his position and received the rank of Lt. Cmdr., Chief of Communications. Concern for others was exhibited in her ability to relate well with her fellow crewmembers. Uhura was respected by Captain Kirk who depended upon her knowledge and abilities. Often she appeared to know what he wished before he commanded it. The crew also found her responsive, sensitive, understanding, and easy to visit with. The sport logs of *Enterprise* record that she held the record for the 100-yard dash in the Pan-American Games of sd2255, and that she loved to fence. She had other talents, especially singing. She knew many songs and music from a variety of diverse cultures and was a master at playing the Edoan *sessica* (Mandel *Manual* 27). Spock encouraged her interest in the Vulcan lyre and she practiced daily. Together they entertained in the ship's recreation area. This interest in music led her to develop an expertise in ancient ballads and other ethno-musical works and to study them as a means of communicating with other sentient life. Most of her contributions to Kirk's missions and others consisted of accurate communications. Kirk had good reason to call upon her and her talents when sent to investigate the possibility of sentient life being killed (Snodgrass *Tears*). This is the one she most often recalled with fond memories for it dealt with a sentient life form that had been killed for their secreted tears. She applied her musical abilities and learned they were responsible for the spacial anomaly in their region of space, and Kirk used the information to stop the slaughter and effect a healing to the region (Snodgrass *Tears*). Her broad and deep knowledge of ancient ballads of Terra and other planet cultures helped her unravel the story that brought together separated segments of a society. When she connected the songs of the Eeiauoans and Sivaoan, she solved a mystery (Kagan *Song*). In a deadly but humorous game at a Klingon outpost, Uhura tried out her Klingon vocabulary and fooled a Klingon sentry at Mortagh Outpost Three (Dillard *Country*). When her medical and military records were opened, few historians chose to reveal any facts about her life before *Enterprise*. The record indicates she suffered a leg tendon injury at Starbase 3, severe frostbite when an environmental computer malfunctioned, sd3138, minor lacerations while on the planet Triskelion ,sd3211 (*GT), and minor radiation after prolonged exposure to Epsilon radiation, sd5577. She suffered from Rigellian fever, sd5843, (*RM) and contracted Damen Auroral plague, sd5276, (Mandel *Manual* 28). Just like other members of the *Enterprise* Bridge crew, Uhura was reluctant to discuss her awards. Her military record declares she has three commendations and four Awards of Valor (Rostler 134). One of these was bestowed by StarFleet Communication Division (Mandel *Manual* 27). However, she would never voluntarily reveal just how many were earned in the line of duty or bestowed for her continual contributions to the field of communications. As considerate as she was toward friends and colleagues, she would not brag about herself. A letter inserted into her records by Cmdr. Spock mentions her receiving an electrical shock at the Bridge Communication Console that led him to investigate several high ranking StarFleet officers and to expose them as Klingon agents (Dvorkin *Timetrap*). Commodore Wesley also included a note of appreciation for her expertise in sign and vocal language in the handling of the Rithra matter (David *Disinherited*). A psychological note included in her record mentions her suffering psychological trauma after Captain Kirk's death. It also mentions that she reported to Dr. McCoy that she "saw" Kirk as a wraith floating in and out of her vision. Her experience with his "ghost" required a few sessions with Dr. McCoy following Kirk's rescue (*TW). Any and all of those she served with gave glowing accounts of her service to the ship and crew. Some included her help with personal problems. Janice Rand remembered her fondly as having helped her adjust to being Captain Kirk's yeoman (McIntyre *First*). Dr. McCoy described her as being as "delicate as ten-penny nails and as defenseless as a tiger," and Chekov lovingly remembered her as always trying to get him to eat some exotic raw dish (Graf *Ice*). In her private moments Uhura questioned the rightness of continuing in StarFleet. Her past remained a large part of her life and pride in her heritage was reflected in the decor of her personal quarters and her off-duty costumes. She always wanted, some day, to be a wife and mother. Tours of duty and volunteer assignments prohibited any action on the matter. Conflicting biographies, especially one by G. B. Love and the official one given by Mandel, confuse the facts of her life, and she did nothing to indicate whether she agreed or disagreed, although she laughingly said she would write her memories some day.

Ul'lud (FF)–Klingon ship captained by Amagh. It was destroyed when one of its impulse engines blew out.

ulu (IT)–Shaped like a wedge piece of pie, this native knife made of bone with a bone handle is extremely sharp. Every adult Kitka carries such a knife he or she has made.

Ulu Clan (IT)–One of several groups of Kitka, native to Nordstral. SEE Nuie.

Umyfymu (DC)–Disguised as an Orion freighter, it was really an Orion T-class destroyer that had faked a distress signal to lure the *Enterprise* close enough to board. Its commander Ondarken spoke Standard quite well. He ordered his ship to chase the *Hawking* carrying Sulu, Uhura, Chekov, and Muav Haslev. On board the *Shras*, Sulu kept the *Umfymu* chasing him until it fired on its own ship the *Mecufi*. Kirk's phaser fire hit an unshielded area, but the ship refused to surrender though it had lost phaser and photon torpedo control and warp drive.

Undiscovered Country, The–Novel by J. M. Dillard. Kirk was attempting to deal with the loss of his son David and Carol Marcus' condition as a result of a Klingon raid on Themis. Both wounds were still raw when he was called to Command and told he would be the "olive branch" to the Klingon Empire who wanted to negotiate peace. Volunteered by Spock, Kirk attempted to carry out his orders but found he retained too much hatred. When the Chancellor's ship was fired upon, and Kirk was told the *Enterprise* had done the firing, he and McCoy beamed to the Chancellor's ship in an attempt to help. After a failed attempt to save Gorkon's life, McCoy and Kirk were arrested for his death. Though the Federation objected, it honored its Interstellar Law and allowed Kirk and McCoy to stand trial where they were sentenced to Rura Penthe, a prison world mined of its dilithium by prisoners. Aided by a chameloid, they escaped but were apprehended before their rescue. A fight between Kirk and the Kirk/chameloid resulted in the death of the chameloid and rescue by the *Enterprise*. Spock told Kirk of the efforts to determine what had happened. On route to the Khitomer peace conference, *Enterprise* engaged in battle with Chang's cloaked ship. The *Excelsior* came to *Enterprise's* aid and Chang's ship was destroyed. Kirk and calvary arrived at Khitomer in time to avert another assassination, this one directed at the Federation President. A plot involving Chang, Nanculus, and Cartwright with many others was revealed. Kirk admitted his ignorance and dislike of Klingons to Chancellor Atzebur and declared his intention to go forward into the future, that "undiscovered country" her father Gorkon had hinted at.

"undiscovered country" (UC)–Kirk told Azetbur that her father's reference to this phrase could be interpreted as "another kind of life" and that "people are very frightened of change."

United Federation of Planets–This federation is composed of allied members who adhere to the principles established at Babel Conferences I and II, most of which are set out in the "Articles of Federation" (Joseph *Technical*). Original members are those planets and systems that participated in the founding. Agencies of the Federation include a Supreme Assembly, a Federation Council, an Economics and Social Committee, a Trustee Council, an interplanetary Supreme Court of Justice, a StarFleet combined peace-keeping force, and a Secretariat (Joseph *Technical*). Historian Margaret Bonnano identifies sd2124 as the date of the installation of elected members from all the worlds of Federation influence into a working viable organization (DC). A precursor to this was the United Space initiative signed in New York, Terra in 2003 (Goldsteins 32). They also identify the year 2077 as an unofficial meeting of diplomats and representatives from Vulcan, Terra, Tellar, and Andor at Alpha Centauri to discuss an alliance. A call for a united federation in 2082 did not meet approval (Goldsteins 86). Yet five years later, in 2089, UFP was incorporated at the first Babel Interplanetary Conference with Harmon Axelrod appointed Secretary General (Goldsteins 98). Historians Okuda and Okuda (*Chronology* 24) identify the date of the Federation founding as 2161. This date may indicate the re-organization that led to a more inclusive alien representational structure familiar to today's Federation. A second Babel Conference was called in 2267 to consider admission of the Coridan planets (*JB). Vulcan Ambassador Sarek spoke in favor of admittance and the vote was carried (Okuda and Okuda *Encyclopedia* 27).

University of Nexqualy (WLW)–StarFleet's Exploration Division granted permission to an archeology group from this university located on Perrin IX to investigate systems within the Dulcipher star cluster. The group consisted of twenty people, including Dr. Abdul Kaul, his two assistants, and their assistants,

University of Oceania (FD)–Terran university that provided classes described as environmental services programs. Moriah Wayne attended. SEE Moriah Wayne.

Unpardonable (GSR)–Ship entrant in the Great Starship Race captained by Lauru ifan Ta from New Malura.

UN Resolution 51 (FD)–Federation ruling established in 2038 determining that no earth (Terran) citizen could be held liable for the acts of their ancestors. A rider confirmed human status to human-variant strains created during the Eugenic Wars. This resolution came to be known as "Khan's Stepchildren" resolution.

ur (FD)–A spring rock lizard native to a seldom-visited world claimed by the Klingon Empire. It produces a neurotoxin whose properties render a victim catatonic. Once awakened the victim has no memory of being stung. Moriah Wayne used this on the two *Enterprise* crewmen on transporter station duty. SEE Moriah Wayne.

'urng (FD)–Klingon craft lost in a skirmish with Variant vessels. SEE Variant.

Ursva (UC)–Fictitious name for a fictitious freighter that Spock and Uhura created to fool the Mortagh Outpost Three, claiming the ship was six weeks out of Kronos and carrying supplies to Rura Penthe.

USS *Farragut* (WLW)–Early in Kirk's tenure of duty on this ship, "the old hands" of the crew cautioned Kirk not to mix Argelian ale with <u>anything</u> else. He failed to listen (WLW). CONSULT *Star Trek Reader's Reference to the Novels: 1990-1991*.

USS *Bill of Rights* (BD)–Excelsior-class starship captained by Alma Orth. It was assigned as part of the Naval Exploration Extension of 2010 that sent ships on exploration runs. The ship was on such an assignment when caught in a trap set by the pirate ship *Shark*. Although it sent a distress call which Kirk received, the ship died in a flushback before Kirk could help it.

USS Exeter (DC)–In DC, Chekov reminded Sulu that *Exeter's* crewmen on their last shore leave had broken Chekov and Sulu's old scoring record for a space game at the arcade on Space Station Sigma One. CONSULT *Star Trek Reader's Reference to the Novels: 1990-1991* for a biography of the ship.

USS *Hood* (FF)–Currently on shore leave at Starbase Seven because its crew were suffering from a rampant virus and required medical help. CONSULT *Star Trek Reader's Reference to the Novels: 1988-1989* for a biography of the ship.

USS *Intrepid* (SS; GSR)–Federation starship NCC-1708 was a sister ship to the *Enterprise*. Its builder was StarFleet Division, Port Copernicus Yards, Luna. Begun on sd2105.07 and launched on sd2437.1, it received its commission on sd2459.82. This one ship, and the only one, was allowed to be crewed entirely by Vulcans. (*IS). In GSR, the ship was captained by T'Noy and was an entrant in the Great Starship Race.

USS *Kongo* (SG; DC). According to Reil's *Ships of the Fleet*, this ship was "Constitution Class 1710" built by StarFleet Division of Port Copernicus Yards of Luna. The keel was laid on sd2107.34 with completion on sd2445.68 and commission after trial runs given on sd2478.21. In SG, Admiral Cartwright sent the *USS Kongo* to support *Enterprise's* investigation of the Romulan space station *Reltah*. In DC, the *USS Kongo* was assigned to an Andorian expedition. On stardate 8747.6, the ship clipped a cosmic string near Perseus causing a containment field breach that left 197 of the crew dead. The list included Assistant Engineer Christopher Dailey, First Officer David Stein, and Second Officer Robert Cecil. The entire aft quarter of the ship was lost and thirteen engineers were trapped in Jefferies tubes. Access tubes and gantries of the Engineering section were torn out, and thirty engineers in main engineering were killed. It took a brace of tugs to maneuver the ship into a docking bay at Sigma One. Memorial services were conducted at Sigma One's docking bay.

USS *Lexington* (SG; Di)–Identified as NCC-1703 heavy cruiser and a sistership to the *Enterprise*. Built by StarFleet Division at Puget Sound Yards, Terra, its keel was laid on 13 September 2220, launched on 21 August 2222 and commissioned on 08 February 2223 (Reil). After some years in service it was drydocked on 09 May 2269 and converted at the Newport News Shipbuilding Yards, Louisiana, Terra. The converted ship was fitted with the "new LN-64 linear warp engines and accompanying intermix shaft assemblies" as well as "the impulse engine configuration integrated with [the] warp drive system" (Reil). Following the completion of the changes, the *Lexington* was re-launched on 13 December 2270 and re-commissioned on 06 July 2271. Trimble (184) identifies this ship as participating in war games against the *Enterprise* fitted with

Daystrom's new M-5 computer. The *Lexington* was badly damaged and suffered many deaths (*UC). In SG, it was sent to support *Enterprise* with her investigation of the Romulan space station. In Di, Commodore Wesley's mission to Rithra was on request from that government. **As** history shows, the *Lexington* name was given to other ships. For further information CONSULT *Yesterday's Son* and *Pawns and Symbols*.

USS Potemkin (Di; FD; SS; FF)–In Di, to support the *Enterprise* and Kirk's notice to the Parath'aa that the Federation intended to monitor their activities, the *Potemkin* took up orbit around the planet. In FD, the ship was part of the escort sent to provide transport to remove the Variants from Discord. In SS, the ship, captained by Gladstone, delivered the diplomat team of Clay and Jocelyn Treadway to the *Enterprise* who delivered them to Ssan. In FF, Yeoman Barrows transferred from *Enterprise* to *Potemkin*. SEE Tonia Barrows.

USS *Republic* (SS)–Historians Okuda and Okuda (*Encyclopedia* 407) identify this ship as a Constitution class registry number NCC 1371. They also mention that James T. Kirk and Ben Finney served together on this ship. Historians Goldsteins (92) identify this as the flagship of space exploration. It carried 224 crew with 12 officers, had the warp capability of 3.25 and was the first UFP sponsored starship class. Builders employed new metal/ceramic alloys for the superstructure. The ship served in the Romulan Wars. Over the years several ships have carried this honored name. In SS, the *Republic* delivered five trainee doctors to Ssan and retrieved them for delivery to Beta Aurelon Three. SEE five doctors.

uterra (SS)–Ssan native predator bird having a long beak lined with rows of sharp teeth, a head that resembles a Terran pterodactyl, and a wingspan of twice the length of a man's height. Generally the birds traveled in mated pairs.

Utilization of an Interim Committee (P)–SEE Romulan Interim Committee.

Vaal (FD)–A computer mechanism Kirk and crew faced on Gamma Trianguli VI. It provided the necessities for the human population. When it threatened *Enterprise*, Kirk was forced to destroy it (*Ap). In FD, Moriah Wayne accused Kirk of being insensitive and violating the Prime Directive in his handling of Vaal.

Valazine (IT)–A powerful sleeping drug which had no effect on those Nordstral personnel who had been aboard plankton harvesters and were suffering the effects of magnetic field fluctuation.

Valdus (GSR)–Romulan Valdus Ionis Zorokove. He was a member of the *Scorah* whose commander Oran deeply hated him, calling him a coward. While the ship was on an exploratory mapping mission, though given an order, he froze at helm controls and was demoted. When members from Gullrey came aboard and caused extreme telepathic fear in all the crew, Valdus managed to get to an ejection pod after sabotaging the ship's controls and causing it to explode. After several days drifting in space, he was rescued nearly incoherent and confused. The rescue ship showed nothing in the area. Shortly after being returned home he was hailed a hero. He never revealed what really happened. Though offered command, he at first refused and then accepted only those ships whose command missions allowed him to remain in the sector where *Scorah* had perished. When he achieved command of the starship *Red Talon*, he drove the crew ruthlessly. In time few requested a duty assignment on his ship for Valdus constantly promoted and demoted crew. Hearing of the Great Starship Race, he requested permission to enter and was granted it by the government of Gullrey. He secreted highly explosive materials on board his ship, planning to board one of the entrants and use that ship to send a fully loaded explosive ship crashing into Gullrey, destroying all life on the planet. He did board the *Ransom Castle*, but Kirk's efforts soon foiled his plan. He and the boarding party were captured. On his orders his second in command Romar took *Red Talon* still carrying most of the explosives and headed to Gullrey. Kirk averted disaster by destroying *Red Talon*. Valdus and his boarding party were tried by StarFleet Command. Probably at a later date, definitely in disguise, he was traded in a diplomatic maneuver.

Valeris (UC)–Vulcan female with straight black hair cut in a short severe style. Her mother was T'Paal and her father Sessel, both diplomats stationed on Zorakis. Her mother named her after an honored Klingon female heroine but her name has roots in a Vulcan word meaning "serenity or inward peace" and "valor." As a young child she suffered through a Klingon raid on the colony. After the death of her mother by Klingon phaser, her father took little interest in her and did not educate her in true Vulcan custom though later she took private lessons to learn Vulcan emotional control. After her father died, she learned of a sponsorship to StarFleet Academy available from the Federation Embassy at ShanaiKahr. She applied, was accepted, and sponsored by Spock who took great interest in her. Her first assignment in deep space was as Helmsman aboard *Enterprise*. Kirk tested her by having her maneuver the ship out of dock on thrusters only. In a conversation with Spock, she learned he planned to retire and have her replace him on the *Enterprise*. Only after the assassination of Gorkon, the arrest and trial of Kirk and McCoy, and the search for evidence did Spock learn of her participation in the conspiracy led by Admiral Cartwright, Captain Chang, and Ambassador Nanclus. In a mind meld, Spock learned of her using Kirk's own words passed to Chang to condemn himself at his trial. He also learned she had killed Samno and Burke in an attempt to cover up her part. She was arrested along with the others at Khitomer Peace Conference.

Valgard (SG)–One of *Enterprise's* shuttles piloted by Jaffe and Corey to the Romulan space station.

Valtane, Masoud (UC)–A descendant of humans who settled a Rigellian world. First Officer and chief science officer on the *Excelsior* under Sulu's command. His personality and duty performance, as well as lack of humor, fit the absent-minded scientist more interested in science than social interaction who took comments as literally as a Vulcan. His medical record which indicated he reported to SickBay with a broken nose also included his explanation that he had run into a bulk head while reading a report.

Vang (FD)–Klingon tactical officer on the *Dagger*.

Vanguard Walkers (FD)–A group of twenty Susuru who attend the leader and the four who are known as They Who Walk in the Vanguard. SEE Susuru.

Van Pelt (FD)–Petite blond female *Enterprise* Security officer who escorted the female Klingon Lu Kok Tak to the Brig. She was a member of the six-member Security team Kirk took with him to board the *Dagger*. Kirk and she were beamed to the Klingon Bridge.

Variants (FD)–The descendants of the genetically altered humans took this term to identify themselves. It refers to all genetically altered human-stock people on Discord. Related term: Vars. SEE Discord

Variizt worlds (P)–Group of planets that have rebelled against Romulan rule.

Vega 9 (BD)–*Enterprise*1701 under the command of Robert April was sent here to defuse a planet-possession dispute. SEE Lorna Simon.

Velikiye (SG)–Chekov's Uncle Vanya kept a small farm near this European city west of Moscow.

vent-forms (FD)–Intelligent microorganic sentient life forms living in colonies near a volcanic vent at the bottom of Hellsgate Rift. Telepathically aware of what was occurring between the Variants and the Susuru as well as between Kirk and Kain, they communicated with Spock, telling him they enjoyed the events that occurred, finding them entertaining. Microorganic life was discovered on Terra after a series of vents were found. Commonly these are found near volcanically active areas where tectonic plates are moving apart. Those under the sea are called smokers. As early as 1949, Terran researchers reported hot brines in central areas of the Red Sea. In 1977 hot spots were marked along the Galapagos Rift and in 1979 research submersibles viewed the vents. These vents sustain vast amounts of life on chemosynthetic food. However, no evidence indicates the Terra vent life forms are sentient.

verti (FD)–Discord term for an aerial vehicle whose wings can be rotated to hover or land in limited space. SEE Discord.

Vheled (FF)–Klingon captain of the *Kadn'ra* carried with pride a scar won in a bloody brawl at one of Alalpech'ch's public drinking houses. As a member of the Gevish'rae, a group located on the northern continent of Qo'noS, he took pleasure in killing Kamorh'dag, another Klingon political group. Councilman Dumeric, his uncle, sent him to Pheranna (Beta Canzandia) to obtain the G-Seven unit believed to be a new Federation weapon. He was told by Grael that his First Officer Gidris would be assassinated by the Second Officer. Vheled questioned Timothy Riordan, one of the Beta Canzandia colony's children about the G-Seven. When Vheled went to search for the team who had been sent to find the other children, Grael killed him.

Victory (BD)–HMS *Victory*, a famous Terran British ship, was Lord Nelson's flagship. It participated in the American Revolution, the French Revolution, and the Napoleonic Wars. Currently drydocked at Portsmouth Naval Base in Hampshire, England, Terra, the ship has a permanent berth and is open to all visitors. Built mostly of oak, it is 227 feet long with a 5 foot ten inch beam, draws a 28 foot draft, carried 104 guns and 850 crew ("Victory." Internet). The ship was capable of doing eight to nine knots and weighted 2,162 tons. George Kirk always planned to take James to visit this ship but duty always seemed to interfere.

Vienna (P)–One of many Terran cities that frequently hold Beethoven festivals with live performances of his music.

Viegelshevsky, Anton (P)–A 23rd century musical composer considered to be this century's most famous composer of electronic music. One of many McCoy reviewed for addition to *Enterprise's* musical library.

Viking (Di)–StarFleet patrol ship investigated the devastation on Gamma Xaridian Three and reported no survivors. It was destroyed during an encounter with Rithra raiders. SEE Rithra raiders.

Vindali 5 (SG)–Planet whose natives have a very active imagination, believing in many supernatural things, including ghosts. SEE Markson.

viridium patch (UC)–An emergency supply of patches are kept and used when subcutaneous transponders are not easily available. The patches are always messier and less elegant but have far greater range. Spock applied one to Kirk before Kirk beamed to the *Kronos One*. Thus Spock was able to remove Kirk and McCoy from Rura Penthe when they got beyond the prison shields.

Vokh (FD)–Klingon *Dagger* lieutenant who refused Kirk's offer of surrender, preferring to die at his station. SEE *Dagger*.

Volk (FD)–A native marine life-form of Discord are able to breach the surface. Description bears strong resemblance to Terra's reptilian orcas.

Volkonsky, Andrei (P)–Twentieth century Russian classical composer (1933-2008) who experimented with 12-tone and serial techniques. His works protested the suppression of freedom. In P, Chekov suggested Dr. McCoy consider Volkonsky as an addition to the ship's musical library.

Vornholt, John – Author of *Sanctuary*.

Vorry (GSR)–Native of Gullrey and one of two scientists on the last Whistling Station Post. He and Dr. Beneon made first contact with aliens — the crew of the USS *Hood*. He participated along with Dr. Beneon in the ceremonies for induction into the UFP.

Vulcan–Planet whose native population is a guiding influence in the UFP. Humans had shown Vulcan that it could influence humans and the Federation. McCoy once remarked that Vulcans are proud to be a part of the Federation and now "urged their sons and daughters into StarFleet Academy...eager to see them participate in the spaceborne operations of a thriving interstellar community...." (Crandall *Shell*). CONSULT *Star Trek Reader's Reference to the Novels: 1988-1989* for a biography.

Vulcan nerve pinch (ST)–Described as finger pressure applied to certain nerves at the base of the neck. It almost instantly renders the individual unconscious. The technique appears to work on most all humanoids. If applied too strongly for too long damage will occur to the trapezium nerve bundles (Okuda and Okuda *Encyclopedia* 550). Spock learned the technique from his distant cousin Selek (*Yy/a).

Vulcan precept (WLW)–As he prepared for a debriefing session with any of the crew interested in the Kh!lict situation, Spock recalled this proverb: "The time required to solve a problem is inversely proportional to the amount of knowledge brought to bear on the subject." He felt confident that the more people who reviewed the data, the greater the chance of one of them "seeing" the key to the entire puzzle.

Vulcan tea (ST)–A spice tea made from Vulcan herbs was always available from the *Enterprise* food replicator. CONSULT Diane Duane *My Enemy My Ally* for the herbs required to prepare tea for Vulcan masters; *Star Trek Reader's Reference to the Novels: 1984-1985*.

wagon passengers (S)–Escaping from the Sanctuary caverns before they could be Reborn, the group composed of Kirk, Spock, McCoy, Renna, Billiwog, an Andorian, and a Tellarite employed a wagon used to transport males to the Reborning ritual. The Tellarite was killed in a skirmish with the Lost Ones. SEE Lost Ones.

Wan, Li (FF)–Black female with a ponytail and delicate features. She was one of the children on Beta Canzandia who followed David Marcus into the hills to escape the Klingons. She also served as bait to lure two Klingons into a pit. SEE Aoras; Gidris.

Wanderer (P)–One name given to the Probe by those it touched in their attempt to identify it.

warp thirty (P)–Speed the Probe is estimated to have achieved on its homeward trip.

War of the Worlds, The (SG)–Novel written by Terran H. G. Wells and published in 1896. Science fiction story about a Martian invasion that is thwarted when the aliens are destroyed by terrestrial pathogenic bacteria. Scotty enjoyed telling stories in the Rec Room in the evening. This is one he chose.

warrants and patterns (BD)–Computer software that keeps robotic vessels or any vessel from hitting another while both are in dock brackets.

waverider (FD)–Floating homestead occupant who patrolled herds of hinds. SEE Waverider Ranch; hinds.

Waverider Ranch (FD)–Floating homestead headed by Aagard din Athos but owned jointly with others who made a living harvesting the hinds. Built to submerge during heavy storms or attacks, it has several levels with the top level being a landing pad for aerial vehicles and a lower level providing space for marine vehicles.

Wayne, Cornelius (FD)–Though he was a human Federation Council member who spent twenty years representing Jotunheim, he opposed StarFleet, calling it a military dictatorship. After his death from a brain aneurysm, his staff told stories of his violent outbursts including his brutalizing, mentally and physically, of his only daughter.

Wayne, John (ST)–A well-known movie star of the Terran 20th century. Many of the films he made were westerns. Commodore Favere had a movie production poster advertising

Wayne in the title role of "She Wore A Yellow Ribbon." Favere had it hanging in his office.

Wayne, Moriah (FD)–Only daughter of Cornelius Wayne. Her dark red hair, stern face with green eyes, and a voice described as being "a rich, well-modulated alto," led many to consider her beautiful. During this mission, as a deputy-commissioner for Interspecies Affairs, her task was to monitor compliance with the Prime Directive. Learning of Sulu's "pet," she attempted to bring charges against him for "transporting dangerous life forms." Though she considered herself a pacifist and an ecologist, she believed all Terrans were out to suppress aliens. Growing up with a limited social life, she quickly became infatuated with the Klingon Captain Kain, accepting all he told her about the situation on Discord. Convinced by his argument that Variants were destroying the Susuru, she drugged the two *Enterprise* crewmen at the transporter station and sent a nuclear device into Harmony's fusion reactor that destroyed the city and all its inhabitants. She even helped the Klingons take control of the *Enterprise*. When Kain and crew were thwarted in their attempt, Kain killed her. Details of her childhood kept secret from the committee that appointed her to Interspecies Affairs revealed her father had brutalized her mentally and physically

Wesley, Robert (Di)–Commander of the *Lexington*. Kirk always spoke highly of him. Wesley considered himself "a good judge of horseflesh" able to recognize the best and the brightest officers in the fleet and to get them on his ship. He sat on the review board when it considered Kirk's readiness for captaincy. He spoke against the promotion, believing Kirk too young and wrote in his report that "despite all the education StarFleet can provide, the greatest single teacher that our officers can learn from is experience" and "in that respect...Kirk is sorely deficient." Though he was the only one on the board to vote nay, he insisted he be the one to deliver the news to Kirk that he'd been promoted. Once the announcement was made, Wesley added his own words: "Kirk, we are a fraternity...a brotherhood...." Following his retirement, Wesley became governor of Mantilles, the most remote planet in UFP (Trimble 251; OMP/a).

West, Colonel (UC)–StarFleet officer who conspired with Admiral Cartwright and Klingon General Chang to interrupt the peace talks at Khitomer in 2293. He was the hit man, disguised as a Klingon who unsuccessfully attempted to assassinate Federation Council President Ra-ghoratrei. Scotty shot him, and he fell from the overhead area.

Whiphand (GSR)–Romulan cruiser and member of the Swarm commanded by Fleet Commander Oran. SEE Oran.

whispering smith (ST)–Possibly a reference to a plant that produces large edible pod-filled husks known as Rigellian husk, that are sometimes served at dinner parties. It also produces a sound similar to a whisper when its leaves are moved.

Whistlers (GSR)–Translated Gullrey term referring to those Reys who manned space stations sending out signals hoping to contact other sentient beings in the galaxy. The last two Whistlers were Beneon and Vorry. SEE Rey.

Whistling Posts (GSR)–Translated Gullrey term referring to space installations designed and manned to send signals into space in the hope of receiving a reply indicating they were not alone in the galaxy.

Windisch (IT)–Female crewmember of the *Soroya* and its pilot. SEE *Soroya*.

Windows on a Lost World–Novel by V. E. Mitchell. On a routine archeological inventory of the Dulciphar star cluster, *Enterprise* discovered ancient ruins on Careta IV. A small team of *Enterprise* personnel led by Kirk and Spock investigated. Accidently Chekov and Dr. Talika stumbled through a transit frame and were locked into Kh!lict bodies. To search for his crewmen, Kirk took Security and went through. They found themselves also locked in Kh!lict bodies. Kirk's efforts to communicate with Spock through the use of Morse code coloration on the back of the creature led Spock to the location of Kh!lict machinery. Kirk convinced the Kh!lict/Talika to activate the machinery and save the *Enterprise* crewmen. *Enterprise's* investigation led to the identification an extinct race called the Kh!lict who employed transit frames to move around their world. This race believed it was the only intelligent race in the galaxy and proceeded to annihilate every race they came across. After they died out, this world was found by those who knew about the Kh!lict and attempted to destroy all evidence of the Kh!lict. What they couldn't destroy, they buried. The events on the planet and the discovery of the Kh!lict led Kirk to recommend StarFleet Command quarantine the planet.

Winnowing (P)–Term used to describe the event in which thousands of Probe's creators chose to leave their home world. Event occurred in the wake of their home world having been attacked. SEE Probe.

Winston (Di)–As aide to Administrator Sharon Jarvis of Beta Xaridian Four, she monitored reports from defense sites struck by Rithrim raiders and sent them directly to Jarvis.

Wise (FD)–Susuru successor as head Walker to Swift. Wise led his people to a peaceful settlement with the Variants and encouraged his people to accept the Federation's offer of resettlement. He also related the history of his race to Kirk and Spock. SEE Susuru.

Wistor (FF)–An old Klingon who had been Karrodh's wet nurse, now elevated to a position of authority in the household after her mistress' death.

Wizard of Oz, The (ST)–Terran classic children's story in which the heroine arrives in a fantasy world aboard a farmhouse caught in a tornado. She and the house fall out of the sky onto a wicked witch, killing her. Kirk mentioned to Torm that he'd better leave Federation space "before somebody drops a house on you...." Chekov told Kirk the original tale may have been Russian and involved a falling tractor and an evil commissar. SEE Torm.

Wlaariivi (P)–Planet in the Romulan Empire. Most, if not all, of its humanoids (Romulan) inhabitants were destroyed by the Probe attack related to its search for intelligent or semi-intelligent sea life.

Worf, Colonel (UC)–Member of the Klingon military assigned as Kirk and McCoy's defense attorney at their trial.

workbees (BD)–One, two, or four-man vessels designed for working on the exterior of ships. These acorn-shaped ships are equipped with claws, magnets, antigravs, hooks, and other tools that enable it to attach to almost any section of the ship it's working on. The pilot can then effect repairs. The size of the ships gave birth to nicknames such as "potatoes, hedgehogs, sandbaggers," etc. Their storage bays are called "pantries."

Worshipper (GSR)–Romulan cruiser and part of the Swarm commanded by Oran. SEE Primus Oran.

wrangler (FD)–The Terran term refers to one who wrangles, i.e. works by moving objects be they organic or not. The term came from the Terran cowboy era. Here it is used to refer to Discord robots designed, and identified by serial numbers, to herd hinds. SEE hinds.

Wu Shanxi (FD)–Federation's leading operatic baritone. McCoy compared Kain's voice to Wu's voice.

Xaridian System (Di)–*Enterprise* was dispatched to this system to investigate small colony outposts that were being hit by Rithrim raiders.

Xenogeologist (UC)–Terran scientists who study the geology of other worlds.

Yarnos Seven (SS)–Diplomatic mission to this planet conducted by Clay and Jocelyn Treadway. A suggestion made by Jocelyn Treadway broke the impasses and led to a peaceful settlement.

Yeshmal (GSR)–Andorian woman ambassador to the Tholian Assembly. She accepted the second place trophy won by Captain Kmmuta and the crew of *552-4* in the Great Starship Race because they could not safely leave their ship. At a later date she delivered it to the ship.

Yosemite (P)–Location of the Terran mountain El Capitan that Kirk once attempted to free climb. CONSULT J. M. Dillard *The Final Frontier: Movie*.

Ytaho (GSR)–One of the entrants in the Great Starship Race commanded by Legarratlinya.

Yuki (FD)–This female native of Discord is known as a Micro. She works on Waverider Ranch. SEE Ranit; Mirco.

Zellich (FD)–*Enterprise* crewmen on duty in the transporter room drugged by Moriah Wayne.

Zeosian (UC)–SEE Dax.

Zeta (UC)–Gorkon's nickname for his daughter. SEE Atzebur.

Zibrat (FF)–One of two Klingon personal guards for Captain Kiruc.

Zicree (S)–Senite who met Kirk, McCoy, and Spock's shuttle *Erickson*. He saved them from the clutches of a giant mollusk the Senites called Old Hemcree. Zicree, as were all Sanctuary residents, plagued by millions of irradiated larvae that grew into giant locusts. Scotty and Donald Mora had released millions of larvae into Sanctuary's oceans in hopes of getting the Senites' attention for a conference.

Zorakis (UC)–A planet in the Boswellia sector of Vulcan space bordering Klingon space. SEE Valeris.

Zoraph (FF)–Klingon crew of the *Kadn'ra* and member of the second search team led by Captain Vheled searching for the children of Beta Canzandia colony.

Zorokove, Valdus Ionis (GSR)–SEE Valdus.

Zorro (GSR)–Nancy Ransom, captain of the *Ransom Castle,* marked supply and/or utility closets with the mark of Zorro, a hastily slashed **Z** to indicate where her crew had put captured and bound Romulans who had boarded her ship. The symbol came from a popular 20th century Terran television show.

Zoth (FF)–Klingon member of the High Council and member of the Gevish'rae.

Appendix A: Stardates

Faces of Fire

3998.6 ....Date given by author Michael Jan Friedman as the beginning of this mission.

Great Starship Race, The

32231.1 Marked the time that *Enterprise* noted the alternating F and F (fixed and flashing) marker in the Race.

Probe, The

sd8475.3 Captain's Log: Notes the Romulan Praetor is dead and interim government installed has extended an invitation to a group of musicians and archeologists to help excavate ruins on Temaris Four.

sd8478.4 Captain's Log: Preparation complete for departure to Temaris Four. Spock has permission to access all records concerning the Probe. Those selected, musicians and archeologists, have much to discuss.

sd8488.7 Captain's Log: Received word that the Probe has crossed into the Neutral Zone which was also sent to Romulus who denied the Probe's existence.

sd8489.1 Captain's Log: First diplomatic meeting is set. Mentions the first musical evening both groups held together in which Jandra was the hit of the evening. Working groups set for the initial assault on the ruins.

sd8492.5 Captain's Log: Mention of another mysterious message from the Empire. Spock has completed first consolidation of data from the Exodus Hall excavation. Diplomatic talks not going well. Romulans have been silent for three days.

sd8493.4 Captain's Log: Mention of Ambassador Riley's injuries. Mention of another mysterious message from Romulus. Probe nearing Temaris Four. Study continues on the data from the excavation and the sounds coming from the Probe.

sd8495.3 Captain's Log: *Enterprise* and *Galtizh* have been "dragged" by the

Probe at warp speeds beyond twenty. Both groups continue to study the Probe as best they can with limited sensor scans. Still concern for Kevin Riley.

sd8501.2   Captain's Log: Mystery of the Probe solved; Probe has returned both ships to Temaris Four. Romulan government moving on information supplied by Captain Hiran. Mention made of Spock's work with the Probe's information center and speculation on events occurring 300,000 years ago.

Shadows on the Sun

9587.2   Date of Kirk's personal log. Noted the arrival at Ssan, the meeting with the diplomatic team of Clay and Jocelyn Treadway; concern about McCoy's actions and feelings about his ex-wife; attempt to show friendship and support to McCoy.

Undiscovered Country, The

sd9522.8   Captain's personal log: Kirk recorded his thoughts about dealing with Klingons. A partial quote was repeated at his trial for the assassination of Gorkon.

sd9523.8   Captain's log: order that Romulan ale would no longer be allowed on board.

Sd9529.1   Captain's log: Kirk believed he was recording his final log as captain of a starship.

Appendix B: Quotations

Best Destiny

1. "What you from fathers have inherited,/Earn it, in order to possess it" (frontispiece). Credited to Johanna Wolfgang Goethe (1749-1832.

2. "Commanding a starship is your first best destiny" (frontispiece). Captain Spock's words to Admiral Kirk (*Wrath of Khan*: movie).

3. "I'm going to be an officer and a gentleman about it (retirement). It's time to lower the pennant..." (Pro). Kirk's words to Spock and McCoy about retirement for he believed this was his last mission.

4. "We're not in Iowa anymore, Toto" (2). Young Jim Kirk paraphrased Dorothy's words from *The Wizard of Oz*. His sarcastic reply was to Lucy who felt unsure on the high seas.

5. "A wise sailor will one time stand upon the shore and watch his ship sail by, that he shall from then on appreciate not being left behind" (7). Stated by Robert April to George Kirk who guessed the quote came from Herman Melville or C. S. Forester. April said he made it up.

6. "There wouldn't ever be another first starship *Enterprise*" (7). Captain April's thoughts as he stepped aboard ship for his mission to Faramond.

7. "...twittering like a mistlethrush" (7). April's description of Sarah April, ship's doctor, who lectured Robert, George, and Jim on being space sick.

8. "W and W...water and weapons" (15). Spacefarer's rule of thumb. Two elements necessary for survival, April told young Jim Kirk.

9. "Sail forth—steer for the deep waters only, /Reckless O soul, exploring. I with thee, and thou with me. /For we are bound where mariner has not yet dared to go,/ And we will risk the ship, ourselves, and all" (37). Quote is from Walt Whitman's "Passage to India" from *Leaves of Grass* 1900. A plaque in *Enterprise's* officer's lounge bearing these words is fixed to the wall near the lift.

10. "Something had changed in the ship's heart. Suddenly she wanted to be part of him instead of the other way around. They had saved each other's lives, and the lives of others. Strange, how things could change" (Epi). Kirk, believing and trying to accept that this was his last mission, allowed these thoughts to

drift through his mind as he prepared to give the last order as the ship headed to home port.

Death Count
1. "K'laxm f'dactla en str'In axltr'dn. Pr'dyn dgreilt jarras'tla en axmb'rerr" (19). Uhura translated this Orion phrase roughly as "Go back to Orion where you will all be charged with treason."
2. "Man does not live by bread alone" (1). The original source is the *New Testament's Matthew* 4:4. Kirk's words to Dr. McCoy who complained about the food.
3. "Man doesn't live by bubble-and-squeak, either" (1). McCoy's reply to Kirk's observation about food. They enjoyed a meal away from the ship with Scotty.

Disinherited
1. "Haven't you learned by now that ensigns are never right" (6). Scotty's words to Chekov when Chekov reported what he thought was a weapon heat signature and Scotty said the signature was a standard pulse pattern and no cause for alarm.
2. "The innocent are the innocent" (14). Spoken by Endris to Commodore Wesley who had declared his surprise that the Rithra were concerned about Wesley's people.

Faces of Fire
1. "Darkness will fall. Enemies will circle us 'round and' round, their swords as numerous as the trees of the forest. But we will not yield. We will wear faces of fire" (Pro). Quoted from Kahless' writing recorded in *Ramen'aa*. Quoted by Kiruc to Emperor Kapronek.
2. "Faces of fire" (Pro). Emperor Kapronek asked Kiruc to identify the meaning. Kiruc declared it had two meanings: (1) the quality of determination, one's strength of will is great enough to surmount any obstacle; (2) one's skill at deception; to remain circumspect in all of one's dealings with enemies or friends.
3. "It is easier to defend oneself with two hands than one" (2). Klingon expression quoted by Kiruc to Karradh.
4. "Lord save me from little minds" (2). One of many pithy saying attributed to Dr. McCoy. This remark to Kirk reflected McCoy's contempt for Ambassador Farquhar.
5. "No technology really mattered unless it could be used as a weapon against one's enemies" (3). Standard Klingon attitude, especially Uheled, whose thoughts were focused on the G-Seven unit.
6. "A position a wise man fears above all others: to be hunted by his own clan" (3). Kiruc's words to Grael which became a threat and ensured Grael's cooperation.
7. "One can never surround oneself with too many beautiful women" (4). Statement made by Yves Boudreau when introduced to Nurse Christine Chapel.

8.   "A plant that can reproduce like crazy and spew out oxygen even faster...a plant that can help turn a freezing ball of dirt into a class-M world" (5). Kirk quoted Carol Marcus' words to her during a discussion of her work on Beta Canzandia.

9.   "Information flows fast and loose where there's liquor to lossen the tongues" (14). Kirk's expressed view toward Scotty's suggestion they frequent an Obirrhat drinking establishment.

10. "No one ever learned wisdom on an empty stomach" (16). Statement made by Omalas to Kirk who was about to be presented with holy Obirrhat texts which Kirk had to read.

11. "For the overly cautious, everything is possible" (17). Statement lifted from the Obirrhat Holy Texts and quoted by Omalas to McCoy and Menikki.

12. "No beast of forest or field shall set itself down on sacred soil" (17). A quote Kirk lifted from the sacred Obirrhat Holy Texts and stated to Omalas as Kirk searched for a solution to the native cubaya treading on holy sites.

13. "You shall adorn the sacred stones with all manner of flowers and growing things, for they freshen memory and quicken the heart" (17). Kirk lifted this from the Obirrhat Holy Texts and quoted it to Omalas as Kirk formed his solution to the Obirrhat and the Mantiel problem.

14. "When one's emperor commands, all other loyalties become secondary. When one's emperor commands, no sacrifice is too terrible, no price too great" (Epi). A quote taken from Kahless' writing titled *Ramen'aa* and quoted by Kiruc to Kapronek who had just told Kiruc that he must die.

15. "Watch your back. Friends may become enemies in less time than it takes to draw a dagger" (Epi). This is considered by students of Kahless to be the most famous saying of all. It is recalled by Kiruc as he left Kaproneh who had just demanded that Kiruc commit suicide.

From the Depths

1.   "Up on that crag a few well-armed warriors could stand off an army" (13). McCoy's sarcastic words in which he referred to the Klingon appreciation for natural beauty.

2.   "Beware of Romulans bearing gifts and polite Klingons" (13). A similar phrase, "beware of Greeks bearing gifts" may have originated from Vergil's *Aeneid* Book II, Line 49: "I fear the Greeks, even when bringing gifts." McCoy's creative words were made to Kirk during their conversation about Kain and his intentions.

3.   "There are none so blind as those who will not see" (16). Kain directs these words to Moriah Wayne in reference to Kirk. Kain, who appeared to have ready many Terran books, may or may not have read "Polite Conversation Dialogue III" attributed to Jonathan Swift, noted Terran writer from which this quote comes.

4.   "He jests at scars that never felt a wound" (19). McCoy's reaction to Moriah

Wayne's insistence that Kirk attack the city where some of his crew were held hostage.

5.   "For what we are about to receive, dear lord, make us thankful" (25). Kirk ironic words just before the final battle between *Leviathan* and *Enterprise*. Words are quite similar to a typicalChristian grace prayer.

6.   "Sufficient unto the day is the evil thereof" (26). Kirk's thoughts to Aileea din Athos' comment about missing the excitement of her job. Consider the source *New Testament: Matthew* 6:34.

Great Starship Race, The

1.   "To see a world in a grain of sand/and a heaven in a wild flower,/Hold infinity in the palm of your hand,/And eternity in an hour" (Preface). The quote is taken from William Blake's *Auguries of Innocence*.

2.   "The long range manned exploration programs will not be reinstated..." (Pro). Opening sentence in the notifications to all Whistling Posts that the government of Gullrey Planetside Assembly was closing all space programs.

3.   "If everyone who goes into the valley gets eaten, then don't go into the valley" (Pro). A Gullrey proverb quoted by Dr. Beneon to her colleague Vorry after they had determined what at first was believed to be an asteroid set to collide with their planet was in fact a spaceship – the USS *Hood*.

4.   "Why run a race where everything's 'fair?' You'll never know how you really did" (1). Kirk's words of rebuke to Captain Nancy Ransom's declaration that it was unfair to allow StarFleet ship participation in the Great Race.

5.   "Credit is negotiable...blame isn't" (1). Kirk's words to McCoy as they discuss the fact that the captain of the ship *Brother's Keeper* has to have a flight master. The captain who was the Surgeon General wasn't about to take any blame for anything negative.

6.   "Look at that ship, Bones...and this time I get a chance to show her off...to be seen by people who only hear about her. The people who paid for her" (1). Kirk's words to Dr. McCoy who had suggested that maybe Kirk shouldn't enter the Great Starship Race.

7.   "I could use a break from roughhousing with the warring Birdbathians as they clash with the Knobheads of New Whatever" (1). Dr. McCoy's heated remarks about Kirk's decision to enter the race. The inspiration may have been taken from Jonathan Swift's *Gulliver's Travels* 1726.

8.   "Fear can do you a service in the right circumstances" (7). Spoken by Valdus to Romar who had mentioned his dread about going to Federation Starbase 16.

9.   "Complacency is what sucks the unready into war" (11). Kirk's words to Tom in explanation of his order to arm the ship's phasers. Kirk wanted to be ready for trouble, if it came.

10. "In space the innocent were rarely treated innocently" (11). Kirk's thoughts about the fearful attitude of Tom toward the events between *Enterprise* and *Red Talon*.

11. "A smart tiger stalks the weak zebra first" (16). Scott's words about the situation of Romulan Valdus going after a lesser target than a starship.

12. "There's nothing more dangerous than a decent man who's convinced he's doing the right thing" (16). Kirk's words to his senior officers after they determined Valdus intended to destroy Gullrey because of his perceived danger to the Romulan Empire.

13. "If the weak survive eventually all are weakened" (17). Valdus declared his belief that his actions were not self-defense but survival for his people.

14. "There is a price to liberty" (23). Statement taken from the Federation President's speech following his presentation of the Spacemanship and Sportsmanship Award to the *Enterprise*.

Ice Trap

1. "You can only cheat death as long as she lets you" (11). Spoken by the native Kitka Nuie to McCoy who told Nuie that Kirk had cheated death many times.

Sanctuary

1. "There is no time like the present" (6). Quoted by the Orion Pilenna, captain of the *Gezary*, to Scotty as she prepared to call Sanctuary's rulers. Quite similar to a sentence taken from Mary de la R. Manley's "The Lost Love' (1696).

2. "Experience is a harsh teacher" (9). Klingon Captain Garvak's words to Scotty before the Klingon left Sanctuary's orbit. He was referring to the situation at Sanctuary. Compare his words to Thomas Carlyle's sentence, "Experience is the best of schoolmasters...." taken from *Miscellaneous Essays* Vol I, p. 137.

Shadows on the Sun

1. "A journey of a thousand miles begins with a single step" (1: McCoy). Originally spoken by Lao-Tzu and put in his collected works, *The Way of Lao-Tzu*. The thought came to McCoy's mind as he packed to leave *Enterprise* and enter retirement.

2. "Men make their own luck" (2: McCoy). Kirk's words to Commodore Montoya's "good luck" offer following the briefing for the Ssan mission.

3. "The most dangerous sort of enemy is one who doesn't mind losing as long as he takes his adversary down with him" (4: McCoy). Kirk's words spoken during a discussion with the Ssan government officials.

4. "A weapon is only as dangerous as the one who wields it" (5:McCoy). High Assassin Andrachis' words during a discussion with his followers about the Federation and its weapons.

5. "An honest day's work for an honest day's pay" (3: Ssan). Paco Jiminey quoted this during a discussion about Ssan assassins in reply to the idea that an assassin cannot turn down an assignment. A popular Terran quote.

Shell Game

1. "There are more things in heaven and earth than are dreamt of in your philosophy" (1). Scotty's reply to McCoy's assertion that logical explanations exist for the disappearances of ships. The original lines are from *Hamlet* Act I, Scene 5, Line 166.

2. "You can't get there from here" (2). McCoy's first thought upon seeing the Romulan space station.

3. "Hours can seem like days" (4). McCoy's thoughts that he changed to "microseconds can seem like years" as he waited for the transporter to take effect.

4. "...Why do I feel like I'm waiting for the other shoe to drop?" (9). McCoy's response to Spock's recommendation that the boarding crew not take the turbo lifts. McCoy wondered why. McCoy had heard this many times, having been raised in the Terran U.S. south.

5. "God willing and the creeks don't rise" (9). McCoy's reply to Chekov's observation about jerry-rigging the doors to ladder access. Another pithy saying McCoy was exposed to growing up in Georgia.

6. "I just thought that once we all retire, I could get you a job as a circus strong man" (9). McCoy's remark to Spock that with his Vulcan strength he should be able to pry open the doors that Chekov had attempted to open.

7. "I shall be enjoying service to StarFleet...long after...you have been put out to pasture" (9). Spock's retort to McCoy's observation about getting a job in a circus.

8. "Not a creature was stirring" (12). Security officer Leno's remark to Chekov who inquired if she had detected any life signs. The line is from the Terran poem "The Night Before Christmas" by Clement Moore.

9. "Shootout at the OK corral" (16). McCoy's thought as he noticed Spock, Chekov, Hallie, and himself had drawn their phasers and were aiming at the creature. Also the title of a popular Terran movie about Wyatt Earp and his brothers.

10. "There were old security guards and bold security guards, but no old and bold security guards" (18). This thought rose to Chekov's mind as he felt helpless to give aid to Hallie. Compare it to a pilot's saying: "there are old pilots and bold pilots but no old and bold pilots."

Probe, The

1. "All I ask is a tall ship, and a star to steer her by...(1). The line is from "Sea Fever," a poem by the Terran John Masefield who lived from 1878-1967. The line ran through Kirk's mind as he considered Admiral Cartwright's statement that a new sector of the galaxy was being opened for exploration and that the *Enterprise* would be considered.

2. "...since Hector was a pup..." (1). Part of Kirk's reply to Admiral Cartwright

that the Romulan Praetor is dead. There had always been rumors about the Praetor. The phrase is a popular American saying.

3.   "Without giving away the store in the process" (2). The Romulan Interim Committee contacted the Federation but sent limited information about the scientific and culture exchange they proposed. McCoy's words were a reply to Admiral Cartwright's decision to respond to the offer.

4.   "A beard more often reveals than conceals" (2). Sarek quoted a Vulcan proverb to the bearded Lt. Kevin Riley when asking if Riley intended to keep the beard.

5.   "Be thou neither hot or cold. Be not lukewarm or I shall vomit you out of my mouth" (2). Sarek's words to Kevin Riley's indecision about his beard. Riley finally decided to keep the beard. Source is King James *Bible*, "Revelations" 3:15-17.

6.   "It would be inefficient to deny existing truth when new truth is what we are all seeking here" (7). The words were spoken by Dajan to Dr. Audrae Benar. Whether they are or are not a quote, the sentiment is just. They had been speaking about the ruins on Temaris Four and Dajan's access to some Federation archeology papers which he admitted he had access to. Dr. Benar was surprised that he would admit such a thing.

7.   "What better way to hasten the fall of peace-minded reformers than to raise the specter of war?" (8). Kirk's thoughts as Ambassador Riley spoke about the possibility of an incident that might provoke a war.

8.   "In for a penney, in for a pound" (17). Sulu's words as a reaction to Kirk's amazement that the speed of the Probe would take them through the Orion and Sagittarius Arms in less than a day. Probably taken from Edward Ravenscroft's *The Canterbury Guests*, Act V, Scene 1 (1695).

9.   "Tortoise and the hare..."(19). Kirk reminded McCoy who was anxious about the Romulans having so much of a head start in the crystal chamber of the Probe. Kirk is referring to an old Aesop fable of Terra.

Starship Trap, The

1.   "You'd better leave before somebody drops a house on you" (1). These are Kirk's words to Captain Torm. The allusion is to the incident in the children's novel, *The Wizard of Oz* when Dorothy's house landed on a wicked witch.

2.   "Law west of the Pecos" (3). A colorful description concerning the western lands of the United States before the territory became settled and established laws.

3.   "I can do as many as six impossible things before breakfast" (8). Dr. Omen quoted this to Kirk, adding that no starship had escaped the Aleph. The line is taken from the Terran novel *Alice in Wonderland*.

4.   "...we are about to go where no one had gone before" (8). McCoy's prophetic words as Omen ceased talking with Kirk and began implementing the Aleph. The original words are probably attributed to Captain Robert April.

5.   "...can this cockpit hold/The vasty fields of France? Or maybe we carm/Within this wooden O the very casques/That did affright the air at Agincourt" (12). Spock quoted these lines from Shakespeare's *Henry the Fifth*, connecting the Aleph to the "wooden O."

6.   "Sometimes it's smarter to fight fire with water than with fire" (13). Scotty's words are a reply to Kirk who wanted to employ *Enterprise's* normal tractor beam instead of waiting for Scotty and Spock to prepare their augmented tractor beam. If the normal beam couldn't hold Omen's ship then Kirk said "we'll try something else."

7.   "...who can do impossible things before breakfast" (13). Kirk fired Omen's quote back at him when Omen demanded to know how Kirk was able to get out of the Aleph and return almost to the point where he and the ship had left. The allusion is to the Terran children's novel *Alice in Wonderland*.

8.   "To murder and create" (15). Kirk's observation that Spock had further questions for Favere and Payton who had eyes only for each other.

9.   "Error in judgment could sometimes be corrected by someone willing to admit he was wrong..." (15). Kirk's thoughts as he watched Dr. McCoy and Franklin Kent, now convinced that StarFleet was necessary, leave together deep in conversation.

Undiscovered Country, The

1.   "Only Nixon could go to China" (1). These are Spock's words to Kirk implying that the Klingons only respect those they fear just as China respected Nixon because of his stance on international relations. The phrase grew out of a series of such references that carried many of the same words and the same sentiment.

2.   "Logic is the beginning of wisdom, not the end" (2). Spock's words are directed toward Valaris who questioned the relations between the Federation and the Klingon Empire and the logic of pursuing it.

3.   "I give you a toast, the undiscovered country...the future" (3). Chancellor Gorkon spoke these words at the first meeting between the Federation represented by Kirk and the Klingon Empire represented by Gorkon.

4.   "But the dread of something after death, the undiscovered country from whose bourn no traveler returns, puzzles the will, and makes us rather bear those ills we have than to fly to others that we know not of" (3). Though the lines were spoken by Chancellor Gorkon, he is not referring to death but rather to the fear of the unknown, which death is but a part. The words are from *Hamlet* Act III, Scene 1, Line 79+.

5.   "To be or not to be...We need breathing room" (3). The first part of the phrase is clearly from Shakespeare's *Hamlet* Act III, Scene 1, Line 56 but are spoken by Klingon Chang who added the last phrase which was spoken by a German in the 1939s to justify their invasions.

6.   "In space all warriors are cold warriors" (3). Chang quoted these words to

Kirk as a challenge toward the militaristic nature of StarFleet. They may be a Klingon proverb.

7. "Parting is such sweet sorrow, shall we say goodnight till it be tomorrow?" (3). Taken from Shakespeare's *Romeo and Juliet* Act II, Scene 2, Line 185. Chang's challenge to Kirk at the close of an evening of challenges.

8. "Out of nowhere. The ships fired out of nowhere... (5). These words of Kwan-mei Suarez repeated in Kirk's mind when he learned *Enterprise* had fired on Chancellor Gorkon's ship.

9. "Better to die on our feet than on our knees" (7). Klingon Keria speaks these words to Chancellor Azetbur urging war against the Federation for the deaths of Gorkon and many of the best minds in the Empire.

10. "Eliminate the impossible, whatever remains, however improbable, must be the truth" (8). The original words were spoken by Sherlock Holmes in the short story "The Sign of Four" (1890) by Sir Conan Doyle. Kirk spoke these words to Uhura, Chekov, Valeris, Scott, and Spock who watched the repeated replay of the firing on Gorkon's ship

11. "Ragnit ascur, unto pram moreoscue shondik" (8). An alien's words tossed toward Kirk during his first minutes in the Klingon prison Rura Penthe. The words are a request for Kirk to swear alliance to the Brotherhood of Aliens.

12. "Quog wok na pushnat" (8). Alien's words forcefully directed toward Kirk. Another prisoner translated the remark to be a request for Kirk's coat.

13. "Fendo pomsky" (8). A female prisoner's words to the alien who had challenged Kirk to a fight.

14. "If the shoe fits, wear it" (10). Chekov's words to Dax an *Enterprise* crewman in whose locker a pair of gravity boots were found. The saying is an old adage that Chekov would attribute to a Russian. It generally means that one should accept the consequences if one is found guilty.

15. "First rule of assassination: kill the assassins" (11). These are Kirk's words upon learning about the deaths of Burke and Samno who had killed Gorkon.

16. "...logic, untempered by compassion, can be used so cold-bloodedly to justify war" (12). Spock spoke these words to Kirk about his discovery of Valeris' treachery and admitted his own prejudices toward those Vulcan who condoned her actions.

17. "Can we two have grown so old and inflexible that we have outlived our usefulness?" (12). Spock spoke these words aloud to Kirk and then wondered if he had made a joke.

18. "Once more into the breach, dear friends...(13). Taken from *Henry V*, Act III, Scene 1, Line 185. General Chang taunts Kirk about he and Kirk being warriors who will have no peace in their time, and then begins firing salvos at *Enterprise*.

19. "There is a divinity that shapes our end, rough-hew them how we may...(13). Kirk quoted these words from *Hamlet* Act 5, Scene 2, Line 10-11 to General Chang for Kirk wished to avoid a battle.

20. "And above all else, to thine self be true" (13). The original words are found in *Hamlet* Act I, Scene 3, Line 78. General Chang directed these works to Kirk implying that both men were warriors and that their nature was to battle each other.

21. "After her...poor thing. If you have tears, prepare to shed them now" (13). Taken from *Julius Caesar* Act III, Scene 2, Line 173. General Chang's words of pride as he prepared to destroy Kirk and the *Enterprise*.

22. "How long will a man lie in space ere he rot" (13). The original line is "How long will a man lie in the earth ere he rot?" taken from *Hamlet* Act V, Scene 1, Line 179. General Chang's words to Kirk.

23. "Our revels are now ended" (13). From *The Tempest* Act IV, Scene 1, Line 148. Almost the last of Chang's taunts to Kirk as the pounding of the *Enterprise* he believed would destroy the ship. It's Spock and McCoy who saved *Enterprise* by re-configuring an atmospheric torpedo to "sniff" out the plasma residue from Chang's ship.

24. "In space no one can hear you sweat" (13). Chekov's words to Dr. McCoy who considered the possibility of smelling Chang's location since the ships sensors were not operating.

25. "Whether tis nobler in the mind to suffer the slings and arrows of outrageous fortune, or to take up arms against a sea of troubles...(13). The source is *Hamlet* Act III, Scene 1, Lines 48-60. Chang's quote illustrated he believed he was doing the best for the Empire by continuing to battle StarFleet and Kirk.

26. "Hath not a Klingon hands, organs...affections, passions. Tickle us, do we not laugh, prick us, do we not bleed – and wrong us, shall we not revenge? (13). The original lines read "Hath not a Jew hands, organs, dimensions, senses, affections, passions?" Taken from *The Merchant of Venice* Act III, Scene 1, Line 61-62, 65, 68.

27. "I am constant as the northern star...(13). Stated by General Chang who took them from *Julius Caesar* Act III, Scene 1, Line 60.

28. "So...the game's afoot...(13). Readers of the Sherlock Holmes stories will recognize these words as they are frequently uttered by Holmes before he identifies the culprit. These are General Chang's response to the arrival of the *Excelsior* to the aid *Enterprise*.

29. "Cry havoc! And let slip the dogs of war" (13). Taken from *Julius Casear* Act III, Scene 1, Line 273. General Chang's words of challenge to *Excelsior*.

30. "It takes one to know one" (13). Kirk repeated this aphorism to Chancellor Azetbur about understanding what Gorkon mean by referring to the undiscovered country as the fear of change.

31. "I grieve with thee...(13). A Vulcan expression that carries deep felt emotions of loss. Kirk spoke these words to Chancellor Azetbur after telling her he wanted her father's killers brought to justice.

Appendix C: Crew Compliment of *Enterprise**

Command:

Commander Officer (Captain)	1
Executive Officer (Lt. Commander)	1
Chief Navigator (Lt. Commander)	1
Helmsman (Lieutenant)	6
Yeomen (Ensign)	4
Navigation Officer (Lieutenant)	3
Navigator (Ensign)	6
Ordnance Officer (Lieutenant)	3
Ordnance Specialist (Ensign)	<u>30</u>
	55

Sciences:

Science Officer (Lt. Commander)	1
Assistant Science Officer (Lieutenant)	1
Scientists (Ensign)	4
Laboratory Technicians (Ensign)	72
Yeoman (Ensign)	2
Chief Surgeon (Lt. Commander)	1
Doctors (Lt. Commander)	3
Head Nurse (Lieutenant)	1
Nurse (Ensign)	21
Medical Technicians (Ensign)	<u>30</u>
	136

Engineering and Ship Services:

Chief Engineer (Lt. Commander)	1
Assistant Chief Engineer (Lieutenant)	1
Engineering Officer (Lieutenant)	4
Transporter Specialist (Ensign)	93

Yeomen (Ensign)	2
Chief of Communications (Lt. Commander)	1
Communication Officer (Lieutenant)	5
Communication Specialist (Ensign)	9
Chief of Security (Lt. Commander)	1
Security Officer (Lieutenant)	5
Security Specialist (Ensign)	<u>84</u>
	239

STAR TREK Blueprints by Franz Joseph Designs. N. Y. : Ballantine Books, 1973.

Appendix D: Diversity of Stars*

To approach stars in any attempt to understand them requires that first we understand that stars are catalogued. Since the dawn of astronomy, those who studied the stars grouped what they saw in the heavens. These groupings, developed in to eight groups, make comparisons possible and inferences too. A Danish astronomer, Ejan Hertzsprung, is credited with initiating a study of stars, their colors, and brightness. To bring order to his facts, he constructed charts to illustrate what he had learned. Together with the American astronomer Henry N. Russell, a chart of color (spectral classes) and brightness (magnitude) was developed. The groupings were illustrated with alphabet letters. Below is a simple chart illustrating spectral types in decreasing temperature. Finer divisions are made by dividing each class into ten catagories.

Type	Color	Temperature
O	Blue	19,300 F+
B	Blue	19,000 F
A	White	13,00 – 19,000 F
F	White	10,300 – 13,000 F
G	Yellow	8,500 – 10,300 F
K	Orange	5,000 – 8,500 F
M	Red	Below 5,800 F

Based on information from Franklin M. Bradley's *The Milky Way: Galaxy Number One*. N. Y.: Thomas Crowell, Co., 1963.

Appendix E: Great Starship Race Manifest*

Vessel	Command	Flag
Alexandria	Pete Hall	Alexandria, VA, Terra
Blackjacket	Ian Blackington	Private
Bluenose IV	Sinclair Rowan	Canada, Great Britain, Terra
Brother's Keeper	Cristoff Gogine	UFP Hospital Ship
Chessie	Samuel Li	C & O Spaceroads, Inc.
Cynthia Blaine	Leo Blaine	Blaine Aerospace Inc.
Dominion of Proxima	Hunter	Proxima Beta
Drachenfels	Helmut Appenfeller	Colony Drachelfels
Elenven	Thais	Andor, Epsilon Indi
Forbearant	Steve Daunt	Argelius
Gavelan Star	Ben Shamirian	Private
Haunted Forest	Buck Ames	Private
Irimlo Si	Loracon	Zeon
New Pride of Baltimore	Miles Glover X	Baltimore, Maryland, Terra
Ozcice	Sucice Miller	Host entry
Ransom Castle	Nancy Ransom	Ransom Carnvale Mining Co.
River of Will	Eliior	Branian College, Eminiar
Specific	Im	Melkot Sector
The Blimp	Charles Goodyear IX	Goodyear Inc.
Thomas Jefferson	Sue Hardee	UFP Museum Ship
Unpardonable	Lauru Han Ta	New Malura
USS *Hood*	Cpt. Kenneth Dodge	StarFleet
USS *Enterprise*	Cpt. James T. Kirk	StarFleet
USS *Great Lakes*	Cpt. Hans Tahl	StarFleet
USS *Intrepid*	Cpt. T'Noy	StarFleet

Valkyrie	Bjorn Faargenson	Shol Brewery, Rigel IV
Ytaho	Legarratlinya	Orion Union
Yukon University	James Neumark	Yukon University, Terra
552-4	Kmmta	Tholus

* List taken from Diane Carey *The Great Starship Race*.

Appendix F: Klingons in *Faces of Fire*

Amagh   Captain of the *Ul'lud*; kept potted fireblossoms in his quarters.

Aoras   crewman on the *Kadn'ra*; sent to search for children on Beta Canzandia; he and Gidris were killed by Vheled who found them in a hole dug by Spock and the children.

Chorrl   member of the second group Vheled sent to search for the children; killed by Grael

Dirat   member of Gidris' team searching for the children; reported failure to find them to Vheled

Dumeric   member of the Gevish'rae; maternal uncle to Vheled; member of Klingon High Council; lost power and favor when his nephew failed to secure the G-Seven unit from the colonists on Beta Canzandia; served in Ia'kriich campaign; won award

Gidris   First Officer on Vheled's ship *Kadn'ra*

Grael   member of clan Nik'nash and Gevish'rae; he killed Vheled; noted for his long braids indicative of his clan; sabotaged the *Kadn'ra*

Haastra   Security officer on *Kadn'ra*

Iglet   crewmember on *Kadn'ra*; member of party hunting for the children of Beta Canzandia colony

Kahless   famed Klingon credited with founding the Klingon race and empire; believed to have come from the Kamorh'dag area

Kapronek   emperor; native of the Kamorh'dag area

Kell   son of Karradh; Second Officer on *Kragh'ka*

Kernod   First Officer on *Kragh'ka*; grandson of Kapronek by a concubine

Kiruc   son of Kalastra; member of clan Faz'rahn of the Kamorh'dag area

Korradh   friend to Kiruc's family; once master of the Second Fleet

Kruge   big-shouldered, tallest of the crew and Second Officer on *Kadn'ra*; came from the S'zlack lands of the home world; intended to assassinate First Officer Gidris

Loutek   crewman on *Kadn'ra*; member of the group sent to find the children of Beta Canzandia; captured by Spock and the children

Mallot   crewman of *Kadn'ra*; possibly Security

Oghir	one of two guards at Kruge's headquarters on Beta Canzandia
Qo'noS	Klingon homeworld
Rogh	member of Gidris' team searching for the children of Beta Canzandia
Shrof	member of Gidris' team searching for the children of Beta Canzandia
Tenrik	assigned to the sensor scanner on *Kadn'ra*
Teshrin	older cousin to Grael who had attempted to assassinate him to gain control of the Nik'nash clan
Torgis	accompanied Kiruc to his initial meeting with Kapronek
Vheled	captain of *Kadn'ra*; native of the Gevish'rae area of Qo'noS; killed by Grael
Wistor	had been Kairadh's wet nurse; now second in authority of Kairadh's household
Zoraph	crewman on *Kadn'ra;* helped search for children on Beta Canzandia
Zoth	member of High Council
Zibrat	accompanied Kiruc to his initial meeting with Kapronek

First group searching for children: Gidris; Loutek; Aoras; Iglat; Shrof; Dirat; Rogh

Second group searching for children: Vheled; Chorrl; Engath; Norgh; Zoraph; Grael

Appendix G : Klingon vocabulary
From the Depths

in order of the chapter in which they appear in the novel

Pro	Qeyn HoD wa'DIch	highest ranking captain in the Klingon fleet.
Pro	Pajwl	possibly a Klingon crewman
Pro	'urng	possibly a Klingon crewman
Pro	luHoHta	There are too few of us to allow me to kill any of you.
Pro	Qighpej	agonizer booth
Pro	tera'ngan	Terran; earther
Chp 6	taj may"Duj tlh Ingan wo'	part of a phrase "Leave this system at once or be destroyed"
Chp 16	luHoHta' Sogh nugneH	Lt. Lu Kok Tak, what do you want?
Chp 16	maj	good; excellent
Chp 16	thlIngan	Klingon
Chp 16	tlheDon	my first captain
Chp 16	luHoHta	one of the few things that can't be wasted on killing
Chp 16	Qeyn	superior captain
Chp 16	bortaS bIr jablu'DI'reH QaQqu' nay	Revenge is a dish best served cold
Chp 20	tera'ngan	human; Terran
Chp 21	Q'reygh	probably the proper name of a Bridge crewman
Chp 21	pItl	done; finished
Chp 22	may'Duj	battle vessel
Chp 23	bIqa' veqlarg'a	Great Demon of the Sea
Chp 25	taj	knife; dagger
Chp 25	Qapla	good-bye; success

Sources Consulted

Alfred, Mark. "The Man at the Helm: Captain Kirk and Hornblower." *The Best of Trek #15*.Ed. by Walter Irwin and G. B. Love. N. Y. : New American Library, 1990: 143-149.

Arima, Colleen. "Sulu's Profile." *The Best of Trek #3*. Ed. by Walter Irwin and G. B. Love. N. Y.: New American Library, 1981: 106-116.

"Beethoven." *Britannica* 2000.

Bonanno, Margaret. *Dwellers in the Crucible*. N. Y. : Pocket Books, 1985.

"Borges." *Encyclopedia Britannica*, 2000.

Bradley, Ranklin. *The Milky Way: Galaxy Number One*. N. Y. : Thomas Crowell, 1963.

"Caposira." Wikipedia. Internet. March 2010.

Carey, Diane..*Battlestations*. N. Y. : Pocket Books, 1986.

...........*Dreadnought*. N. Y.: Pocket Books, 1986.

..........*The Final Frontier*. N. Y. : Pocket Books, 1988.

Carter, Carmen. *Dreams of the Ravens*. N. Y. : Pocket Books, 1987.

"Chagall." *Encyclopedia Britannica*, 2000.

Clowes, Carolyn. *Pandora's Principle*. N. Y. : Pocket Books, 1990.

Cogswell, Theodore. *Spock, Messiah*. N. Y. : Pocket Books, 1976.

DeWeese, Gene. *Renegade*. N. Y. : Pocket Books, 1991.

.........*Chain of Attack*. N. Y. : Pocket Books, 1987.

Dillard, J. M. *Mindshadow*. N. Y. : Pocket Books, 1986.

.........*The Final Frontier: Movie*. N. Y. : Pocket Books, 1989.

.........*The Lost Years*. N. Y. : Pocket Books, 1989.

.........*Demons*. N. Y. : Pocket Books, 1986.

Duane, Diana. *My Enemy, My Ally*. N. Y. : Pocket Books, 1984.

.........*Spock's World*. N. Y. : Pocket Books, 1988.

.........*The Wounded Sky*. N. Y. : Pocket Books, 1983.

Dvorkin, David. *Timetrap*. N. Y. : Pocket Books, 1988.

Ecklar, Julia. *Kobayashi Maru*. N. Y. : Pocket Books, 1989.

Ferguson, Brad. *Flag Full of Stars*. N. Y. : Pocket Books, 1991.

.........*Crisis on Centaurus*. N. Y. : Pocket Books, 1986.

Fontana, D. C. *Vulcan's Glory*. N. Y. : Pocket Books, 1989.

Ford, John M. *How Much for Just the Planet*. N. Y. : Pocket Books, 1987.

Friedman, Michael J. *Double Double*. N. Y.: Pocket Books, 1989.

..........*Legacy*. N. Y. : Pocket Books, 1991.

Gerrold, David. *Galactic Whirlpool*. N. Y. : Pocket Books, 1980.

Goldstein, Fred and Stan and Rick Sternback. *Star Trek: Spaceflight Chronology*. N. Y. : Pocket Books, 1980.

Graf, L. A. *Traitor Winds*. N. Y.: Pocket Books, 1994.

Haldeman, Joe E. *Planet of Judgment*. N. Y. :Pocket Books, 1977.

Hambly, Barbara. *Ghostwalker*. N. Y. : Pocket Books, 1991.

..........*Ishmael*. N. Y. : Pocket Books, 1985.

"Huerta." Wikipedia. Internet. March 2010.

Johnson, Shane. *Mr. S cott's Guide to the Enterprise*. N. Y. : Pocket Books, 1987.

.... *Worlds of the Federation*. N. Y. : Pocket Books, 1987.

Joseph, Franz. *Star Trek Blueprints: General Plan of the USS Enterprise*. Set of 12 sheets. N. Y. : Ballantine Books, 1973.

...........*Star Trek StarFleet Technical Manual*. N. Y. : Ballentine Books, 1997.

Kagan, Janet. *Uhura's Song*. N. Y.: Pocket Books, 1985.

Klass, Judy. *Cry of the Onlies*. N. Y. : Pocket Books, 1989.

Kramer-Rolls, Dana. *Home is the Hunter*. N. Y. : Pocket Books, 1990.

"Klingons." Internet. May 2010.

Krophauser, Bill. "Montgomery Scott: A Short Biography." *The Best of Trek #5*. Ed. by Walter Irwin and G. B. Love. N. Y. : New American Library, 1983: 140-147.

Larson, Majliss. *Pawns and Symbols*. N. Y. : Pocket Books, 1985.

Lorrah, Jean. *The IDIC Epidemic*. N. Y. : Pocket Books, 1988.

Love, G. B. "She Walks in Beauty..." *The Best of Trek #4*. Ed. by Walter Irwin and G. B. Love. N. Y. : New American Library, 1981: 139-146.

Mandel, Geoffrey. *USS Enterprise Officer's Manual*. N. Y.: Interstellar Association, 1980.

...........*Star Trek Star Charts: The Complete Atlas of Star Trek*. N. Y.: Pocket Books, 2002.

McIntyre, Vonda. *Enterprise: First Adventure*. N. Y. : Pocket Books, 1986.

..........*The Voyage Home*. N. Y. : Pocket Books, 1986.

..........*The Search for Spock*. N. Y. : Pocket Books, 1984.

..........*The Wrath of Khan*. N. Y. : Pocket Books, 1982.

"Milky Way Galaxy." Wikepedia. Internet. April 2010.

Mitchell, V. E. *Enemy Unseen*. N. Y. : Pocket Books, 1990.

Morwood, Peter. *Rules of Engagement*. N. Y. : Pocket Books, 1990.

Morris, T. A. "All About Chapel." *The Best of Trek #9*. Ed. by Walter Irwin and G. B. Love. N. Y. : New American Library, 1985: 84-85.

Okuda, Michael and Denise Okuda. *The Star Trek Encyclopedia: A Reference Guide to the Future*. N. Y. : Pocket Books, 1997.

..........*Star Trek Chronology: The History of the Future*. N. Y. : Pocket Books, 1993.

Okrand, Marc. *The Klingon Dictionary*. N. Y. : Pocket Books, 1985.

Palestine, Eileen. *Star Trek StarFleet Medical Reference Manual*. N. Y. : Ballantine Books, 1977.

Reil, Calon. *Ships of the StarFleet: 103ed*. Wilbraham, Mass: Mastercom Data Center, 1988.

Reeves-Steven, Gar and Judith. *Memory Prime*. N. Y. : Pocket Books, 1988.

Roddenberry, Gene and Setphen E. Whitfield. *The Meaning of Star Trek*. N. Y. : Ballantine Books, 1968.

..........*Star Trek: The Motion Picture*, 1979.

Rose, Pamela. "Speculations on Spock's Past." *T he Best of Trek #2*. Ed. by Walter Irwin and G. B. Love. N. Y. : New American Library, 1980: 176-181.

Rotsler, William. "Sulu." *Star Trek II: Biographies*. N. Y.: Wanderer Books, 1982: 119-131.

Rotsler, William. "Chekov." *Star Trek II: Biographies*. N. Y.: Wanderer Books, 1982: 91-117.

Rotsler, William. "Uhura." *Star Trek II: Biographies*. N. Y.: Wanderer Books, 1982: 133-149.

Rotsler, William. "Spock." *Star Trek II: Biographies*. N. Y.: Wanderer Books, 1982: 91-117.

Rotsler, William. "Scott." *Star Trek II: Biographies*. N. Y.: Wanderer Books, 1982: 69-89.

Rotsler, William. "Kirk." *Star Trek II: Biographies*. N. Y.: Wanderer Books, 1982: 27-53.

"Shostakovich." Wikipedia. Internet. April 2010.

"Tallyrand." Wikipedia. Internet. April 2010.

Thompson, Leslie. "A Brief Look at Spock's Career." *The Best of Trek #3*. Ed. by Walter Irwin and G. B. Love. N. Y. : New American Library, 1980: 117-133.

.... "A Brief Look at Kirk's Career." *The Best of Trek #2*. Ed. by Walter Irwin and G. B. Love. N. Y.: New American Library, 1980: 123-133.

Trimble, Bjo. *Star Trek Concordance*. N. Y. : Ballantine Books, 1976.

Underwood, Alva. *Star Trek Reader's Reference to the Novels: 1980-1983*. AuthorHouse,2002.

..........*Star Trek Reader's Reference to the Novels: 1984-1985*. AuthorHouse, 2004.

..........*Star Trek Reader's Reference to the Novels: 1986-1987*. AuthorHouse, 2006.

..........*Star Trek Reader's Reference to the Novels: 1988-1989*. AuthorHouse, 2008.

"Victory." Wikepedia. Internet. April 2010.

Voyage Home, The. Movie: 1986.

Wolterink, Katherine. "A Lexicon of Vulcan." *The Best of Trek #10*. Ed. by Walter Irwin and G. B. Love. N. Y. : New American Library, 1986: 115-121.